GASP

Julie: Eco-Cop #2

by

Charles & Lidia LoPinto

GASP: Julie Eco-Cop #2

Imprint: Green Leaf Publishers
Greenleafpublihers.com

Div. CAE Consultants Inc.

For information:

CAE Consultants Inc.
746 Vivian Court
Baldwin, NY 11510
(914)963-3695

For copies on demand contact
Createspace.com
or any retailer.

For bulk orders contact
Greenleafpublishers.com

serve and protect.

Recent Reviews:

"All the good stuff is here for a thrilling read. Frighteningly current and pertinent." Book Reader, CA

"I truly enjoyed the fast pace of this exciting story! The LoPintos drew on their combined experience as chemical engineers, knowing the weaknesses of petrochemical processing and transportation of chemicals. They studied at least six incidents, all believed to be "accidents" but no one knows how they happened..." Ann Thomson, Rocky Ford Daily Gazette, CO

"Authors Charles & Lidia LoPinto tell an exciting story that weaves together the worlds of environmental destruction, blackmail, and politics."Thomas Biblewski, Baker Street Dispatch

"Poised to be the E-Files of the Environment, within the first few paragraphs the reader is caught up in the story's plot."Mason Canyon, Chatooga Press

"I wondered if this novel could possibly live up to being WORTH the asking price. I'm happy to report that if environmental stories are what you like, this new series is for you: if you are as new to them as I, let these authors make you a fan! A well written 'Cozy' with thought provoking information..." Reviewed by Ottilee Bastgen of Concord, CA for the January issue of Cozies, Capers and Crimes Newsletter

"A griping, shocking and exciting novel that keeps the reader relentlessly turning pages until the end. Riveting and highly recommended."James Cox, The Midwest Book Review.

"I enjoyed both of your books and think that you two have created what could be a marvelous franchise for a film and television property. Sean and Julie are strong characters. With Sean, you have an archetype that fits nicely into the hero's journey. He's a reluctant hero and Julie's younger character, a feisty Latina, spurs him into action. There's nice chemistry between these characters... they would be two meaty film roles."

Scott Petri, Hollywood screenwriter

Dedication;
This book is dedicated to all the real heroes of the environment and in remembrance of the victims of terrorist attacks around the world.

Chapter One

Gasp! Worst Case Scenario

The thundering sound reverberating through the house woke Jeremiah from a sound sleep. As he reached for the lamp on his night table, another loud roar — like a car crashing right outside the door — shook the lamp and toppled it. Louise awoke and started coughing; acrid smoke burned her eyes. As she reached for the nearest piece of cloth to cover her mouth, she realized that her face was wet. She turned on the overhead light and saw blood on the towel. "Get the children!" she yelled, fighting back frequent coughs.

Jeremiah ran to the bedroom where his 3-year-old daughter was crying as she rubbed her eyes. His 5-year-old son was coughing and crying, but between sobs managed to say, "Papa."

Jeremiah ran to the kitchen, grabbed some towels and soaked them under the faucet. He ran back and placed a towel on his son's face and told him, "Hold it there and breathe through the cloth." He grabbed his daughter and son, holding them tightly in his muscular dark arms and ran to the door as he yelled, "Louise, come on!"

As the family ran toward their beat-up pickup truck, they saw others running away from the railroad tracks, which were less than a mile away.

This was the poor part of the quiet Virginia town. On this side of the tracks lived the "colored folk." The houses were clean, small, and simple, with white or gray wooden shingles. Some had earth-swept yards. Most had open porches with large wooden chairs where residents enjoyed the cool shade on hot summer days. Air conditioning was a luxury most could not afford, with antiquated wiring often incapable of handling even

the basic necessities. It was a peaceful area, not like the slums in the city. Those who lived here were proud people. The men usually worked at the local chemical plants or far-away factories, with a few still holding on to the family farm. Those who finally got an education moved to Charleston or New York. On Sundays, the old folks went to church, sang, listened to a sermon, met their friends, and later enjoyed a picnic. But on this day, this sleepy, peaceful town awoke to a sight of such horror that some town folk could not run, but stood frozen, staring back at the tracks in disbelief. The black plumes reached high into the sky. Blazing orange and yellow light from the fires illuminated the derailed cars and some of the homes. The faces of the people staring back at the fire had an orange glow; their eyes reflected the light. As Jeremiah passed a woman he heard her say, "O God, the gates of hell have opened up, please protect us!"

"Come on Mary," he yelled, pushing her along while holding the children, "We've gotta get out of here, it's a chemical spill!"

The smell was stronger now, but the breeze pushed aside the smoke enough for Jeremiah to pause for a second to look back at the tracks and see the bright orange light of a fire out of control. By the streetlights, he could see a yellow haze hanging ominously just above the ground and creeping up the road like some eerie creature from hell.

He knew that smell: sulfur aerosol formed when sulfuric acid and caustic soda mixed. He often endured the acrid fumes before he put on the heavy gas mask and suit during maintenance at the chemical plant. On hot summer days, the heat was so intense inside the gear that he took off the mask for a moment and held his breath.

Suddenly he realized that this was just what they talked about at the last safety meeting: the *worst case scenario*. He looked up and saw fire trucks around the tracks spraying water on the fire in an attempt to stop the spreading flames. Jeremiah gasped as he realized what was coming. "God, not water! Don't let them! Run Louise!" he yelled desperately, but his now-hoarse

voice could barely be heard above the screams of people, sirens, and cars.

Fire trucks sped by, followed by police cars with flashing lights as Jeremiah tried several times to get the pickup truck started. The entire population of the town — now crowded around Main Street — was trying to get away from the suffocating fumes.

The truck finally started and Jeremiah drove toward Main Street. He met a few firefighters wearing respirators and heading toward the tracks. Traffic on Main Street was deadlocked. Police officers with protective gear worked desperately to evacuate the people. An officer wearing a gas mask stood on the sidewalk directing pedestrians into cars that had spare seats. The officer's instructions to "Move! Move!" were muffled by his mask.

Several people climbed into the back of Jeremiah's truck. Holding wet towels tightly to their faces, they crouched down, seeking whatever shelter the truck sides could provide. The line of cars began to move past the town's business district.

Louise watched the store windows, which reflected the parade of fleeing residents. Without saying a word so she wouldn't alarm the children, she pressed Jeremiah's arm, pointing with the other hand at one of the windows that faced an open road leading to the tracks. The huge flames lit up the window. A fireball was followed by a deafening thundering sound.

Jeremiah stomped on the accelerator and drove on the sidewalk, but he could not outrun the oncoming hot scorching wind that blew past the crowd as people screamed in agony from the burning gases. Some people on the street fell to the ground. Emergency response teams in gas masks worked furiously to pick up the injured and place them into any available vehicle. Jeremiah couldn't take time to stop and help. He wanted his family out of there as fast as possible. He sped up Main Street to the highway, leaving devastation behind.

At the schoolhouse on the west side of the tracks, there were already ambulances, cars, lines of people, and volunteers handing out water, burn ointments, oxygen, and food. Because the local hospital had to be evacuated, only those with serious burns were sent to the hospital in the next town. As Louise got out of the truck and walked toward the school, she could barely speak because the choking fumes had further irritated her lungs; blood dripped from her nose. She held Shayla tightly in her arms and noticed the blood drops on her daughter's still little body. Suddenly Louise stopped, dropped to her knees, and holding the infant tightly to her chest, let out a deafening scream. Her daughter was no longer breathing.

When Sheriff Samuel Williams, a heavy-set man who was far too out of shape for his job, arrived at the scene of the train wreck, he was met by the emergency HazMat team leader, who had just arrived by helicopter. The tall man wore a yellow rubber suit, with full mask and respirator. He handed the wheezing sheriff a full respirator with air pack to replace the flimsy filter mask he was wearing. "You'll need this," the HazMat leader said, helping him put on the gear with expert hands. By the time the sheriff got the mask on, he could barely speak.

"Come on! We need to get further away so we can breathe. We've got to plan the evacuation. How far is your office?" asked the HazMat leader.

The sheriff put up two fingers to indicate two miles.

"Good enough. Lord save us! Come on!"

The men got into the sheriff's car and drove past the poor part of town near the tracks. Paramedics were picking up lifeless bodies of those who had been trampled by the frenzied crowd or whose systems just couldn't stand the heavy fumes. There were bodies everywhere and too few volunteers available to pick them up. There were still a few people trying to get out of town, walking on the side of the road. All the cars had left.

The sheriff stopped in front of the church and five people got in. A man, red-faced and eyes tearing spoke. "Where are the rest of the rescuers? We need transportation. Some people hid in basements or even freezers where the fumes couldn't get in."

No one responded. The sheriff was barreling toward his office as if something imminently evil was pursuing him.

When they arrived at the sheriff's office, the five passengers got out and approached the nearest vehicle heading out of town. The air was still foul-smelling but breathable, for the moment.

Once inside the sheriff's office, the two men removed their masks. Sheriff Williams was silent as the HazMat team director removed his gloves and headgear.

The tall man had very dark skin, with red blotches where the mask had pressed against his face. His tightly curled hair was wet with perspiration and his eyes were red from the gas.

"Harry Jones," he said extending his hand.

"Sheriff Williams." He did not extend his hand. He was still trying to take off the mask and gloves.

Harry said, "We've called the National Guard but it will take time for them to arrive. We need all available resources down by the tracks. You need to evacuate all the residents right now!"

The sheriff looked at him defiantly. "We have everyone available on the job. We just don't have enough equipment. The OC Chemicals plant manager mobilized all available personnel and equipment."

"There are dead bodies and injured everywhere near the tracks; it looks like Bhopal here sheriff! I don't understand why you're investing all your resources evacuating the north part of town while there are still residents trying to get out of the area closer to the wreck!" yelled Harry.

"The state safety board approves the emergency evacuation plan, and we follow it. It's too tough to change plans on the fly.

Besides, we don't have enough gas masks. I know we need more people working the area near the tracks, but you can't force people to risk their lives. The residents just ran; I didn't see them helping!" snapped the gasping sheriff, his eyes wide and his hands trembling.

"We see this thing all the time. The town plans evacuations for the affluent whites or blacks, because they're the ones on the boards. The town's poor, generally black, are left behind. In this case they were the ones closest to the wreck," said Harry, trying to compose himself.

"Dammit, there was no time. We did what we could. I didn't cause this thing and you Yankees always have to turn this into a race thing. You come here with a lot of prejudices of your own, boy!" said the sheriff.

Harry looked like he was going to explode.

"Wait, before you bite my head off. I call everyone younger than me boy. No offense, Mr. Jones. Look, it wasn't a racist plan. There are blacks on the board; we just weren't prepared!"

"Never mind this shit! Look, we have to work together. I have the federal authority to take over and direct the operation. This town is going to blow. The rail cars were either not labeled correctly or someone purposely changed them. The fact is, the First Response Team dumped water on sulfuric acid and caustic soda. That triggered a second explosion, which spread the flames closer to the propane and solvent-filled rail cars.

"Right now we have a Worst Case Scenario. A fire out of control and organic solvent tanks and propane tanks that'll blow up like the Fourth of July as soon as the fire reaches them! Call your volunteers and have them pick up the few remaining residents in the area near the tracks before the explosion!"

"I can't ask my people to risk their lives like that without proper gear. When is the National Guard going to get here?"

Harry heard the sound of trucks outside. "They're here. We have work to do."

Harry and the sheriff went outside to meet the officer-in-charge and brief him on the situation.

The news media vans started to arrive, but they were allowed no closer than two miles from the accident. There were daredevil helicopters from news agencies filming from above. It was now dawn; the horror of the wreck was excruciatingly evident. Live news feed started going through to news agencies and television stations around the nation.

Inside the sheriff's office, the television set showed the horrible pictures from the helicopters: burning railroad cars twisted and broken everywhere; flames from the chemical fires leaping high into the early-morning sky. The fires had reached cylindrical tanks containing propane and solvents.

"In Wilburn, Virginia, a small town near the railroad tracks, the worst railroad accident in U.S. history has devastated a town. A train carrying chemicals and fuel derailed at 3 a.m. today near the most populated and poorest part of the town. The initial explosion sent residents running out of their homes. A secondary and more powerful explosion about an hour later killed and injured many townspeople. At this point, crews are attempting to rescue the few remaining residents before a third explosion, which can occur at any moment, as flames are about to reach the tank cars containing flammable solvents and propane. Our TV van is parked about two miles from the site, yet we can feel the searing heat of the fires."

The live TV image fed to horrified audiences showed towering flames rushing toward the camera, followed by a thundering sound that visibly shook the van. "Let's get out of here," said someone, as the camera crew rushed to beat the scorching wind that followed, while still sending live video to viewers.

The bright orange flames rose for nearly a mile and all aircraft turned around in an effort to keep a safe distance away.

The National Guard didn't have time to move closer to the wreck to pick up the remaining residents before the explosions began. Guardsmen huddled behind their trucks to avoid flying debris: metal, glass, wood, and other projectiles that flew past them and crashed into cars and buildings. The sheriff and Harry had run back into the sheriff's office, a solid concrete building that provided them with needed protection. Once inside, they tried desperately to communicate with rescue teams by radio. Helicopters were brought in to dump water and sand on the periphery to stop the fire from spreading; everyone knew that was all that could be done. There was no putting out this fire; it had to burn itself out.

The guardsmen did their job well. The streets were deserted. Bodies were taken to the morgue; the injured were taken to the hospital. They proceeded to evacuate residents who survived the explosions by hiding deep in basements or concrete shelters.

Chapter Two

An Agent Back on Track

Juliana was at peace on the warm sand, watching the turquoise sea splash on the shore. The cool shade of the palm tree sheltered her from the bright sunlight. She placed her hand on the neck of the brown pony that kept her company on her beautiful native island of Vieques.

Suddenly, the loud ringing of the phone awoke her. She was only dreaming; she was back in her New York apartment.

It had been several weeks since she returned from Alaska. Her last assignment had taken a toll on her self-confidence, as a woman and as a Federal Bureau of Investigation consultant. She thought of returning to the relative safety of her job at the Environmental Protection Agency's Criminal Investigating Division (EPA CID), where, before she had taken on the FBI assignment, she'd spent days researching documents, doing lab tests and preparing for her cases.

It was obvious that on her last assignment the FBI had overestimated her capabilities as an agent, and she'd made things worse by going out on her own without backup. She broke several FBI procedures that nearly got her killed and endangered her partner Sean. But, after her return from Alaska, Deputy Assistant Director Anna Gutierrez gave her another opportunity to remain in the FBI Environmental Crimes Unit (ECU) on the condition that she attend training classes.

The last two weeks of FBI training further eroded her confidence. It was obvious to her that she did not excel at self-defense. Gone were her arrogance, high spirits and dreams of a career in environmental law enforcement. She now regretted not taking her mother's advice and going to law school. She seemed better suited to paperwork.

The engineering and environmental science graduate degrees served her well at the EPA. Her scientific and analytical skills were well-known and she moved up the ranks quickly. But she thought it was the opportunity of a lifetime when Assistant Director Gutierrez had asked her to join the FBI Environmental Crime Division as a consultant. She would remain on EPA's payroll and try things out at the FBI. The ECU division needed people with her skills to fight the new breed of environmental criminals.

The ringing got louder and Juliana reached for the lamp on her nightstand, knocking over the glass of wine she'd sipped a few hours before, to help her sleep. "Hello" she said groggily.

"I'm sorry to wake you up so rudely but I have an urgent assignment for you, Agent Del Rio. You're going to need your FBI training. You need to fly to Wilburn, Virginia, ASAP to investigate a new case."

"Good morning Mrs. Gutierrez. Ahh it's 5:30 in the morning, ... What's the case?"

"Turn on the television. The newscasts will fill you in. You're leaving on the 7 a.m. flight and will be in Wilburn by noon. All details and orders will be on your e-mail. Good luck, Agent Del Rio." Mrs. Gutierrez hung up abruptly, as usual.

Juliana jumped out of bed, annoyed at Gutierrez's arrogant, domineering, and rude attitude. "She just thinks she's the queen bee," she muttered. "Damn that bitch!" she said out loud, and then quickly hung up the phone, hoping that Gutierrez hadn't heard her. A dial tone told her that Gutierrez had hung up. Thank goodness.

Juliana turned on the TV. A newscast had interrupted all programming. She turned the volume up and ran into the shower, leaving the door open.

"A second chemical explosion has devastated what remained of the town of Wilburn, Virginia. Hundreds are dead and we do

not yet have an accurate count on the injured but that, too, may be in the hundreds.

At 3 a.m. this morning, a train containing numerous rail cars filled with assorted chemicals, headed for the town's chemical plants, derailed close to Main Street. The smoke and fumes from the resulting fire drove terrified residents from their homes and into the street in an attempt to flee the town. Shortly after the fire started, firefighters poured about 600 gallons of water on the fire. That was followed almost immediately by an explosion that killed many fleeing residents and sent everyone around running to any shelter that protected them from the choking fumes. The second explosion further fueled the fire, making evacuation difficult. Before rescuers could get to the few remaining residents – living no more than one mile from the tracks – a third explosion, of a propane tank, leveled several nearby buildings and homes, killing hundreds of residents and injuring countless others.

More on this accident later. But now a special report from our Washington correspondent:"

"A number of black leaders are demanding that federal agencies conduct an official investigation of the Wilburn accident to determine its cause and why the evacuation procedures failed to move the mostly black population out of the area closest to the blast in a timely manner. More than 150 residents of Wilburn are dead and possibly 350 are critically injured from the series of explosions that took place early this morning.

The derailment of the 120-car train containing more than 30 cars full of hazardous chemicals happened at the crossing near Main Street, the poorest part of town. The derailment sparked a huge fire and an initial explosion that sent nearby residents running for safety. Less than an hour after the derailment, a second explosion occurred when sulfuric acid and sodium hydroxide reacted violently with water that was sprayed from fire trucks. The rapidly spreading fire caused a third explosion when the fire reached tank cars containing flammable solvents.

Most of the residents injured and killed are black or other minorities, and elderly. Many of them lacked transportation. There weren't enough rescue personnel to get the remaining people out before the second explosion. The National Guard, called to the scene within an hour of the derailment, was unable to get residents out before the third explosion. Yet, organized town volunteers evacuated other parts of town, particularly the wealthier suburbs, with no incident.

EPA sources say the second explosion, which unleashed suffocating gases, was not as extensive but deadly just the same. It was caused by the mistaken dumping of water on leaking concentrated sulfuric acid and caustic soda. According to officials, water should never be used directly on those chemicals because they react violently with water, releasing deadly fumes. In this case, officials said that the tank cars were mislabeled and firefighters were not aware that the tanks contained sulfuric acid and sodium hydroxide."

Juliana knew her reservation was already made and she needed to get to the airport fast, but she didn't know from which of the city's airports she was leaving. La Guardia was the closest to her apartment. A quick check of the Web site showed that her plane was scheduled to leave from there.

That gave her some time to take out the garbage and throw a few things in a bag: jeans, safety shoes, deodorant, a dress (just in case) and plenty of long-sleeved shirts to protect her delicate arms. She reached into the back of the closet, where she kept a spare gas mask that she used for training and a couple of spare chemical filter cartridges made especially for the kinds of fumes she had heard described in the newscast. She remembered Sean's advice and placed her gun in her shoulder holster and made sure she had her new shiny FBI badge. She looked at it for a minute with a sort of disbelief. "I guess I am an agent after all," she thought.

She left a message on her landlady's answering machine, giving the cell phone number where she could be reached.

Finally, she called the limo service, which picked her up at the door. She was nervous now: The last assignment taught her to expect the worst.

She arrived at the airport early and had time to pick up the newspaper – which did not yet have the story.

Unlike her last assignment, where she had to disguise her identity, she proudly displayed her FBI badge as she went through airport security. However, the guards pulled her aside, asked for her picture identification card and took it inside to check the records on the computer. As she waited for what seemed like forever, she grew more annoyed by the minute. "No one believes I'm an agent; I don't even believe it myself!" she thought.

Feeling humiliated and embarrassed, she finally got through security. She headed for the candy stand. Juliana loved to gorge on chocolate to calm her nerves. This ordeal called for chocolate. After devouring a candy bar, she took out her palm top computer, made some notes, and decided to forget about the incident at the security point. Nevertheless, she was happy to have seen the expression on that annoying security guard's face when she found out that her FBI badge was genuine. The male guard suggested in a patronizing manner that she "keep the bullets in her purse and the gun hidden."

On boarding the plane, she took the window seat as always, and like a child, delighted in the colors of the dawn as the sun begun to peek over the horizon and illuminate the sky. She relaxed and smiled, looking forward to the special view of New York that this dawn flight would offer. It was close to takeoff and the plane started taxiing. She was so mesmerized by the sunrise that she did not notice someone had sat down next to her. She felt a tap on the shoulder and turned to see Sean's smiling face.

"Lassie. How are you?"

"Sean Ryan, are you on this case, too?"

"Someone's got to keep an eye out for ye."

"So, they don't trust me alone anywhere?"

"Do you forget I'm your partner, Julie?"

"I heard you didn't want to work with me anymore. Did that bitch Gutierrez twist your arm?"

"Hey, where did you hear that? And, no one twists Sean Ryan's arm, I volunteered because... well I did."

"Really? You volunteered to work with me after what I did in Alaska?"

"That's water under the bridge. You'll know better this time. You're just getting started, you know. We're still partners until someone says differently. And what do you have against Gutierrez? She's a good person."

"I hate her arrogance and her commanding attitude. She calls before dawn and expects you to just go. It's as if we don't have a private life in this job. I don't think she cares about her agents."

"Well, that comes with the job, you know. And, you're no stranger to arrogance, but as far as Gutierrez not caring, you're wrong. She's a bit abrupt, I admit, but she puts her heart into her work."

"Is there something going on between you and her?"

"No! But I admire the lady. She's gone through a lot and built the Environmental Crimes Unit single-handedly. No one wanted to fund it. She fought and scratched to get what she wanted."

"And she got you, I see."

"That she did, but I had no chance on the force anymore. The drink was doing me in. If it hadn't been for the lady, I might have been retired early. Did you know she lost a child to leukemia and blames pollution they found under her home?"

"No, I didn't."

"She's sworn to do polluters in. That's why she works day and night, never rests. Doesn't want to go home and feel the void the child left in her heart."

"Oh... Well, maybe I was a bit harsh. After all, if she was a man I would just think she was an assertive leader."

At that, Sean and Juliana settled in for the flight to Virginia.

The flight was full of conversation and fun this time. Unlike their first trip together to Alaska, Sean actually drank juice, stayed awake and initiated conversation. He talked about his latest case, tracking a mob-run hazardous waste-dumping operation.

"So I could hardly believe it Julie. I saw the guys loading that crap into the trucks, and when the inspectors stopped them, the truck was empty. Time and time again we couldn't figure out what they were doing with the hazardous waste. Finally, one night I got under the truck before it took off. There I was hanging from the axle as the truck sped down the highway."

"Sean, always trying to be the big hero! You could have been killed."

"Anyway, as I was saying, there I was hanging from the axle when I noticed the valve right above my head was dripping the stuff on my face, and suddenly I realized what they were doing. They never actually went to a site; they just spread it all over the road and then went on to the next client and charged an enormous amount of money for waste disposal. We arrested them all. It was a good collar."

"So, you're now the official FBI Pollution Avenger, Sean. And you hated this job at first! You thought this stuff was too easy. I've never seen you looking more animated. And, I noticed you didn't touch a drop."

"I'm on the wagon again. The department sent me back to AA. This time I hope to make it."

"So Sean, how's your love life?"

"Well... don't know if it's right for us to discuss that."

"Gee, mine is an open book to you, after the last case. Partners should share. Come on, I want the details."

Sean took a quick sip of water and unfastened his seat belt. "Excuse me," he said getting up and heading to the restroom.

Julie's face was flushed and she was perspiring from embarrassment. She looked out the window at the clouds. When the beverage cart passed by her seat, Julie ordered a small bottle of rose wine. She poured it into an icy glass and took a big swallow. Her hands were shaking.

When Sean returned, Julie smiled and tried to appear calm. Sean had a glass and some bottled water with him and looked over at Julie's icy glass of wine. After a few moments of silence Julie finally spoke.

"I didn't mean to pry into your private life. I'm sorry if I upset you."

"You upset me? No, it's just that I'm not used to all this darn water and fruit juice so eerly 'n the mornin," said Sean pouring the brogue on, as was his custom when he wanted to make Julie smile.

He took a sip of his water, while eying Julie's glass and took a deep breath. "You were asking about my love life, I believe. Well, I went to see Alexandra, Harrington's wife, after we got back from Alaska to let her know how her husband died. We took a liking to each other. I've been seeing her for the last month. She has a couple of nice kids. They don't even seem to mind this old Irishman courting their widowed mother."

"Well, she seems to have a wonderful effect on you. You look younger, and have more enthusiasm. Just don't be such a hero. She just buried one guy she loved."

"I wouldn't go as far as love, Lassie. It's too soon for her and maybe too late for me. We're good company for each other and

we have a lot of stories to share. She lived with a narcotics agent for 25 years and she understands what I went through."

There was an air of familiarity and friendship now between Sean and Julie. The two were bonded by the life-death events of their last case. "Sean, is it always this way with your partners? Having placed my life in your hands so often on the last case, I feel I can tell you anything and I just assumed you felt the same way. I'm sorry if I crossed the line. Perhaps we women are accustomed to sharing a lot more."

"Hey, you know, it's fine. I'll let you know if that time comes." The conversation continued for a while before both settled back and watched the movie. As they landed, Sean noticed the smoke coming from the south. "Julie, look. I think I can see the wreck from here. How far is Wilburn?"

Julie pulled out her notebook that contained the Internet printout of directions to the town.

"What's this?" said Sean looking over the papers with an air of skepticism.

"They're the directions, according to Zigmap.com. We're only about 30 miles from the wreck."

"Humm. We'd better ask. If you make a wrong turn it could be hours before we find our way back. This area looked pretty mountainous from the airplane."

After picking up their bags, Sean approached the car rental office. "Could you direct us to Wilburn?"

"Sure. Here are the directions," said the clerk, handing Sean a sheet of paper. "There've been a lot of reporters going that way today. If it weren't for this train derailment I wouldn't have known where Wilburn was either," said the clerk.

Sean gave the clerk his card, and he and Julie boarded the shuttle on their way to the car. Julie was quiet as she led the way.

"Would you mind doing the driving?" asked Sean handing her the keys.

Julie smiled as she took the keys. As soon as they were on the way, Sean fell asleep. Julie was glad he trusted her to get them to Wilburn on time.

Chapter Three

The Smoldering Fires of Hell

The 45-minute trip took them through some parts of the South that Juliana had never seen before. Alongside the corn and tobacco fields were poor homes, with weathered siding. Sometimes she could see the black residents resting on the shady open porches, escaping the scorching midday sun.

Julie noted that there were distinct areas where everyone was black. There were other areas where no residents where in sight, but by the looks of the housing and cars, Julie knew they were white. This kind of racial segregation was not as pronounced in Puerto Rico, although she was familiar with the wide discrepancy between rich and poor on her native island and in New York.

All of a sudden she looked in the rear view mirror, as if realizing for the first time which side she was on. In Puerto Rico, her mocha skin and fine features were the objects of desire for her many suitors, dark or light. Julie was a beautiful Caribbean woman who thought of herself proudly as "Puerto Rican."

In multicultural New York, Julie never felt different. At her job at the EPA, she was always attending meetings to encourage minority professionals, and she had black superiors. In New York, she rarely thought of the color of her skin, except when picking out makeup or a new outfit. She lived in a Manhattan apartment where racial issues hardly ever came up.

But here, in what was a new environment to her, she felt black. She felt she could relate to the people she saw and she suddenly said out loud, "I'm one of them." That knotted her stomach. She knew she would have to endure the humiliation of racial bias, from both whites and blacks.

Her muttering woke Sean from a sound sleep. His face wrinkled in disgust at the pungent chemical smell that filled the car. He opened the window, but that only made the chemical smell more irritating.

In the distance, they saw a solid column of black smoke touching the clouds. The temperature was well over a hundred degrees in the sun. He closed the window and turned up the air conditioning. It didn't get rid of the smell, but did cool the air to a bearable temperature.

As they approached Wilburn, the smoke became thicker and more irritating. They saw signs pointing to the HazMat Team's temporary shelter – a local bar, near the tracks. It was far enough from the wreckage so that the air was breathable – although it still smelled bad – and close enough for the workers to use as headquarters.

There were several people inside, some shedding heavy rubber suits and masks and others drinking non-alcoholic beverages. Alcohol and chemical exposure don't mix. The combination could be fatal and these men knew it. Julie looked around, but most of the emergency workers on their break barely looked at her. They were exhausted and drenched in perspiration.

Julie approached a tall black man seated at the other end of the bar, talking on the radio and making some notes on his clipboard.

"OK, we'll have to dig a trench to contain the spill before it reaches the creek. We'll need a digger. Call the nearest town. No, don't use water, sand or soil, and don't try to drop lime on it yet," he said to the man on the radiophone.

"Juliana Del Rio, FBI Environmental Unit," she said flashing her new shiny badge.

"Harry Jones, EPA, now please excuse me... NO, Lieutenant, NO, we need that equipment now! Use any small diggers in town and get your men to start digging... We flew in a batch of extra suits and packs this morning. Have someone come and pick them up. Are your men trained in the use of air packs?"

Sean looked over but didn't approach Julie and Harry. At the other end of the bar, he was drinking his club soda and already talking to the workers. Looking at Julie, he realized it was as if she had taken off her training wheels and he was watching her go solo.

"We're here to investigate the wreck," Julie explained to Harry.

"Look lady, this is a bad time for the FBI to start its investigation. We're fighting the clock. The chemicals will be spilling into the creek and public water sources in less than a hour unless we can stop the flow."

"Could you spare a rubber suit and an air pack? I'd like to help."

"In the basement. Get your gear. Wait. Do you have training in the use of this gear?"

"Yes I'm a special EPA consultant to the FBI, of course I'm trained...."

But before she had a chance to feel insulted, Harry said, "Never mind. Get out there and train those soldiers on putting on their gear properly.... please. That's what we need right now."

When Julie hollered at Sean, he turned and she signaled him to join her.

Sean excused himself and walked to the other end of the bar.

"This is Harry Jones, EPA. He's asked me to help with some training out in the field. We'll need to wear gear if we're going to get close to the wreck."

"Look Lassie, I've got a lot of people to talk to in town and at the hospital. You go ahead without me. But remember to call me if you need anything."

"I'll call you in two hours," she said walking into the basement. She emerged wearing a yellow suit, mask and air pack.

Sean looked at her and put his hand on her shoulder. "You be careful, don't try to be a hero. OK?"

Julie nodded.

Harry got up and said, "Can I offer you a ride?"

"Sure. Sean — you'll take the car then?"

Harry and Julie went out the front door and Sean returned to his interviews. He was going to head for the hospital next, but first he wanted to look around town.

Julie tightened her mask and checked her suit. As they approached the site near the tracks, the smells grew unbearable, and the heat suffocating. Already-suited National Guardsmen were digging trenches by hand while waiting for mechanical diggers. Harry directed Julie to a nearby tent where some soldiers were rummaging through the suits and air packs.

 Harry announced: "Ms. Del Rio will demonstrate how to put on your protective equipment PROPERLY. Remember that the gases out there could easily knock you down and the heat could kill you. Buddy system - two together at all times. Work as groups and stay within sight of each other. Team leaders, head counts every 10 minutes. Who's the team leader here?"

A man raised his hand.

"OK. You're responsible for this group. Here's a radio. Report to me every ten minutes or if something goes wrong.

"Men, your job is to dig a trench parallel to the creek leading to a tank that will be installed to catch the runoff. We want to catch all that acid. That is concentrated sulfuric acid; so before

you remove your suits, go to the decontamination station. Be careful with your masks and gloves. DO NOT take that mask off. Good luck out there.

"Ms. Del Rio, proceed with the training."

Julie began demonstrating the use of the suit and the men listened attentively. When they were all ready, she checked for leaks, and sent them off.

Harry was not far away directing the trenching operation. Julie reported to him when she finished the training. "Look, I need to start investigating the site now; I'll stay within view."

"Where's your partner? You can't be running around this site alone."

"Sean is trying to cover the hospital and town. There's suspicion of sabotage here."

Harry wasted no time and pointed to a man standing by in a rubber suit.

"OK. You, accompany this FBI officer on the investigation. Keep her in sight at all times."

The man who was assigned to accompany Julie looked tired and he seemed relieved to be away from the digging. Julie walked closer to the charred rail cars and started backtracking their path. She walked for about ten minutes, looking down and around the area. She stopped and looked down at a deformed piece of scrap metal. It could have been from the train wreck, but it wasn't charred. Part of it was flattened as if the wheels had gone over the three-foot piece of steel. She waved her companion over to help her lift it. It weighed almost 50 pounds.

She and her companion carried the piece of metal all the way back to the camp in blazing heat that sapped a person's strength. At one point her companion stopped to take off the suffocating

mask, but Julie signaled a definite NO, with her hand. It was too dangerous.

When they finally got back to the camp and inside the temporary headquarters, Julie took off her gear and phoned Sean. Julie wrinkled her nose at the smell of the chemicals, which was not noticeable when she was breathing through the mask. It was an uncomfortable feeling that took time to adjust to, but it wasn't necessary to wear the mask inside the building.

"Sean, you need to get over here. There's something you need to see."

Meanwhile her companion disappeared.

Julie continued to examine the chunk of metal, and while she waited for Sean she scraped some of the powdery material from the metal and placed it in a sample bag, along with a label and instructions.

Harry stopped in to see how things were going. "What's in that sample bag?"

"I don't know exactly, but I scraped it off this metal piece I found on the tracks less than a quarter-mile from the wreck. I'm going to send the sample bag to the lab. By the way, why were those tanks mislabeled? The sulfuric and caustic soda tanks don't indicate their contents from overhead. It almost looks like someone obliterated the labels with spray paint, from what I can see. I need to be able to get close to a tank to take a paint sample."

"That may not be possible until we contain the spill. That's our priority now. Sorry, Agent Del Rio, but you realize that we have to stop the contamination of public drinking sources first. I just can't spend time or resources on your investigation until we get that done."

"I understand, Mr. Jones, and thank you."

"For what? I'm not even helping you?"

"For giving me your respect as an agent."

"You're welcome. If it helps, there is a local FBI agent somewhere around here by the name of Bud Manner. He may be able to get that sample to the lab. If you wish, I can see that he gets it."

"Thank you Mr. Jones. That will help. Here's the sample bag."

"Ms. Del Rio, I'm glad you're here. Maybe tomorrow I'll be able to help you more."

As Harry walked away, Sean arrived, looking pale and breathing heavily. For miles around, the hot, polluted air was taking a toll on anyone outside.

Sean sat at one of the tables and wiped his forehead. "Alright, what is it you wanted me to see?" he asked Julie.

"Sean, you're out of breath. You need to breathe some oxygen to stop your wheezing." Julie walked over to the pile of air packs and brought one over to the table. "Wear this tank for a while; the oxygen will help." Sean welcomed the soothing flow of oxygen, which offered relief to his parched throat and lungs.

Julie put on her mask, picked up the chunk of steel and signaled Sean to go to follow her to the car.

As they got into the car, they removed their masks and were assaulted by the foul-smelling fumes. Sean floored the accelerator to speed away from the acrid, contaminated air. He kept driving until he saw the school that was being used as a shelter. They got out of the car and Julie removed her protective yellow suit.

"God, we both stink and I am soaked. I think we need to shower," said Julie wiping the dripping perspiration from her wet and sticky hair.

"The car smells like we drove straight out of hell. What is that stink? They'll never take the car back at the rental agency," said Sean inspecting the car inside and out.

"It comes from the spilled sulfuric acid. It smells strong, but it won't kill you at this concentration. Forget the car smell and please help me hide this evidence in the trunk and put these suits over it. I have a feeling someone may not want us to keep it."

"What makes you think that?"

"Harry Jones didn't want anyone alone out there and he assigned a guy to walk around with me while I investigated the site. He saw me pick this up and even helped me carry it back to the campsite. Then he left without saying a word. I was so concerned that I took a sample of the powder I found on the metal and gave Harry a sample bag to give to a local FBI agent to send to the lab. I believe his name is Bud Manner."

"Humm... did you get a bad feeling right here in your gut when your guy left?"

"Well yeah, but it could be the chemicals. Are you making fun of me?"

"Oh shut up. This is serious; this piece of evidence is not safe in our car. The car could be stolen or ransacked. There must be a gymnasium where we can take a shower and put this thing in a locker," said Sean lifting up the large chunk of metal.

Sean managed to hide the chunk of metal under the yellow safety suit and was making an effort to carry it without letting anyone know how heavy it was. As they entered the school building, the welcoming volunteer approached, but took a couple of steps back as he got a whiff of the agents.

"Hi, I'm Agent Juliana Del Rio and this is Agent Sean Ryan," she said flashing her now dull and tarnished badge. The chemicals had spoiled the finish.

"Lad, could you kindly show us to your nearest shower in the gymnasium? We just came from that hellish train wreck," said Sean.

"Sure. We also have fresh clothing supplied by a number of organizations in nearby towns. The public has been very responsive to our needs. Many residents just had to discard their clothing. That smell doesn't come off in the wash. Follow me," said the volunteer.

When Julie and Sean got to the locker room, the volunteer said, "There's a place to remove your clothes before you take your shower; you'll find clean clothes where you leave the shower. Now, if you'll excuse me, I must help some other victims."

There were lines of people waiting to use the showers and bathroom. Juliana took her place in the line leading to the women's shower. Meanwhile, Sean found an empty locker and placed the coverall-wrapped evidence into it, securing the locker with his own combination lock – something he always carried. He then joined the line to the men's shower, but was eager to continue the investigation.

"Sorry for my stink, buddy," said Sean to a man standing in line. "What part of town are you from?"

"About two miles from the wreck," said the short, stocky man with pale skin and just a few hairs on his head. "I work for the Wilburn Herald; I'm a reporter. I live near the newspaper office in downtown Wilburn."

"So, did you take note of how the evacuation went?"

"I don't share my story with other reporters, mister."

"No, well ... mister, could you hold our place for a minute?" Sean asked the man behind him, before taking the reporter aside to the lockers.

"My name is Sean Ryan, special FBI investigator," he said showing his badge. "Your cooperation will be appreciated."

"George Reed," said the reporter, shaking Sean's hand. "Well, I have the real story and the story that my editor will print."

"Listen. Join us at the bar in two hours. After we clean up here, we're headed for the hospital."

"Can I tag along? I didn't cover that today."

"You know, we just can't allow reporters to join us in an official investigation. FBI rules, but we can meet and talk afterward," said Sean, thankful that the rules were finally helping him out. He didn't want this guy tagging along.

Before showering, Sean put his clothing in a plastic bag and sealed it. After his shower, he put on a T-shirt that said Wilburn HS and jeans that barely fit around his waist.

While Julie waiting for her turn in the shower, she was talking to a very tired volunteer who related an incident about a three-year-old child who had stopped breathing, at the steps of the school.

"After some CPR, I managed to revive the child and personally drove her to the hospital. They wanted to make the family wait while they tended to people who weren't in such critical condition. Black families are seldom seen in this private hospital. When they asked about insurance and weren't taking the child inside, I yelled, 'There's no time for this! Do you want this child's death on your hands?' Then, the mother said, 'My husband works for OC Chemicals. We are fully covered but I just don't have the card with me. Can you check the computer?' But they just sent her in without any more questions. I guess they realized that there was going to be trouble. The little girl was admitted and is in critical condition battling the chemically induced pneumonia."

"There seem to be only a few blacks here, yet there were many blacks at the wreck," said Julie to the black volunteer.

"Well, I think many went to the hospital and some traveled to their nearest church. The school downtown wasn't used. It's too close to the wreck."

Juliana showered and changed into the only outfit available: a pair of gym pants and a T-shirt that was too big. She picked up the sealed bag with her dirty clothes, and walked out to meet Sean, who was already talking to one of the victims. She was a slender white woman holding a child. Her face looked as if she had sunburn.

"I was working at the all-night gas station when I heard the blast. At first I thought our tanks exploded or maybe a plane had hit us. The smoke soon got to us and I ran out and got into the pickup truck. I was on the road heading away from the tracks when I saw a light. When I stopped and turned to see what it was, that's when the hot cloud hit my face. I got what feels like a sunburn. I was coughing up bloody specks. I stopped by the baby sitter's house, but she was gone with my son. I found him when I got here. Thank God he's OK!"

Sean and Julie got back into the hot odoriferous rental and drove two miles to the local hospital, searching for more clues.

"So Sean, what did you find out?" asked Julie now in the passenger seat, combing her hair.

"It looks like we have a racial problem in this town that began with a federal mandate forcing the biggest employee, OC Chemicals, to promote blacks and women. A few whites who were working there for years were passed by for minorities coming from other parts of the country. Blacks from the town weren't promoted. There was resentment on both sides, so I don't know which side has the biggest motivation."

"What sides are you talking about?"

"Blacks and whites, of course."

"Gee, I didn't hear that at all, but then I've only been talking to black women. It could also be labor and management."

"You ain't going to get much cooperation around here. These people are going to have a problem accepting a black and Hispanic woman investigator. I'm sorry I had to say that. It stinks just like the rest of this hellish town, but it's the truth."

"That's OK, but you're bigoted yourself to assume that everyone will treat me like that."

"No Lassie, I'm just being practical. The ones who have the information are going to avoid you, or worse. For now, I probably have access to people who may not talk to you. You should concentrate on those who have no problem with you. We'll work the interviews together later. But Julie, for God's sake, don't try to go off on your own again to prove me wrong. These people are dangerous. I'm not kidding, Julie. For once please trust my experience and considerable age, which is good for something other than just gray hair."

"OK. You're very worried about me. Thanks for caring. I do appreciate it Sean, but I'm part of this team, too, and you can't be the only one that sticks his neck out."

"I care more than you think," said Sean in a low voice, and then quickly changed the subject as the car passed the sheriff's office.

"Stop. I think the sheriff's in. We need to talk to this guy."

Sean got out and said, "You park the car. I'll meet you there."

Sean walked toward the sheriff's office, making sure his gun showed by strapping it over his T-shirt and pulling out his FBI badge. Storming into the sheriff's office with an air of authority, Sean walked up to the busy sheriff, who barely looked at him.

The sheriff was wet with perspiration and reeked of sulfur. He breathed heavily and didn't look good.

"Agent Sean Ryan, special investigator for the FBI, sheriff," Sean said in a deliberate, antagonizing tone. "We're here to investigate this terrorist attack."

"Terrorist attack? What the hell are you talking about, boy?"

"I don't think you realize the seriousness of this situation. In other words, we need to find out who's behind this before there's another attack. We need your cooperation, sheriff."

"This was an accident. A train derails every day in this country. This was just another derailment that turned fatal."

"Why are you so resistant to the idea that this could be terrorism? The fact is that we have evidence to prove this was no accident, and have agents trailing perpetrators right now. You have to cooperate with the FBI and answer our questions."

"Do you realize that we're working to stop the chemicals from destroying the water system? We have no time for you feds now."

"I understand that there are well-equipped crews out there working on just that right now. From what I can see, you have the time to answer questions now!"

At this point Julie walked in. She had taken the time to straighten her hair and put on some makeup.

"Girl, the shelter is up the road," said the sheriff barely looking at Julie.

"This is Dr. Del Rio, special EPA consultant to the FBI and an agent."

The sheriff looked skeptically at Juliana. "Could I see your badge?"

Juliana took a deep breath, ground her teeth and pulled out the badge and her ID. She showed him her gun for good measure. "Satisfied now, mister?"

"Your badge could use some polish, and you'll refer to me as Sheriff Williams," he said sarcastically. "Look honey this is no place for women. Take a look at me! Why don't you go up to the high school or the hospital? We have too much to do. There'll be time for questions of this kind later."

"Listen, I just donated my time to train those soldiers and spent about an hour walking those tracks, mister."

"Dr. Del Rio, proceed with your questions," said Sean, looking at Julie as if saying "follow my lead".

"I just received a copy of the town's risk management plan and the plans for evacuation. The downtown area was clearly identified as a source of gridlock. Why were resources allocated to the northern part of town?"

"Look, the plan went as indicated. All resources available were deployed as fast as possible. We didn't have time to evacuate before that second explosion. Besides these... people... neither listen nor follow directions. They fled town and left people behind to die. We had to order people at gunpoint to take passengers. You know, it's typical."

"Typical of what?" asked Julie indignantly.

"I've told you all I know and am willing to say. You feds go back where you came from. Until I get official notification that I got to talk to you, I'm busy."

"Were there any arrests made for racial problems prior to the accident? Is there any history in this town?" asked Julie, defiantly ignoring what the sheriff just said.

"If you're looking for racial motives and conspiracies I can't help you. There was a group that protested the frequent trains carrying lethal materials, but the feds at Department of Transportation did nothing, and now look. It's what they said would happen."

"What about brawls in bars, racial slurs, and so on. Has there been an increased incidence of arrests lately?" demanded Julie.

"Can't say. We arrest people when they commit a crime, not when they call each other names, lady! How long have you been in law enforcement! Look, you see those firemen out there? They are black and white working side-by-side right now risking their health along side those soldiers, many from our town. You come

here thinking we southerners are just a bunch of bigots and hate-mongers. You're the bigots. Don't waste any more of my time."

"We could get a court order right now if we have to," snapped Sean.

"Look, if you want more information, talk to Reverend Jefferson up the street. He preaches at the Baptist church. He's black and a good friend to me, by the way. He'll tell you what goes on in this town."

"We heard enough for today, Sheriff Williams, and if you want official notification, you got it. You'll get a fax from the FBI office today and a court order if necessary."

"You go right ahead, boy. You feds do what you have to do and we'll do what we have to do." The interview obviously over, Sean and Julie walked out to the car.

"Dammit, they flattened two tires," said Sean kicking the rear wheel.

"And they broke the lock and took my spare tire and it looks like someone has been searching for something."

"Dammit, the rental agency is going to be pissed. Julie, could you call the rental agency and have another car delivered to the Wilburn Hotel? Meanwhile I'll fetch us a couple of tires from that gas station!" Julie stayed in the car making a phone call while Sean went up the street.

Only a few minutes had passed when a guy dressed as a deputy came out and stood by Julie's car. "Get out of the car." Julie complied, but held her badge out.

"Spread them," he yelled. As he frisked her, he took her weapon out of her holster and asked, "You have a license for this weapon, bitch?"

"It's in my wallet," Julie said, grabbing her gun quickly and pointing it at the guy.

"Just give me a good reason," he snarled, taking out his gun while kicking her and knocking the gun out of her hand. "On the ground, nigger!" he ordered, kicking her once in the groin. "On the ground I said, bitch!"

As the guy approached Julie to handcuff her, he felt a gun on his head. "Now asshole, don't make a move. Give her the guns easy. Both of them.

"Agent Del Rio, point this gun at him and keep your finger on the trigger. Now asshole, kneel down easy in front of her. What possible good reason did you have to arrest this woman? She is an officer of the law. Are you aware of that? I see you have her badge and ID in your hand."

"Lots of criminals have fake IDs and she had a gun that she pointed at me."

"So, you saw a black woman in a rental car, making a cell phone call and you assumed she was a criminal!" Sean said with a snarl. "Agent Del Rio, you may return that favor to him." Julie kicked him in the groin as hard as she could, making the deputy double over.

"OK, now take off that uniform slowly, all of it."

The guy took off his shirt, and pants. "The underwear too, bastard, we want you buck naked."

When the guy was stark naked Sean inspected the uniform. The guy tried getting up and Julie shot to his side. He went back down to his knees.

"Here it is, a screwdriver and the trunk lock. It looks like you've been busy. Now... change the tires, asshole!" and Sean fired a shot. The sun was scorching. There was no one around to see this spectacle. The guy took out the jack and started changing the tire. When he tried to swing at Julie, Sean kicked him in the groin again.

Just then, the sheriff stepped out. "What the hell is going on here? Put the guns down," he said, pointing his own gun at Julie and Sean.

"Before you shoot, both you and your deputy here will be dead," said Sean pointing his gun at the sheriff.

"This deputy flattened the tires on a federal agent's car and tried to kill me. Now he's sorry and wants to make amends," said Julie. "Put your gun down, sheriff, and no one is going to get hurt."

The sheriff complied and watched as the naked deputy changed the tire, sometimes burning his skin on the hot metal.

"By the way, he's not my deputy. I don't know who he is. He's all yours," said the sheriff.

"We'll find out. He's under arrest for attempting to murder a federal officer."

As the sheriff went back inside, Sean handcuffed the suspect and shoved him in the back seat.

"Julie, we need back-up. Call the office and ask for two armed men. We'll drop this guy in the next town and refuel."

The ten-mile trip to the town of Forkbend was uneventful. The assailant was allowed to wear a shirt and underwear but not his pants. Sean told Julie that in cases like this humiliation was a good immobilization tactic.

Arriving at the Forkbend Sheriff's Office, Sean showed his badge and said, "I'm an FBI agent. This man is under arrest for attempting to murder a federal officer. You're to hold him here until the federal agents come to pick him up." Sean filled out some forms and signed them while the sheriff made a verification phone call to check out their badges.

The guy, who said his name was Steve Howard, was given the opportunity to call his lawyer. The deputy took statements from him, Julie and Sean. As a deputy put Howard behind bars,

Sean and Juliana left for the next town. Steve would be held at least through the evening.

As they got into the car, Juliana looked far into the horizon and asked, "Do you think he'll go to jail?"

"He'll be out on bail. There'll be a trial, months from now. Don't know if the FBI can make the charges stick, Julie."

"I felt so humiliated. He made me lie on that scorching pavement and called me 'nigger'. I've never even seen murderers treated that way."

"He's up to something. He was trying to intimidate us. He wanted that piece of evidence we have. The racial part is just him. He was dressed as a deputy to be able to rip off the car undetected. Or at least I think so. The sheriff at first seemed to want to protect him, but then he denied he knew him. Julie, in this business you get called all kinds of names. You can't let it get to you, or they win."

Julie yawned, "Listen, it's late; let's go to a hotel and check in. I'm beat."

"What do you think of that bed and breakfast over there?" asked Sean.

"Well, it's certainly quaint; it has a lot of antiques, but Sean, this is an FBI mission, not a honeymoon. Gutierrez won't approve."

"Hey, there were no other rooms in town because those who evacuated Wilburn came up this far. I have a feeling this place may have rooms, but more than that, I may find the lead I'm looking for right here. How about if you go in and get us two rooms, while I bring in the luggage?"

As Julie entered the neatly landscaped home, she noticed that there were quaint antiques in the entrance way, and smiling couples were eating dinner. The hostess and waitresses were dressed in starched uniforms.

"Two rooms please."

The clerk smiled and asked, "Do you have a reservation?"

"I'm afraid not, we work in the next town," replied Julie.

"Well I'm sorry, but we are currently booked. You could try the Ramada off the highway."

"Thank you, I will," Julie said over her shoulder as she headed out the door.

Sean was already unloading the bags. "They didn't have a room. They said they were booked. Let's drive to the Ramada. They have rooms there."

Sean got on the cell phone and called the Rose Hill Bed and Breakfast number. "Do you have any rooms?"

"For which night sir?" asked the clerk.

"Half hour from now. It's for my wife and myself."

"Well, we have a honeymoon suite. It's $250 per night."

"Two hundred and fifty dollars? We'll take it."

"Sean, what the heck are you doing!" interrupted Julie.

"Shhh..."

"Are you going to pay by credit card sir?"

"Yes, Amex."

As Sean rattled off the specifics, Julie got into the car and shook her head. After what seemed like an eternity, Sean finally got back into the car.

"What are you doing?"

"I'm testing my theory. We're all set for the honeymoon suite."

"What theory? And, I thought they just told me they didn't have rooms."

"Exactly. Now, let's hold hands and go right in, like we're a couple."

"Again, does every mission have to be like this? I better not find out this is some male trick to get me into a room with you."

"Julie, if I wanted that to happen, I wouldn't need any tricks."

"Ohh, excuse me."

"This is an idea I have for a lead, OK? So just go in, keep quiet, smile and give them our reservation number, 184B."

"What do you mean? They just told me they didn't have rooms and I told them I didn't have a reservation."

"Julie, go ahead, I need you to go in and ask for the reservation."

Despite being ticked off at Sean's request, Julie walked back into the big Victorian home.

"Hello again," said the clerk.

"Hello. As I recall, my husband did make a reservation. Sean Ryan, 184B. Oh, here he comes now."

"Oh, yes, well, I'm afraid there has been a mistake. We're booked," said the clerk as Sean dragged the bags up to the desk.

"What do you mean? I just made this reservation." Sean replied.

"Well," said the clerk, "let me check. Oh yes, but I'm afraid that the honeymoon suite was reserved for someone else who had not arrived, but the couple just called in and confirmed that they were arriving late."

"What do you mean? You took my credit card," said Sean.

"Well, of course, there will be no charge to it. I'm sorry, but we do at times overbook when clients don't come in time, but if

they do finally come in or call, we honor the first reservation if no one else is actually in the room."

"Well, that's a darn good way to build repeat business, because I know my wife and I won't be coming back."

"I am sorry sir."

"I want to see the manager."

The clerk looked nervous and went inside. The manager came out and asked, "What's the problem?"

"Agent Sean Ryan, FBI. I want to know what's the real problem?" He said showing his badge. "It seems that Agent Del Rio came in asking for a room and there were none. We made a reservation half an hour later and my reservation was confirmed on my credit card. Now, when agent Del Rio came in alone, the reservation was lost. Is this hotel for whites only?" asked Sean.

"Of course not! Why that's illegal and we don't discriminate here. The truth is we're bad businesspeople for overbooking like this. I'm sorry you were upset. How about a coupon for a 50 percent discount next time you and Agent Del Rio visit town? Just call this number, give them the coupon number and they'll let you know if they have a room available."

"We'll take two of those and we will call."

"All right," said the clerk.

Sean and Julie stormed out. Julie got into the car without a word. Sean drove to the highway and followed the signs to the Ramada.

"Why in the hell did you put me through that second humiliation today?" snapped Julie fighting back the tears. "I didn't even see it coming. That's how stupid I am!"

"Because I need to determine how bad the racial problem is in this area, and if it extends to this town. There is a possibility that this might be a racially motivated terrorist act. Julie, you may have to endure this. This isn't going to be your first or last

encounter with these bigots. I recommend you keep your gun handy and loaded at all times. And stay close to me until we get backup. No matter what the motive was, there are people here that don't want us finding the truth."

"But if they are true terrorists, they'll want to advertise what they have done, isn't that true?" asked Julie.

"Yes, but so far, no letters to the newspaper or TV and no threatening note. I don't know if the racial prejudice I've seen scattered here and there is bad enough to motivate someone to commit this kind of terrorist mass murder. We'll have to see."

"Well, we're assuming that people are the target, but could it be the land? I mean, what if this brought real estate values down and some company needs the space for a factory?"

"It's a possibility. We can't discount anything at this point," said Sean.

They arrived at the Ramada and the black clerk checked Sean and Julie into their separate rooms after Julie upgraded her reservation to a Jacuzzi room. "Hey, I don't care about Gutierrez, I need a good soaking," she said smiling. "I'll pay the difference on this great salary of mine."

"Hey Lassie, want to join me for a drink at the bar?"

"No, and you don't want one either. I'm going to bed. Thanks for everything today Sean."

"Thanks for what?"

"For coming to my rescue. If it wasn't for you, I think that guy would have killed me."

"That's my job, remember?"

"Thanks anyway," repeated Julie, smiling as she kissed Sean quickly on the cheek and walked to her room.

Sean stood there, with his hand caressing his cheek and muttered to himself. "Good night Lassie, I'm sure glad you're still with me."

Chapter Four

Local Exposure

The ringing of Julie's cellular phone woke her. She slowly got out of bed, stumbled to grab her purse and pulled out her phone, just in time to prevent the call from automatically rolling over to her answering service. Julie attempted to push the desk chair with one hand while answering the phone, "Hi, this is Juliana." However, her right foot hit a leg of the hard wooden chair. "Hey! This better not be an omen for the day, I had enough abuse yesterday."

"Hello, Julie? What did you say? This is Peter." came a reply from the other end of the phone.

Julie's smiled and blushed, "Peter! That was nothing. Just forget my ranting." Julie paused, but when Peter did not speak she continued, "It's been a few weeks. It's good to hear a friendly voice."

"You sound like you're in trouble already," Peter replied.

"It's just that I'm on a new assignment and, well, it's just not a nice group of people."

"I expect that working in the FBI you would meet a lot of bad people. You know, not every assignment can be like your last one. Most of the time you have to work in hostile territory."

"You sound like Sean. Just a few hours from the capital and I feel like I'm in a war zone. In just one day, I've been insulted, humiliated, called names, kicked, segregated and exposed to poisons. I already have black and blue marks."

"Oh, you shouldn't be so quick to judge all southern hospitality. Look I'm going to be in Wilburn within the hour, and ..."

Julie interrupted, "How did you know I was in Wilburn?"

"Everyone has heard about the Wilburn accident by now, and you know that my environmental organization has resources tracking who and what is happening. I called your apartment and found you were out of town, so I did some checking at the agency. I assume you and Sean are working together again. So how is Sean?"

"He's fine. He seems to know how to get along with these folks. But why are you coming to Wilburn?"

"This chemical release is big news, but the major networks are playing it down. You know they always try to underplay these incidents, first by passing them off as simple accidents and then by giving vague or incomplete information. But I know this was no accident."

"How do you know that? We're just starting our investigation."

"You'll have to see me to find that out. I'm heading to the KCAMP trailer park. It's outside of Wilburn. It's not a large facility, but with all the people who have evacuated the area they have room for my trailer. Julie, the trailer sleeps five, so you and Sean can stay with me if you wish."

"OK. Actually it would be great to see you and get out of this hostile environment. And I'll drag Sean along. Look, Peter, I'm going to wake Sean and have breakfast first. We should be there in about three hours."

"That's fine. It'll give me time to set up the trailer. See you then, Julie."

It didn't take Julie more than two minutes to grab the hotel phone and get transferred to Sean's room. "Sean. Get up! We're going to meet Peter. Get dressed and meet me in the hotel restaurant for breakfast in fifteen minutes. On second thought, we'll stop for breakfast along the way to save time."

"OK Lassie, see you in fifteen." Sean was surprised by the enthusiastic tone in Julie's voice and didn't want to object to whatever was making her happy. He walked over to the bathroom and began to shave and wash up, thinking that it would be interesting having Peter around. Yet, he was also disappointed that he would not have Julie's full attention on the case.

Sean sat comfortably on a lobby couch waiting for Julie. He wondered why it was taking her so long. However when he saw her come out of the elevator he decided not to ask. Instead he stood up and said, "You look cheerful this morning."

"Yes, I am. I'll try to put yesterday behind me and start fresh today. Let's get some breakfast." They walked side-by-side to the car, stowed their luggage in the back seat. Sean drove to the highway, looking for the nearest place to eat breakfast.

"Julie, there's a restaurant up ahead. Do you want to stop there?"

After a short pause, "No, let's go a little further, I recall there were a couple of fast-food places on the way to Wilburn."

Sean cleared his throat and continued driving. They stopped at a McDonalds and had a quiet breakfast during which Julie told Sean about her conversation with Peter.

After breakfast, Julie went to the restroom and Sean used his cellular phone to call the FBI office in Washington, D.C. "Mr. Dowling, this is Sean Ryan. I want to know if you had any information on the man we arrested and dropped off at the local police."

"Ryan, I don't know how to tell you this, but this morning when I called the sheriff at Forkbend, he said he handed the prisoner over to two FBI men late last night. The problem is we didn't send anyone there last night; we were going to do it this morning. I don't know what to say. We can't figure out how they just handed over this guy to the wrong people. The sheriff's

people say that they have signatures of the agents and that the agents had badges."

"Do you know who the agents were?"

"No. They had fake badges. The sheriff should have confirmed their IDs before he let them take the prisoner, but he didn't."

"I'm upset, but I'm not surprised. You see, around here there's a lot of loyalty to the local authorities, and it doesn't take much to persuade someone to try such a scheme. Oh well, at least we still have the evidence." Sean hung up the phone and casually looked around at the other people in the food stop. When he saw Julie walking to the table, he stood and walked over to meet her. "Lassie, let's get back on the road," he said, taking her arm and leading her out."

"Sean, what's the matter? You seem uptight."

"The man we arrested yesterday got away."

"How? Did he escape?"

"Well, not really. He walked out with a little help from some of his friends."

Sean glanced up just in time to see a black limousine pulling out of the parking lot. Tinted class prevented him from seeing who was in the car. He immediately assumed a protective mode and escorted Julie to the passenger door and let her in. As he walked around to the back of the car he paused when he noticed a piece of gum stuck to the trunk's lock. He picked off the gum, noticed the loose lock and continued to the driver's side. Once in the car, he stared at Julie with a puzzled expression.

"Sean. What's up?"

"It's just that this chunk of metal we found at the tracks, then our prisoner escaping and now..." Sean paused.

"And now what?" asked Julie.

"Now, this limousine, this gum and breaking the trunk lock. It's just too coincidental. It reminds me of something, but I can't recall exactly what. You could say it's bad vibes."

"Then maybe it's a good thing we're going to see Peter. He may be able to help you figure it out, Sean."

"I hope so. I'm afraid this case is going to get more complicated before it's over."

Sean started the car and slowly pulled out onto the main road.

"Don't think about the case for now; just concentrate on driving for the next hour. That should relax you," Julie said.

Sean looked at Julie and smiled.

"I'll put some music on, that will help," said Julie tuning in the radio.

There were few stations, and those were mostly static.

"Too many mountains to get stations far away, Julie. This isn't New York, where there are hundreds of different stations and clear reception.

"Just turn off the radio. I need some answers. I need to know what physical symptoms will be experienced by the people who were exposed to the chemicals."

"Anyone who was exposed to the fumes or vapors will experience burning or irritation of eyes, nose or throat, maybe even headache, nausea, dizziness, and difficulty breathing. If the exposure was long enough, they may be drowsy and lack coordination or mental function."

"So, someone could be exposed and not be able to get to a hospital?"

"Yes, a person could be unconscious for a long time. But these are the immediate effects."

"You mean there are others?"

"Long-term exposure to concentrations over the limits set by federal standards can produce adverse long-term health effects ranging from mild flu-like symptoms to asthma, pneumonia and death from complications."

"Can you detect the chemicals by smell?"

"Only within a certain concentration range. For example, hydrogen sulfide, the gas with that pungent rotten-egg odor, can be detected only at low concentrations. If you can smell it, it's not dangerous. At higher, more lethal concentrations, the human nose can't detect it. People die of hydrogen sulfide poisoning because they can't smell it."

"If the chemicals get into the river or standing water, you may eventually smell decaying fish or an odor of ammonia from the decaying materials."

Julie leaned forward in her seat. "I think we're getting closer to town."

"Did you see a sign?" asked Sean.

"No. I smell smoke."

"I don't smell anything."

"Just like smokers don't smell smoke, your nose may have been desensitized."

"Between the chemicals and the smoke ..."

"Sean, we're near the trailer park where we're to meet Peter. The sign back there said to turn at the next left and follow the road for two miles."

"OK, Lassie." Sean made the next left and followed the road. The smell of smoke got stronger, and Sean noticed considerable debris along the road as he carefully drove the next two miles.

"There, another sign for KCAMP trailer park. We make a right here."

Sean turned onto gravel and dirt road. The car bounced from side to side with every bump and dip. Sean stopped to stare at a burned-out shell of a camper along the side of the road.

"Julie, this wreck has not been here more than a day. It's still smoldering. I suspect it was a result of an accident when someone was trying to get out of the camp in a hurry."

Julie said nothing, but stared at the wreck and shook her head. A half mile up the road, they reached a large open area and a small cabin, which was the trailer camp's main office. The park had room for fifty trailers, but only three camper pads were occupied. Julie turned to Sean; "Looks like most people evacuated the area after the crash. It's not hard to tell which is Peter's trailer. It's got to be the large shiny one over there."

As Sean pulled up next to Peter's trailer, Julie scrambled out of the car. Before she got to the trailer door, Peter called out, "Hi Julie! Hi Sean! Welcome to my home away from home. Just come in, the door's open."

Julie looked around at the trailer and noticed a camera and speaker on top. She looked over to Sean, who shrugged his head; "I guess he has the whole contraption wired and under surveillance."

"Sean, you're correct. I wouldn't want to venture into unknown territory without the proper equipment." As Peter's voice beamed through the speaker, Julie opened the door and stepped into the trailer. She spotted Peter at the other end of the trailer and walked over to him. Sean followed about ten feet behind. Peter was sitting at a desk operating a pair of computers.

Sean said, "The only thing I want to know is whether you have something cool to drink."

"The refrigerator is well-stocked. Help yourself."

Julie leaned over Peter, who was intensely scrutinizing the information on the computer screen and said in a friendly tone,

"How are things? The last time we spoke you said you had some environmental business that took you out of the country."

"One of our member groups in France was having a rough time with the French government about storage of nuclear waste. I went over there to help them present the case to the courts. It was tough, very tough."

"What was the outcome?"

"The courts haven't announced their decision, but I don't expect it to be in our favor. Anyway, I fear there will be more confrontations before that issue gets resolved."

Sean, who had been sipping a cold soda at the other end of the trailer, put the soda down and walked over to Julie and Peter. "What are you two talking about?" he asked. "It would be great to hang around here and chat, but I'm getting paid to do some investigating."

Julie shrugged her shoulders, and ignored Sean.

Sean continued, "It's best I see what the local FBI agents are doing. I don't expect you want to come along, Julie."

Julie remained bent over Peter's shoulder, but turned her head. Sean grabbed the doorknob, but hesitated before opening the door and turned back to look at Julie. Julie saw Sean's face and said, "You see what they're doing. I think that I better get as much information as I can from the computer. Maybe it will give us a lead." Julie quickly turned back to the computer, not noticing the grim expression on Sean's face as he left the trailer.

"Peter, what evidence have you found?"

"How about you tell me what you found, Julie?"

"You know I can't discuss the case. Maybe if you have something interesting we can exchange information."

"Well, I've been following the Internet chat rooms since the accident and found a lot of local discussions about the train wreck."

"That's not unusual after such an accident." Julie moved into the chair next to Peter.

"Yes, but the discussions involve members of several local organizations accusing each other of causing the accident and denying their own involvement."

"Wouldn't these messages come from environmental groups to manipulate the media?"

"No. These accusations came from extreme hate groups. If just one of these accusations is correct, then this train wreck was no accident."

"But Peter, is there any evidence of who caused the wreck?"

"No. I went back into computer records of the discussions before the incident, but none of these groups had mentioned anything that would imply its involvement. Of course there are a lot more records to check, and it will take time."

"Then I guess we better get moving," said Julie as she started typing.

Normally, it would be a short ride to the FBI offices in town; however, this was not a normal day. There were ambulances with screeching sirens, crews and slow-moving vehicles sluggishly maneuvering city streets. There were deputies at numerous checkpoints. Sean chuckled when he saw two policemen struggling with a reporter and a camera crew.

Sean parked the rented car across from the sheriff's office, where the FBI agents from the Richmond office had set up temporary offices in an empty warehouse.

Sean walked in and introduced himself to the first agent he met, a tall, blond-haired man in his late thirties, "Hi, I'm Sean Ryan from the New York office. I'm reporting in. You have a snarl of traffic out there. It seems these deputies would have

difficulty getting a chicken to cross the street, and now they have to handle Times Square traffic."

The agent shook his hand, "I'm Agent Hilbaum. Frank is my first name. I'm running this makeshift office, probably because I grew up here and know these people." Frank paused, "It's good to meet you, but I was told to expect two agents."

"Yea, my partner is checking out some computer information about the released chemicals. You know she's an EPA employee and enjoys that type of stuff." Walking over to the coffee machine, Sean continued, "I'm sure she'll be joining us later."

"Oh, the agent is a woman. They hadn't mentioned that."

Sean spoke as he poured himself a cup of coffee, "Well, I guess it's one of those don't-ask, don't-tell type things." However when Sean looked at Frank, Sean realized he was giving the wrong impression and added, "Juliana Del Rio is a good agent. If there's any environmental evidence in this case, she'll find it."

Frank introduced Sean to the other agents, pausing in front of a short but muscular man with light brown hair. "This is Agent Bud Manner. He also grew up in this town and is now stationed in Richmond."

Sean held out his hand and Bud shook it, but neither said anything.

Frank motioned toward the man standing next to Bud. "This is Agent Zack Greenburg. He is currently stationed in the Richmond office, but only on temporary assignment."

Sean noticed Zack's dark hair before he extended his hand and asked. "Where's home, Zack?"

"Washington, D.C. My father was a congressman from New York for twenty-five years, but I really grew up in the capital."

"We'll it's good to have you here."

Sean turned toward Frank, "So what do you have on this so-called accident?"

Frank paused before carefully responding, "We still list it as an accident, since as of now we have no evidence to the contrary. We're reviewing the statements from the people on the train. The engineer, who actually survived the accident, reported he saw no one on the tracks, and there were no lights. So we assume there wasn't anyone around to set off an explosive."

Sean shook his head, "It could have been set off when the train passed over it, or it could have been remotely detonated. It was dark and the engineer wouldn't be looking that carefully at the tracks."

"Yes, that's all true, but we don't have any solid evidence. There was no warning and no one has come forward claiming responsibility. Generally when terrorist groups cause this type of disaster they claim responsibility. Right Sean?"

Sean glanced at Frank. "You're probably right. So what are your men doing?"

"Bud's checking out the local supply shops and stores, seeing if there were any unusual purchases of explosives and equipment lately. And Zack's following up with the inspectors on the findings at the crash." Frank stared at Sean. "And I'm coordinating with our Sheriff Williams."

"Yeah, I met your congenial Sheriff Williams. I doubt you'll get much assistance from him."

Bud spoke up, "You just have to talk their language around here and…" but Bud stopped when Frank turned and stared at him.

Sean refrained from commenting and instead turned to Frank. "What about the explosives that Agent Del Rio found?"

"If they are explosives they're probably standard type and readily available. Bud will check it out."

"What do you mean, IF they are explosives? What did the lab say?" asked Sean.

"We didn't get the sample to the lab yesterday. We were busy," replied Bud.

"What could keep you too busy to send an important piece of evidence for analysis?" Sean snapped angrily.

Frank interceded, "Don't worry, we'll get the sample to the lab today."

"I'll report this to the office," Sean told Frank.

"Look Sean, we have an agent who is undercover in a local group and we expect he'll be able to provide information if this was caused by a local group."

Sean left the building, convinced that the agents from the Richmond office were not doing all they should. He thought they were inexperienced and decided to hold off reporting them to Gutierrez. Sean drove to the high school. It wasn't as busy as it had been the day before. He stopped in front of the building to question a deputy. "What's the status of the school shelter?"

"Sir, most of the medical cases have been taken to nearby hospitals and those people who still have homes were sent back. Only a few people who lost their homes and family are here. But they will be sent to the Red Cross or other charitable shelters by tomorrow and the school shelter will be shut down."

"So then I guess you won't be guarding the school after tomorrow."

"That's right. There won't be any need for us."

"Thank you, deputy." Sean walked down the long hall, bypassing the main gymnasium, until he got to the end, where he turned right. Out of sight of the deputy, and making sure that no one else was around, Sean walked to the lockers, took his key and opened the locker that contained the evidence that Julie had found. It was still wrapped in the yellow overalls. He carried the bundle out, but before leaving the gym, he grabbed a sandwich

and soda and dumped them into a sack. Food and evidence in hand, Sean walked back to the hall and toward the deputy.

"I'm going to need some of these work cloths from my locker," Sean explained when the deputy spotted the coveralls. "Have a good day deputy."

"You too sir," replied the deputy.

Sean walked out of the school and to his car. He placed the metal piece into the trunk, got into the car and dialed Julie's number from his cellular phone.

"What's up Sean?"

"I met the FBI agents from Richmond assigned to Wilburn. You should come the next time I meet with them. They're not much help, but we should try to keep up appearances."

"OK Sean, I'll be there tomorrow. For now I have a lot of work checking out these local companies."

"Well, OK Julie. And by the way, I've taken the evidence and will bring it over to Peter's trailer."

"Why didn't you give it to the local FBI?"

"I just don't feel comfortable with them. I want to make sure it gets to the lab. I'll see you later, after I check out the crash site again to see if they found anything else. Take care, Lassie." Sean ended the call and placed the phone in the glove compartment. Taking a deep breath he sat back in the car, opened the paper bag and ate his sandwich. When he finished eating, he started the car and drove to the crash site, where he approached Mr. Jones.

"It's nice seeing you again, Mr. Jones, Can you update me on the status?"

"It's Mr. Ryan, right? My teams have the spill contained and under control. We have prevented any major contamination of the river. Most fires are out, although there are some smoldering spots that we have to watch carefully. In a way we were lucky

that the crash didn't happen in the canyon area or we wouldn't have been able to get to the fires so quickly. However, on the other hand, we would have had fewer casualties."

"Mr. Jones, did you find any additional evidence pointing to the cause of the crash?"

"No. Nothing since your partner found that piece yesterday."

"Well, I'm going to walk around and see if there's anything unusual about this crash."

"Be my guest, but I suggest you put on coveralls."

"Yea. I have some in the car. Thanks." Sean went back to his car and put on the coveralls, but because the air was now clear, he left the mask off. He started walking, enjoying the visibility that was now considerably better. He looked at the ruins of the homes and other structures. The fire had consumed the entire first row of homes next to the track. The next three rows of homes had been knocked down by the blast and looked like matchsticks carefully arranged in one direction.

Sean walked for hours, inspecting most of the track along the crash site as well as the surrounding area. He didn't find anything of interest, but did take notes and tried to recreate the events of the crash using crude sketches. Between the surrounding damage and the location of the train cars, he pinpointed the location of the initial derailment. He determined the spot where the third car in the train left the tracks. He studied the information, but was tired and thirsty.

He walked back to the car and took off the coveralls, stashing them in the main clothing bin in the parking area. He drove toward town. By now the sun was setting and Sean's stomach was growling. He parked in front of a bar and walked in. Taking a seat near the restroom, he ordered a hamburger and a soda. While waiting for his food, he went into the restroom. Among the vulgar writings on the wall, he noticed a message that caught his interest. It was a dialog between two bigoted men complaining about the blacks and other minority groups. The

note went on *"White power! We won't let them take our rightful place. Take action today! Meet at JB's place this Wednesday."* Sean didn't know the place, but made a note to check it out later.

When Sean returned to the bar, he had just started to eat when he noticed the reporter, George, whom he had met at the high school, at the other end of the bar. The reporter approached Sean and asked, "So, Sean how do you like our town?"

"It takes some getting used to."

"That it does. There are some very powerful people in town and they control the authorities."

Sean leaned forward and listened intently to the reporter.

"The sheriff and his group don't like a reporter poking around, even a local reporter. I can imagine he doesn't like the national attention and the FBI. What have you discovered about this accident?"

Sean sat back in the chair and sighed. "You know I can't discuss the case with the media. You have to talk to the agent in charge."

"You mean Frank Hilbaum. That's worse then dealing with the sheriff."

"Well I can't help you," Sean answered, sipping his soda.

The reporter stood up and left the bar.

Sean finished his hamburger, paid the bartender and left a couple of minutes later. As Sean approached his car, he heard noises in the bushes. He walked over to investigate and saw three white men beating up the reporter. "Stop! I'm an FBI agent."

Two of the men turned and started toward Sean. They were slightly smaller than Sean, but stocky and solidly built. Sean maneuvered to avoid being cornered. One of the men took a swing at Sean but missed. The other tried to get behind Sean, but Sean moved away quickly and landed a right hook on the

second man, sending him three steps backward. The third man knocked down the reporter, and turned to Sean. He was the same height as Sean, but thinner. He and Sean exchanged a few harmless punches before Sean tripped over a rock and fell to one knee. The third man threw a punch that caught Sean on his chin, sending him backward; he landed flat on the ground. The other two men started to grab Sean, but stopped when a powerfully built large young black man suddenly appeared from the other side of the bushes. He pulled both men off Sean and tossed one to the ground. The faces of the white men turned red with fury.

Sean was trying to get to his feet and gasping for air. The two white men tried to grab the black man; however, he grabbed both men, knocked their heads together and tossed them against a large tree.

The black man looked at Sean. "Are you OK?"

Sean shook his head affirmatively and whispered, "Yes, but check out the reporter."

The black man picked up the reporter and carried him to the parking lot. Sean lagged behind and spoke as he pointed. "Put him in my car. It's the one over there."

After putting the reporter in Sean's car, the black man turned and walked away without saying a word.

Sean called out, "Wait!"

But the black man was already out of sight.

Sean started the car and looked over at the partially conscious reporter. "You need medical attention."

The reporter slowly turned his head and stared at Sean and said, "Don't take me to the hospital. *They* will only attack me again."

"Who are they?" asked Sean as he drove the car out of the parking lot, but the reporter had lost consciousness.

It took Sean ten minutes to get to Peter's trailer. Peter helped Sean carry the reporter into the trailer, while Julie got some water and towels. Julie stopped the bleeding while Sean told Peter and Julie about the incident in the parking lot.

"When I came out of the bar, I heard noises and saw three white men beating up the reporter. I took on two of them, but when the third man joined in they had the best of me. Then this huge black man appeared from nowhere, picked up the white men and tossed them into a tree."

Peter asked, "Can you describe the black man?"

"He was 250 pounds with a wrestler's physique and very quick and powerful. He carried the reporter into car, but disappeared without a word."

Peter walked over to his desk, opened a drawer, pulled out a photograph and showed it to Sean. "Is this the man?"

"Why, yes! Who is he?"

"Billy Justice. He's a member of our organization and he's investigating this incident."

"Why did he disappear?" asked Julie.

"He's working undercover," replied Peter.

Sean stood up and walked over to the now-sleeping reporter. "It's good for our reporter here that Mr. Justice was in the right place at the right time."

"Justice has that ability." Peter spoke as he turned to Sean. "It's been a long day and you took a beating, too. You and Julie can stay here tonight."

"Thanks Peter; for one night only though." Sean looked to Julie and she nodded in agreement. "We can discuss our strategy in the morning."

Chapter Five

The Dark Side of Town

The morning sunlight streamed through the narrow windowpane above Julie's bed, and was reflected into many brilliant colors by the shinny metal bed frame. Julie slowly opened her right eye and watched the multicolored display on the wall of the trailer. She was too restless to go back to sleep and it was too early in the morning to wake the others. She quietly dressed and, after checking that the reporter was comfortable, left the trailer and followed the main horse trail that led to town. She walked briskly. In fifteen minutes she left the forest and entered the more-populated area just outside of town and parallel to the railroad tracks.

Julie walked past several old houses occupied by black families. The conditions reminded her of the communities that hugged the coastal roads of her beloved island of Vieques and the hilltops of Puerto Rico. Children were playing in front of one house and Julie heard a mother calling to the children. "Adam, Christy it's time for breakfast!"

Julie stared at the mother for a while then walked up to the house and faced the woman standing on the porch.

"I saw you the other night in town. Weren't you staying at the school?" asked Julie.

The woman looked at Julie, shrugging her shoulders, and answered, "Yeah"

Julie waited for the woman to continue, but after an uneasy silence Julie asked: "Could you tell me why you were in town, ma'am?"

The woman picked up a small boy, turned and walked toward her front door and then spoke. "That's what I want to know. If you can answer that, then come inside and tell me."

Julie followed the woman through the front door and into the kitchen. The mother sat the little boy at the table, next to three other children. Julie's eyes widened when she saw the table set with plenty of food; fried potatoes, bacon, biscuits and eggs. "This looks very appetizing."

The woman responded kindly. "Would you care to join us? I have coffee on the stove. Help yourself."

Julie nodded and walked to the stove, "Thank you. I hadn't realized how hungry that walk made me." Retrieving a cup from a small hook above the stove, Julie poured the coffee and sat next to the woman.

The children were fidgeting, but none of them touched the food. Instead they all focused on the mother, except for a few quick stares at Julie.

The mother turned to the oldest child, "Luana, please say grace this morning."

Luana lowered her head and clasped her hands together.

Julie studied Luana, who was about fourteen years old but already seemed much more mature.

Luana prayed, "Bless us Lord for this bountiful food and for keeping our family together."

The mother looked at Luana.

Luana continued, "Oh, and bless all those less fortunate, especially those that suffered from the terrible accident." Luana looked at her mother, who now nodded affirmatively and Luana finished, "Amen."

The older children began serving themselves, while the mother helped serve the youngest boy.

Julie remained still, with her head lowered. She remembered the many times that her grandmother and mother asked her to say grace at the dinner table. She felt a little guilty, having stopped such practices since leaving home.

"Please help yourself to the food," said the mother, having served the little boy.

Julie looked up and responded. "Thank you."

The mother continued. "My name is Grace. You were correct. I saw you the other night in town. Our whole family, and almost everyone else in this area, was forced to take shelter at the school. They said it was to protect us from the effects of the chemicals." The mother poured a cup of juice for one of the children. "There always seems to be something that adversely affects this community. We spent one night in town, but when we came back to our homes we found that those houses that had not been destroyed had been searched."

"What do you mean searched? Did you report this to the police?"

"We did. Actually we accused the police."

"What did they say?"

"They said it must have been burglars, and that they had their hands full and couldn't help."

"They could have protected the area while you were gone," Julie said angrily.

Grace shook her head. "The point is, it was the police who searched our homes, probably hoping to confiscate weapons and find valuables."

"How could they do this during such a tragedy!" Julie declared.

"It was terribly wrong, but then the police have this 'holier-than-thou' attitude. If it was us, they'd call it looting and put us in jail, but if they do it they hide behind the law."

"Grace, my name is Julie and I work for the FBI and the EPA. I know the sheriff is a bigot. He really didn't want to take the extra effort to evacuate this area."

"Sure. He didn't want to have to put all of us into their school. But once he had to, he made sure he got something out of it; his way of getting revenge," Grace replied.

"That's awful. But I know how that feels." Julie took a biscuit, broke it in half and began eating.

Grace let out a long sigh. "They always find a way to keep the blacks separated from the whites in this town. Frankly I'm glad. I don't want to associate with most of them. But my children deserve better. Our community is very upset at the moment. This accident cost many lives, including some of our children; the Reverend lost his daughter, for one. I'm a good friend of him and his wife. For now this community is in mourning."

Julie lowered her head and started to pray.

A gunshot reverberated through the crisp morning air, making Julie jump, and startling the children. Grace hurried the children to the far end of the kitchen. "Get into the bedroom and stay with your father," Grace ordered.

Julie ran to the front door and looked outside. A police car was parked a hundred yards up the street. Another gunshot was fired, and Julie turned to Grace. "Sounds like it came from behind that brown house on the other side of the street." Julie ran out the front door, down the porch, and carefully made her way toward the police car. Grace followed her out to the porch, but remained there.

Julie stopped at the police car and stooped down, behind the driver's door.

Grace screamed, "Don't shoot!"

A third shot was fired; the bullet whizzed by Julie's head and ripped into the side of the police car.

Julie pulled out her gun and badge and turned to face the shooter. "Stop! FBI!" But fifty yards away she saw an armed deputy.

The deputy had his gun cocked and aimed at Julie. The two stared at each other. The deputy's hands were shaking, but he shouted, "Put the gun down!"

Julie was scared and lowered her hands. The deputy walked toward Julie while repeating, "Put the gun down, and raise your hands or I'll shoot."

Julie was incensed, but held her gun at her side.

Grace ran toward Julie, yelling, "She is with the FBI! Don't shoot!"

The deputy kept his gun on Julie, but asked, "Why are you here?"

Julie put the gun on the ground and stood up slowly, " I was having breakfast with this family."

The deputy slowly lowered his gun.

Julie was relieved but angry. "What are you doing here and why did you shoot at me?"

The deputy replied, "I was patrolling the area and spotted a male suspect and chased him behind that house," pointing to the brown house. "When I saw you behind the car I thought you were the suspect hiding."

"Do I look like him?" asked Julie.

"Well, no, but I didn't get a good look at the suspect."

Grace walked in front of Julie and faced the deputy. "And what did you want the suspect for?"

The deputy responded sarcastically, "He was a suspicious character, I wanted to question him."

"By shooting him?" Grace asked, throwing up her arms in disgust.

"It was a warning shot," the deputy walked toward Julie and ignored Grace.

Julie remarked, "Well, the one you fired at me was no warning shot."

The deputy became defensive. "At that point I thought he... I mean you, were armed."

Julie turned to Grace, "Let's get back to breakfast. We'll let the deputy make up whatever story he wants. He seems good at that."

Julie and Grace slowly walked back to the house. Meanwhile the deputy shook his head while looking at the hole in the side of his car.

Julie whispered to Grace as they walked toward the house, "He'll have to explain that bullet lodged in his car door!" and they both laughed.

With their mother back, the children again sat at the table and finished their breakfast. Grace's husband was also at the table. "Jason. This is Julie from the FBI. We were just outside when a deputy shot at her, thinking she was a suspect." Jason listened and ate, but remained quiet.

Julie asked Grace, "Can you tell me something about the hate groups in this town?"

"I don't know anything about them. I've been taught to fear them and I want no part in finding what they did or who they are."

Julie responded, "I believe the best way to handle such groups is to expose them for what and who they are. We aim to learn as much about them as we can. When we understand what they do, their numbers, who their members are, and how they

operate, we can prevent tragedy by exposing them publicly, thus eliminating the power they get from secrecy."

The children finished breakfast and went out to play. Jason went off to work his shift at the chemical plant. Julie helped Grace clean off the table and they continued their conversation. When Julie left, she thanked Grace for the food and Grace thanked Julie for her company.

Julie walked down the road and back toward the trailer park. She looked at her watch. It was almost 10 a.m. She picked up her pace when she remembered that she still had many things left to do today.

When Julie returned to the trailer, Sean was dressed and having breakfast. Peter had just gotten up; the reporter was awake but still in bed.

"Good morning Sean." Julie greeted vibrantly.

"And a great day to you too Julie." Sean replied.

"How is our guest today?" Julie asked as she walked over to George and looked at his bruises. "Looks like you'll be fine. You may have some pain for a couple of days, but there are no broken bones."

George turned onto his side. "Ouch, I guess you're right. I think another day of rest though will help before I get back on my feet."

Julie responded, "Good."

Pulling out a chair next to Sean, she said, "I have a story to tell."

As she sat down, Sean's cellular phone rang.

"This is Sean Ryan."

"Hello, Mr. Ryan. This is Agent Hilbaum. We have an important development in the case. Can you join us in town?"

"We'll be there in ten minutes."

"Oh, and will Ms. Del Rio be joining us?" Frank asked.

Sean noted Frank's sarcasm and quickly responded. "Sure, she's part of this team too! See you shortly." And he hung up, without waiting for a reply.

"Julie, we have an important meeting in town."

"OK. I guess my story will have to wait. Anyway it's time I met the other team members," Julie replied.

"Well, don't expect them to treat us as part of their team. We'll have to do most of this on our own," Sean warned, opening the trailer door.

Julie grabbed her purse and turned around. "Peter, can you continue the Internet investigation on your own?

"Sure Julie."

George looked at Julie and then at Peter, "I'd be glad to help the investigation, too."

Sean raised his brow, "But remember, this is a confidential FBI investigation and there will be no news stories unless I approve them first."

"That's OK, I've learned my lesson. I suspect my next story will be an after-the-fact recounting of these events. Hopefully by then the perpetrators will be in jail."

"Good. It's about time someone starting cooperating with this investigation," said Sean as he followed Julie out of the trailer and to their car.

"Sean, I got the feeling you meant me," Julie said just before entering the car.

Sean withheld his response until he was in the car. "Well I'm a little upset that you have spent all this time with Peter. It doesn't look good to the FBI agents on the scene and I don't want things to get worse."

"I don't think anything will look good to the law enforcement in this town. This morning I was shot at by a deputy! How much worse could it get?"

"What do you mean you were shot at?" asked Sean looking puzzled at Julie.

"Keep your eyes on the road Sean. It happened this morning near the tracks. I had breakfast with one of the families I met at the high school. There were gunshots and when I walked over to a police car to see what was happening, the next thing I knew a bullet missed me and hit the car. I pulled out my gun and badge and turned around. The shooter was a deputy. He ordered me to lower my gun. When he found out that I was an agent, he said he mistook me for a male suspect he was chasing. But that's highly unlikely. He didn't care to check things out. To him, I was a black person and that gave him the right to shoot first and ask questions later."

"Look, Julie, I'm sorry you had to experience this, but don't let your feelings interfere with your objectivity in this case. We have to concentrate on the facts and get this investigation back on track. I know these people are bigoted, but we have to rise above that." Sean started the car and drove to the main road.

It was a short, quiet drive to town, but each could feel the tension.

Julie entered the FBI office ahead of Sean. She approached the first agent.

"Hello, Miss Del Rio, I presume? I'm Frank Hilbaum, in charge of this investigation, and this is agent Bud Manner."

"It's my pleasure," Julie responded as Frank took a long look at Julie.

Sean stood behind Julie, let out a long sigh and said, "So Frank, what's the new information you called about?"

Frank turned to Sean. "Oh, Yes. An extortion note was sent to one of the plant managers, a Mr. Hugo Arias, demanding half

a million dollars. This is a copy of the note. I'm sending the original note off to the FBI labs for analysis," Frank said, handing Sean a piece of paper.

Sean took out his glasses and read the note aloud. "IF YOU DON'T WANT AN ACCIDENT TO HAPPEN TO YOUR PLANT, PAY UP $500,000. YOU WILL BE GIVEN INSTRUCTIONS FOR DELIVERY IN TWO DAYS."

Frank walked to his desk and sat down. "Sounds like a typical ransom note. There's no name or contact given and it was delivered to his home and left in his mailbox without an envelope. I talked to Mr. Arias, the plant manager of the OC Chemicals facility, and he said he never received such threats before. I told him the FBI would send a team to check out the plant and determine how to protect it from terrorists."

"Is the company going to pay the ransom?" Julie asked.

"Mr. Arias said it wasn't likely. They don't want to set a precedent. But the final word will come from the corporate office tomorrow," Frank answered.

"It will be a major effort to protect a whole chemical plant," Julie said, thinking out loud.

Bud quickly responded. "Oh, we'll prevent any terrorist from getting into the plant."

Sean coughed, drawing the attention of the others, and asked. "Any idea who sent the note? Are there any groups in the area that are capable of causing such damage?"

"We have some local groups that are quick with the verbal threats and tough talk, but none with a history of this type of violence. I sent Zack to check them out," Frank answered.

"Then I guess all that's left for us to do is to continue to check the train wreck site for further evidence. Frank, may I keep a copy of this note?" Sean asked.

Frank shifted his position in the chair. "Well, I guess so Sean, but I don't know what good it will do."

"It may turn up a clue or two. And Frank, can you arrange for me to meet with Mr. Arias?"

"I'll see what I can do. But Mr. Arias is a very busy man."

"I hope he's not too busy to catch the people responsible for this environmental disaster," said Julie.

Sean folded the copy of the note and handed it to Julie. "Let's check out the site, Julie."

Once on the street Julie asked, "What do you make of this?"

"Julie, it just doesn't make sense to bring this extortion out in the open now - unless it's meant to divert us from the truth."

"So what do we do?"

"We let the local FBI and sheriff follow up, while we look in other places."

"And where would that be?"

"I'd like to say the local pubs."

Julie laughed, seeing Sean crack a smile while he spoke. "We did that in the last case! But seriously now, where do we start?"

"We check out these local hate societies. I don't think Zack is going to learn anything from his investigation. He's inexperienced and isn't one of the locals. I'm surprised that Frank sent Zack on this assignment. He should have sent Bud or done it himself."

"But aren't we also outsiders?" asked Julie.

"Yes. But I don't intend to let that stop us," Sean replied as he opened the car door for Julie.

Sean drove out of town and stopped at a small bar. "Julie, I'm going to question some of the patrons. Maybe they know where we can find some of these local organizations. Stay here, I'll be right back."

"OK. But are you sure you're not going in for a drink?"

"No Julie. I promise I'll be good," said Sean as he walked to the bar door.

Julie remained in the car. Five minutes later Sean returned.

"I was told about a political meeting today at a place two miles down the road."

Ten minutes later, Sean parked the car across from a large stone building. Men were entering a door, above which was a sign: "White Brothers Unite." Sean turned to Julie, but before speaking, Julie said, "I'm coming with you! I'm your backup."

"I'm not going to stop you. But be careful," responded Sean.

Slowly Julie walked behind Sean. Sean entered the building and paused. He saw a large auditorium and motioned to Julie to follow him over to some chairs at the back of the hall. On stage, were ten men; in the center was a man speaking at the podium. Julie looked around the hall, tapped Sean on the shoulder, and pointed to the hanging banners.

Sean leaned over and whispered to Julie. "This is a conservative political meeting, and the leaders are recruiting volunteers to help in the campaign for their candidate.

Julie whispered. "This is a presidential election year, Sean."

"Yes, Julie. But it seems like this rally is geared to the local candidates."

"Why are there only white men at this rally?"

"This is a right wing political group with close ties to white supremacy organizations."

"Sean, I've been to political rallies in New York and Puerto Rico, but this place gives me the chills."

"Well Lassie, I know how you feel. It's easy to get caught up in the group mentality. For me it was a religious battle in Ireland. Here it's a racial battle. In the end it's the same hatred and it's not something that's easy to change."

"So what do we do here, Sean?"

"We wait. This rally will be over very soon. Then we'll see the speaker. He likes to talk so maybe he'll be willing to tell us something useful."

As the speaker continued, the crowd got more thunderous. Julie and Sean could no longer hear each other and it became impossible to hear the speaker. Sean motioned for Julie to stand up and she followed him to the front of the hall and into a small backstage area. Surprisingly, it was empty. When the last of the shouting was over, the speaker and the other men who had been on the stage made their way toward the area where Sean and Julie stood. The other men made it difficult for Sean and Julie to get through to the speaker. One of the men blocked them, stood face-to-face with Sean and blurted out, "What do you two want? This is a private place and we don't like women in here." Sean maintained his ground and kept silent. The man kept his eyes trained on Sean.

Julie stepped sideways and slipped past two other men, who were not sure how to handle the situation. Another man asked Julie, "What do you want?" But Julie ignored him. Reaching the last man between her and the speaker, Julie stopped.

Julie shouted at the speaker, who was now only four feet away: "Sir, I'd like to speak to you, please."

Sean had used Julie's distraction to also slip past the men and was a few feet behind her. When he heard Julie shout, his eyes widened and he held his breath.

The speaker turned to face Julie. "Are you with the press?"

Julie smiled, and waited a moment before she replied, "Not really."

The speaker now had a good look at Julie. He approached her with his hand out and returned her smile.

Julie shook his hand. "I apologize for the timing, but my partner and I are investigating this train accident and we thought that you might be able to help us."

"Well, I'm very careful about who I talk to, but if this isn't for publication then I'll be glad to straighten you out. Follow me." He led Julie and Sean to a small room where just the three of them could talk in private.

"My name is Ralph Raymond. I'm a teacher and the party speaker."

"Which party is that?" Julie asked, while showing her FBI identification.

"The Sovereignty Party."

"Who do you support?" asked Julie.

"We concentrate on local candidates. We don't have a presidential candidate; instead we have our agenda and we get people to join our group. But I don't think you came here just to find out about our political beliefs."

"You're correct. We're investigating the train accident," Sean reminded him.

"Our group had nothing to do with that!"

"So you know what group was involved in the incident?" Sean asked quickly.

"No! I understood it was an accident. You just said so."

"That's the official story, but we have evidence to the contrary," Julie replied.

Sean asked, "Do you know any group that would have a reason to do this?"

"No." replied Mr. Raymond.

"What do you know of a Mr. Hugo Arias?" asked Sean.

"You mean the plant manager at OC Chemicals? He's a greedy and misguided bigot and a member of a small society that meets every Thursday evening. Beware of him; his kind can be dangerous."

"Why do you say that?" asked Julie.

"Well girl, you see his form of bigotry is tainted by his quest for money and greed. He has no real moral or political agenda. His kind will lie, cheat, and deny as long as it serves him personally."

"Thank you," Sean said as he motioned for Julie to follow.

Mr. Raymond quickly moved to the door. He took Julie's hand and rubbed it gently. "Thank you. Come back for one of our big rallies," he said as he opened the door for Julie and Sean.

Leaving the hall, Julie and Sean drove toward town.

"Sean, what is it with this Mr. Raymond? Why is he inviting a black woman to his all-white male rally?"

"Julie, he doesn't expect you to accept. He's playing the part of the salesman. It's a good front that these guys put on."

In town they stopped for dinner at a small restaurant and discussed the case. Julie used her cellular phone and called FBI headquarters in Washington. She asked the records department to run a check on the plant manager, Hugo Arias. They told her the report would be e-mailed to her within the hour. After dinner, they drove back to the trailer, where they found Peter still at work at the computer.

"Peter, I need to check out my e-mail."

"Sure, Julie. That computer is connected to the Internet." Peter pointed to the table next to him.

Julie sat down and began to type.

Sean sat on a small couch and relaxed. "Peter, where's George?"

"Billy drove George back to his apartment."

"Here it is Sean," said Julie. "FBI report on Mr. Hugo Arias. Single. Both parents are deceased. Has one living brother. Arias currently plant manager of OC Chemicals. He worked for OC Chemicals for twenty years. Born in Wilburn. Has a passport - so he probably travels for business. Member of several business organizations; Institute of Chemical Companies (ICC), National Organization of Chemical Chemicals (NOCC); American Society of Chemical Engineers (ASCHE). Member of local organizations including Circle of Knights (COK)."

Sean asked, "Can I get a copy of that report?"

Peter added, "Julie, I'm going to search the Internet for any recent travel itineraries for Mr. Arias."

"OK," replied Julie as she printed a copy of the FBI report. Taking the printout to Sean, she added, "What does this mean? Do you think he's involved?"

"It's possible, but we'll need solid evidence to convince the authorities. Right now they all think he's the victim."

Sean yawned. "It's getting late, Julie. Are you ready to head back to the hotel?"

"Sean, I'd like to stay here a while and continue this computer investigation of Mr. Arias. However, you look tired. Why don't you go back to the hotel and I'll join you later. Billy can give me a ride when he gets back."

"Well, OK," said Sean. "Good night, Peter." Sean left the trailer and drove back to the hotel.

Meanwhile, Peter and Julie continued their computer search.

"Julie, I have Mr. Arias' travel history on the computer. He made several domestic trips to St. Louis. It happens to be the location of his corporate office. He also flew overseas: two trips to Buenos Aires, Argentina, and one to Frankfort, Germany. I'll see if Mr. Arias has any airline reservations."

After a few keystrokes Peter added, "There is a reservation to Buenos Aires for Mr. Arias on Argentine Airlines tonight." Peter typed a query into a search engine. "I don't find any company office in Buenos Aires, and there are no known relatives of Mr. Arias in Argentina either."

Julie moved close to Peter. "Maybe I'll stay here tonight, Peter."

Peter continued to look at the screen. "You can stay if you wish. But what about Sean?"

"Oh, Sean will be OK."

Turning to Julie, Peter said, "He's your partner and I don't want to cause any trouble between you two."

"Partner is all that he is, Peter," Julie answered as she moved back to her computer.

"Maybe we should look into OC Chemicals Company," said Peter. "Can you find out if the plant has reported any chemical releases or accidents? You know that they have to report such incidents to the EPA and OSHA. Meanwhile, I'll check out any companies that do business with OC Chemicals by searching press releases and announced contract awards."

A few minutes later Julie interrupted Peter. "The EPA records indicate that the plant has had three recent chemical releases, none of them serious. But each has been attributed to software or valve failure."

"Julie, I have a contract award to several local companies in the last month. One is for cleaning services, another for pipe components, and one is for computer hardware and software."

"What is the computer company?" asked Julie.

"It's Forsythe Systems."

"Do we know what this company does?" asked Julie.

"I'm looking at its Web site now," answered Peter. "They advertise that they provide computer and software services to the process industry. They promote several software products that they say improve plant control and reduce maintenance and operating costs."

"Sounds like a kind way of saying they can eliminate employees," responded Julie.

"Forsythe Systems lists many local companies as clients, including several OC Chemicals sites. It appears that many of the OC Chemicals plants use its software services."

"Julie, I'm going to check with Billy. Maybe he has something about Mr. Arias."

Peter made the phone call from his computer. "Billy, we need to know more about this Mr. Arias. Did you find out anything today?"

"Peter, I spoke with one of our members who is a member of an organization that Mr. Arias belongs to."

"Is it the Circle of Knights?

"Yes," replied Billy.

"This informant says that Mr. Arias and several others in this organization have formed a small group. He doesn't know what they do. He said they keep their plans very secret. He did say Mr. Arias meets regularly with two other men: Mr. Ashland and Mr. Forsythe"

"Bingo!" shouted Peter. "See you later, Billy."

"What do you have?" asked Julie.

"A connection between Mr. Forsythe and Mr. Arias. They meet at their secret society."

Peter looked at the blinking icon on the computer. "I have a message on my ICQ." Peter clicked the icon. "I'm going to connect it to the speakers so we can both listen."

"Peter, this is Carla. How is the investigation going?"

Julie looked at Peter. "Who's that?"

Peter answered, "It's an audio message from Carla. She's at the New York office. She just sent this message. I'm going to connect live with her."

"Hi Carla, this is Peter. I have Julie here and we're checking out our suspected terrorist's travel plans to Buenos Aires this weekend."

"Hey Peter, haven't you been reading the newsletter?"

Peter raised his eyebrows, "What do you mean?

"There's an Environmental Conference in Buenos Aires this weekend. It's at the Regency Hotel," answered Carla.

"That's right! I'll check where Mr. Arias is staying," said Peter.

"Why would Mr. Arias want to attend an Environmental Conference?" asked Julie.

"That's a good question." Peter smiled and turned to Julie, "But Mr. Arias is booked at the Regency, so I guess we'll have to find the answer to that question," said Peter.

Julie stood up, "Thank, you Carla, for the information. I'll notify the FBI office. Good-bye." Julie took Peter's mouse and clicked the "disconnect" button, cutting off Carla.

"I need to call Mrs. Gutierrez with this information."

"Don't you think you should talk to Sean first?" asked Peter.

"He's tired. He's probably already asleep," replied Julie.

Julie took her cellular phone and punched in the FBI office number and waited for a response.

"Hello, may I please speak with Mrs. Gutierrez?"

"She's gone for the evening. Do you want to leave a message?" asked the answering service.

"No. I'll e-mail her."

Julie explained to Peter, "If she checks her e-mail she may get it tonight."

Julie began to type:

Email to Mrs. Gutierrez

cc:

Subject: Investigation of Mr. Arias

From: Juliana Del Rio

We are investigating leads that may connect Mr. Hugo Arias, plant manager of OC Chemicals, to local and foreign terrorist groups. We do not have evidence and we don't want to tip off the on-scene FBI with this information just now. We know Mr. Arias is attending an Environmental Conference in Buenos Aires this coming weekend and we are concerned that he may be involved in some terrorist activity there. We would like to follow Mr. Arias to Buenos Aires to check out his contacts. In the meantime, we suggest the authorities in Buenos Aires be notified."

Sean arrived at his hotel room, washed up and undressed. He turned on the TV and listened to the news person.

"On the national scene, clean-up crews in Wilburn have finished removing chemicals from the scene of the train accident. The authorities have not indicated any official cause, but some sources report that it was a train mechanical failure."

"I hate it when the media makes up the news. This mechanical bullshit is just that. Bullshit. I wouldn't be surprised if the local authorities leaked that just to get the media and FBI off their backs," Sean grumbled to himself.

Sean turned off the TV and rested his head on the pillow. In a few minutes he was asleep.

The clock showed 11:45 p.m. when Sean's phone rang. "Hello," Sean said sleepily.

"Hello, this is Mrs. Gutierrez. Did I wake you, Sean?"

"Yes, Mrs. Gutierrez, but that's OK. I'm surprised to hear from you at this hour."

"Well, I had some questions I wanted to discuss by phone about your report," said Mrs. Gutierrez.

"Our report?" asked Sean.

"Yes. In your report this evening you requested to follow Mr. Arias. I wanted to know if you had any other leads to follow in Wilburn?" asked Mrs. Gutierrez.

Sean hesitated but managed to answer, "Nooo."

"Then I'll make arrangements for you and Julie to attend the conference in Buenos Aires this weekend."

"Wait a minute. Mrs. Gutierrez, I guess I have been out of the loop on this, but I don't know anything about Buenos Aires or this report you mention."

"Didn't you and Julie prepare a report and e-mail it to me?"

"No. At least I'm not aware of one. Maybe Julie sent it directly to you."

"Is Julie there?"

"I left her with Peter this evening. They were going to do some computer investigation of Mr. Arias. I don't know if she is back yet."

"Who is this Peter?"

"Peter is an Envirotechie. He helped us with information on our last case together and he has a trailer he brought to Wilburn. He's a member of an environmental group. I think it is called Citizens Against Pollution. The group fights environmental crimes and..."

Mrs. Gutierrez interrupted, "Yes Sean, I know something about that organization. The members are known to do more than provide information. They have interfered in some cases."

"Yes, I'm aware of that too, but so far they have been helpful to us. I make sure not to compromise the FBI."

"And what about Julie?"

"She's OK, but I am concerned about her relationship with Peter."

"Is she compromising the FBI?"

"No! However, I suspect she and Peter have a personal relationship."

"Well I can't tell her what to do with her love life, Sean. But I can tell you that you two ought to work as a team. If you send in any more reports, you better make it clear whether you are both aware of the contents. In the meantime, I'll arrange for all of us to attend the conference."

"You too?"

"Yes, I'll coordinate with the local authorities. You and Julie will attend the conference and follow Mr. Arias and his acquaintances."

"OK. I look forward to seeing you."

"I'd like to see your collaborated report in the morning. Goodnight," said Gutierrez and she hung up.

Sean put the phone back on the nightstand, turned over and fell back to sleep.

Chapter Six

A New Beginning

The next morning, the rains started early in Wilburn, washing away the lingering odors of the recent chemical tragedy. Sean was writing his report to Mrs. Gutierrez as he sat on his bed. He had finally taken a computer course last month at the agency, but these "laptop contraptions" as he called them, were a struggle for Sean. His report read:

At 1600 hours yesterday, the HazOp crews packed up and left. Chemicals were pumped into trucks the day before and sent to a hazardous waste site. Most of the media are now gone and the town's people are moving back into their homes but the place is far from normal. There is a lingering odor that no one knows how to get rid of. Farmers in the surrounding areas worry about the crops that did survive and have few people to turn to for help. When I asked them questions they asked me more questions. Special Agent Del Rio offered her assistance, guiding them with information on the chemical compounds, but once they knew the potential problems they felt worse. Another EPA employee spoke at a town meeting and provided the residents with material safety data sheets on the spilled chemicals. This caused more worry about unborn fetuses, farm animals, elders, etc. People are worried about their children. Will they develop cancer? Will their parents?

Mr. Hugo Arias has been unavailable and our investigation in Wilburn has led to dead ends.

Recent orders are to follow Mr. Hugo Arias to Buenos Aires, where he will attend the International Environmental Conference. We'll catch a flight to Argentina tonight.

Sean connected the laptop to his phone line, and e-mailed the report to the agency. After the report was sent Sean's computer

message popped up, "You've got mail". The message said: "*Your tickets will be at the counter at the airport check-in. Your flight is US Air Flight 210 at 6:22 p.m. tonight from Richmond to Miami. Then you will change over to Argentine Airlines Flight 1402 to Buenos Aires. I'll arrange for you to be met at the airport when you land and to stay at the conference hotel. Assistant Director Gutierrez.*"

He took a sip of his soda, placed it on the night table and started dressing when he heard a knock at the door.

"It's Julie."

Sean opened the door and found Peter and Julie. They barged in excitedly. "We found out something. We may have solved this case!"

"What is it?" Sean hurriedly tried to put on his pants.

"It's a connection. We found out that all of OC Chemicals' plants are controlled by the same software package," said Julie gleaming as she looked at Peter.

"It's not unusual for one company to use one vendor," replied Sean skeptically, as he took off his undershirt and combed his hair. He took out a crisp shirt from his bag and carefully put in on while gazing Julie. Her eyes, however, were focused on Peter.

"They've had a series of accidents lately, and in all cases, the failed components are controlled by the software," said Peter.

"Accidents always happened at night and weren't consistent. No one was hurt," finished Juliana.

"So, they run a bad operation. They have a poor safety record or bad software. What does this prove?" asked Sean.

"There's more..." continued Peter. "There have been some large payments made to the software company lately. So, they are getting more contracts despite their poor performance. And one of the officers of the company resides here in town and has been seen talking to Hugo Arias, the plant manager."

"There's nothing unusual there, they work together," replied Sean while buttoning his cuffs.

"No, I mean, at Hugo's secret society meetings. They belong to the same organization. It's a white supremacist group, you know the Circle of Knights. An informant working for our group has told me," said Peter.

"That's different. Now we're getting somewhere," Sean finally acknowledged. "And now Arias is going to be in Argentina, at the environmental conference. Mrs. Gutierrez wants us there Saturday. Julie, we're leaving tonight. She called me last night. Apparently she followed up on your report - which by the way you didn't share with me first," said Sean, while he loaded his gun and slipped it in his holster.

"I didn't have time to call you last night."

"I'll bet," snapped Sean.

"Don't you see, it could be a fascist group planning to terrorize the conference," said Juliana. "They caused this accident, you know."

"Wait a minute. How do we know that? What evidence do you have?" asked Sean. "The metal part we sent to the lab the other day was analyzed. The report shows that the deformation was caused by the wheel of a train going over it, and that it may very well have been the cause of the derailment. See, here's the report. I just got it this morning," said Julie now sitting on the bed next to Sean, who took the report from her and glanced through it.

Julie, in the meantime, picked up Sean's soda from the side table, her arm crossing over his chest, and took a sip. She sat closer to Sean, to view the report over his shoulder. Her body now nearly touched his. Sean tensed and responded by standing up abruptly.

"But there is something else..." continued Peter. "No one bothered to point out to us, and we realized this later, that

typically, chemicals going to the local OC Chemicals plant are diverted through another set of tracks that passes through the other side of town, near the plant. This train was diverted by the train's control system to pass through the town. This metal object was conveniently placed just in the right spot to derail the train at this particular location."

"So, this was deliberate," said Sean.

"Absolutely, a carefully staged accident. These townspeople were executed," said Julie. "There's more. The paint samples came back from the lab. Those tank cars were recently sprayed to conceal the words Sulfuric Acid and Sodium Hydroxide. So, the firefighters had no idea they were dumping water on water-reactive chemicals," finished Julie. She walked over to Peter.

Sean stared into the mirror for a moment, following Julie's reflection. "And... how is this connected with the software manufacturer?"

"Well... it turns out this fellow, his name is Jeff Forsythe, was a systems engineer for Transportation Data Systems, about four years ago, before he started his own company, Forsythe Systems. Most of his business now comes from OC Chemicals," said Peter.

"So... what's the motive?" asked Sean.

"Sean, I think these guys are trying to kill blacks in general. Arias and Forsythe both belong to that group. They are a hateful, murderous bunch. I've been persecuted because of my race since I arrived. They've abused me, tried to kill me, and called me a Nigger!" exclaimed Julie in frustration.

Sean put on his jacket and He walked over to Julie and Peter. Looking directly at Julie, he placed a hand on her shoulder.

"Lassie, that's just how a lot of towns are. Racism is an illness that plagues this country everywhere I've been. It proves nothing in this case. These bigots will occasionally murder some poor black man, run him over with a car, or terrorize a family. But, to date, they haven't been known to stage such a large-scale

incident. I'm sorry you had to suffer this way. I know it's been hard on you, but we can't let how you feel cloud our thinking."

"A recent FBI case published on the Internet indicates that FBI agents infiltrated a KKK group and stopped them from causing a chemical accident designed to kill residents. So racial motivation for environmental crimes is plausible. If one white supremacist group uses those tactics, groups with similar views will use them too!" stated Peter, now annoyed at Sean's skepticism. Sean casually walked back to the bed, and picked up his laptop computer. He started carefully placing it and the wires into the case.

"But they didn't prove racial motivation for that environmental crime. That's the point," said Sean. "I know that case, and that is only what the FBI announced publicly in trying to make its point to fund the Environmental Crimes Unit. The perpetrators in that case were part of a small isolated group acting on their own - a couple of idiots - who were going to just loosen a valve by hand," said Sean.

"Racially motivated terrorism is a reality," insisted Peter.

"No, this kind of thing takes time, money, expertise and planning. A group will not do this for only revenge or to annihilate a race. There's another motive here," said Sean, sure of himself.

"So, there's plenty of money behind racism! Why do you refuse to believe that these people's hate is so deep that they will go as far as genocide? Didn't the Nazis exterminate six million Jews?" asked Julie, frustrated.

"They didn't exterminate them just because of their hate; there was an economic motive. They wanted to eliminate their enemies so they could take over Europe. Hate was just a tool for the Nazis to motivate the Germans, but it was not the ultimate motive. It never is. Money, resources, water, land and greed are." Sean answered in a cool, almost arrogant tone.

"I think you underestimate man's capacity for hate," argued Peter.

"No, I don't underestimate it, but it is only exceeded by his capacity for greed, or maybe for competition and survival. They want to call these wars 'ethnic cleansing', 'genocide', and hide behind so called 'nobler' reasons such as religious freedom, but all we're really after is **land**, **water** and **power**. That's what drives wars, and the killings. American Indians were exterminated to control the most fertile lands and water. The Israelis would like to control the source of the water in Lebanon and the fighting will never stop until they do. The rest of the world fights over land and resources, and as these dwindle due to our continued greed, so will wars escalate, and the suffering," said Sean emphatically.

Peter didn't have a comeback for such an elaborate speech. Julie contemplated for a while, realizing there was more to Sean than she gave him credit for. "So, what's your theory?" she finally asked.

"We'll find out when we go to Buenos Aires. I think Arias is the key here. Are you packed?"

"It'll take me just a few minutes."

"There's no time for that now. You'll have time later to throw some things in a bag, but now we need to go to the sheriff's office. This guy knows something. Peter, you better not be seen with us," said Sean as he grabbed Julie's hand and pulled her out of the room, leaving a bewildered Peter.

Sean returned, peeked into the room quickly and with a sly smile said to Peter, "Lock up, will you please?"

Julie was sitting in their rental car, which still reeked of chemicals despite five different air fresheners that Sean had placed in it. "What's the matter with you?" she asked.

"I think you're seeing too much of that guy," said Sean starting the car.

"Number one, we're good friends, and two, *que carajo te importa!*"

"Look you always end up getting hurt with these guys."

"What guys? Yes, I fell for the wrong guy back in Alaska. I admit that was a mistake, but Peter saved our lives on that case. He has been so helpful. What do you have against him now?"

"No he hasn't! I remember that he took his time coming to our rescue in the warehouse. He doesn't have what it takes. He was paralyzed by fear."

"Sean, what now? Are you my dad or are you jealous?"

"Neither! You are gallivanting around with Peter forgetting that we're on a case and I just wish you would remember that we're partners. He is not an agent. He hesitates in the face of danger. He is a good source for research but you're placing yourself in jeopardy by working with him. Your job is to work with me," snapped Sean, speeding to the sheriff's office.

"You seem to be acting like some damned bull in heat. I don't appreciate this kind of attitude from you. We are partners... that's all Mr. Ryan. Just partners."

"Look, this is business. You're jeopardizing the case by abandoning me and going off with Peter. Yes, we're partners. Let's keep that in mind from now on and start acting accordingly."

"You don't even appreciate all the work we did trying to solve the case," said Julie, frustrated.

"I do appreciate it, but I just wish you had kept me in the loop instead of firing off that report without checking with me first."

"What was this visit about? It was about keeping you in the loop."

"Never mind, let's interview the sheriff. We have a flight to catch."

When they arrived at the sheriff's office, Sean said. "OK, I'll lead, but I want you to try to charm him into answering some questions about the plant manager."

"Me? Charm this bigot?"

As they headed into the office Sean was still frowning, but Julie managed to put a big smile on her face.

"Sheriff Williams, it's so nice seeing that you're OK. How are you feeling? Have you been taking care of that cough?" asked Julie.

"To what do we owe this pleasure?" asked the sheriff.

"We have a few more questions for you and then we're out of here. We need to know more about Hugo Arias. For example, do you know where he was the night of the accident?" asked Sean.

"He was at the plant, making sure everything was OK. He called the safety team and issued them masks. He sent us all of the resources he had and was very helpful to all of us," the sheriff answered indignantly.

"Do you know anything about the Circle of Knights Society?" asked Sean.

"No. It's a private club and I don't belong. It's never been any trouble."

"Are you aware that Arias belongs to this group, and they peddle racial hatred?"

"What are you suggesting?"

"You tell me. We have a bigot society here in town, having meetings, spreading racial hatred, and then we have a chemical 'accident' where a lot of blacks are killed. What do you God damn think is going on!" asked Sean, his voice controlled and hard as steel.

"I've told you before that the train derailment was an accident. That's all, an accident. There was no racial motivation or terrorism."

"That's not what the lab shows, Sheriff Williams," said Julie.

"What do you mean?"

"The FBI has proof that this was no accident. We're leaving, for now, but other agents will be around. This group is under careful scrutiny."

Suddenly, from the back came a voice: "Hey, can you bail me out?"

It was George. He was sitting in one of the jail cells.

"What the heck is he doing here?" asked Sean.

"He was drunk and disorderly last night."

"What's his bail?"

"His stay is over; he can go," said the sheriff unlocking the cell.

"George, I thought you were going home to rest last night," said Sean.

"I got sidetracked."

Sean and Julie started out and the reporter followed. "What do you mean this was no accident. What can you tell me?"

"Nothing, only that we suspect terrorism."

"What's the evidence?" asked George.

"We can't go into it now. We're in a hurry. Call the FBI office and they'll give you the official story."

"Where are you guys going?"

"We can't tell you, you know that."

"I'll find out, you know."

As Sean and Julie got into the car, George came up to the passenger window. "Come on, give me a story."

Sean simply drove away and left George standing on the street.

On the way to the hotel, Julie was quiet. Sean pulled the car into the hotel's parking lot, still annoyed at Julie and at George. He walked into his room and grabbed the bags before going next door to Julie's room.

Julie was folding her clothes into the bag, and said nothing.

"You know, it's winter in Argentina. Those outfits are going to be too light," said Sean.

"Unfortunately, I don't have the time to go shopping."

"There's a mall next to the Richmond airport and we may have time for you to buy a coat. That suit looks warm enough."

"I'll get a nice outfit in Buenos Aires. I always wanted to shop there."

"I'm sorry I snapped at you that way. It was unprofessional. I should have told you earlier that having you go off on your own was not the way I wanted to investigate this case. You know, there have been a lot of close calls here, and we need to work as a team at all times – particularly in Argentina. We may be in danger and we'll be on our own."

"I was wrong to go off with Peter and not include you in the investigation. You're right, I am attracted to him and I forgot myself. I needed a refuge after the way I was treated in this damn town and he was very comforting to me."

"I know how that feels, but don't forget, it's my job to protect you. That's the deal. You're still an environmental consultant. This case is getting very dangerous. Peter is not an agent. He is young and relatively inexperienced, and his group may be placing you in danger. It's best they're used for information but

not a good idea that you're seen together, at least when we're on a case."

"I know it's your job, but I want you to know I appreciate your dedication. Thank you for the times you've saved my life. I will be more discreet with Peter, but just to let you know, we are seeing each other, as friends, outside of the job. I know that could be a problem with Gutierrez, so if you want, I'll bring it up to her."

"There is no need to mention it to her. Your private life is your own. Just keep it separate from your job."

"It's hard to do that. Sometimes you have feelings for people you work with," said Julie now looking at Sean. "What am I supposed to do, turn off all emotions while on the job?"

"You may have to bury your feelings for the sake of this job. I always have," said Sean now picking up her bag. "OK, let's go. We have a long trip to the airport." Once back at the car, Sean tried to lighten the mood. "Boy, that rental agency is going to charge the FBI extra to clean this stinking car."

"I can't wait to get some fresh air. Do you want me to drive so you can rest? You look a bit tired."

"Would you mind? I need some sleep, I've been struggling with that computer since early this morning to get the report out."

"No problem, partner!"

Sean got into the passenger seat, as Julie slid over to the driver's spot.

Sean was asleep in minutes and snored all the way to the airport. Julie tried to close his mouth a couple of times. He didn't budge.

What a protector, she thought, and brushed the reddish hairs away from his face.

Sean woke as they pulled into the airport. "Our flight to Miami is in a couple of hours. Do you want to shop?"

"OK. Meet me here in an hour, I'll get a coat."

"I'll come with you. I don't trust anybody around here. Besides, I happen to like shopping."

"Well, I hope Gutierrez will pay for this, I had to get rid of a lot of good clothes that the chemicals ruined. The suit I have on now is new. I got it in town."

"Looks good. Gutierrez is going to give us a hard time, you know. She watches her budget like a hawk."

"Well, I'll call the EPA. This is several hundred dollars' worth of clothing."

Sean and Julie went into the store. Julie walked around the racks of new fall coats. "There's nothing warm enough here."

As Julie tried on a coat, Sean walked toward her, looking around at the periphery of the store, his hand now inside his coat holding his gun. "Someone is following us."

"Where?" whispered Julie.

"He's hiding behind the third rack."

Julie's adrenaline surged and perspiration covered her forehead. She instinctively slipped behind the clothes rack and walked toward the door. Sean followed.

They took a quick look back and walked out the door. Julie was wearing the coat she was trying on. As she went through the door, a piercing alarm alerted the store guards, who soon appeared. "Please stop right there!"

Sean already had his badge in his hand and flashed it at the guards. "Sean Ryan, FBI. We saw a suspicious character behind one of the racks. He seemed to be observing us, and hid when I noticed him."

The guard spoke into his two-way radio: "Joe, check the cameras. Is there a guy hiding behind one of the racks?"

"Yeah. I saw a guy who looked suspicious. He didn't take anything."

"We can't stop him. You guys have to do it. We have no evidence to arrest him."

"We'll handle this from here Phil, and thank you for your assistance," said Sean noting the guard's name tag and shaking the guard's hand.

A man in the long, black unseasonably warm raincoat and hat came out and attempted to walk toward his car unnoticed. "Hold it right there," warned Sean pointing his revolver at the man's back.

The other man stopped and raised his hands.

Julie also pulled out her gun and pointed it at the man, her hand slightly trembling. "Turn around slowly," she said.

As he turned the man said in a trembling voice: "It's me, George, the reporter. Don't shoot me please!"

"What the hell are you doing here?" demanded a surprised Sean.

"I got nothing from your office and I decided to follow you to find out where you're going."

"I find it hard to believe you're doing all of this for a story. We could arrest you on suspicion of trailing an officer of the law."

"I just want to know what's up. I was planning to sell the story to one of the networks and maybe get out of this now literally stinking town of Wilburn."

"You know more than you've told us," said Sean walking toward George.

"Sean, we can't waste any more time on him," said Julie pointing at her watch. "We have to catch a plane to... New York, so you can go to the office, remember?"

"You are booked to a flight to Buenos Aires leaving from Miami. I checked with Peter."

"You know too damn much," said Sean, as he turned and walked toward the car with Julie trailing behind. The reporter ran to catch up with Sean and walked along side.

"Why are you going to the same environmental conference as Hugo Arias is attending? What do you suspect about him?"

"We don't know yet, but if you've warned him you'll have jeopardized our operation and then we'll arrest you as a co-conspirator."

"You can't arrest me for exercising my constitutional right to freedom of the press."

"I can arrest you for attacking an FBI officer," growled Sean, as he grabbed him by his collar, nearly lifting him off the ground.

"Sean, come on. Leave him, please. We'll let Franz take care of him while we're away. He'll make it look like an accident," said Julie taking Sean's arm. "Come on, we're late. Let's go."

"You don't fool me. You can't touch me and you know it. Franz? Who the hell is Franz? I'm not worried. He can't touch me either...Maybe I'll just sic my dog Adolph on you, you morons."

Sean and Julie ignored George's ranting, got into the car and headed toward the nearby terminal.

"We'll leave the car on the lot and do a quick checkout. They'll send the bill to the agency," said Sean.

"They're going to charge Gutierrez an arm and a leg for this. But we're out of time," said Julie as they ran toward the departure gate. They passed through security, showing their badges.

Again, the guard wanted to check Julie out, but Sean balked. "Look, we're both agents. Here's more documentation. We better not miss this flight on your account."

"You can't take those guns on board loaded," said the security guard.

"We're putting them in our bags, OK?"

Sean and Julie ran toward the gate and barely made the flight. Julie took the window seat, as usual. They both waited to catch their breath and finally Juliana said: "Dammit."

"What?"

"I didn't pay for the coat!"

"Well, I'm sure Gutierrez will get a bill for that, too. They took my badge number. They'll probably triple the price for the government's benefit."

"Where did she book us?"

"We're at the Regency Hotel in Buenos Aires," said Sean, stretching a bit in his seat.

"I can't wait!"

"Ah....Julie, it wasn't my idea but she booked us in the same room. She said it's safer and it saves money. We're booked as Mr. and Mrs. Trillian, again!"

"That is sick! Again! Is she playing a joke on us? Just like it was in our last case. Well, I just don't care at this point. I wish we were there; I need a shower!"

"Well, it's a twelve- hour trip, so try to sleep."

"I can't sleep. I'm angry with myself. I didn't notice that reporter following us!"

"You should be angry at yourself. This lack of concentration can cost you your life! Have you been paying attention at all to what I've been trying to teach you?"

"OK, dammit! It took you twenty-five years and a lot of bullet holes to learn all that stuff. I finally admit that I am just not trained as an agent. I don't have the experience. I am just an EPA consultant and have to stop trying to play detective! Yes, I was arrogant to think I could do it, but I finally bow to your greater wisdom and experience, Mr. Ryan! Are you happy now? I do my own job very well, thank you!"

"And by that you mean I don't?" quipped Sean.

"NO! I mean we're a team, let's stop competing and work together, I know my own limitations and you pointing them out to me constantly doesn't help our relationship .... as partners!"

"I think I need a drink!" Sean grunted. "Stewardess!"

"No, I ... please..." pleaded Julie realizing she could be pushing Sean off the wagon with her stubbornness. "Please don't take a drink because of me, I apologize, really, I should keep my mouth shut!"

The stewardess stopped by their seat and Sean said "Ginger Ale."

"Me too, lots of ice please," she said with a smile of relief. There was a short silence while the stewardess prepared the drinks. When the stewardess left Julie said: "I'm really sorry. I tend to carry on like that when I've been in a tense situation. It's my nerves."

"I know."

"How do you know?"

"When you work with someone as much as I have with you, you get to know her."

"It's only been a couple of months since we teamed up on our first case."

"I still have spent more time with you than with Alexandra, and saved your life a few times in those two months. I know you pretty well by now. You needn't apologize, we're both going to be

under a lot of stress from now on and we can't keep apologizing every time one of us snaps at the other. Partners forgive these things. It's part of the job," said Sean.

Nothing much was said during the trip to Miami. Sean put on his earphones and Juliana read a book on environmental testing techniques. Sean glanced at it and closed his eyes while shaking his head.

As Sean and Julie made their way through the Miami airport terminal, Sean didn't say much. He was on the job now, watching Julie and anyone that came near them.

When they sat down at the gate waiting to board, Sean noticed a man reading a brochure. Sean got up and walked past the man, glanced at the brochure, and noted it read Forsythe Systems.

Julie got up and caught up with Sean. "I'm going to the ladies room."

"I'll stand guard."

"What for?"

Sean insisted and stood guard outside the restroom.

Exiting the ladies room, Julie stopped in front of Sean. "Don't you have to go, too? Why don't I stand guard for you?" she asked jokingly.

"My makeup is just fine," snapped Sean as he started walking ahead of Juliana.

Then once again, getting more serious, "What's going on with you? Do you see someone suspicious?"

Sean nodded and said nothing. On the way back to the boarding area Sean made a sudden move and pulled Julie into a corner. It was a quiet spot where they couldn't be seen. Julie was now only about a foot from Sean, and felt uncomfortable being so close to him.

"What's going on?"

"That guy from Forsythe Systems. I happened to glance at him reading a brochure of the company and saw that his leather briefcase had the initials JF. That may be the guy Arias does business with and he's on his way to Argentina too, possibly the conference."

"Could it be he's there to sell services?" asked Julie slowly moving away.

Sean pulled her back. "He's standing against the window, so act naturally and don't give him any reason to suspect he's being followed. I doubt that he's going to Argentina on his own. I don't know what he could be selling there."

"Well, I think that he and Arias are going there as a team to make some kind of deal. Maybe they're selling terrorist services to international anti- or pro-environ-mentalist forces. I mean, I believe Peter. Arias and this guy Forsythe made the train wreck happen, but maybe there is another motive," said Julie.

"You know Lassie, you're a pretty smart woman. They must be selling their services," said Sean, looking now directly at Julie. The look and the closeness made Julie nervous.

Suddenly Sean started walking toward the terminal, leaving Julie to catch up with him. "Are you sure that's him? I mean you never met him. Maybe it's someone who works for him?"

"We'll find out soon enough," said Sean as they walked toward the boarding area.

Chapter Seven

The Argentine Way

The long flight to Buenos Aires was uneventful. Sean avoided Forsythe, who sat several rows in front of him, and Julie said nothing about the case during the flight. Instead, she read a novel. Sean dozed, occasionally peeking at the on-board movie.

Upon arriving in Buenos Aires they were met by Mrs. Gutierrez.

"Julie, Sean, so glad to have you here!" She surprised Julie and Sean by hugging each of them. Gutierrez was not the stern director; today she was Anna, warm, friendly. However, she changed back to Gutierrez the FBI assistant director as soon as they got into the black sedan with the tinted windows. Sam, a stone-faced large black man, who kept his semiautomatic weapon at his side at all times, was sitting next to the driver.

"Sam is my bodyguard. We felt this was needed. There is additional support at the conference. While in Buenos Aires, I urge you to treat me as an old friend while in public, and please speak Spanish. Refrain from public conversation regarding the case and our mission. The two of you have been checked into a large suite. You'll be able to monitor the street and the conference. The equipment you'll need is in this suitcase. Because of the possibility of sabotage of this conference we're working with the local law enforcement agency. The contact is Ricardo Ortega, whom you'll meet later. He'll coordinate surveillance with you. There are a number of undercover Argentine agents working in the hotel."

Sean leaned forward and whispered to Gutierrez: "My Spanish is good Anna, but my accent is heavy."

"That has never been a problem in my career Sean," Gutierrez said, before continuing with instructions. "This is a global conference and you'll be representing an international delegation. You're sharing a special suite that will give you an excellent view of the street entrance. As far as the front desk is concerned, remember you're married to Ms. Del Rio and you're registered as Mr. and Mrs. Trillian. The office has booked you for a number of sessions during the conference. Here's the list."

Upon arriving at the hotel, the group separated. Sean and Julie carried their bags into the lobby.

"OK Lassie, Español from now on, but you better not even snicker once."

Julie smiled, but as soon as Sean looked at her, she tried to look serious.

Sean approached the desk clerk and said quietly, in his Irish brogue-tinged Spanish, "We are Mr. and Mrs. Trillian and we're attending the conference."

The clerk took down the information, looked up their reservation and handed them the electronic key-cards. A bellboy took their bags and walked with them to their suite.

The two agents kept quiet. Any hint to the bellboy of who they were might jeopardize the operation. As the bellboy opened the door, Julie's face lit up when she saw the opulent suite. The bellboy placed the bags inside and as he walked out Sean handed him some of the pesos that Gutierrez gave them to spend while in town.

When the bellboy was gone, Julie took a deep breath and let out a sigh as she plunged into the luxurious couch.

"Now this is a hotel room! I'm beginning to like Gutierrez. I can't wait to get in the tub. Ohh, there's only one bedroom in this suite. You can take the bedroom Sean, I'd rather sleep out here so I can watch the large-screen TV."

"Fine with me."

"Why don't you shower first, since I want to soak for a while? It's nearly morning and there won't be time to sleep before the conference, which starts at ten, but at least I can look presentable. I'm going to have something to eat downstairs later."

"I want you to watch the street while I'm in the shower. The delegates and visitors are starting to trickle in the front door and we may catch something. You watch through the telescope I've set up," said Sean.

"OK, go ahead. Nice new shiny equipment. Oh, yeah, did the new budget come through? Can't believe how they're splurging here," said Julie.

Sean went into the bathroom and Julie watched the street with the high-tech telescope. She took some time to focus away from the building and test the zoom lens. As she was observing the delegates coming in through the front door of the hotel, she noticed a group from India - the woman wearing a colorful wrapped skirt and the man a turban. There were Chinese representatives and dark-skinned delegates in African garb. The unusual mix of races that filled the street stood out against the mostly white European immigrants who lived in Buenos Aires.

This was an important international environmental conference where issues like global warming, ocean dumping, nuclear terrorism and toxic contamination were going to be discussed. Top leaders from the world's most prominent environmental organizations wanted to be heard.

Suddenly Julie saw a familiar figure below and she zoomed in on his face and briefcase. "Sean, come over to the window quickly!"

Sean ran out of the shower with a towel loosely wrapped around his waist.

"I think one of them is Forsythe, the man you saw at the airport, and the other might be Arias. I only saw pictures of him, so I can't be sure," said Julie.

"I actually never met either of them," said Sean as he adjusted his towel. He looked into the telescope and studied the faces, using the zoom lens to get a better view. "Yes, the one on the right is the man I saw in Miami, but I'm not sure who the other man is. Do you have a photo of Arias?" asked Sean.

"No, but let me take one. I believe I can send it to Washington for an ID." Julie picked up the digital camera, zoomed in on the men, and snapped. Within seconds a close-up of Arias and his companion appeared on the small screen of the camera. Julie connected the device to her computer and plugged the laptop to the phone line. "I'm e-mailing the file to the lab in the states for verification and to Peter because he might have their pictures handy. We should get an answer quickly. I could access the files myself but it would take too long."

"And you can dial into the FBI network from here?" asked Sean.

"Sure, the FBI networks are worldwide. I just type in the country here and the system dials into the closest phone number to connect and e-mail. Simple."

"I have got to get more training on these things," sighed Sean frustrated at his lack of understanding of basic high-tech gadgets.

"I thought you knew everything," said Julie in a teasing tone. "It looks like there might be something I can teach *you* after all."

"Humm? You go take your bath. I'll keep watch," said Sean.

As Julie walked away, satisfied that she finally had one up on Sean, she quickly turned and casually said "By the way, looking good. Buff, and trim; going to the gym lately? I guess Alexandra is keeping you in shape!"

"I had to pass my physical, or I wouldn't be on this case! Now get into your bathtub already. We've got work to do this morning."

Feeling somewhat uncomfortable at Julie's remarks, Sean quickly put on a shirt. However, he didn't want to take the time to get fully dressed until he finished watching all of the delegates enter the hotel. He looked carefully at each delegate, often taking digital pictures.

Julie closed the bathroom door and shouted, "This bathroom is terrific! Gutierrez outdid herself!"

Sean didn't stop his surveillance to put on his pants. He saw the man who he thought was Arias, and his companion Forsythe, going into the hotel.

He called Gutierrez from the secure cell phone the assistant director had provided. "Mrs. Gutierrez? Can we get our contact to confirm if Hugo Arias has checked into the conference? I believe I saw him outside with Jeff Forsythe and someone else that might be from that computer company."

"We'll have our contact report to me if he checks in. If he does, we'll make sure you get into the conferences he is attending."

Before hanging up Sean heard a knock. He opened the door, still wearing the towel and an open shirt, and saw a young, dark-haired man who presented a badge.

"Ahh, El Señor Ryan?" said the man somewhat surprised to see Sean practically naked.

"Yes."

"Ricardo Ortega of the Argentine police. Your Assistant Director, Señora Gutierrez must have told you I was coming to discuss how we can coordinate our activities."

"Yes, yes, come in," said Sean in his broken Spanish.

"Excuse me while I get dressed please, I was showering after our long trip from Wilburn, Virginia. Are you aware of the chemical accident that occurred there?"

"Yes, I was briefed on it by Señora Gutierrez."

Sean carried his pants into the bedroom. "Sit down; I'll be right out!"

Julie's voice could be heard from the bathroom, which was accessible from the living area where Ricardo was standing. "Sean, could you bring in the robe that's on the bed please?" Sean came out wearing his pants and partially buttoned shirt, holding a terry robe provided by the hotel. He slowly opened the bathroom door and quickly placed the robe inside.

"Officer Ortega from the Argentine Police is here," he whispered in English to Julie, who was in the tub, covered in suds, with her eyes closed. Sean took a quick peek and dropped the bathrobe on the nearest chair. "Thanks. Now get out please," she said.

Sean came out, somewhat embarrassed.

"Can we offer you something to drink? Soda or water," he said, pointing at the small bar in the suite.

"Thank you. I seldom have a chance to be in such luxurious surroundings. I see Washington treats its agents well."

"Well, this is not typical, but yes, we get to work in some nice areas. Last case my partner Juliana and I were on a cruise. Of course, then I ended up in a radioactive chamber, but that's another story."

"I would enjoy meeting with you off duty and hear your stories. You seem very experienced. I want to join the FBI one day."

"I'll be happy to. But let's discuss this case now. Do you know that Mr. Hugo Arias is here in Argentina and is suspected of chemical terrorism in the states? We haven't been able to prove anything yet, but we have some leads. He has been seen with another suspect, Jeff Forsythe, head of Forsythe Systems, a contractor to OC Chemicals, the plant that Arias runs outside of Wilburn. We have evidence that the recent train wreck occurred as a result of a deliberate derailment, and that Arias has

connections to a group that may have caused the derailment and possibly other random chemical spills. We have no proof. But their attendance at this conference, and it being a target for terrorists, was enough reason to follow them here."

"We will help you in any way we can. Señora Gutierrez has promised to assist us in locating possible terrorists who may disrupt this conference. And, by the way, your Spanish is excellent. Did you live in South America?"

"Well, I know I carry a heavy Irish accent, but I worked for the CIA before I joined the FBI and I spent a lot time in Colombia."

"And your partner, the lady in the bathroom?"

"Julie? My partner, Juliana Del Rio is posing as my wife during the conference. She is a consultant to the FBI from the US Environmental Protection Agency. This is our second case together. We work exclusively on environmental cases that involve sabotage, terrorism, and similar crimes."

Ricardo looked away from Sean and focused on Julie, who emerged from the bathroom looking radiant, wearing a white terry robe; her hair piled on top her head and held in place with a big colorful clip. Small black curls framed her mocha face and she looked relaxed and especially beautiful. Even Sean took a second look, as if he had never noticed before that Julie was an attractive woman.

"Hello Mr. Ortega," she said, while holding her robe tightly around her. "Please excuse me while I go into the bedroom and change."

Ricardo followed Julie with his eyes all the way into the bedroom.

"Mr. Ryan, I understand you are posing as a couple, but, are you?"

"Are we what?" asked Sean.

"A couple."

"Not that this is any of your business Mr. Ortega, since you're here to assist us, but, no, we are only partners."

"Well, I just thought, you seem very close, I didn't want to... I mean, she is a beautiful woman. Is she seeing anyone?"

Sean rolled his eyes and muttered in English "Here we go again. Mr. Ortega, may I remind you that you are here to assist in this international investigation, not to romance US officers. Miss Del Rio is off limits to you sir. She is on assignment, and I would urge you to respect that. I may have to ask Mrs. Gutierrez to assign another officer to this case if you don't. Is that clear?"

"So you are involved I see."

"My involvement with her is professional. She's my partner and we need to stay focused on this case right now, but I also don't want to see her hurt. Is that clear?"

The subject was dropped as soon as Julie emerged from the bedroom. "It's a pleasure to meet you," she said extending her hand to Ortega. He stood up as he reached for her hand, holding it gently and bringing it to his mouth to kiss the back. "I am honored, Ms. Del Rio."

Julie was flushed and smiled, slowly retrieving her hand from Ortega's as Sean looked on with his typical frown. He walked toward the hotel bar and almost reached for the small bottle of whiskey, but then switched, choosing the can of ginger ale instead. "May I offer you a drink, Mr. Ortega?"

Ortega took a while to respond, his eyes fixed on Julie, making her extremely uncomfortable.

"Let's discuss your strategy, Mr. Ortega," said Julie to break the awkward silence.

"Yes let's!" interrupted Sean. "Julie, should you be checking the e-mail, to see what the ID on those guys is?"

"Oh yes. They may have already responded." Julie walked to the laptop computer and keyed in some codes to retrieve the e-mail. "Peter responded. It's Forsythe and Arias we saw."

"Come here, Officer Ortega; these are their pictures. These are the men I was telling you about and who are at the conference."

Ortega walked over to where Julie was sitting and put his head close to hers to view the photographs. He placed his arm around her back and held on to the chair nearly surrounding Julie. "Yes, I have seen them. I'll point them out to our contacts and we'll make sure they are followed."

Ortega walked away from Julie and his eyes focused on Sean. "We have a few other suspected terrorists on our list Mr. Ryan, and we're looking out for any connections or meetings with Hugo Arias and his companion Jeff Forsythe. We'll also tap their phone lines. We have officers – disguised as staff – on duty at the conference in a number of locations. For example, one of the bellboys, and some people at the registration desks work for us. They will be relaying the registration information to Señora Gutierrez so you can attend the same conferences they do."

"Good. Well, I think we'd better run along to the conferences, which are starting soon. Good-bye, Mr. Ortega."

"Here is my cellular number if you need to reach me; may I have your phone numbers?" said Ortega.

"We were just issued new local phones; here's my number and here's Ms. Del Rio's."

"Ms. Del Rio, will I see you tonight at the reception?"

"Yes, we'll be there."

"Good-bye Mr. Ortega," said Sean showing him the door.

"I'll be running along too, Sean. I wanted to grab some breakfast before the conference starts," said Julie grabbing her handbag and heading out the door with Ricardo.

"Why don't you join me for coffee downstairs?" asked Ricardo.

Sean frowned as he watched the two of them walk side-by-side until they were out of sight.

"Well, he seems to work very fast. I hope his police work is as good," Sean muttered to himself.

Julie spent about a half-hour before the conferences started getting acquainted with the handsome police officer. He was a personable and very interesting man. He loved to discuss politics, and made Juliana feel intensely feminine with all of his chivalrous attentions. It didn't take long for the two to realize that there was a special chemistry between them.

"I understand that Forsythe is going to be attending the transportation conference. I have to go, Ricardo. It was great meeting you."

"I'll see you tonight at the reception. You're a very special woman and I hope to see more of you. Until tonight," and Ricardo kissed her on the cheek, a gesture that is typical between good friends or simply acquaintances in that part of South America. Julie was surprised but she then kissed him back, more tenderly, her lips lingering a bit longer, a gesture that Ricardo immediately responded to by holding her hand for a minute and letting it slide through his as she walked away.

Julie continued to smile as she went over to the ballroom where the transportation conference was being held. As she walked in, she spotted Forsythe sitting in the second row and took a seat just behind him. She put on her reading glasses and concentrated on a notebook and brochures.

The speakers presented slides, and Forsythe seemed to be taking notes on a notebook computer. But Juliana put on a pair of magnifying glasses and she could see the icon that indicated he was online via the wireless service; he seemed to be typing e-mail. She glanced away and when she looked over at the screen again, she saw a diagram. It looked like pipes, valves and vessels, and part of a chemical processing plant. Forsythe

seemed to be typing commands and clicking on various parts of the diagram.

That evening there was a reception in the Grand Ballroom. All the environmental representatives attended the formal dinner and dance. A live tango orchestra would be playing, a gift from the government. The delegates would enjoy an evening of classic tango, sung by Argentina's best.

Sean came into the suite to change and found Julie standing in front of the mirror working on her hair. The slenderizing simple black gown she wore cost her a week's salary, but the effect was stunning. She didn't look like the Julie he was used to seeing. She was like a child in anticipation of her date with Ricardo in such a romantic setting. As Julie put on makeup and sprayed on cologne, Sean stopped for a minute and took a long look at her, but could not figure out what to say. As he walked past, he glanced at her shapely back and quickly moved his eyes away, looking down as he went into the bedroom to change.

Gutierrez's words at the recent sexual harassment seminar seemed to echo in his head. Since that day at FBI headquarters, when Gutierrez led the new seminar, Sean had been more sensitive and cautious about his relationship with Julie. But this new sensitivity put a damper on some of the fun they were having together, at least from his point of view. He remembered the time he held her and kissed her, as part of the charade on the Alaskan cruise line case. She was furious, and told him in no uncertain terms that theirs was going to be a professional relationship, and nothing more.

But Sean now resented Ortega because there were no obstacles that prevented the man from showering Julie with well-deserved compliments, and what made it worse for Sean was that, instead of rejecting them, she seemed to eat them up. Ricardo was moving in fast on Sean's partner and he felt threatened; his male ego was hurt, and he couldn't do anything about it because it wasn't his business. His stomach tightened

into a knot whenever he thought about Julie and Ricardo together.

"You seem quiet Sean. What's the matter?"

"Oh, nothing. It's been a long day," he replied from inside the bedroom.

Sean changed into a tired old navy suit and standard issue FBI tie. His choice of attire never did justice to his rugged Irish face and tall, muscular slender body.

Juliana finished with her hair and makeup, picked up her beaded pocketbook and slipped her gun inside it.

"Sean, are you done? I'm going downstairs."

Sean emerged, wearing his slightly wrinkled suit, and Juliana frowned.

"Are you wearing that?"

"Yes," said Sean annoyed.

"I thought you had a gray suit."

"The gray suit stunk from our trip to Wilburn."

"I sent it to the cleaners for you, I think it will be OK. Try it."

"You sent MY suit to the cleaners?"

"Yes, and 'thank you Juliana for being so thoughtful'," said Juliana sarcastically.

Sean rolled his eyes and took a deep breath, but went back into the bedroom to change into the newly pressed gray suit. As he put it on, he noticed the smell of sulfur from the train wreck that had penetrated the fibers was gone, replaced now by the aroma of the cleaning solvent. He wrinkled his nose and walked toward the mirror.

As he gazed at his reflection, he smoothed his hair, and moved his face closer to the mirror to take a closer look at his

face. He traced around what used to be wrinkles on his face but now was smooth. He stepped back and realized he was still a good-looking man. The years of alcohol abuse had taken a toll on Sean's good looks, but in the last eight weeks his body had miraculous been brought back to life.

The pollution had been expelled from his body and his soul. His face was smooth, his hair seemed to have that flexibility it lacked before and he was able to stand erect and tall. His muscles had been toned at the gym. With his new suit, and new confidence he emerged thinking to himself that perhaps he could teach Ricardo and Peter a thing or two. His male ego was now sufficiently swelled for him to think of himself as a true contender. He walked out and dared to look Julie in the eyes.

She smiled and said, "That's more like it. Now you look presentable."

Sean looked at Julie, his ego having been deflated sufficiently now, and said, "You, too."

Julie picked up her pocketbook, started walking out the door. As Sean followed her out and closed the door he said, "Don't forget to put your gun in your pocket."

"I'm carrying the gun in my purse. There are no pockets in this dress, as I am sure you've noticed."

To that Sean dared not respond, but he did take the opportunity to gaze approvingly at Julie's shapely figure as she was walking to the elevator. He followed, smiling to himself.

The Grand Ballroom was all aglow, the orchestra already playing a song by Gardel, *"El Dia Que Me Quieras."* ("The Day You Fall in Love With Me")

Julie saw Ricardo sitting at Gutierrez's table, and walked toward him with a smile on her lips. He planted a kiss on Julie's lips, right in front of her boss, but Gutierrez was not the FBI director today. She was soft, happy, and smiled approvingly at Julie and Ricardo.

Gutierrez was a slightly plump woman, short, her hair dyed red. Her gold-rimmed glasses framed her slightly wrinkled face. She always wore a skirt suit, even to parties. But for this event, she wore a red gown. Sean sat next to Gutierrez, as Ricardo took Julie's hand and led her to the dance floor.

"I can almost forget work today," said Gutierrez.

"Buenos Aires is one of the most beautiful cities in the world. It was known as the Paris of the Americas in its day," said Sean.

"You're looking better Sean. I see you took my advice and have been taking care of yourself," said Gutierrez.

"Yes Anna, I have. I'm glad you approve," said Sean smiling. "Would you care to dance?"

"Yes, I haven't done this in years, thank you."

Sean led Anna Gutierrez to the dance floor and she smiled as they both awkwardly danced the tango. Sean glanced at Julie occasionally when he thought his boss wasn't looking. However, Gutierrez was a true FBI agent. She didn't miss a thing.

"How are you and your partner getting along these days, Sean?"

"Well ma'am, we have ironed out a few problems. I'd say we get along better. We're friends now."

"More than friends, I think, by the way you're looking at her."

"No... I was looking at the man up front. I saw something suspicious."

"Really? How interesting."

Sean saw something from the corner of his eye and quickly turned his eyes away from Gutierrez and toward the front. He saw Hugo Arias casually walk toward a table where three dark-haired men, who could have been delegates from the Arab countries, were sitting. Forsythe followed Arias and sat at the table with the four men.

Sean grabbed Gutierrez's arm and said, as he walked her toward the lobby, "Come on Anna, we'll make our way to the lobby so we can get a closer look."

As he passed Julie and Ricardo on the dance floor, Sean cut right in and whispered something in Julie's ear.

Placing his arm on Ricardo's shoulder, Sean led him to the bar.

As Julie and Gutierrez walked to the ladies' room, Anna pretended to twist her foot and she fell near the table where Arias and the other men were sitting. Gutierrez casually dropped her glasses as Juliana was helping her up. As she was walking away, one of the men from the table ran after her and returned her glasses.

At that point, a waiter walked over to the table and placed a basket of bread near Arias's seat.

"Thank you," said Gutierrez, sounding slightly tipsy. "You're a gentleman."

The two women walked past the entrance and toward the ladies' room. Gutierrez put her glasses carefully into her purse, inside a plastic bag. "We'll have this analyzed tomorrow," she said to Juliana. "We have at least one print." She walked over to the waitress and said to her in Spanish. "Table 31. All utensils to the lab for prints."

In the ladies' room, Gutierrez made sure they were alone before she explained: "The waiter is one of our own operatives. He doesn't work for Ortega and I don't want Ortega to make this collar. If these guys are up to something, we'll be able to trace them. We'll analyze DNA and prints," explained Gutierrez, now back in her role as boss. "Ms. Del Rio, I need you to attend a few more technical meetings and observe these individuals tomorrow. And I hope that you will be careful what you say to Ortega."

"Yes ma'am."

"Let's go back now."

Julie and Gutierrez entered the dining room and approached the bar where Sean and Ricardo were sitting and sipping club sodas.

The listening device, hidden in the bread basket the waiter had placed on the table, was picking up the conversation between Arias and one of the other men. As the women approached Julie started: "Ricky, let's go back to the dance..." but Ricardo pointed to the earphone and held up his hand. "Let's get out of here!" said Sean.

Sean and Gutierrez started walking to the lobby, followed by Ricardo and Julie. The four met at the elevator and went up to Sean and Julie's suite. Sam, the bodyguard, was standing outside, his face without expression. They said nothing as they walked to the door. When they entered the room, Ricardo and Juliana sat on the couch, and Sean poured himself a soda from the small bar before settling in to report to Gutierrez.

"What did you hear out there?" asked Julie.

Sean ignored Ricardo and proceeded to explain in English. "Arias said he was going to demonstrate a powerful new technology that will allow them to control and infiltrate systems remotely from any location."

"That makes sense. Maybe that's what I was looking at this afternoon. Forsythe was viewing what looked to me like a plant schematic and I thought he was sending something over the Internet. I got word from Peter that there was a minor release at Arias's plant. No damage; a valve was opened accidentally and some solvent spilled."

"For all we know, what he was looking at was a new Web site and the release was either a coincidence, or judging by that horrid place OC Chemicals, a common event. If we're going to prove something is going on, we need to trace the transmissions," continued Sean.

"I can have my men follow Forsythe," said Ricardo. Sean raised his eyebrows upon hearing Ricardo's impeccable English.

"I think that's a good idea, but I want *my* agents to follow them tomorrow. We have a few technical tricks of our own," said Gutierrez.

"They'll be using their laptop computers, I'm sure. They might even try another test while at the conference. We have their schedules, don't we?" said Julie.

"Good idea. The two of you will follow Forsythe and one of the men. Ricardo, I want you to be in close contact with the operatives and particularly some of the other suspects on the list," said Gutierrez.

"Señora Gutierrez, with all due respect, I don't think you have authority over my department."

"This is a cooperative mission. You don't want to interfere with the investigation."

"You seem to want me out of this piece right now. I detect some mistrust."

"It's not that. We just want to retain control over these suspects. Arias and Forsythe are Americans and we want to bring them to trial."

"Well, they are subject to our laws while in Buenos Aires, and if they break the law, we'll arrest them and have first crack at them."

"That's what I am afraid of."

"This isn't a third world nation, Ms. Gutierrez."

"This suspect may be the one responsible for the recent train wreck in Wilburn, Virginia, where hundreds of people died Mr. Ortega!" said Gutierrez.

Wrapping her arm around Ricardo, Julie quickly tried to turn the conversation: "Ricky, I think we have another half hour

to dance downstairs. Our work is done for today, and we can consider ourselves off duty. Isn't that right Mrs. Gutierrez?"

"By all means."

Ricardo and Julie went back to the dance, leaving Gutierrez and Sean to discuss the details of the case. Sean took the opportunity to tell Gutierrez how he felt about Julie's relationship with Ricardo.

"Ma'am, I have to make this comment about Julie's relationship with the police captain. I don't think this is appropriate, and it's hurting the case."

"How so?"

"Well, I think that Ricardo is taking too much time away from Julie's investigation."

"So far, she has provided very good information, and I have no problem with her performance as an agent. As far as her relationship is concerned, I have to say selfishly that it helps this case. Not that I'm encouraging this for that reason, but I feel that my agents are entitled to a private life. Why are you *really* concerned Sean?"

"I told you why."

"Sean, I'm an old woman and it doesn't take an FBI agent to see what is going on. You have become interested in your attractive partner and you're having difficulty separating your own feelings for her from your work. I just wanted you to know that I understand how you feel, and I really don't want to interfere here. I can assign a new partner if this is affecting your work."

"I... don't want a new partner."

"Then, I'm afraid you'll have to deal with this issue yourself. We've all been there, Sean. I was a young agent once, too. When you work with people this closely, it's bound to happen."

"I'm surprised to hear you admit that, particularly after the last seminar you gave."

"That was business and necessary, but people are people, and we can't do anything about that. Just be careful. As long as you are caring and sensitive and you don't place any demands on her, you're OK."

Sean sipped his soda and finally said: "So how did you cope with your feelings?"

Gutierrez smiled and changed the tone of her voice, realizing that Sean was beginning to accept his feelings. "I didn't really do a good job. It was a struggle, and sometimes I buried feelings for years, not for fear that it would be unprofessional for me to express them, but for fear that I would be rejected. Don't make that same mistake. Before you know it, it will be too late. This job is no substitute for family. That I learned the hard way."

"Thank you, Anna, I'll keep that in mind."

Changing her tone again, Gutierrez took charge. "OK. Tomorrow, I want you to follow Forsythe to the morning seminar with the new 'Cyclops' device to record his moves. At this point, we're not sure if what Julie saw was a real transmission. We need to intercept that communication. Keep your eyes peeled on him, and do whatever is necessary to find out what they're up to. As far as Ricardo is concerned, I don't want him involved at this point. I want to drag these bastards into a U.S. court and see them behind bars," ordered Gutierrez, as she walked out of the suite.

Sean changed into comfortable clothes, climbed into bed and began studying the manual on the Cyclops device; he made notes as he went, but kept drifting off. It wasn't long until he was sound asleep.

Ricardo held Julie tightly as they danced to the sounds of the *bandoneon*. The orchestra was playing a medley of classic romantic tangos, to wind down the evening.

"I want you with me, don't go back," said Ricardo holding Julie's face close to his.

"I've been working to get to this point for years now. I love what I do. It makes a difference. I just can't give it all up and move to Buenos Aires."

"I need you Julie."

"I can't ... you can join me in New York."

"I'll be just another Hispanic with no position there. It would take me years to make captain."

"I... just can't think about this now, while I'm this case."

Ricardo kissed Julie tenderly. "Marry me Julie. You don't need to work. You can be my wife and the mother of our children. I make a good salary. What kind of job is this for a woman like you, always in danger, working with toxic chemicals? Julie, this is not for you."

"I have known you for less than 24 hours ... you must be crazy to..."

"Yes, crazy for you." Ricardo continued to run his fingers over Julie's back, holding her more tightly as he kissed her again.

Pulling away, Julie started, "I don't think I'm used to this kind..."

Before she could finish the sentence, Ricardo pulled her back into his embrace and tightened his hold. "The men you are involved with don't appreciate you if they don't desire you as I do."

Taking her hand, he walked toward the lobby and into the elevator. As the door closed, he drew her into a long, passionate kiss.

When they reached her floor, he held her close to his side as they walked to the suite. At the door, Ricardo once again pulled Julie into an intimate embrace.

"I think we better say goodnight here," said Julie looking at Sam, the bodyguard at the door, whose expression seemed to be one of disapproval.

When Julie opened the door, Ricardo quickly stepped inside. Pushing the door closed, Ricardo picked Julie up and carried her to the couch where he began making love to her. She had no time to react. Before she knew it, the top of her dress was torn off and Ricardo was kissing her breasts and removing her undergarments, as he positioned himself on top of her.

"What if Sean comes out? I think he's inside. Please...stop now," begged a slightly frightened Julie.

"I don't care about him, I love you Julie. You know you want me."

Julie was uncomfortable, her earlier feelings of sexual excitement gone. She tried to push Ricardo off, but he was heavy and he wasn't budging. His erection frightened her and suddenly she realized he was going to penetrate her. As she continued to struggle against Ricardo, reality hit her like a lightning bolt: She was going to be raped! She froze as fear gripped her body and mind. Ricardo's strong hands dug deep into her thighs leaving painful marks as she struggled in vain against his heavy body.

"Get off me," she demanded, hoping her fear wasn't evident in her voice or eyes.

"Julie, you know you love me..." and he continued to move inside her.

"I SAID GET OFF ME!" she yelled, loudly enough for the bodyguard to hear, but Ricardo was oblivious to anything but his own needs. He was obsessed.

When Julie yelled again, Sam stormed in, his heavy body slamming the door back against the wall, his gun pointed at Ricardo. "Stop right there or I'll shoot!" At the same time Sean ran out to see what was happening. Ricardo quickly lifted

himself off of Juliana, leaving her to try to cover her body with what was left of her torn dress.

"If he hurt you, we can take care of this bastard right here," said Sean.

"No, it was a misunderstanding. Ricardo won't bother me again," said Julie with more conviction than she felt as she fought to hold back the tears..

Ricardo gave Julie a piercing stare before being ushered out by the bodyguard.

Julie was barely able to get to the bathroom and lock the door before she began sobbing uncontrollably.

Sean looked at the couch and saw shreds of Julie's dress and undergarments. "That bastard is going to get what's coming to him," he mumbled.

"Julie, come out. I'll talk to Gutierrez about this asshole's behavior. We can have him arrested."

Julie continued to sob. "No, I don't want anyone else to know. This was my fault. I led him on. I don't want Gutierrez to know."

Sean sat on the floor and leaned against the door. "Julie, let me tell you a story. Once there was a man down on his luck. He was a tough guy, fighting drug traffickers in the Colombian jungles. But he didn't care about the drug addicts, or the people he was helping. He cared about himself, his glory. Each kill, each victory validated his existence. He thrived on the death and destruction of war. He needed no one but a bottle, to put him to sleep at night. But one day, something happened."

"What?" asked Julie still sobbing.

"He was shot. Although the doctors patched him up, they couldn't do anything about was his failing liver. If he didn't stop drinking, he was dead for sure, they said. He realized that he wasn't going to die a hero, but as just another drunk."

"So what happened to him?"

"Well, he came to New York, joined this crazy Environmental Crime Fighter's group, as we call it, and met Mrs. Gutierrez and a tough woman named Juliana Del Rio. She made him realize that the world needs people like him and that one man can make a difference and change things for the better. He realized that when he died, he wanted to be remembered for having done something. He also realized that there are people out there who are willing to accept you and will trust you enough to place their very lives in your hands. You trusted me, Julie, back there in Alaska."

"And you came through. You are a hero."

"No. You are. You were fearful when you went into that warehouse. Yet you went ahead and put it all on the line to save some dolphins, the oceans, the environment, and follow those ideals of yours. I still don't totally understand what drives you, but I really admire that conviction."

"You didn't think much of this job when you started," said Julie.

"Well things changed after I met you."

Julie opened the door and Sean got up. "You OK, Lassie?"

Julie embraced Sean and held him close to her for a while.

"Let's go to sleep," said Sean.

"Oh, don't get any ideas Mr."

"As I have already told you many times, Ms. Del Rio, if I did have any 'ideas' about you, I wouldn't have to resort to tricks. We have a long day tomorrow. The Global Warming Conference starts and there have been several threats from radical groups. I have to follow Forsythe around and you have a lot of research. We both need a good night's sleep."

"Don't say anything to Gutierrez about Ricardo. Honestly, he misunderstood me. He had asked me to marry him and ..."

"There's no excuse for what he did. Julie, I have no respect for men that force themselves on women. That's a crime in any country and it was certainly NOT your fault."

"Nothing really happened. He comes from a different culture. He misunderstood me."

"What culture is that! I've never had to do what he did to get a woman's attention! Women were always forcing themselves on me!"

"Oh, I see, hot stuff you were."

"In my day, Julie… I was a different lad."

"Well, I'm glad you changed, because we could never solve any cases together if you had to constantly be beating off women with sticks!"

"Thanks a lot. So, I see I've put a smile on yer face again. Go to bed."

Sean went into the bedroom and closed the door. Julie put on a T-shirt and pants, opened the sofa bed and crawled in. It had been a long exhausting day, she realized, before falling asleep.

Ricardo managed to get a couple of hours' sleep, but his rest was cut short by a 5 a.m. call to come to the hotel and check out the place for possible sabotage. He drove through the empty streets of Buenos Aires, reliving the incident of the night before. He was angry with Julie for rejecting him and for her humiliating screams. He was tired and irritated, but as he arrived at the hotel he knew that he had to put thoughts of last night out of his mind; he had work to do. Once inside the lobby, Ricardo met two special investigators with trained dogs.

Ricardo spoke to the lead investigator: "We need to check out the entire area by 9 a.m. We received a call this morning from a right-wing group threatening to blow up the Global Warming Conference this morning. It could be a tactic to disrupt and delay the conference or to eliminate the delegates, we don't know. We're proceeding as if an actual bomb has been planted."

"Understood. We'll check out the conference area, the restrooms and all of the closets, and so on. What about the delegates' quarters?" asked the investigator.

"We've been surveying the entire area since the delegates began arriving. However, we suspect that these explosives might have been planted some time ago, way before this conference. The members of this group are focused on disrupting the Global Warming Conference, and we suspect that is where they may have planted the explosives," said Ricardo.

"OK, let's get going," said the investigator, pulling the dogs by the leash.

"I'll come along with you," said Ricardo.

The dogs sniffed all of the crevices, closets, restrooms, and other spaces. No spot was missed. Finally in the largest conference room, Ricardo noticed a small trap door near the podium. It was the housing for some electrical switches. "Did you check the breaker boxes in every room?"

"No, we would have to get platforms for the dogs to get up that far."

"Do it! Check inside every switch box!"

The investigators used chairs as makeshift platforms from which the dogs could sniff the boxes. Handlers and dogs went from one box to the next. When they reached the largest room, where the conference was to take place, the German shepherd climbed up on one of the chairs and sat down immediately, signaling his master that he had smelled explosives. Ricardo ordered the men to open the breaker box.

At first glance, there appeared to be nothing out of the ordinary in the box. But looking closer, the investigator noticed that there was an extra wire attached to one of the breaker connections, and a hole in the wall. The extra handlers and dogs were ordered to clear the room, leaving the lead investigator, one of the dogs, and Ricardo to continue the inspection.

Ricardo moved in to take a closer look at the connection with a small flashlight. He couldn't make out what he was looking at. "We need a team in here," he said turning to the investigator. As Ricardo turned, his flashlight fell on the wire. Just as he was about to retrieve it, the investigator said. "Don't, sir! We better clear this room immediately."

As they were running out the door, an explosion blew the men to the ground. The German shepherd let out a loud yelp as it was hit by a sharp object. Then the dog lay on the floor motionless. Ricardo raised his head, but a sharp pain in his arm was too much for him and he passed out.

Juliana woke to the muted sound of a blast. She got out of bed and looked out her window. She saw an ambulance and heard the sirens of vehicles rushing toward the hotel. She ran to Sean's door and knocked. "Sean, Did you hear that? Get up!"

Sean opened the door. "Yes, it sounded like an explosion. Let me call the lobby."

"Go ahead, I'm going to the bathroom to get dressed," Julie answered grabbing a pair of slacks and a shirt.

Sean dialed and waited. "The front desk must be flooded with calls. I can't get through."

Just then Julie's cellular phone rang, and she grabbed it from her purse.

"Julie, this is Mrs. Gutierrez."

"Yes, Mrs. Gutierrez, what's up?"

"I have some bad news for you Juliana."

"What's happened?"

"Ricardo has been injured in an explosion downstairs. There was a bomb in the room where the Global Warming Conference was to take place, and they couldn't defuse it in time."

"I'll be right down."

Turning off her phone, she turned to Sean. "You were right; there's been an explosion and Ricardo was hurt. I'm going down to the lobby."

"I heard you. I'll meet you there later."

As Julie grabbed her purse and headed for the door, Sean handed her an orange juice. "Drink this before you go rushing out there, and remember, this accident doesn't make what he did last night alright."

Julie drank the juice and rushed out the door without commenting.

Downstairs, she met the ambulance. Ricardo was on a stretcher, his arm bandaged. He had a few cuts and bruises on his head, but he smiled when he saw Julie. "Mi amor, you came to see me."

"I'm glad you're OK, Ricardo."

"It is just my arm, I'll be off duty for a while, but otherwise, I was lucky. Will you come with me to the hospital? I don't want anything to happen to you. There have been other threats."

"I have to stay. This is just too important."

As the doors closed and the ambulance pulled away, Julie began looking around the building. Nearby, a special agent with a bandage on his head sobbed like a child as they took the body of the German shepherd out of the building and into a van. There was a police barricade in the lobby. A TV crew was filming. One of the environmental organizers spoke to the TV reporter:

"We will not allow terrorists to derail our mission. This conference will continue as scheduled. The issues being discussed here by the delegates have a global impact and benefit all of mankind. Those who seek to stop these efforts are

criminals seeking to destroy not just this effort, but all of humanity."

Chapter Eight

The Rats Below

Julie returned to the lobby and saw Sean in the coffee shop talking to a delegate. Sean was to follow Forsythe today, and although he had never actually met Forsythe, he took the precaution of disguising himself with dark beard, a pair of dark-rimmed glasses, and a cap to cover up the crop of thinning reddish white hair that normally hung loosely about his face. With his old tweed jacket, the look was complete. Julie stood at the door and signaled. Sean excused himself and joined her.

"What's with this outfit?" snickered Juliana.

"Never mind that. I don't want Forsythe to recognize me. What happened to Ricardo?"

"He's OK. His arm was injured, but the police dog died," said Julie.

"Well, too bad it wasn't the other way around."

"That's a terrible thing to say!"

"Yes it is and I meant it. What are you doing today?"

"I told Gutierrez I was going to attend the environmental crime sessions. We're trying to find common threads with international incidents."

"OK, Lassie, my conference session is about to start. I'll see you tonight."

Sean rushed past the police barricade and over to the conference room, where the topic was to be chemical safety. He knew Forsythe was scheduled to attend this session and Sean wanted to make sure he sat near him. When he arrived, Forsythe was sitting in the middle of the room concentrating only on his

computer screen, seemingly oblivious to what was going on around him. Sean moved toward him. He sat one seat to the right in the row immediately behind him so that he had a clear view of the computer monitor.

The speaker was presenting a dull series of slides on a rather uninteresting topic, except perhaps to the few chemical safety specialists in the room. Sean pretended to concentrate on the slides and the monotonous voice of the less-than enthusiastic speaker, but he kept an eye on Forsythe. Sean was wearing the "Cyclops eye", the new high-tech gadget Gutierrez had sent in the briefcase.

The device consisted of a camera "eye" disguised as a button in the middle of his cap. The eye was wired through a device that resembled a hearing aid. The images captured by the "eye" were transmitted directly to a small pocket computer with a wireless connection to the Internet. The encrypted images were sent to the FBI lab in real time, so that other agents could see and analyze exactly what Sean was seeing. The device could also store images for later viewing.

Sean looked awkward, pretending to type on the tiny keyboard with his large hands. In a small window on the screen he was glancing at the images on Forsythe's screen, which he was capturing with the tiny camera. Suddenly, his eyes fixed on diagrams that were displayed on Forsythe's computer screen. He could make out a chemical storage vessel, piping and electronics like the control panels he had seen on his previous investigation at the nuclear manufacturing facility in Alaska.

Sean was also in direct communication with the FBI agent in the lab via a keyboard chat, so he typed:

"Did you see that, what do you make of it?"

The agent back in the lab replied:

"The party you are surveying typed V-104 Open. The graphics suggest this could be a valve somewhere, but we can't trace the communication to

its destination. We will note this and cross check later."

Sean noticed that Forsythe was looking around, and quickly slid the small computer into his pocket.

Forsythe got up and left the room abruptly. Taking care not to be seen, Sean followed him to the side door of the hotel and out to the parking lot. He hid behind a doorway as he watched Forsythe get into a sedan and drive off. Sean quickly flagged down a Buenos Aires taxicab, with a reputation far more notorious than New York cabs for driving through traffic. As he climbed in he said in Spanish:

"There is extra money in it for you if you follow that black sedan stopped at the corner."

"Don't worry, this is the worst time for traffic, he won't get away," said the driver sounding excited at the prospect of a chase.

The sedan went down the *Avenida de Mayo,* past *Plaza de Mayo,* and toward *El Congreso,* the government's house. Forsythe's sedan parked near *El Congreso* in what was a tow-away zone. The driver and Forsythe got out and walked quickly toward the great fountain adorned with cherubs and other great statues, and past flocks of pigeons that regularly cooed for food that visitors gladly provided.

It had rained for the last few days, saturating the ground and leaving the benches damp and tacky. The air seemed damp and smelled of the Rio de La Plata, the river that merged with the Atlantic at the Buenos Aires coast.

Near one of the black Cherubs, which in fact was pissing into the fountain, (something that amused Sean to no end) the duo met two men, one with dark hair and beard, perhaps an Arab. Sean sat on a park bench feeding the pigeons crackers. He placed his hat on backwards so that the "Cyclops Eye" could record the

conversation and adjusted the controls to full volume. The device's amazing range and filtering features enabled him to hear their conversation clearly, while masking other sounds. The men planned a meeting that evening at a garbage dump in *Quilmes,* which is located outside of Buenos Aires.

Sean was puzzled, but had no time to think it through because it began raining. It was just a few drops at first, but suddenly it became a deluge. Soon the pigeons disappeared into their hiding places as the heavy rain soaked the men, who turned up their collars and walked quickly toward the car. Sean attempted to follow; the rain soaked his tweed jacket, making it heavy and uncomfortable. The wet ground could hold no more water and deep puddles formed, making it difficult to walk. As Sean approached the clearing of the Plaza, one of the men pointed to Sean and said in English:

"Isn't that one of the delegates from the conference?"

"What the hell is he doing here? Let's find out!" The two men ran toward Sean as Forsythe ran back to his parked sedan and sped away. Sean turned and ran toward the street. One of the men took a shot at Sean, but missed. The rain had chased everyone else away, so there was no one else in the Plaza to see what was happening.

The rain quickly flooded streets. Water splashed several feet in the air as the men's feet hit the ground. Sean noticed that the men had split up and one had actually run around and was coming toward him, while the other was coming up behind him. He ran into a narrow side street but they followed. Sean quickly realized there was no exit to this street, and the depth of the water was slowing him down. As more shots were fired, he zigzagged from side to side to avoid the bullets. He felt a sting on his arm. Blood soon became visible through the tweed fabric of his wet jacket. As he ran, he tried to call Julie on his now-soaked cell phone but he couldn't get a connection. He pressed the emergency button on the special phone, which ensured the Geographic Positioning System tracked his location. Seeing no

visible signal, he placed the phone in the jacket's inside pocket and buttoned it.

Now trapped and in pain from his wounded arm, he noticed water going down a round metal cover on the street. It was the sewer. The men were almost upon him as Sean opened the cover and slid quickly down the metal ladder into the dark hole, closing the cover above him with his left arm.

The men were confounded as they stood over the manhole, looking for Sean. Then one of them pointed to the loose cover. "He's down here!" yelled the dark bearded man.

The men opened the cover and slid down the ladder. Sean had made his escape down the now nearly flooded pipe, which carried the storm water. He made his way to the larger main line, which collected storm water from all of the streets.

Built a century ago, the storm water system was a marvel of engineering, designed to keep Buenos Aires dry during heavy rains. But as the city grew and the old cobblestones where covered with layers of asphalt, the volume of water also grew. No longer was the water filtering down through the permeable cobblestones into the soil, but it was rolling instead down the sleekly paved modern streets, and into the storm sewers. Heavy rains were too much for the ancient system. Flooding during heavy rains was a recurring story in local newspapers.

As Sean walked, he could see light filtering in the distance from the storm drain above. The dim light revealed the gray/brown furry bodies of the long-tailed rats that had been traveling unnoticed with Sean all long. They climbed up the walls to escape the water. Some were screeching as they swam past him and others were already dead. Sean ignored the floating rodents, soda pop cans and assorted debris as he pushed ahead toward the light. He made his way toward the opening as quickly as he could in thigh-deep water, but the storm drain was too narrow to escape and what looked like a small waterfall was pouring down the side.

As the water continued to rise, Sean looked at the dark tunnel ahead of him; escape seemed impossible. The men were catching up with him. Another shot bounced off one of the walls. He tried to run, but the water was up to his waist.

Floodwaters on the streets above grew steadily deeper until the pressure of the rapidly moving water forced opened a manhole. A sudden gush of water from above knocked Sean down, his head hitting the walls of the passageway as he sank beneath the surface of the water. He managed to get up and get a breath, his arm now no longer throbbing, but numb. A rat attempted to climb on him to escape the water and he pushed it away. Water was pouring in quickly from all directions and rising rapidly; it was up to his neck. Soon he was swimming in the conduit, barely able to take a breath.

The men behind him screamed as another gush of water flooded into the sewer from up above. "Let's get out," said one of them. "I can't breathe, help me," said the other. Then silence.

Sean swam to the next manhole. He took a breath in the only bubble of air available and he climbed up the flooded stairs. He pushed up on the manhole cover with his left arm to no avail. He was pushing against four feet of water rolling down the street above. Nearly out of breath, Sean turned back and desperately sought one of the few pockets of air at the top of the flooded pipe and took a breath. He swam to the second, and then the third manhole, breathing the small layer of air above the floodwaters.

As he swam, he felt the bodies of the drowned men move past him. Their limp and loose hands and legs caught against Sean's body and swept him down as he furiously tried to kick the dead limbs away from him. Once in a while he could feel a rat desperately trying to share the little air that was left or biting down on his cheek. He could feel the tail, whiskers and sleek wet fur brush against his face. The rats let out a pathetic screech as they drowned.

The air smelled of sulfur and petroleum, a byproduct of the hundreds of thousands of cars that packed Buenos Aires streets

during the day. It is ironic, that a town called "Buenos Aires", meaning good air, was now so polluted by car exhaust. The underground river of rainwater would end up in the shimmering "Rio de La Plata." The river of silver was now tarnished by countless polluters, such as tainted rainwater and the city's billions of gallons of sewage dumped a mile from the shores every year, which the tides carried back to shore and into the river.

Nearly out of breath, Sean swam up a small passageway leading toward a dim far-away light. The water level receded until he was able to walk rather than swim. He could see the dry bottom of the conduit ahead. The light filtering from storm drains revealed the decaying urban litter dropped into storm drains by the well-dressed urbanites.

As Sean reached the ladder and started up, rodents feeding on the debris, jumped on his pants and ran up his leg to get a sip of the blood now dripping from his injured arm and bitten cheeks. He pushed them away in disgust. Suddenly a glint caught his eye. He stopped and turned back down the ladder; he found a box hidden in the corner. It contained various chemicals including a bottle of arsenic, now empty, and nitric acid, plus a full bottle of glycerin. Who put that there and how long ago? Seemed like the perfect hiding place for raw materials for explosives – among these rats. No one seemed to maintain this area. Sean made a mental note of the material and its location, but was too exhausted to investigate further.

He made his way back up the ladder, pushed open the manhole cover with his left arm and pulled himself up into the deserted street. Once on the surface, he walked toward the entrance hallway of one of the buildings. Blood soaked his right arm and dripping from the rodent bites on his face; he felt weak. As he stumbled into the hallway, he managed to press the button of his cell phone one more time before he passed out.

Sean opened his eyes to see Juliana.

"Sean? Wake up! What happened?" asked Julie as she brushed Sean's matted hair from his bitten face.

"It's good to see yer, Lassie." Sean reached for Julie's hand and held it close to his heart for a minute in a rare moment of tenderness. Julie didn't move her hand, but smiled.

"The Argentine police found you in a hallway, covered in blood. They thought you might be a victim of the flash flood, so they sent you to this hospital. They found your badge and called the main office. The doctors said the bullet wound was superficial and you'll be OK soon. They gave you a tetanus shot when they realized that those look like bites. What happened?"

"The guys that met with Forsythe drowned in the sewer like the rats."

"What are you talking about? What guys and what rats?"

"I was following Forsythe and he met with two men at the *Plaza del Congreso*. They were talking about a second meeting in *Quilmes*. When they realized I was following them, they shot at me and chased me around town. I tried to hide in the storm sewers but they followed me. The flash flood came so quickly that I nearly drowned and they did for sure. I saw them float by me, along with a lot of other rats in the sewer. Before the water did them in, those men shot at me a number of times. They intended to kill me!"

"I saw Forsythe at the conference this afternoon doing 'business'. I assumed you were somewhere around. We're continuing to monitor Forsythe, but there's been no arrest."

"He should be arrested!"

"Well, if you file charges, we can have Ricky arrest him."

"Ricky? I thought he was in the hospital," growled Sean letting go of Juliana's hand.

"His arm is in a sling, but he'll recover. He's back on the case."

"And you call him Ricky now? After what he did?"

"He asked my forgiveness. He misunderstood me, I told you."

"Never mind. I'm feeling sick; call the nurse." Sean turned his face away from Julie.

Julie went outside. "Ricky, come on in."

Ricardo walked in, "Hello Sean. How are you?"

"You have some nerve showing your face around here."

"I apologized to Julie and I want to apologize to you, Sean."

Sean turned his head and said nothing.

"Ricky, Sean says that Forsythe met with two men at *El Congreso*. They were planning a meeting in the *Quilmes* dump. Then the two men pursued Sean into the flooded sewer and shot at him several times before drowning," said Julie.

Ricardo explained: "*Quilmes* is outside of Buenos Aires. Sometimes criminals bury bodies or toxic chemicals at the dump, unnoticed by the authorities. The whole place is an ecological time bomb. It's going to stop operations soon. There's water contamination and pockets of methane gas that could explode, but that's another matter. I'll check out the morgue. The men who followed Sean may have been found floating in El Rio de La Plata by now and taken to the morgue."

"Sean, do you know what the meeting in the park was about?" asked Julie.

"No, but the lab might know. They were receiving the conversation up in Washington through that Cyclops contraption. Maybe they got the whole conversation. They're trying to determine if the test Forsythe conducted back at the conference coincided with any plant release. By the way, where's that device now?"

"It was still in your jacket, but the water ruined it. It will go in for repairs. They don't allow cell phones in here, so I'm going out to call the office to see if they have any further information on the meeting in the park. I'll be right back," said Julie, walking out and leaving Sean and Ricardo alone.

Sean's expression was defiant as he faced Ricardo. "You should get as far away from Julie as you possibly can if you value your life Mr. Ortega. She is unwilling to press charges against you, but that doesn't matter. Once I'm out of here, you'll have to deal with me."

"I have already apologized. I was drunk, I was just... she has forgiven me; we are getting married."

"You weren't drunk. I know what you were drinking. You just like to get your way with women and won't take no for an answer. Marry her, is that what ye wants to do? So you can load her with children, keep her from a job and slap her around any time she doesn't do what you want? I know your kind. I had a father like you. Thank heaven he died. You are pathetic. Since when does a guy like you become an *environmentalist?*"

"Mr. Ryan, you are totally wrong and totally out of line. If you weren't in that bed right now, we'd be outside!"

"Any time, loser, any time!"

When Julie returned, the men stopped talking.

Wanting to get Julie alone, Ricardo said, "I think Sean is getting tired and we'd better go."

"You go ahead, Ricky; I have something to discuss with Sean."

"I see. Please don't worry about *me*," said Ricardo sarcastically, and walked out, slamming the door behind him.

Julie waited a bit, went out the door and checked to make sure no one was listening, and then walked over to Sean, her face close to him and whispered:

"Sean, the office says that they identified the two men on the videos you transmitted. They are known terrorists and they made out the word 'Sarin' in one of the conversations that were garbled. They were planning another terrorist attack they think because Sarin is an organo phosphate gas, which the media

claims was used by the military in Chile to kill their enemies. It's undetectable and simulates a heart attack. What's worse is that it has been used as a spray on a pillow to simulate death by suffocation. That is why the office wants you out of here right now. You need to come with me to the hotel where Gutierrez has protection."

"And you didn't want to share this with Ricardo?" questioned Sean.

"I was ordered not to. They don't want to share anything with the Argentine police, in the event there might be terrorist informants in their ranks."

"And you suspect Ricardo?"

"No, it was just orders," said Juliana looking down.

Sean got up with some difficulty and started dressing in front of Julie. She didn't attempt to look the other way as Sean removed his gown and put on his underwear. He found a new suit in the closet.

"I brought you that this morning. The clothes you were wearing had to be discarded."

"You know me too well, Lassie. The right size."

Julie and Sean got into the waiting black sedan. The chauffeur drove them to the hotel, with Sam sitting in the front seat, his expression blank.

Sean's arm was in a sling and his face was drawn. He looked away from Julie and focused on the Buenos Aires scenery during the ride for a few minutes, before closing his eyes and putting his head back. He was exhausted. "The doctor told me I lost a lot of blood and maybe I am a little anemic. I have to take some pills and he recommended I eat a good steak tonight."

"I guess we're in the right place for that. Can I join you?"

"I'll be in no mood for conversation Julie, I just want to eat in my room and rest."

"I'll make sure you're not disturbed. There will be a guard at our door all night. I'll sleep on the pull-out couch as I did last night and you can have the bedroom, it's quieter." Sean had no strength to answer. He simply nodded and closed his eyes.

When they arrived at the hotel, Sean slowly walked to the elevator. Julie offered her arm for support. He took it gratefully.

The guard was posted at the door. As soon as they entered the suite, Sean walked silently into the bedroom and got into the bed.

"Sean, let me order your dinner. I'll get you a 'lomito', it's great."

It didn't take Sean long to fall asleep. When room service arrived, Julie went into the room to wake him up. He looked pale. Julie looked at Sean for a while. His strong muscular six-foot-five-inch frame looked slim and lax. The bites on his cheek complimented his many scratches and scars on his rugged Irish skin. His stubbornly straight, fine, red hair hung around his face. She decided to let him sleep for half an hour.

Later, when she brought him his dinner, she placed her hand on his face to wake him. Sean opened his eyes and sat up. Julie had placed a tray on his bed and turned on the bedside light.

"How about some TV?" she asked, handing him the remote.

"That sounds fine. Just close the door on your way out please."

Julie looked at Sean but he would not make eye contact. Before she closed the door, he said "Thank you. Goodnight."

Julie smiled, and walked out, not saying a word. She changed into a pair of men's pajamas she traveled with and climbed into the pull-out couch. She turned off the light and fell fast asleep.

Julie hadn't been sleeping long when there was a knock at the door. Julie groggily got out of bed, turned on the lamp and opened the door. It was Ricardo. "Mi amor," he said hugging her.

"Come in; can I offer you something to drink?" asked Julie, deciding it was time to get the record straight.

"I'll have some scotch and soda, if you have it."

"We just have soda in this room."

"That's fine. I came to apologize to you again for what happened."

"I told you; it's forgotten."

Ricardo reached for Julie and held her. She didn't resist but she didn't return his embrace this time. "Ricky, sit down, we need to talk. I'm so flattered you feel this way toward me, but what happened last night shows we are from different worlds. It's not just that you thought you had the right to force yourself on me, but you assumed I wanted to be a wife and have children. You just don't know who I am at all. You see me only as a woman."

"And what a woman you are!"

"Ricardo, let me tell you about my island, Vieques. It's a beautiful place. A paradise in the Caribbean. I don't know of any other island as beautiful. Have you ever seen a phosphorescent bay? It's a magical place, where the plankton emit light. At night when the tour guides churn up the water with their motor boats, it glows so bright that it looks as if the stars were emerging from the bay. During the day you can see beautiful colorful parrots flying free, wild horses roaming the beach, and clear aqua waters.

"But one side of the island is held hostage by the military, which has used it for training exercises for many years. Poison bullets litter the ground and sometimes are eaten by birds, killing them. War games pollute our beautiful island.

"One day, many years ago, the love of my life, Antonio, joined a group of protesters. They were young and stupid, so they crawled under the fence thinking they were going to stop the target practice with their own bodies. Antonio was the first one to run onto the field. Before the sergeant in charge noticed him, it was too late. A bullet ended Antonio's life.

"Seeing the daily assault on my little paradise all my life made me want to do something about environmental crime, so I became an EPA investigator. I worked very hard, just like you have, for my position, and now I have an opportunity with the FBI to make a real difference. Yes it's dangerous, but just like you, I accept the risk. You're unwilling to give up your job, and neither am I willing to give up mine. So you see Ricardo, I don't have time to be a wife and mother. I don't want children, I have a mission in life."

"I think it's a shame. You'll wind up a lonely old woman, Juliana. This job is not for a woman. What will happen when you get shot or disabled? Can you face that kind of danger every day? I just don't think women have that kind of strength."

"Women have the strength to give birth to the entire human population. I don't think you could survive that kind of ordeal. I guess you expect me to be a wife and sit and wait while YOU face danger every day. I just don't want to be sitting on the sidelines."

"A woman should not have to face that kind of risk in her job. Women bring life into the world. It's wrong to expose them like this. I'm sorry Juliana, I agree with what you are trying to do, but I just don't think it should be you risking your life."

"If not me, who?"

Ricardo put down his drink and started out the door, his head down. "Good-bye Juliana, I will always remember you. Good luck."

"Good-bye Ricardo."

Julie got another soda from the small refrigerator, and sat on the bed. Sean opened the door and came out, looking somewhat better.

"You're up?"

"Yes. I think it's time to go home. I just got word from Gutierrez. She told me they arrested two men in *Quilmes* who were Forsythe's clients. They were in the toxic cleanup and disposal business. They had a deal with some of the *Quilmes* administrators. They let them dump anything they wanted, for a fee. They thought that by using the software Forsythe was peddling, they could drum up more business cleaning up spills they caused themselves."

"Sounds like a pretty disgusting business. What about the two terrorists that died in the sewer?"

"I think they were potential clients for Forsythe. They had heard about his software, too."

"So, did they arrest Forsythe and Hugo?"

"They can only detain Forsythe on trying to sell security software to the Arabs. Otherwise there is nothing preventing him from selling his software to clients in North or South America because he can't be held responsible for how his clients use the software. I think Forsythe will get a fine and a slap on the wrist because they can't really connect him directly to the accident or the terrorists. As far as Hugo's concerned, we have nothing on him yet but we'll keep him under surveillance."

Sean took a soda from the fridge and sat next to Julie on the bed.

"I ...happened to overhear what you told Ricardo."

"I knew you were listening. I saw the door was ajar. I had closed it."

"Is it true?"

"Is what true?"

"That you have decided to have no children."

"Well, yes, right now, I don't think this is a good job for a mom. Sean, I come from a large family. There are plenty of children in this world. I just don't see any reason right now to have a child. What for? The world is going to hell anyway. What life or future will he or she have? Overpopulation, declining quality of life..."

"I guess if our mothers thought that way, neither one of us would be here to talk about this, or *save the world.*"

"I could ask why you didn't have a family all these years."

"I liked my job too much, too. I didn't want anyone to tie me down. I was selfish."

"Well, you've managed to find company lately. I guess eventually I'll find someone who doesn't mind my job and wants what I want. But for now, I think I need to concentrate on my work."

"I'm going back to bed. I think the plane leaves tomorrow morning."

The next morning as they were packing to leave, Sean was watching the news. "Julie, come in, they found the rats that nearly killed me."

"Two men were found floating in the Rio de la Plata this morning. They are believed to be terrorists connected to the recent bombing at the International Environmental Conference held in Buenos Aires. More details later in the show."

"While Buenos Aires is the focus of the International Environmental Conference, it faces its own local environmental crisis. The town of Berazategui is suing Aguas Buenos Aires for 300 million pesos for environmental damage to their shores. Two million cubic meters of raw sewage are dumped by the city daily,

only a mile and a half from shore. The sewage regularly washes back to shores of nearby towns, infecting their beaches. They fear that soon, irreparable contamination of the wells that supply Berazategui's drinking water will occur, as the waste seeps into the aquifer. Mr. Ramirez, what are your comments on this lawsuit?"

"It's time to build a plant to handle Buenos Aires waste. This will attract tourism and allow us to rebuild our coastline."

"That is so ironic," said Julie.

"What's ironic?"

"That they call this place *Buenos Aires*. The air is far from good; that Riachuelo smells like an open sewer. Sean, you never really told me how you managed to survive in that storm sewer. What happened out there?"

"Well, I was swimming in the tunnel, and these rats started climbing on my shoulders, biting my face and trying to lick the blood from my arm."

"Ohh, that's so gross! Not before breakfast please! Why are you always getting into these situations? Couldn't you find a better place to run? Why did you have to follow them into the park alone?"

"Does it never end Lassie! What about you hiding in that toxic waste truck on our last case? I nearly choked trying to rescue you. What were you thinking! Were you thinking?"

"Never mind that. We have a few minutes to grab some breakfast and go to the airport. After a short stop in Miami, we'll be back to wonderful New York."

"I can't wait. I can see how my cat is doing."

Chapter Nine

Stranger In Town

Sean stepped off the plane, followed closely by Julie and Mrs. Gutierrez, who tapped Sean on the shoulder. "Sean, I want you to see the company doctor today. You suffered severe blood loss and I want you checked out. That's an order!"

When they reached the baggage area, a man approached Mrs. Gutierrez. "This is Agent Drago. He's here to drive you two home and take me to the New York office. I want to see both of you at 4 p.m. Drago will update us on the case and then we'll decide how to proceed."

Since Drago had arranged for their expedited departure from customs, it didn't take them long to reach the airport exit, where a dark town car was waiting. Gutierrez was in the front and Drago was driving.

Sitting back and relaxing, Sean said, "It's good to be back in New York."

"I don't know. I liked Buenos Aires. It's a prettier and cleaner city than New York, and quite safe," countered Julie.

"If you call getting shot at and swimming in the sewer safe. And what about men hitting on you constantly!"

Before Julie could answer, Mrs. Gutierrez interrupted. "It's nice as a woman to get such attention. But in the long run it can be a nuisance and a barrier to us, Julie."

Sean looked over at Mrs. Gutierrez and smiled.

Drago parked in the reserved lot of the FBI office, got out, and opened the door for Mrs. Gutierrez. "Assistant Director, I'll hold your luggage. You have a 9 p.m. flight to Washington." Mrs. Gutierrez looked up to the tall agent. "Thank you, Drago." Before

leaving, she looked back into the car. "I'll see you at four sharp," she reminded Sean and Julie.

That afternoon, Sean entered the FBI office, where Drago and Mrs. Gutierrez were already at work. Walking toward Drago, he asked, "Agent Drago, do you have the latest report from Wilburn?"

Drago handed a pile of papers to Sean, who remained standing and quietly began studying the report.

Sean looked up as he heard quick footsteps approaching and saw Julie enter. She was well-dressed, but in very conservative business attire. She wore her gold chain and matching earnings, but was bare of any rings or other jewelry. Julie stood at one end of the table and greeted the group. "Good afternoon Assistant Director Gutierrez, Agent Drago, Sean." Sean's eyes followed Julie around the table as she walked over and sat across from Mrs. Gutierrez and next to Drago.

Sean stepped to the side so he was directly behind Julie. He bent over slightly and said softly, "Good afternoon, Julie," before taking a seat next to Mrs. Gutierrez.

"Agent Drago, please give us an update on the case," requested Mrs. Gutierrez.

"On Saturday, while the FBI team was in Buenos Aires, there was another chemical release at the OC Chemicals Plant."

Sean interrupted, "Yes, I believe I saw Forsythe trigger that event."

Drago continued, "There were no injuries or exposures. The release was liquid and the sump contained the entire spill. The chemical was an emulsifying agent used in the polymer-processing unit. An FBI team will check out the OC Chemicals plant this week.

"Today, the sheriff of nearby Victoriaburg found the body of Zack Greenbaum in the wreckage of his car off Route 33. It

appears that he went off the road and into a gully and died from a concussion."

Julie shook her head, "That's dreadful! He was so young!"

Sean leaned forward in his chair, "I wouldn't rule out foul play. Why would he have a concussion? Didn't the air bag open?"

"We don't know at this point."

"Zack was investigating the local terrorist groups; they could have done it. And then there's the evidence that Zack was supposed to have brought to the lab. Has that been located? So many unanswered questions," said Sean, shaking his head. "Frank should not have put Zack on that assignment!"

Mrs. Gutierrez shook her head and quietly spoke: "We've ordered an autopsy, and have a forensics team going over the car. I already had two phone calls from Congressman Greenbaum asking about the circumstances of his son's death. I understand his loss. I just hope this incident doesn't become a political issue." Looking up she continued in her more demanding tone, "Anything else, Agent Drago?"

"Agent Frank Hilbaum said that with Zack's death, he'll have to take over the investigation of the terrorist groups."

Mrs. Gutierrez looked around the table. "Any comments?"

Sean held his head.

"What's wrong?" asked Gutierrez

"I have a headache. Agent Drago, can you get me some aspirin?"

"Sure," replied Agent Drago, as he left the room.

Sean waited until he was gone before speaking. "I see no new leads on who caused the train accident." Shaking his copy of the report, Sean continued. "The only thing in the report is that Mr. Arias returned home today. There's no mention of his associates,

or other suspects they have investigated. It's as if the local authorities are just waiting for the next terrorist attack. They're always a step behind. I'd say we need someone on the inside."

Julie added, "Since Forsythe Systems provides services to the OC Chemicals plant and other plants, I think we should get someone with the latest computer and control systems skills; maybe someone with an engineering background."

"Does either of you have someone in mind?" asked the director.

Julie smiled and replied, "I had a college roommate who is a chemical engineer and who worked in a refinery for three years before getting her computer degree and joining the FBI. She's currently working in the new Internet Crime Division in Washington D.C. Her name is Sharon Goody. She grew up in Georgia and can handle herself well with these local townspeople. I can call her tomorrow if you want."

Mrs. Gutierrez quickly replied. "No, I'll contact her when I get back to Washington tomorrow. If she's right for the assignment and wants to do it, I'll let you know, Julie. You can then join us in Washington to brief her on the case."

Sean coughed and sat up in his chair. "I suppose I should get back to Wilburn and do some more investigating."

"Not so fast, Sean. I saw that doctor's report and you need some rest. You're on medical leave for a week. Julie will return to Wilburn as soon as we plan out this undercover assignment," stated Mrs. Gutierrez. "For now, this stays among the three of us."

"But Mrs. Gutierrez..." Sean began to complain before the director cut him off.

"Sean, is Julie able to carry on this case without you for a few days?"

Sean sat back in his chair and chose his words carefully. "Sure she's able," he answered softly.

Agent Drago returned with the aspirins and water.

"Thanks," said Sean taking the cup and the pills from him.

"Sean, I understand your concern. Agent Drago will also go to Wilburn. He'll work with Frank Hilbaum and investigate Zack's accident. If Juliana needs assistance, she can contact Drago." Turning to Drago, Mrs. Gutierrez warned, "Be careful of the local authorities. Don't trust anyone."

Mrs. Gutierrez stood up, "Then it's set. Juliana, I look forward to seeing you in Washington soon. Good-bye Sean and Agent Drago."

[Four days later, on a road about thirty miles outside of Wilburn]

"Fill it up with premium. I don't want to ruin this baby," Sharon told the station attendant.

The attendant looked down the side of the long red truck. "This is a beauty. I don't see too many of these souped-up Ford F-350s in these parts. What do you use it for?"

"Well, my ex-boyfriend left it behind. He had to get out of the country fast and didn't know what to do with it. Now I use it to hop around from job to job. It comes in handy for towing and trucking heavy loads." Sharon walked over to the soda machine, dropped in four quarters and selected a bottle of water. Walking back to the truck she took a long sip and slowly opened the passenger door halfway. Speaking softly, she held out the bottle, "Here Grady. Com'on boy have some water."

A large chocolate Labrador stood on the passenger seat. Sharon held up the bottle and squeezed out a little water into Grady's open mouth, spilling some of it on her pants. Patting Grady on the head, she said, "Lie down, we'll get going again shortly." As she closed the door and turned around, the attendant was right behind her. Pointing to her wet pants, he held out several paper towels.

"Thank you," she responded using the towels to wipe her pants.

The attendant smiled. "Nice Lab you got there."

"Yes, he is. Do you have a dog?"

"Yep. Why, between hunting or protection or just loneliness most people around here do."

"Well, Grady is my protection. He knows who the bad guys are." Sharon dropped the paper into the trashcan next to the pump. "So, how much for the gas?"

"Twenty-five bucks."

Sharon reached into her front pocket and took out a small stack of twenty-dollar bills. "Got change?" she asked handing the attendant two of the bills.

"Sure, just one minute," said the attendant, heading for the office. Sharon got into the truck and glanced at Grady.

The attendant returned, and handed her the change through the passenger window.

"Thank you," she replied, sliding the bills into her blouse."

The attendant raised his eyebrows and cleared his throat. "You're welcome."

Sharon smiled at the attendant and drove away.

The attendant stood smiling and watching the truck until a customer interrupted, "Hey, can you fill it up?"

The attendant was still smiling as he walked to the pump. "Yeh. Don't be in such a hurry."

Taking one hand off the wheel, Sharon reached over and patted Grady's soft ears. "You think we had our act together for that attendant, Grady? I thought we did a good job. We're going to have to be careful when we get into town so that we don't make anyone suspicious. Julie has already warned me about the

bigotry in the sheriff's department and much of the town. We're going to have to make these folks feel like we belong here."

Grady rolled over on his side, lightly pawed Sharon's hand and then made a vain attempt to lick it.

"You must be hungry, Grady. We'll be in Wilburn in a few minutes. First we have to find a place to stay, then you can eat." Sharon paused. "Most of the media have left town, but there still probably aren't any rooms at the hotels. We'll have to try some of the boarding houses or maybe someone is renting a spare room. You'll have to behave yourself. Got that? We don't want to be kicked out."

Sharon entered Wilburn from the south, and headed up Main Street. She slowed down to look at the Victorian style homes that lined most of the streets near the center of town. She drove past the sheriff's office, and a few blocks later turned onto Jackson Avenue. "Grady, there's a large gray house with a 'Rooms for Rent' sign out. Let's stop and check it out."

Sharon pulled up to the curb and parked. She looked at Grady as she rubbed his ears. "Now boy, you stay here for a minute and I'll be right back." Sharon opened the passenger window about three inches to let air in before getting out of the truck. She walked up to the front porch, looked back at her truck, took a deep breath and then whispered, "Here we go." She rang the doorbell and waited quietly.

Thirty seconds later an elderly well-dressed woman opened the door. "Hello. May I help you miss?"

"Yes, thank you. I'm looking for a room to rent. Do you have any available?"

"Yes. We had a newsman check out this morning. Come in. My name is Mrs. Snow. If you follow me I'll show you the room."

Sharon opened the screen door and followed the woman. "Mrs. Snow, my name is Sharon Goody, I'm looking for work at the chemical plant – I'm a computer specialist. I just needed to

get away from my ex-boy- friend. I'd like to rent the room for a week for now, maybe longer once I get the job. I have money and can pay you now."

Mrs. Snow asked, "Where are you from?"

"I grew up in a small town in Georgia, named Cottonville. My father was pastor of a small church. My parents died in a car crash five years ago."

Mrs. Snow took a key that was hanging from the wall and opened the door marked Room 3. She motioned for Sharon to enter first. "This is the room. It comes with a continental breakfast. There's a bathroom at the other end of the hall that you share with one other guest. The room is $200 for a week, with half due up front."

Sharon walked over to the bed, sat down and looked around. "It's fine...if you allow pets. I have a Labrador dog. He's well-behaved and will only be in the room at night when I sleep." Sharon approached Mrs. Snow and took out a roll of bills from her pocket. "Here's $100."

"As long as he doesn't keep us awake, the dog can stay. If he destroys anything you'll have to pay for it. This is the key," said Mrs. Snow taking the money.

"Thanks," said Sharon closing and locking the door before joining Mrs. Snow, who was already on her way down the hall. "Can you tell me where the grocery store is?"

Mrs. Snow stopped and faced Sharon, "Half a mile north on Main Street."

"Thank you," replied Sharon as she left the house and went to the truck. "Grady, we have a place to stay. Mrs. Snow is our landlady. She is a little stiff, but we should be fine. Now let's get you some food."

Sharon drove to the market, and left Grady tied to a post outside the store, while she bought dog food and a few other items. She carried the two bags out to the truck and temporarily

placed them in the back. She walked around to unlock the passenger door and opened it a few inches. She turned to pick up the two bags, but stopped when she saw a large man standing at the end of the truck. She looked at him and stepped backward toward the passenger door. The man moved two steps forward and leaned on the side of the truck.

Sharon looked around the parking lot, but there was no one around. She straightened her back. "Excuse me, I want to put those bags into the front." She waited, hoping that the man would move out of the way or maybe help with the bags.

The man spit tobacco juice onto the ground. "Girl, you seem to be alone. A pretty blond with green eyes, that's not right. Maybe we can find something we can do together?" Then he moved a few feet away from the truck, blocking Sharon from passing him. Cars were parked behind and to either side of her; the menacing man in front of her. She slipped her right hand over the passenger door edge. "I'm not alone."

"I don't see anyone else here. Come on, let's get this show on the road!" he said, taking a step toward Sharon.

"I don't think so!" screamed Sharon as she flung open the passenger door and shouted. "Stop, Grady."

The man was within two feet of Sharon and about to grab her when Grady jumped out of the front seat onto the ground and dug his teeth into the man's left leg.

The man cringed from the pain. "Oouch. What in tarnation is this dog doing! Get him off of me!" He tried to grab Grady, but Grady's grip made it impossible for him to pull the dog off without ripping apart his leg. "Lady, do something!"

"So now it's 'Lady.' You still want to do something with me?"

"No, no. I don't want anything from you. Just get the dog off me and I'm history."

"OK. Grady, stand by!"

Grady let go of the man's leg and sat next to Sharon. The man turned and muttered, "That damn dog," as he limped away. Grady had been well-trained by the FBI to defend his partner and he did it in true FBI style.

"Good boy, Grady. Now let's get back to our room. We're both hungry, and you deserve a treat. After supper, we have a meeting with Julie."

Back in her room, Sharon unpacked her clothes, ate and fed Grady before leaving for her meeting. It was nighttime and a nearly full moon provided sufficient light for her to drive and read the road signs. "Grady. There's the road to the trailer park," said Sharon, turning the truck onto the side road. "Grady, we're going to meet Julie again, and there will be other friends there who you should be nice to. I see the trailer office and a couple of trailers and cars over there."

Sharon parked the truck next to the cars and opened the passenger door. "Grady, come!" Grady took his place next to Sharon and together they walked over to a trailer. "From the way that Julie described it, this looks like Peter's trailer." Sharon knocked on the door, and to her surprise Julie answered through the intercom next to the door. "Hi, Sharon. Nice to see you and Grady again. The door's open, come in."

Grady entered first, and then Sharon. Once inside Sharon looked at the display of electronic equipment, noticing the camera shots of the outside. At the other end of the trailer, Julie was standing and two men were sitting in front of computer screens. "So this is the setup you mentioned, Julie."

Moving to stand behind one of the men, Julie smiled and said, "This is Peter. He works for Citizens Against Pollution or CAP. They are here to investigate these incidents and they also help us out."

Sharon approached Peter, who was still looking at the screen. "Hi, nice to meet you."

Peter turned to Sharon and looked up. He paused, surprised at the strikingly fine Southern beauty of this woman. "It's great to have you join us," said Peter, standing and shaking hands with Sharon.

Julie took a step to the side. "And this is Justice, also a member of CAP."

Justice quickly stood up and looked directly at Sharon extending his hand. "Thank you for helping us out."

Sharon turned toward Justice. Her eyes opened wide and she smiled as she noticed his physique. The heavy muscles of his arms extended to his broad dark shoulders. "It looks like I'm in very good company," she said, shaking hands with Justice.

Once everyone was introduced, Julie stepped forward and embraced Sharon. "It's great to see you again! Did have pleasant trip?"

Sharon stepped back, "Grady and I had a wonderful trip. That truck the FBI provided is great and the trip gave Grady and me the opportunity to get to know each other and get our act together. We rented a room at Mrs. Snow's Lodging House in town."

As Justice knelt over to pet Grady, Sharon warned. "Don't do that! Grady is trained to be an expert defense dog. He'll grab you and not let go until he's ordered to stop." Sharon bent down and patted Grady on the head; "Grady, Rest!" Turning to Justice, she said softly, "Now you can pet him."

"I see you've learned the commands for Grady." Julie commented.

"Yes, and not too soon either. Earlier today Grady saved me from a harasser."

"Did you report the incident?" asked Julie.

"No, the man ran off. Anyway he didn't do anything, and I didn't want to get the local sheriff involved. He might have

checked into my background and I didn't want to explain things."

"You're right. Anyway I am glad to see you're OK. We have a lot to go over."

Sharon sat down next to Justice as Julie returned to business. "When I got back to town this morning I met with the sheriff and then with the local FBI. They still believe that the train wreck and the recent explosion at the plant were accidents. I told them what I saw in Argentina and they shrugged it off. I was furious when they told me that the sample bag, which I suspected contained the explosive that I found at the site of the train derailment, didn't get to the lab. I thought it was supposed to be there when we left for Argentina." Julie took a deep sigh and then continued. "Agent Hilbaum told me that Agent Greenbaum was delivering the sample when he disappeared but the authorities didn't find the sample when they searched Greenbaum's car after his accident. And they haven't been able to establish Greenbaum's last contact."

Sharon stared at Julie. "So now what? Do you trust this agent Hilbaum?"

"I'm not sure."

Peter interjected, "Julie, you can't trust him! He's probably tied into this conspiracy - or at least covering for them."

Julie turned to Peter. "So you don't think we should tell Agent Hilbaum about Sharon?"

"Definitely not! You'll only put her life in danger."

"Sharon, would you be OK if you worked directly with us? You won't have the local authorities as backup."

"Yes, but how do we communicate?" asked Sharon.

"Peter, any ideas on maintaining communications with Sharon?" asked Julie.

"We could set up a dedicated e-mail address or a Web site," replied Peter.

Sharon had another idea. "Why don't we set up a fake Web site for a white supremacy group and use a chat room? Peter can monitor communications and it will serve as a cover."

Julie asked, "Can you set that up, Peter?"

"I'll do it tonight. I'll send you an e-mail about the site. You can communicate through your laptop modem or any other networked computer." Peter continued, "So what's the plan?"

Julie looked at Sharon before turning to Peter, "Sharon is going to try to get a job at Forsythe Systems. She has some personal references and the required qualifications. All she needs is the opportunity. That's where you can help out, Justice."

"What can I do?" he asked.

Sharon replied, "I'll explain the plan to you." Looking at Julie, she added, "Why don't you and Peter work on that Web site?"

After thirty minutes, Julie noticed Sharon and Justice were laughing and talking. Julie walked over to Sharon, "Let's get some fresh air."

Peter interjected, "You have some secrets to discuss?"

"Oh, Peter, it's just girl talk."

As Julie and Sharon left the trailer, Peter replied. "All the more reason to join you."

Julie walked Sharon over to the parked cars. "So, Sharon how do you feel about this plan. Are you comfortable with your part?"

"Julie, I'm ready. I want to get them as badly as you do."

"I know. The first week I was nauseated all day from the chemicals, but I had to stay. I saw parents bury their children, and I saw this little girl gasping for breath. Someone needs to pay."

"The worst part is that no matter what we do, we can never make things right. This is irreversible damage. All we can do is make sure it doesn't happen again."

"Sharon, you know you'll be exposing yourself to these criminals. I want you to have a gun just in case. I talked to Mrs. Gutierrez and she approved." Julie unlocked her car trunk, took out a handgun and gave it to Sharon. "I know you're trained to use a gun."

"You know me better than that. I don't like to use guns or carry them. That's why Grady is here."

"Then keep the gun in the truck, just in case."

"OK." Sharon walked over to her truck, placed the gun into the glove compartment and locked it. As Sharon returned, Julie smiled.

"And now for our 'girl talk'. I saw you eyeing Justice. You like the strong handsome type?"

Sharon smiled and blushed. "I hope I wasn't too obvious in there."

"Justice will be keeping watch on the suspects and also on you. He already helped Sean out of a jam. He's a real nice guy."

"How is Sean doing?"

"He's recovering from the injuries he sustained in Buenos Aires. I expect that he'll be joining us soon."

"What's up with you and Sean?"

"We're partners. I help him stay sober and I'm getting him more interested in environmental issues. He helps me get

through these tough cases and shows me the ropes. He protects me."

Sharon laughed. "Something like Grady does for me?"

Julie chuckled. "He's the one that keeps calling me 'Lassie'."

"Lassie?"

"When he first used the word back in Alaska I didn't know it was an Irish thing. I thought he meant the television dog. Now it's more of an inside joke."

"It seems you have a very close relationship."

Julie paused for a minute and then said quietly, "It's too close lately."

"Is he getting fresh with you? I know I had to fight off a few 'partners' in my time."

"The first time we worked together, in Alaska, Sean tried to take advantage of the situation. He's like most men. But that's not the problem any more. He respects me, but his male ego is too much. Sometimes Sean acts like he owns me or something. He makes a fool of himself competing with Peter, of all people, and in Buenos Aires, he was jealous of Ricardo. I mean, he was furious; he tried to hide it, but he couldn't. When Ricardo tried to rape me, Sean was ready to kill him. I know he threatened him."

"But can you blame him? I remember your e-mail about Ricardo. That louse, you should report him."

"No, I think I was at fault.... But as far as Sean's concerned, I made the mistake of confiding in him too much and leaning on him too heavily. You can't treat a man like a girlfriend. They think you're coming on to them right off."

"That's when a canine partner comes in handy. I can tell Grady anything. And, he'll always be his sweet furry self!"

"Well, men are men, you know... I don't think Sean knows where to draw the line."

"Do you?"

Julie, paused, took a deep breath and let out a sigh. "I care about him as a friend, that's all, really. Why can't men understand that?"

"I don't know... What about Peter? Is there anything between you two?"

"Peter's a friend. He and I share our love for the environment. We don't threaten each other with a complex relationship." Julie paused and then said "And... I don't think Peter is interested...in women."

"Oh! That's just fine!" exclaimed Sharon. "It's always the cute ones! Let's get back inside! Grady and I need to get back and rest for our big day tomorrow." Julie and Sharon laughed as they entered the trailer.

"Peter; Justice. It was nice to meet you. Grady and I are going back. Come on Grady."

"Thank you, and good luck," said Peter.

"I'll see you tomorrow, Justice."

Grady followed Sharon back to the truck and jumped in when she opened the door. "Grady, it's been a long day and we need some rest. Did I ever tell you what a great partner you are, boy? You are just the best!" Sharon petted Grady and he put his head down on the seat, enjoying the attention. Sharon drove back to town, ready for a quiet and restful night.

It was a bright sunny morning. Sharon parked her truck across the street from the Forsythe Systems offices. Grady was left back in her apartment, sheltered from the burning sun.

The offices were just two blocks south of the center of town in a group of recently renovated buildings. Far from the train wreck, these buildings showed no sign of the hellish explosion just weeks before. Sharon crossed Main Street, entered the office and walked up to the receptionist's desk.

"I'd like to see the President, Mr. James Ashland."

"And what is it in regard to?"

"It's in reference to a job," said Sharon handing the receptionist a letter.

The receptionist read the letter, picked up her phone and dialed. "Mr. Ashland, there's a woman here, Sharon Goody, who would like to see you regarding a job. She has a letter of introduction from a Mr. Kingman of Remote-Com Corporation." After a brief pause, the receptionist said, "OK. Mr. Ashland."

She hung up the phone and turned to Sharon, "Mr. Ashland's office is at the end of the hallway," she said, handing Sharon her letter.

"Thank you." Sharon walked down the long hallway, and went into Mr. Ashland's office.

A middle-aged, rather large man was seated behind the desk. "Please come in and sit down, Miss Goody."

Sharon sat in the chair across from Mr. Ashland and handed him some papers. "Here is my resume, reference list and letter of recommendation from Mr. Kingsman of Remote-Com Corporation. I'm looking for work, and Mr. Kingsman recommended I see you."

Mr. Ashland took a minute to review the papers. "I see you have experience in plant control systems. Mr. Kingsman has a fine company. Can you tell me why you left and came here?"

"Mr. Ashland, I had worked for Mr. Kingsman for over a year, but I had some personal problems with an ex-boyfriend and

I needed to get away from him and his town. I didn't have any specific place to go, until Mr. Kingsman suggested Wilburn."

"We work for many of the operating chemical plants in Wilburn. Much of our work is in controls for these plants and maintenance of the computer systems. Are you interested in this type of work?"

"Yes. I've worked in chemical plants. I'm familiar with the operation of the major computer control systems and can program in the software languages indicated on my resume."

"Your experience and credentials are impressive. We aren't looking to hire right now, but I can talk with our chief executive and get back to you. We're always interested in qualified people. Meanwhile, can I have a phone number where I can reach you? I'll get in touch with you in a couple of days."

"Thank you," replied Sharon as she and Mr. Ashland walked to the reception area. Sharon wrote her name and Mrs. Snow's boarding house telephone number on a piece of paper and handed it to Mr. Ashland.

"Thank you, Miss Goody. I hope you enjoy your stay," Mr. Ashland said, extending his hand.

Sharon shook his hand. "It was a pleasure meeting you Mr. Ashland."

As she left the building, Sharon saw Justice standing against the back of her pickup truck. He had picked up Grady from Sharon's apartment and let him lose so Grady was standing next to him now. "What are you doing with my dog boy? You better stop it. Stop, Grady."

Justice straightened up and yelled back, "That damn mutt of yours growled at me. You should have him on a leash!"

Grady ran up to the back of the pickup box, barking and growling at Justice. Hearing the commotion, Mr. Ashland and another man came running out of the building. "What's going on here?" he asked Sharon.

"That black boy over there is annoying MY DOG!" she replied.

"You! Boy! Better leave my dog alone or I'll have him rip you apart," shouted Sharon.

Justice backed away, muttering several obscenities, and walked down the street.

Sharon turned to Mr. Ashland. "It was because of people like that I left my last town," she said before crossing the street.

The other man, who had been quiet until now, turned to Mr. Ashland and asked, "What's up?"

Mr. Ashland replied, "Miss Goody came into our office looking for a job, Jeff. I was starting to tell you about her when the dog started barking."

Jeff turned his attention to the departing Sharon. "Miss Goody, I'm Jeff Forsythe. I own the company. Jimmy here tells me you're looking for work?"

Sharon turned around and slowly walked back across the street. "That's correct, Mr. Forsythe."

"If you can hold up your computer skills like you can your people skills, we may have a spot for you. Come back tomorrow. Meanwhile, we'll check out your references and if you pass, you're hired." Jeff smiled at her.

Sharon returned his smile, "Thank you." When she reached the truck, she patted Grady on the head, looked across the street at the men entering the building, and whispered to Grady, "Nice show Grady. I think you're ready for Hollywood."

Chapter Ten

Julie's Turn

The morning sun filtered through the trailer window and sparkled across the keyboard as Peter typed in his password. "Is there anything on the Internet?" asked Julie.

Peter clicked the icon to open the Web site he created the evening before. He checked the messages for Sharon's code name. "Nothing yet from Sharon, but we already have a few extremists leaving their comments. I just hope she's OK."

"Don't worry about Sharon; she knows how to handle herself. She'll give a good performance; I'm sure Forsythe will hire her." Julie placed her hand on Peter's shoulder and leaned over to view the screen. "Now, what do you mean we have some comments by extremists?"

"Julie, it's just some whacked-out hate group talk. After all we did disguise this site to serve as a way to communicate with Sharon without blowing her cover." Peter's fingers relaxed and his hands slid off the keyboard and onto his lap, "I'm not worried about her getting hired. But I am concerned about what they might do if they find out she's an agent. There are too many people who are associated with these terrorists and it only takes one to point a finger at her!" said Peter shaking his right index finger at Julie.

"I can't call these guys 'terrorists'. All they are is crooks. From what we saw in Argentina, they use technology to cause chemical releases at will. They make money by convincing legitimate businesses to hire them to clean up messes they leave behind and then to provide software systems to prevent further releases. It's just like the old storefront window scam to me."

"I don't know that scam."

"You know: Throw a stone through a window, then sell the store owner new glass the next day? Simple but effective."

Peter stood up and walked down the length of the trailer, grabbing his half-filled cup of coffee. "*Terrorists* is what they are! Environmental terrorists! They do irreparable harm to the environment –ecocide that future generations will have to pay for!" Peter threw the cold coffee into the sink and poured a fresh cup.

Julie followed Peter to the end of the trailer and waited until he took a sip. "I want to catch these guys too, but I need proof that a jury will accept and convict on."

"Damn! This is too important to be worried about protocol anymore!"

"I feel bad, too, when I know there's environmental abuse but don't have the means to put the responsible parties in jail. That's the most frustrating part of this job."

The red warning light above the trailer door flashed. "It's George!" said Peter as he unlocked the door. George spotted Julie inside and quickly squeezed through the door, almost knocking Peter down with the bundle of papers he carried in his left arm. Julie went to the computer screen and checked out the parking lot. It was empty.

"What's up, George?"

But George didn't answer Peter. Instead, he smiled at Julie and led her to the other end of the trailer. "I know you and Sean were following Mr. Hugo Arias and Mr. Forsythe so I did some investigating." George looked across the trailer at Peter and frowned. "Unfortunately, I don't have the computer skills you have! But I do know where and how to get my hands on all the past newspapers. If you carefully read through them, as I did for the last three days, and you know what to look for, you can get to the truth and unravel the entire conspiracy."

Peter locked the trailer door and sat next to Julie. "Show us what you have."

"It's not easy getting this information. There are many people in town who would cut my throat if they knew what I was doing. I'm not even sure they don't already know, so you'd better be careful. Is Justice or Sean around? We may need them."

Peter remained quiet. Julie almost responded but decided it was better not to tell George about Sharon. "Justice is busy today and Sean is on other FBI business."

"I guess we'll just have to take care of this ourselves, but I'd be careful," said George squirming in his chair.

Uncomfortable, Julie quickly changed the subject. "What information do you have?"

"Well, it's a rather long story and has many pieces."

"Just take it slow and give us the complete story, George."

George loosened his tight grip on the papers and placed them on the table. "You have to go back ten years, maybe longer. In my first piece here, I have an article from 1990. It announces the establishment of the Forsythe Systems Company and says that its first client is OC Chemicals Company. There's a quote here from Mr. Arias, *'We have awarded a contract to the Forsythe Systems Company to automate and computerize the plant systems. In the last five years we have experienced poor control reliability and as a consequence have been the recipient of several fines. We are taking this step today to show to our community that we intend to take an active role in keeping our plant, our employees and the community safe'.*"

"Sounds like typical company hype," said Peter.

"But now for the rest of the story," continued George picking up another story from the pile. "In this article from 1992, Forsythe Systems announced its reorganization. It also contains a short bio on the principals of the company."

George handed the paper to Julie and she read the headline out loud, " 'Forsythe Systems Grows and Moves to New Offices'," and then continued reading the article, " 'This week Forsythe Systems will move into it's new offices on Main Street. After just two years the company has increased its net sales from $250,000 to $5 million. This explosive growth is partly due to the fast-expanding use of intelligent computer control systems, says its new chief operating officer Jim Forsythe.

"'Mr. Forsythe, the founder and president of the company for the last two years, takes on his new position in his growing company as he welcomes new management. Mr. John Ashland joins the company as the new president. Mr. Ashland had been Manager of Engineering at Inland Chemical Company for ten years and a resident of Wilburn since graduating from college. Mr. Forsythe grew up in Wilburn, has worked at OC Chemicals for five years and for several other companies before starting Forsythe Systems'."

"You see, Julie!" George said excitedly. "This shows a connection. Mr. Forsythe had to know Mr. Arias at OC Chemicals since they worked together. And Mr. Ashland worked for Inland Chemical Company." George thumbed through some more articles, pulled one out and handed it to Peter. "Now read this one."

Peter reluctantly took the paper and read: " 'Wilburn Gazette, Nov 12, 1991. Inland Chemical Suffers Tank Fire - Yesterday the Inland Chemical Company reported that a tank fire occurred in one of its fuel tanks. The company spokesman, Mr. Ashland, stated 'The fire was caused by a control system failure. The fire was quickly put out and there was no damage to the rest of the plant'."

George pointed to another spot in the article, "Peter, skip to the area highlighted in yellow."

Peter continued, "'Mr. Ashland said that Inland Chemical Company was hiring Forsythe Systems to propose improvements

in the plant's reliability and controls.' So? I still don't understand," said Peter handing the paper back to George.

George insisted, "See, how these guys are working together? First, there's a problem at the Inland Chemical plant, and then Forsythe Systems gets a contract. Years later Forsythe hires Ashland, the person on the inside. It's a perfect case of sabotage and conspiracy. Who knows how much he offered these guys?" George pounded his hand on the table, knocking some of the papers to the floor.

"These are just clues, not proof. I can't use this in court!" Julie said, frustrated.

"But there's more stuff linking these so called 'accidents' to Forsythe Systems in these articles. Look at this one." George pushed a paper into Julie's hand. "Read the highlighted section."

Julie glanced over the whole article and then began. "Wait, look at this: *'Bill FitzPatrick of Yoland Chemical Company was responsible for saving the life of two coworkers and preventing significant damage to the plant with his timely shutdown of a critical high pressure catalytic process and control system. The unit experienced a failure in the safety systems, but thanks to Mr. FitzPatrick the event was not catastrophic.'*"

George hurriedly added, "A facility in Texas was not so fortunate. When they experienced a similar type of failure it caused a fire that destroyed the plant. You could say that Mr. FitzPatrick was lucky to have been in the right place at the right time. However," said George shaking another piece of paper, "in this here article – just three months later – Mr. FitzPatrick joined Forsythe Systems as chief of Plant Operations. His first project for Forsythe Systems was at the Yoland plant. Can't you see? Forsythe Systems is growing by paying off insiders to cause the problems it is hired to solve!"

Peter had seen and heard enough, "OK, I agree. There seems to be something going on."

But Julie was still looking for some direct proof. She looked at the pile of papers. Slowly and methodically she read to herself one of the articles that appeared on the back of the Mr. FitzPatrick article. "'Sheriff *takes Man in Custody. Mr. Jammer was arrested for disorderly conduct in front of the OC Chemicals Company's employee entrance today. He had been standing at the entrance shouting obscenities at all black employees as they entered the plant. He also displayed a sign with the words 'Black Go Back! Leave our jobs for us whites'. Mr. Jammer, an OC Chemicals Plant spokesman said, was a past employee who was laid off three months ago. Mr. Jammer claimed that he was let go by the company to be replaced by a black employee because of affirmative action. He took his case to court. The court ruled against Mr. Jammer earlier this week.'* Well, it looks like Mr. Jammer took his case to the street," said Julie and she threw the paper back on the table.

"George. Do you know of any racial problems at the chemical plants?" asked Julie.

Before George could answer, Peter asked, "What does that have to do with Forsythe Systems?"

"It probably doesn't have anything to do with Forsythe Systems. But it could have something to do with the accidents," said Julie, shrugging her shoulders.

"I thought Sean convinced you there was no racial motive here."

"Well, we didn't discount it completely."

"Wait, Julie may have something here. I remember years ago, at a time when the economy was slow, a white supremacist group demonstrated in front of OC Chemicals when a court ruling forced the hiring of more blacks through affirmative action. There was a confrontation with the sheriff and both blacks and whites were arrested. At the time, whites were laid off and replaced with blacks. The group claimed the layoffs were discriminatory and the policy was racist," said George.

"Well, that was a few years ago, and doesn't connect anyone with these crimes. Getting back to Forsythe Systems: what are we going to do about George's articles? If you don't want to do anything about them, I can make good use of them on our Internet Web site," said Peter.

"No, I don't want these articles on the Internet right now," said Julie realizing that such a move might jeopardize Sharon.

"Can't the FBI use them?" asked George.

"I would like to show these articles to my superiors, but I think they'll want to know what the local FBI and authorities think."

"Oh, you don't want to get the sheriff's office involved in this. They'll just harass me as they always do when I try to print the truth," replied George. "And these local FBI agents aren't going to like any accusations either."

"Well, I think it's about time we tried shaking the tree, as Sean would say," said Julie walking toward the door.

George, reluctant to follow Julie, yelled, "I don't want to see that sheriff again!"

"Come on George, you know you want to get the big story on this. How can you do that by staying out of it?" Julie asked, giving George her most persuasive smile.

But George wasn't moving, so Julie added, "Peter can come with us."

Peter was surprised at Julie's suggestion. The FBI's policy had been to use CAP's help only indirectly, and off-the-record. This was an opportunity he has been waiting for since the Alaskan case, so he jumped at the chance. "Why not? This trailer-bound existence is starting to drive me crazy. I'm coming along."

George slowly got up. "I guess I better come along. I know it'll be useless, but at least the three of us and these articles

should show that we mean business," he said, hurrying to catch up with Peter and Julie before they reached the car.

Julie called Hilbaum from her cell phone.

"Agent Hilbaum. This is Agent Del Rio."

"Oh, Yes *Miss Del Rio*, I heard you were back from your little excursion to Argentina. What can I do for you?"

"I have some information that connects the Forsythe Systems Company with numerous chemical plant incidents over the last ten years. My associates and I can bring it to you."

"Sounds like you have some solid evidence."

"It's good enough, I think, to start a federal investigation of the company."

"Ms. Del Rio, to save some time, why don't we all meet over at the sheriff's office?"

"OK. We'll be there in about fifteen minutes."

"Fine, I'll see you there."

It was a quick drive, during which George sat in the back and organized the articles and Peter saw the town and the countryside in daylight for the first time since he arrived. Julie was happy and confident. She parked the car across from the sheriff's office and the three of them crossed the street and walked through the glass doors together.

Inside, Frank Hilbaum was already talking to the sheriff. Julie interrupted as she approached them. "Sheriff Williams and Agent Hilbaum, I'm glad we're all here."

"It's a pleasure seeing you again, Ms. Del Rio. What can we do for you?" asked the sheriff.

"I want to show you some past newspaper articles that George Reed put together. They present a disturbing picture of Forsythe Systems Company and their forced relationships with

local chemical companies. OK George, tell them what you told Peter and me."

George laid out the papers on the desk. He held up one paper and read from it. When he finished, Peter read a second article. The two alternated for about 10 minutes, each story sounding more sinister than the last.

Frank abruptly grabbed Julie's arm and led her to a corner of the office. "These two friends of yours are not the type of people the FBI relies on for help. For all I know they're responsible for the train wreck! I'm not going to listen to their *stories*. And you, my dear, should know better. I suggest you drop this now!" Frank hissed as he loosened his tight grip on Julie's arm.

Juliana was furious at the way the sheriff had treated her and his refusal to even listen to what appeared to be bonafide evidence. But when Frank's hand slid down Julie's arm and carelessly moved to her hip, Julie kept a tight rein on her temper. She refused to let this guy intimidate her and she gently took his hand and held it for a moment. Frank relaxed when he thought Julie was returning his affection, but his wry smile changed to surprise and then to pain when she swiftly jammed her knee hard into his crotch.

"That's what I think of your suggestion!" she said loudly enough to cover up the short growl that Frank gave as he bent over. The sheriff, Peter, and George were involved in their own discussion, and the rest of the office was so busy that the scene went unnoticed by everyone except for two men standing at the front entrance. One was tall and wore a dark brown cowboy jacket with fringes and a large western hat. The other was of medium height and less conspicuous, wearing jeans and a short-sleeved T-shirt. Frank looked over at them, acknowledging their presence with eye contact. As Julie walked away, she noticed that Frank nodded at the two men. Curiously, they both turned around and left the office.

Julie returned to Peter and George and tried to concentrate on the discussion with the sheriff.

"I can't take any action based on these articles. I don't see the connections you are drawing," said the sheriff, who was surprisingly calm.

Frank joined the group, gathered up the papers, and handed them to George. He forced a smile, and politely told Peter and George, "I think you made your point, but the sheriff isn't going to do anything, so why don't you leave."

"Let's go George, we can make better use of our time. There are other methods for informing the public," said Peter.

Julie remained inside as George and Peter left the building. She looked at Frank and her eyes widened when she noticed that he was nodding his head at the two men outside. She watched helplessly as the two men jumped Peter from behind. Peter fought back, haphazardly throwing punches at the men. George turned, saw the fighting, and moved toward the man now hanging onto Peter's back. But before George reached the assailant, the man in the cowboy hat ran up, grabbed the papers from George's arm, and pushed him to the ground. "Stop him!" yelled George as he fell to the pavement.

"Sheriff, do something!" yelled Julie as she ran outside, followed by the sheriff and two deputies. George was on the ground pointing down the street, but the man in the cowboy hat had turned down a side street and was no longer in sight. Meanwhile, two deputies separated Peter from the man in the T-shirt.

Peter shouted, "This man jumped me."

"He started it. He came out of the building and ran into me."

Peter turned to the sheriff. "That's a lie!"

George added, "And there was another man who jumped me, but he got away. He was wearing a cowboy jacket and hat."

"I saw what happened," said Julie.

The deputies escorted Peter and the man in the T-shirt into the office, and began taking their statements. Frank pulled the sheriff aside and said something to him in a hushed voice. When Frank was done speaking, the sheriff walked over to Julie and George. "Ms. Del Rio, we must detain Peter and the other man for disorderly conduct. They will be held in custody up to 48 hours so they may cool off. I have to do this in order to keep this town from falling into total disobedience."

Julie looked at Frank defiantly, but kept quiet. She approached Peter and whispered in his ear. "I'm sorry Peter. We'll straighten this out for you, but I can't do anything now. I have to call Gutierrez first."

"Julie, you and George should go. I'll be fine. I don't expect this to go to court."

"I'm sorry I got you into this mess."

Peter tried to lighten the guilt for Julie. "I should have seen this coming. But don't worry. I've been in much worse jails," he said, before lowering his voice to a whisper. "Be sure to check on Justice and Sharon. Keep an eye on that Internet site."

"I will. Good-bye, Peter." She turned her attention to George, who was holding a handkerchief on his forehead. "Come George let's get you cleaned up."

Julie helped George to her car and they drove back to the trailer.

Chapter Eleven

Sharon's Turn

Sharon stood impatiently at the door. "Come on Grady, I don't want to be late on what could be my first day of work."

Grady had a habit of pausing to sniff every object in the room. It was an asset when he was the top narcotics dog at the FBI, but Sharon found it annoying. She rolled her eyes and scolded Grady, "That's enough. Let's go!" Grady nonchalantly walked through the door.

Sharon wanted to appear confident when she saw Mr. Ashland this morning. She wore a pair of slightly worn, snug-fitting jeans and a crisp light blue shirt. She made sure her hair was meticulously combed, her makeup perfect and her shoes clean.

Reaching her truck, she let Grady in on the passenger side. Sharon didn't go anywhere without her canine partner. His cuddly shiny coat, white teeth and lovable grin provided a great cover for a trained animal capable of killing a grown man with a single bite to the jugular. Grady made Sharon feel safe. She could always count on him to be there for her, with unconditional love and protection. Grady always did his job. He was a far cry from the partners she had in prior FBI assignments, who in the end, always wanted the same thing from the lovely blond agent with the sculptured body. Sharon wanted no more of those "partnerships." She was happy with this new arrangement; she liked to be the one in charge, she realized as she drove to her meeting.

Arriving at the Forsythe Systems office, she put Grady in the back of the truck and ordered him to stay before entering the building.

"Hello, I don't know if you remember me, but I'm here to see Mr. Ashland."

"Yes, I remember you. Mr. Ashland is currently busy, but you can wait over there," said the receptionist pointing to the area across from her desk.

Sharon chose the seat near the wall adjacent to Ashland's office. Just as she was sitting down, she heard raised voices coming from Mr. Ashland's office. She leaned back and turned her head to the side so that her right ear, which was equipped with a barely visible listening device, pressed against the wall.

She tried to remain perfectly still, determined to concentrate on the conversation, but the texture of the wall against her ear triggered memories of a time in kindergarten. During midday nap she would place her ear on the floor to hear what others were saying or doing. Mrs. Hazelton would scold her. Her mother's voice echoed in her head: "From now on, Sharon, pretend that you're sleeping during naptime."

Sharon learned early on that she could get what she wanted by pretending. She understood how to turn human frailties like lust or bigotry into an advantage. All she needed to do was flaunt those blond curls, tight body and perfect features. Predictably, no one would suspect she was a cunning expert in computer security with a Ph.D. in engineering. She had often used her good looks as cover when working with the FBI. She was so good at it that she was always on demand as an undercover consultant and could name her price. But this assignment was different. She wanted to help her friend Julie – someone who shared her passion for the environment and who was a true friend. She believed in this one and was determined to get these guys at any cost.

Suddenly realizing that she had been letting her mind wander, Sharon turned her attention back to the situation at hand. The voices were barely audible even with the latest listening devices the FBI could provide. Listening closely, she determined there were three men's voices. She could hear most

of the words and identified two of the voices as belonging to Mr. Ashland and Mr. Forsythe, but she didn't recognize the third voice.

Mr. Ashland spoke softly and clearly. "We have two employees besides Mr. FitzPatrick at your plant. Any of them could provide the authorities with damaging information."

Mr. Forsythe responded more loudly, "I don't want to leave them there while the FBI is searching the plant. It's too dangerous!"

The third man sounded annoyed. "Jim, I want your employees to stay. Pulling them out may tip off the FBI, causing them to dig even deeper. I'm not comfortable with you taking them out. We're walking a very fine line between using the FBI to our advantage and providing the FBI with enough knowledge to send us to jail. If it wasn't for the train derailment we wouldn't be in this situation."

Forsythe quickly responded, "Hugo, don't worry. The FBI won't find out anything. I have a perfectly good excuse for pulling the men out. I'll tell them that I'm pulling out all non-essential employees as a precaution in case of a terrorist attack at the plant. Isn't that why the FBI is investigating? They don't know we sent those threatening letters. To them there's been a threat to the plant and I'm just trying to protect my employees. For appearances' sake, I'll leave Mr. FitzPatrick there and maybe we can put someone new in the plant. Someone who knows nothing about our operation, just so we have a scapegoat if we need one."

Hugo asked, "What about Mr. FitzPatrick? Can he be trusted?"

Mr. Ashland answered, "FitzPatrick is a company man. He won't turn against us; he has just as much to lose as the rest of us."

Mr. Forsythe led Hugo to the door and added, "By keeping FitzPatrick there, we'll have someone who'll be able to keep an eye on the FBI."

Hugo laughed and said, "Yeah, and we all like the idea of having someone spying on the FBI."

Hearing the approaching footsteps, Sharon jumped up and scrambled to the chair farthest from Ashland's office. She made it just as Forsythe turned the doorknob and partially swung open the door. "Jim, make the changes as we agreed with Hugo," he said, putting an arm around Hugo and escorting him out of the office.

"OK, Jeff, I'll do it right now. Good-bye Hugo," said Mr. Ashland. He waited until the door closed before dialing FitzPatrick's number, "Bill, I need you to reassign Pat and Mark to the Buyard Chemical Plant."

"Why, Jim? Is there something urgent that has to be done at the Buyard plant?"

"No, but we want to get our people out of the OC plant before the FBI agents start asking questions and investigating. Tell them that we're using the excuse that we decided it wasn't safe for them to be at the plant while there's a risk of a terrorist attack. That's a pretty good cover story that the FBI should buy."

"What about me? You want me to leave the plant?"

"No. You stay and keep an eye on what the FBI is doing. I don't want them to find anything."

As Forsythe and Arias walked to the exit of the building, Sharon saw that the receptionist was walking with them, so she took a position outside Mr. Ashland's office. She listened but couldn't hear the conversation with FitzPatrick because Ashland had turned his back to the door.

Sharon heard the receptionist say goodbye to the men and saw her turn back to the reception area. Immediately Sharon knocked on the door and poked her head in.

Mr. Ashland turned to face the door. He pointed his index finger toward Sharon, indicating that he would be with her in a moment. Sharon stepped back and waited for Mr. Ashland to finish his conversation.

Mr. Ashland straightened his back and spoke quickly, "Bill, you do what I've told you, I'll call you back shortly. I have a visitor."

Mr. Ashland hung up the phone and walked to the doorway. "Miss Goody, please come in," and he led her toward his desk. "Take a seat. I assume you're here for that job we talked about yesterday. It's nice to find someone who's eager to work these days."

Sharon sat, crossed her left leg over her right and looked directly at Mr. Ashland, who sat down and smiled at her. "I like to be prepared and get right into my work, Mr. Ashland."

"Good, because I've checked out your references and they are very good, especially your experiences with plant control systems."

"I spent three years supporting operations as a control engineer," said Sharon, as she smiled back at Mr. Ashland.

"That's what we're looking for. We have an opening for a system maintenance engineer at a local plant. Your responsibilities will include installing and fixing control hardware and configuring software. Can you do that?"

"Yes."

"The job pays thirty-five dollars an hour. We expect forty hours a week, and sometimes there's overtime. Sometimes you'll be on call and we'll provide you with a beeper."

Sharon leaned forward, "That's OK with me. When can I start?"

Mr. Ashland leaned back. "You can start today if you want. Report to Mr. FitzPatrick at the OC Chemicals plant. He'll be

your supervisor. I'll arrange for your badge. You can pick up your employment papers from the receptionist." Mr. Ashland stood up, walked around his desk, and extended his hand. "It's nice to have you aboard. I wish you the best."

"Thank you," said Sharon as she stood and shook his hand.

Mr. Ashland walked her to the door. "Tell the receptionist that I asked you to fill out the employee forms."

While Sharon walked to the receptionist, Mr. Ashland returned to his desk. He dialed Mr. FitzPatrick, "Bill, did you tell Pat and Mark to report to the Buyard Chemical Plant?

"Yes, Jim, they'll be there this afternoon."

"I'm sending you a new employee. Her name is Sharon Goody. She doesn't know anything about our plans, so keep it that way."

"OK, Jim. But why are you sending her here?"

"She won't be able to tell the FBI anything about what we've been doing, but she'll be a perfect patsy should we need someone to take the blame, should the FBI find anything. Just make sure she doesn't cause any trouble."

"Sure thing. When will she start?"

"She'll probably be there in an hour. See that she has her badge ready and show her the plant procedures. And, Bill, keep me informed on the FBI."

"They told us that the FBI would be here today, but so far I haven't seen them."

"Just keep an eye out for them. Good-bye," said Ashland ending the conversation.

Sharon finished filling out the payroll and employment forms and handed them back to the receptionist. "Here are the papers. Thank you," Sharon said to the receptionist, left the office and walked across the street to her truck.

Grady was sitting in the back. "OK Grady, I have a job. Or maybe I should say we both have another job. Come on. Let's get started." Grady followed Sharon to the passenger door and got into the front of the truck. Sharon walked around to the driver's side and looked across the street. Justice was standing on the corner looking at her. Sharon nodded and Justice responded in kind, smiled and then turned and walked down the street. Sharon got into the truck and drove away.

It didn't take her long to reach the OC Chemicals plant, which was at the northwest end of town. She parked in the contractor's parking area, instructed Grady to stay in the back of the truck and walked up and into the guardhouse. A tall slender man in the company blue and white guard uniform asked her, "Yes, can I help you?"

Sharon smiled, but the guard remained expressionless. "I'm starting work today. I'm from Forsythe Systems. I'm supposed to report to a Mr. FitzPatrick."

"Oh, yes. I have a badge ready for you and you have to fill out this form." The guard handed Sharon some papers and a plastic card tied to a long shoelace. "You must wear this badge at all times and place this parking sticker in your windshield."

Sharon hung the badge around her neck and placed the sticker into her pocketbook. "Anything else?" she asked.

"Yes, all workers must take safety training before they can enter the plant. There's a twenty-minute video. At the end of the video you'll have to answer ten questions regarding the plant procedures. If you get eight correct answers you pass. If not, you repeat the training until you pass. Here are the questions. The room is over there," the guard pointed to a small room located just past the water cooler.

Inside were three chairs, and Sharon sat in the chair closest to the TV. Sharon had taken similar safety tests, and knew that the purpose of giving out the questions before seeing the video was to make it possible for the viewer to identify the answers

while looking at the video. This made passing the test a lot easier. The guard walked up to the VCR, pressed the play button, turned on the TV and closed the door as he left the room.

Twenty-two minutes later Sharon walked out the room and handed the question sheet to the guard. She walked over to the water cooler, took a small cup and sipped the cool water. She casually walked up to the guard, "So did I pass?"

The guard continued checking the answers, then looked up at Sharon, "You did fine. I can give you directions to the control room building. You'll find Mr. FitzPatrick there." As the guard gave Sharon directions, the main siren for the plant went off, repeating three short bursts.

Sharon asked the guard, "Are they testing the siren today?"

The guard nodded. "Yep, there are some federal inspectors here today. They're checking the plant's security systems. Don't be surprised if they check your badge."

Sharon smiled at the guard. "Thanks for the advice. I think I better get to work," she said, as she headed for the control room building.

The five-minute walk took Sharon past several process vessels, including two tall distillation columns and a large catalytic reactor. She could not resist the opportunity to look straight up at the equipment that seemed to reach toward the sky. The sights were familiar to Sharon. After spending eight years in the chemical business, she had seen many types of process equipment. As a young engineer, it was the variety of machinery and processes that attracted her to the business, and gave her a feeling of awe.

But after years in the industry, those feelings turned to disgust, because at every opportunity she faced the stark reality of the business, the greed of the companies and the complacency of those she worked with. By the time she left the industry, she had come to despise those very symbols that once she admired.

While looking up, Sharon heard a hissing sound, and she looked down just in time to see a burst of steam come from a nearby steam trap. Although the trap was about ten feet away, the steam shot directly in front of her. Had she taken three more steps, she would have been hit with the scalding steam. Luckily, she only felt the hot, moist air as the steam dissipated. From now on she was going to keep an eye on the ground and her ears tuned for sounds. She knew all too well the dangers that a chemical plant hid; her pair of safety boots and hard hat were definitely not protection from every hazard.

The single-story control room was built of solid concrete and without windows. It was designed to withstand an earthquake measuring nine on the Richter Scale, but it was mainly built for an unnatural disaster. It was designed for a man-made explosion, which was more likely to occur than an earthquake in this region, and could cause as much or more damage. This was the safest building in the plant, so logically most of the workers stayed inside unless they had to go out. For the operators and control systems personnel it was the main work place. There was no slacking off while in the control room. It contained some of the most sophisticated and complex systems in the entire plant; they always needed fixing, fine-tuning, or monitoring for some operation that was undergoing startup or shutdown.

Sharon opened the heavy vaulted door and entered the small front hallway. It contained two racks for storing hard hats on one side, with a long wall of shelves that held overalls. Many of the operators had their names printed on the shelves and their hard hats. Sharon took lipstick from her purse and used it to place a big red "S" on her hard hat before placing it on the rack.

She walked toward the open area in the center of the building, but stopped once she saw that it was the main control room. The area contained the plant monitoring equipment, which consisted of twelve video monitors, divided into four stations, each with three monitors. An operator was seated at each station, looking at the screen, calling up data from the computer, or talking to someone via radio. Control panels

surrounded the stations and rose to within two feet of overhead trays. Hundreds if not thousands of wires were strung from the trays to the panels. Only a few years had passed since Sharon had been in a chemical plant control room, but even in that short period there were significant technical advances. The monitors were larger, and provided complete touch control. Detailed information on every piece of process equipment was available at the touch of the screen, and every control device could be monitored from the station. Lights and recording devices on the control panels were gone, replaced by process information databases. Sharon stood behind a clear plastic window that surrounded the central area and stared into the room.

When one of the operators came into the hallway she asked, "Can you tell me where I can find Mr. FitzPatrick?"

"Yes, Ma'am. He's the white man standing by that panel," he said, pointing to the far side of the control room. "Excuse me I have to get out to the tank farm."

She saw Mr. FitzPatrick talking with a black operator but could not hear their conversation because of the plastic partitions that provided a noise barrier. She walked around the partitions and heard Mr. FitzPatrick barking out instructions to the operator. "God damn it! I told you to adjust the gain on this meter. Do I have to do everything? When are you going to get off your black ass and do something right around here?"

Another black operator turned to Mr. FitzPatrick. "Hey Bill, don't start dumping on my operators. Get one of your own people to fix that meter."

Mr. FitzPatrick mumbled, "Maybe I would if I had one of my own people."

Sharon walked over to Mr. FitzPatrick and asked, "If you want I can fix that meter."

Mr. FitzPatrick stopped what he was doing, looked at her and asked, "You must be Sharon?"

"Yes, I was told to report to you."

"Great, then you can take care of this meter. It's been recording higher than the other two meters in the line. It's a feed meter used in determining the cost of raw materials and it's triple redundant. If two of the meters don't agree, OC Chemicals could end up paying more than it should. Because these are critical, they're located in this climate-controlled room." Mr. FitzPatrick stepped aside to allow Sharon to work. She looked through the open tool kit next to Mr. FitzPatrick, took out a number 2 Phillips-head screwdriver and started working. Mr. FitzPatrick watched as she worked, even cracking a smile now that he had someone to do his work.

Looking at the operator sitting at the nearest station she asked, "What does the meter read?"

"Ten point two five."

"And what do the other meters read?"

"Nine point five."

"OK, then tell me when this meter reads nine point five," instructed Sharon as she began turning the set point screw on the meter.

The operator read out loud, "Ten point zero, nine point seven five, nine point five."

"That should do it!" she said, putting the screwdriver back in the toolbox.

"Good job," said Mr. FitzPatrick, smiling at Sharon.

"It's an old meter and will continue to cause problems unless you replace part of the mechanism, or replace the whole meter with a modern smart meter," Sharon warned.

Mr. FitzPatrick chuckled, "It'll be a cold day in hell before they change these meters. They'd have to change all three meters, which would cost them over a hundred thousand dollars. It's cheaper to make a minor repair every week."

"It's no skin off my back. They pay me to make the repairs."

"And you did it very well."

"Thank you."

"Look Sharon, it's noon, are you hungry?"

"Yeah."

"Then let's go to lunch. After lunch I'll give you the 'FitzPatrick' tour of the plant and show you where we do our work."

Bill led Sharon to the main office building, which housed the cafeteria. After selecting sandwiches and soft drinks, they sat at the far end of the room.

"Are you new to Wilburn?" asked Mr. FitzPatrick.

"Yes, I've only been here for a couple of days."

"Then I assume you don't know what happened?"

"I heard some stories, but I don't follow the papers."

"I'll give you my inside story," Bill took a bite and chewed before continuing, "Almost two weeks ago there was a train accident. It caused a chemical spill and a huge gas cloud that exploded and killed a lot of people. Authorities believe it may have been the work of terrorists who are now trying to do the same to this chemical plant. That's why the FBI is investigating the plant. They may interrogate all of us, so don't be surprised. Just tell them what you know.

After taking another bite Bill continued, "I hope they ask me, because I'll tell them the truth. You see, some people think a white supremacy group did it, but that's ridiculous. I know this town and I'm convinced a group of blacks bombed the tracks because they were not happy with the local authorities. The federal government knows, but they don't want to make it public because they're afraid it will upset their liberal political friends."

"An interesting analysis and thanks for the advice." Sharon took a bite of her sandwich and thought about Mr. FitzPatrick. She found him pretentious. She was accustomed to such people and normally didn't let them bother her, but in this case he was also dangerous. She decided she was going to have to be very careful in her relationship with him.

Mr. FitzPatrick's words caused Sharon to consider how she would handle questioning by the federal investigators: 'Whose truth would I tell? Mr. FitzPatrick's truth about a political cover-up, or Forsythe Systems' truth that they are perpetuating this investigation, or my truth that I'm an engineer supposedly looking for employment but that I'm really working for the FBI?' she wondered.

Mr. FitzPatrick thought Sharon looked sad. "Don't worry dear, you'll be fine. This is probably too much for a girl to handle, but it'll all blow over in a couple of weeks. Let me help."

Sharon winced. She had heard the same damn words from previous bosses. When Sharon was a young engineer, she ignored these advances, hoping the harassers would stop on their own. She soon learned that her silence was interpreted as acceptance. In this case, she had to decide whether playing the game with FitzPatrick would gain his trust, or whether it was best to make him respect her technically. She opted for the latter. "Mr. FitzPatrick, I appreciate your support, but ours is a professional and not a personal relationship. I can handle my job and I am not your 'Dear'."

FitzPatrick leaned back, fumbled with his sandwich, and said, "Oh, I didn't mean to imply there was a personal interest. I think you misunderstood."

Sharon stood up with her tray and said, "Look, I've been through this before. I know what you want and what you imply. I'm just not interested. Now, what about that tour of the plant?"

FitzPatrick looked up at her, "Ah...". With trembling hands he picked up his tray, along with the uneaten part of his

sandwich. He threw the food into the garbage, but took his half-full can of soda and followed her.

Sharon held the door for FitzPatrick. "So where do we start?" she asked.

"Over there," said FitzPatrick as he and Sharon walked outside side-by-side. "This is a 40,000 barrel-per-day refinery producing gasoline, diesel fuel and some basic chemicals. It's a medium-size plant, definitely smaller than the large plants located in the Middle East or even along the Gulf Coast. The crude oil feed has to be converted into a hydrogenated gasoline. To do this, we must first heat it and crack it over a catalyst. This is done in that large reactor, which is the heart of the complex. Operating at high pressure and temperature, it must recycle the catalyst, which consists of very costly palladium attached to a ceramic substrate. After being cracked and cooled the products are separated in these two tall columns."

"I saw these columns as I walked to the control room."

"Yep. You can't miss them. They are the tallest structures in the plant, and for that matter in the whole town. Opposite these columns are the heating furnaces and the sulfur removal units, while on the other side of the furnaces at the north exit is the plant flare."

FitzPatrick and Sharon walked across the road and up two levels. Standing next to the railing he pointed down: "If you look there, the pipe rack from the reactor runs east and you can see the tank farm. Behind the tank farm is the water treatment pond." Turning slightly FitzPatrick continued: "To the south you can see the main entrance and the plant offices. The control room is on the west side of the plant, between the reactor area and the warehouse. I hope this is sufficient description for you.

"Let's head back to the control room. I have some work I have to do," said FitzPatrick, leading Sharon down the stairs and toward the west end of the plant.

Sharon took a moment to look at the reactor as she passed it before asking, "Mr. FitzPatrick, how long have you been working here?"

"I've been working at this plant for three years, but I have also worked at some of the other nearby plants. Forsythe Systems has more than a dozen clients in the area. But this plant is thirty years old, and there has been talk of closing it down. Usually a plant like this will run for three years without having to shut down to perform major maintenance. But between accidents and lower foreign gasoline prices, the plant has averaged less than eighteen months of continuous operation."

"Are there other Forsythe employees on site?" asked Sharon.

"Not now. It depends on the amount of work we have. We always have at least one employee on site. We're coming to the control room. I'll show you your workspace. And Sharon, why don't you call me Bill. We don't bother with formalities around here."

FitzPatrick led the way into the control room building, crossed the hallway and walked down the corridor until he reached an open doorway that led to a room with three desks. The other end of the room was directly open to an endless series of control panels and wires that led to the main control room. The control room, as its name implied, was just that. Not because its purpose was to control the environment that the operators had to work in, but because it was the heart of the plant operation.

FitzPatrick stood at the doorway and said, "This is our workspace. It gives us direct access to the control room, but allows us some privacy too." Sharon walked into the room, ahead of FitzPatrick, who placed his left hand on Sharon's back and led her over to the far desk.

Sharon turned to Bill, "Look we'll get along fine, just as long as your hands and mouth do not wander where they shouldn't.

I've seen your treatment of the workers around here, and I'm not going to sit by and take your shit." Sharon turned away from Bill, walked behind the nearby desk and sat down. She turned on the computer, while Bill stood staring at her with his mouth open.

Sharon added, "I'll check out the plant control system on the computer."

FitzPatrick quietly walked to his desk, sat down, opened a side drawer, pulled out a small flask, unscrewed the top, and took a quick sip.

Sharon heard the drawer close and then smelled the slight hint of Scotch.

Sharon worked quickly, spotting the various computer programs that were controlling the plant systems, reporting data to the operators and communicating with the rest of the facilities. She was most interested in any program that tied into outside systems – such as telephone communications or Internet connections. She expected OC Chemicals and Forsythe Systems used sophisticated technology to communicate. She was determined to find the links between the two companies.

She had the passwords to the standard computer systems that allowed her to see what was happening in the plant and to make modifications to the control systems. However, she couldn't change the plant conditions. This was common when it became necessary to change a valve or retune a controller while the plant was operating. In such instances the operators would bypass such a control while the modifications were being made. Sometimes this required someone to work on the control panels, adjusting or changing a malfunctioning component.

For now, the plant was running smoothly. Sharon spent two hours monitoring the systems and learning the operations. She was able to access a process diagram and study the equipment and the location of various critical control items. As she worked,

Sharon's keen sense of smell told her that FitzPatrick had opened the flask at least three more times.

Sharon was restless and her computer investigation was not leading to anything especially useful. She decided she had to get into the control panels, but she needed an excuse.

She called up the temperature controller on the main catalytic reactor. This was a critical system, and as such it had multiple temperature sensors. It was common for one of these sensors to malfunction: they had to operate in very harsh conditions, being subjected to high temperatures and in a location that was under mechanical vibrations and in a corrosive atmosphere. She called up one of the temperature sensor recording devices, identified as item TE-2001B.

Sharon removed the 'B' sensor from the control operation, leaving the other two devices identified as 'A' and 'C' to control the reactor temperature. Sharon knew from the process diagrams that this would not interrupt the plant operation, because the system was designed to operate with two of the three sensors functioning. If one of the sensors stopped operating, the other two automatically became the active controllers. She called up the sensor control properties on the computer screen, and changed the type of sensor from 'R' to 'N', and put the sensor back in operation.

Two minutes later the operators sent a flashing warning message to FitzPatrick's and Sharon's computers, 'Temperature controller warning, item TE-2001B is outside of acceptable operating range.'

As soon as Sharon saw the message, she re-opened the controller properties screen and changed the sensor type back to 'R'. When FitzPatrick, who had been busy putting the flask back in his drawer yet again, noticed the warning message on his computer screen, he opened the controller properties screen and read the information. "Sharon, a thermal couple is giving an incorrect reading. I don't see any problem with its properties so

either the element is broken or there's a problem with the connections. Why don't..."

"While the operators go and change the element, I'll check out the connections," Sharon said as she got up and walked behind the control panels out of sight of FitzPatrick.

Sharon moved in and out of the narrow passages, opened various panel doors and looked at the wiring. There were almost thirty panels that comprised the complete plant control system hardware. This area was the most congested part of the whole facility. The control room had been well-designed. It was necessary to locate the control panels as close to the operating stations as possible. Unfortunately, this also meant that space around central operations was at a premium. The hardware was spaced as close together as possible, while still allowing space for an engineer to work.

At times, Sharon found herself surrounded by multicolored wires or wedged against metal boxes and door panels. There was barely enough space to breathe. Although Sharon was somewhat claustrophobic, she was not uncomfortable.

Had it not been for the powerful air- conditioning and fans, it would be unbearable. One of the benefits of working in the control room was the controlled temperature and air quality. The outside plant was either too hot or too cold, and fraught with potential hazards and unpleasant, if not lethal, odors.

The climate control in the building was a side benefit to the workers. Its main purpose was to protect the delicate equipment. In either case, Sharon was glad for the conditions inside.

Sharon had checked out panels one through twelve when she heard footsteps. It was difficult to tell exactly where they were coming from, since what little pathway there was twisted and turned around the panels. She closed the door to panel twelve and proceeded directly to the panel marked eighteen, and opened it. She was glad that the panels were well numbered and each was given a name referring to the section of the plant. She

had seen this numbering on the instrument drawings on the computer. She knew that panel eighteen contained the wiring for the temperature controller and sensor TE-2001B. As she opened the panel door, the footsteps stopped. She saw a pair of work boots, visible from under the door. She closed the door and found herself standing eye to eye with the black operator FitzPatrick had scolded earlier. He was wearing the standard operator shirt with his name, 'Clyde', embroidered on the pocket.

He frowned as he spoke, "I'm supposed to tell you that we changed the temperature element and when you're ready we can test it out."

Sharon smiled, "I'm finished here. You can put the sensor back in operation. OK, Clyde?"

Clyde grinned and said, "Sure Ma'am," before he turned and walked away.

Sharon returned to panel number twelve and continued her methodical search. All of the panels looked very similar. Inside were hundreds of tiny color-coded wires that were fed from the top and dispersed to three or four dozen terminal strips. Some panels had backup power supplies or control components with blinking lights or a small LED panel with numbers. When Sharon opened panel number sixteen, marked 'Reactor Feed Control System', there was something else hidden behind the top terminal strip.

It was a small metal box, which on closer inspection had a label which read 'Deckman Control Panel, PC C2260. ATX-standard automation.' Sharon knew this was an advanced control box, and that the other plant equipment predated the ATX standard. This type of box was typically used with Windows NT or Windows 2000 software, instead of the plant's custom software. She was not familiar with the purpose of the box, but tried to follow the connections. A pair of wires led from the box to a terminal strip, which was marked number R17a-141 and 142. On the side of the box a power cord was connected to an uninterruptible power supply, but there were no other wires into

or out of the box. There was a blinking LED panel that read, 'Status: Ready'.

"What are you doing?" came a voice from behind her.

Startled, Sharon turned to see FitzPatrick.

"I was just looking around at the panels."

"They said the sensor was working properly now," said FitzPatrick, annoyed.

"Yeah, I found a loose wire in panel eighteen and reconnected it."

FitzPatrick glanced over Sharon's shoulder and saw that the door to panel sixteen was open and shrugged his shoulder, "Sharon, I don't want you snoopin' back here."

Sharon slid to the side, now sandwiched between the panel door and FitzPatrick's body, and spoke softly, "Look Bill, I'm sorry. There's just so many panels around here I thought I'd see what was what." Sharon touched her finger against Bill's nose, "I'm not nosing around, I'm just getting used to this operation. Let's go back inside." Sharon was so close to Bill that she could feel his body shaking and she almost gagged from the alcohol on his breath. "Let me help you." She put her arm around his and walked him to his desk.

Sharon returned to her computer, looked up panel sixteen and searched the entire diagram for information about the Deckman control box. She thought, *no mention of that control box, so it does not appear to be part of the plant.* She clicked on her connection to the Internet, and looked up information about the Deckman Control Panel, PC C2260 box. She read the housing specifications and then the features. The control contained an Intel Celeron 833 MHz processor and used a Pentium III ATX motherboard. This type of product had only been on the market for a year or two. Sharon continued reading until she got to the Options, which read:

1. *Field bus interface, network adapter, serial interface card*

2. *CP-Link interface cards to connect Control Panels*

3. *ISDN adapter, or modem*

4. *Wireless communications adapter*

5. *Un-interruptible power supply UPS*

Sharon's eyes perked up. She read the options list over again, concentrating on items three and four, and looked over at Fitzpatrick, who was dozing in his chair. She closed the door to the room and went to look for an operator. She saw Clyde standing by a panel. "Clyde, I want to check out some of the control valves; I'm going out to the plant."

"Do you want me to take you there?"

"No thank you Clyde. I left Mr. FitzPatrick in his office, I don't think he wants to be disturbed for a while."

Clyde laughed. "No Ma'am, I wouldn't want to be the one to disturb him."

"I didn't think so," Sharon responded and chuckled.

On her way out to the reactor area, Sharon grabbed her hard hat from the rack and took spare overalls from the shelf, putting them on as she walked. *"I've got to get to FC-2244, the feed control valve,"* she thought. Making sure no one was around, Sharon read the shiny stainless steel tag on each control valve. But, FC-2244 was not at ground level. *"Damn, they probably put it upstairs!"* She climbed the stairs to the first level, where she found two more valves. *"Oh, these are only three-inch valves. It's probably right at the feed to the reactor."*

The bright sun and the searing heat of the reactor made Sharon perspire profusely. She thought briefly about FitzPatrick

and wondered what story she was going to tell him. She'd worry about that later.

She looked around to see if anyone was coming, before climbing the narrow metal stairs. The hot handrails made it difficult to hang on as she climbed the three levels to the top of the reactor. When she reached the top, she enjoyed the breeze for a moment before spotting three large valves, each hanging away from the platform she was standing on and next to a maintenance platform that could be accessed only by a special crane. Sharon instantly recognized the 12-inch feed valve she was looking for. "Damn," she exclaimed, kicking the railing.

Sharon hung over the railing as far as she could to see if she could spot the special receiver that could only be controlled by the Deckman. She then looked at the connecting pipe from the feed line to the reactor. *"It just might work...I just won't look down,"* Sharon took a deep breath, climbed over the railing, straddled the 12-inch pipe, and began inching her way to the valve. She only needed to slide about three feet to get a better look. But as she looked down she saw someone coming up the stairs She scrambled back to the platform and waited to see who was coming.

A man wearing yellow overalls and a red hard hat approached. "May I know what you are doing up here?" he asked.

Sharon looked puzzled. This was not the typical operator; his speech and style were very cosmopolitan. "I'm checking out the control valves."

"I'm Warren Fieldman, FBI," he said, flashing his identification. "We're here to investigate terrorists' threats to this plant. I saw you from the ground and followed you up here. Are you an operator?"

"No, I work for Forsythe Systems. I'm an engineer."

"Where is your security badge?"

"I have a temporary badge, I'm waiting for them to get me one with my picture. This is my first day." Sharon slipped her hand under her overalls, pulled her badge over her head and handed it to Warren.

He looked at the badge and said, "This doesn't look good, finding you out here with a badge that doesn't have your picture. I'm taking you down for further questioning."

Sharon thought of telling Warren about her suspicions about the valve and the control system, but was afraid he would blame her. Warren held her right arm and led her to the stairs, letting her descend first. He took her to a small room at the rear of the control room that generally served as an eating and smoking area for the operators. Now, it had been taken over by several FBI agents. Warren told Sharon, "Sit down and take off your overalls and hard hat. I'm going to check out your story. Do you have some identification, maybe a driver's license?"

Sharon handed Warren a copy of her employment form, which she had placed in her pocket earlier in the day. "I don't have my driver's license on me; this will have to do."

Warren looked over the form, which contained her Social Security number, driver's license number and name. Sharon bit her lip as she watched Warren read the form. She wanted desperately to prevent Warren from looking at her pocketbook. She had her FBI badge in there and if he found it, her cover would be blown. The fact that her pocketbook was locked in her desk did little to ease her apprehension; the desk was only about 20 feet down the hall.

Warren tried to use his cellular phone, but immediately put it back into the case and turned to another agent. "This damn phone! It's not getting through."

The other agent looked up at Warren: "This building is designed to minimize outside electronic interference. It would take a special receiver to get reception in here. You have to go outside."

"OK. Watch her while I go out and check her identification."

Shortly after Warren left, Clyde entered the room and walked over to the soda machine. He bought a soda and walked over to Sharon. "Did you find the equipment you were looking for, Ma'am?"

Sharon looked at the FBI agent, who ignored the two of them. "Yes, Clyde. But can you do me a favor? Can you tell Mr. FitzPatrick that I'm here and am being questioned by the FBI? I know you don't want to disturb him, but he'll want to know where I am."

"OK, Ma'am. I guess he had enough nap time. Anyway it's almost time to quit. You have a good evening now."

"Thanks, Clyde. You too."

Warren returned as Clyde was leaving and sat next to Sharon. "Your identification checks out. But what were you doing in the plant?"

"I told you, I was checking out some control equipment. There was an item that was giving a bad reading," said Sharon just as FitzPatrick walked into the room.

Warren wasn't satisfied. "I still find it strange that you just started today and I find you out in the plant alone."

"She's not alone, I'm her supervisor!" said FitzPatrick as he approached Warren.

Warren stood up and asked, "And who are you?"

"I'm William FitzPatrick. The Forsythe Systems supervisor, and she works for me."

Turning to Sharon, FitzPatrick continued, "I've been looking for you. Have you finished your work in the plant? You know we have to get that system operating before tonight or the plant will have to shut down. It will cost lots of money if we don't!" FitzPatrick looked back at Warren, "Can she go now? I need her to help finish our work."

Noticing FitzPatrick's unsteadiness Warren thought, *'the last thing I want is some half-drunk plant worker falling down on my time.'* He shrugged his shoulder and said, "OK, you can both go."

As they left the room Sharon said to FitzPatrick, "Thanks for getting me out of the hot seat."

Bill replied, "I did that for the company. But then again I enjoyed it. I don't like those feds snooping around here. I'm just happy to throw a wrench into their investigation."

Back in the office, Sharon took her pocketbook out of her desk and said, "It's five o'clock."

Sharon and Bill walked to the contractor's gate and went to their respective vehicles. Sharon let Grady out of the back and walked him around the lot. She kept an eye on FitzPatrick as he drove out of the lot. Once FitzPatrick was gone, Sharon walked Grady back to her truck. "You stay here a little longer Grady; I have some more investigating to do."

She returned to the plant. She thought of going back to check the valve, but she didn't want to run into the FBI again. Instead she went to FitzPatrick's computer and tried to logon under his name, but did not have his password. She tried 'Bill', 'William', and other passwords but they all failed.

She took a lock pick out of her pocketbook and opened FitzPatrick's desk. Inside she found only business cards and phone notes; no clue to his password. She found his flask, opened it and took a small sip, "Not bad. It's probably Johnny Walker Black," she said softly. She put the flask back and locked the desk and stared at the screen. Again she tried to logon and typed 'User Name: wfitzpatrick' and 'Password: scotch'. Sharon smiled, as the computer accepted the password. She read a number of directories and files, but the contents were mainly about work orders and requests from OC Chemicals Company.

She opened Bill's e-mail program and browsed his outgoing messages. There were messages describing new technology and

recent additions to the plant control system and correspondence with other chemical companies. From the information, Sharon was able to put together a theory of how they were running their operation. The correspondence helped build a case against Forsythe Systems, but it did not discuss any current plans.

Sharon opened his Internet connection, and began to read the recent URL's that FitzPatrick had looked at. She recognized several of the typical URL's, some well-known search engines and several technical sites. Sharon was not familiar with a site named controlit.com, and typed the URL and waited for the page to open.

When the screen appeared, it requested a login name and password. Sharon tried the same username and password she had used to logon to the computer. Bingo! From the menu she saw three categories. She read the page for the first category entitled, 'Latest Control Techniques'. It contained several articles on using remote control devices. One of the articles was about the perils of wireless communications. Sharon read the following:

> 'The Wired Equivalent Privacy (WEP) protocol (also known as IEEE 802.11) has major security flaws' according to the Internet Security, Applications, Authentication and Cryptography (ISSAC) research group at the University of California in Berkeley.
>
> A cracker just needs to have some easily obtained equipment to be able to intercept wireless transmissions, change the data contained in those transmissions and access the contents of a wireless network.
>
> It is recommended that anyone using an 802.11 wireless network not rely

*on WEP for security, but instead em-
ploy other security measures to protect their wireless network.*

*Cracking WEP is accomplished using
some sort of wireless Ethernet interface — such as a PC card or another similar device, along with the
ability to modify a few driver set-
tings. Doing so will allow you to access supposedly encrypted data that
was sent wirelessly.'*

Sharon moved to the second category, entitled 'Our Services and Products'. This section listed several electronic devices and a description of their uses. It allowed the user to send e-mail to the webmaster. The third category was entitled 'Priority Users'. When Sharon clicked this page she was again asked for a login name and password. For the third time she typed *wfitzpatrick* and *scotch*. But this time the screen turned red and flashed, 'Warning – You are not authorized for this site. If you try to proceed you will be reported.' Sharon did not want to alarm the webmaster, yet she knew that such security measures likely meant there was sensitive data that might be incriminating.

Sharon looked at the time and thought, *'I can try this site from the safety of my room'*, and tidied up the desk and left the building.

She dialed Justice's number from her cellular, "Hi, Justice. I have some information about Forsythe Systems, but I would feel safer if you met me at the contractor's parking lot. I'm hungry and I thought we would pick up something at a drive-through and take it back to my place."

Justice replied, "I can be there in fifteen minutes."

"Good. I'll see you soon," and she placed the phone into her pocketbook and walked to the parking lot.

Chapter Twelve

That Knot in Her Stomach

It was a bright afternoon when Julie and George drove back to the trailer park from the sheriff's office. The chemical odors were less noticeable and, unlike the yellow, dry, and singed trees near the train wreck, the surrounding woods were green. There were a few large trailers in the park, some bearing the names of news stations.

The bright sun and clean air didn't make Julie feel at ease. As she got out of the car and helped George into the trailer she felt tightness in her stomach. Peter was in jail and she was powerless against Hilbaum and the sheriff. When she entered the trailer she quickly disarmed the alarm and looked at the camera that monitored the front door. George went to the nearest bed and sat down, wiping his perspiring forehead with his sleeve. Julie turned on the air conditioner and one of the computers, and then turned her attention to George.

"What can I get you George? Do you need a doctor?"

"No, I'm OK, I just need to get out of this business, that's all. I could be writing about the latest movies, or better yet, obituaries, but no, I have to be playing secret agent games all of the sudden. What the hell was I thinking!"

"Calm down George."

"Calm down? This is the second time in as many weeks that someone beats me up in this fucking town! I mean, agent Hilbaum and the sheriff are as crooked as they come! I know who sent the cowboy to attack us! Hilbaum, your FBI friend. He signaled them. I saw him nod at them when they came in the door. Didn't you notice?"

"Yes, I'm sorry. I had no idea what they were going to do. I had other things on my mind."

"You led me into the lion's den; now they're going to be after me, and you can't do anything to stop them Ms. Del Rio."

"Well, I know at least one person who can."

"Who?"

"Assistant Director Gutierrez. She can investigate Hilbaum. In fact, I better call her right now." Finding her cell phone in her handbag, she started to dial, and then said, "Shit the battery is dead!"

"Don't you charge it every night?"

"No, I forgot." When she plugged the phone into the power cord the cellular displayed two voice messages from Gutierrez.

"Oh no! She called and I didn't answer."

She pressed the dial button. "Hello, Mrs. Gutierrez please."

"Hello, Assistant Director Gutierrez."

"Ms. Del Rio, why didn't you answer my calls? I was ready to send agent Hilbaum to see if you were alright."

"I'm sorry Ma'am, but the cell phone wasn't working."

"Please be sure that the battery in your communications device is operational at all times. We must maintain communications in the field."

"Yes Ma'am."

"Agent Hilbaum called to brief me on the situation."

"And what was *his* story?"

"He tells me you are working with two civilians, a reporter George Reed and Peter Wells. He is holding Wells on a terrorism charge. He believes he is behind the recent accident."

Julie's stomach tightened and she blurted. "What? What is he talking about? We brought the evidence to him to show that it's Forsythe and his group who are behind the accident."

"Yes, but the evidence you brought was insufficient, and that is what made him suspicious. Why is this man Peter so interested in finding culprits? Why is he involved?"

"You know who he is, Mrs. Gutierrez. He helped us out in Alaska. He works for Citizens Against Pollution, an organization that investigates all kinds of environmental crimes, ecocide terror cases, and prosecutes polluters."

"A vigilante group. That's our job!" snapped Gutierrez.

"With all due respect Ma'am, citizens have a right to protect the environment privately. They can't just depend on government agencies."

"Well, this Peter has been sending suspicious messages from his computer to environmental and extremist groups. We have a National Security Agent report on him. FBI intelligence intercepted the messages and traced them back to his trailer. Frank believes he may be part of an eco-terrorist group that has been burning buildings and destroying property back east."

"I was with him when he sent those messages. He monitors many extremist groups this way and sometimes he pretends to be one of them, but he had nothing to do with the attacks. He is not an eco-terrorist!"

"Well, right now, that's not how it looks. I'm afraid your friend Peter is going to be staying in jail for a while."

"Look, Mrs. Gutierrez, if anyone is crooked here it is Frank Hilbaum and his friend the sheriff. They are hiding something."

"Do you have any evidence, or are you just making blind accusations? The local FBI has hard evidence against your friend Peter. And Frank Hilbaum is a veteran of the FBI with a good record. As far as the suspect, Peter Wells, is concerned, you

need to keep your distance – when and if he gets out of jail! Is that understood, Ms. Del Rio?"

"Yes Ma'am."

"While Mr. Ryan is recovering, you will report to Frank Hilbaum. He is taking over the investigation then."

"But Frank Hilbaum made lewd moves toward me; I had to knee him to get him off. He's a bastard, I'm sorry to say."

"Are you making a formal sexual harassment accusation?"

Gutierrez's question made Julie think about making a formal accusation. Julie thought for a minute and then replied, "Absolutely, Mrs. Gutierrez, and you know the procedure, as you clearly pointed out at the seminar. You need to investigate any sexual harassment accusation."

"Very clever, Ms. Del Rio, but this better not be an excuse to have him investigated."

"I assure you that he really did do what I said. He probably has the black and blue marks down there."

"You're putting your career on the line here. You'd better be sure."

"I'm sure. He's crooked. I just need more time. I believe Sharon will come forth with good information."

"Well, for now, Ms. Del Rio, work with him as if we never had this conversation. I'll conduct the investigation and get back to you."

"Thank you, Ma'am."

As Julie pressed the disconnect button on her cell phone, George looked at her and shook his head.

"What?" she asked.

"Are you crazy, opening up an investigation against this bastard? He'll fry you and your partner."

"I'm not afraid of him. I need a reason to have him investigated and this is a good excuse. Besides, it's true, he did attack me back there."

"Well, Julie, it's your funeral. I'm taking off and getting as far away from you as possible."

"Can you get a copy of those articles George? I'm going to need the evidence for Gutierrez."

"I don't know why I should help you, but yeah, I have a list of the articles. It shouldn't be more than a day to copy them from the library. At least I'll be safe there. I think."

"Thanks George. I really appreciate this. You can leave when you feel like it. I'm driving back into town. I have to do a little shopping and see about bailing out Peter."

Julie drove toward the sheriff's office. It was late in the afternoon and there seemed to be more people walking around town. Traffic was heavier than usual. News trucks and trailers were parked around the streets. Julie didn't pay attention to what was happening because her mind was on Peter and how to get him out of jail.

She parked her car in front of the sheriff's office, in the very spot where a few weeks ago a man dressed as a deputy humiliated her and called her a "nigger". *'Where is that guy now and who got him out of jail?'*, she wondered as she walked into the sheriff's office.

"Sheriff, good afternoon. I'm here to see Peter Wells and arrange for his bail."

"He'll be arraigned tomorrow and you may be able to bail him out then, but tonight he'll stay here. You may see him," responded the sheriff, without even looking up from his computer screen. Julie could see he was writing e-mails, but the text was too small for her to read.

The sheriff rose from his chair and signaled for Julie to follow. He unlocked the door to the jailhouse and let Julie inside

the cell. As he walked back into his office, he pointed at the camera above. "When you're ready, just signal, I'll come and get you out."

As soon as the sheriff left, Julie hugged Peter and he returned a warm hug, but as usual, nothing more. "Thank you for coming to see me."

"Have you called your lawyer?"

"Yes. CAP is sending the group's lawyer. He'll be here in the morning, along with a representative to help out. As you may know, they're accusing me and CAP of terrorism."

"That's just a smoke screen, you know that. They know we're getting close and they're desperately trying to divert everyone's attention. I'm glad your lawyer is coming, Peter, because I was given orders to stay away from you. In fact, I may have to move back to the hotel. But I'll keep an eye on the trailer tonight."

"I appreciate that... You don't believe these accusations do you?"

"No, and I don't think Gutierrez does either. I think she has to play along with the sheriff until I get some hard evidence."

"And how are you going to get that?"

"At this point we're waiting for Sharon to come through, and I'm following some leads of my own."

"I wish Sean was here."

"Gutierrez ordered him to rest when he returned from Buenos Aires. He was in pretty bad shape. But he's resilient; he'll bounce back. Meanwhile, I can take care of myself. I've been in the environmental business for a long time."

"Yes, but this is a different type of business. This is dangerous, Julie."

"Well, according to Gutierrez, I have to report to Frank from now on."

"That's ridiculous! Didn't you tell her what happened?"

"He claims he arrested you for suspicion of terrorism and the other guy says *you* attacked *him*. She has no evidence to the contrary except for what I told her I saw, but that wasn't enough."

"What a mess! I can't wait until my lawyer comes."

"Look Peter, I'm going to go food shopping so I can eat in the trailer tonight and keep checking those news groups. I also have to think this through and figure out where to go from here. Take it easy and I'll be in to check on you tomorrow. OK?"

"Take care of yourself Julie."

Julie kissed Peter's cheek, but he didn't return the affectionate gesture. "Good-bye Julie," he said as she left.

Julie walked out of the jail cell toward the door. The sheriff came in, locked Peter's cell, and let Julie out without a word.

That evening, as Julie drove into the dark trailer park, the quiet made her uneasy. She missed the symphony of beautiful sounds the Caribbean night offered: coqui frogs, crickets, night birds, the sound of a radio playing Latin music and the laughter of neighbors. Vieques was alive with activity at night, with neighbors visiting, laughing and talking outside. Visitors sometimes were surprised by all the noise. This trailer park near Wilburn had an eerie silence.

In the aftermath of the accident, birds had left the area or suffocated and died. There were no sounds of crickets and frogs, owls or bats. Juliana wondered if anyone had noticed their absence. "Rachel Carson's Silent Spring, it's happening!" she said out loud. She left the car door open and the headlights on as she walked toward the trailer. She opened the door, turned on the outside light and walked back to the car to turn off the headlights. She saw a few more trailers tonight.

She wearily stepped into the trailer with her bag of groceries and checked out all of Peter's security and computer systems.

Page 214

She felt a heavy burden as she looked around at the empty screens and the silence tightened her stomach even more. It was a fear that she had never experienced before, even during that dark night in Alaska when she realized Sean had been captured.

As she put the food into the refrigerator and sat down, her mind went blank. She just couldn't think of what to do next; she was panicking. "Get a grip on yourself," she said.

She took a deep breath and walked over to the computer to write her report to headquarters. She struggled for a while, but then decided that it was best to include Peter and George in the report. Rather than her usual crisp and curt report, Julie rambled on. She wasn't sure how to finish it, and finally decided that the report, just like the case, had no clear direction. She grudgingly e-mailed it to headquarters.

Julie started cooking dinner. She didn't like the local cuisine. Back in New York she was satisfied with a salad or a quick Pita sandwich for dinner. She rarely had time to cook and she was always on a diet to maintain her slim figure. But since early today, she yearned for a home-style meal. She felt guilty telling Peter that she had to "go food shopping" and by doing so cut short her visit. But, Peter wasn't making her feel safe or loved lately, and in fact, he never did.

She had bought all of the ingredients for a Puerto Rican feast. She turned on the television and began frying the onions, and adding the achiote and other ingredients for the Spanish rice. She cooked the canned beans, flavoring them with her favorite spices. She took out a plantain from the bag, something she thought she might never find locally, and fried it along with a fish fillet. The smells and the textures of the food calmed her nerves. She was momentarily transported back to her beloved Vieques, where she recalled lazy days cooking with her grandmother in her island home.

Julie enjoyed her meal while watching the news on television. The local news was now carrying more stories about the aftermath of the train wreck. She realized that all of those

trailers and media vans in town were there to cover the story. As she was about to get up she saw Hugo Arias, the plant manager and the sheriff on television.

"So you are saying that this could be a terrorist act?" asked the reporter.

The sheriff made a statement. "We have reason to believe that this was the work of environmental extremists or eco-terrorists who have been burning property in New York and California. Environmentalists have wanted to close our plant for a long time and we believe this was an attempt to destroy the plant, except something unexpected happened. The train passed through town, and not by the plant that day."

"Have there been any arrests?" asked the reporter.

Frank Hilbaum, who had been standing in the background, stepped forward. "The FBI has arrested a suspect who we believe has been involved in the conspiracy. We traced messages to his computer that implicated him and his group and there is other evidence that we can't discuss right now."

"Oh God! Frank is involved! That bastard!" Julie said out loud.

Her stomach tightened. She felt she was walking a tightrope without a net and she had the urge to hold on to something, or someone. She entertained the possibility of calling Mrs. Gutierrez. But why? She didn't have any evidence to offer her.

The computer, which had been idle for a while, was flashing the small e-mail icon. It was a message from Sharon over the public instant message chat that was sent from the Web site that Peter originated.

"Sometimes the best place to hide something is out in the open," Peter had said when he set up the Web site and explained the code they might use so that the conversations couldn't be interpreted by the terrorists or the National Security Agency.

Julie opened the message from Sharon:

'Mom - Got the new job today, we are ready to kick ass tomorrow. How are things back home?'

Julie read the message with some satisfaction. She thought that finally something worked out as she had planned. Julie clicked the new message button and typed, *'Mom is fine, but Dad got into a fight and got arrested. Wish I could get in touch with Dad's friend.'* Julie sent the message and continued reading the other messages on the screen.

By the time Julie got to the end of the screen, she had gotten another e-mail. Julie looked back to the first screen, and read the top message: *"Sorry to hear about Dad, I'll let Dad's friend know."* Julie exited the Web site. She sat for a minute gathering her thoughts, and looked up the Wilburn Chamber of Commerce Web site. She entered the zip code and category; all the local chemical plants came up on her screen. She looked at the addresses and located them on the map to see if something made sense. But she couldn't concentrate because her mind was now elsewhere. Even with the sounds of the television in the background, the large empty trailer seemed too quiet and eerie.

Suddenly she jumped, and ran to the door and locked it. Her heart began pounding. The loneliness and silence were too much. Her mind kept revisiting memories of her and Sean in Argentina, and in Alaska. She felt empty and the knot tightened in her stomach. She listened for sounds outside and kept her gun in her hand, ready to fire.

She finally walked over to the bed, undressed and put her head down on the pillow, but she couldn't sleep. Her mind kept returning to Sean, his face, and how safe she felt with him around. But another part of her felt shame. *"I don't need him to feel safe; I can take care of myself,"* she thought as she lay in bed. After tossing and turning for ten minutes she got up and paced around the phone. She wanted so badly to hear his voice again, but her pride wouldn't let her call. Finally, as if she had no control, her hand went to the phone and she dialed Sean's

cellular, wondering if he might be angry that she woke him so late at night.

"It's me," she said.

"Julie, are you OK?"

"Well, yea, but Peter and George got beat up and...."

"Why, what happened?"

"George found some articles that point to Forsythe, Hugo and other local managers conspiring to get more contracts by creating chemical accidents. It's the same scheme we found in Argentina, but the evidence is circumstantial."

"So, send the articles down."

"We don't have them. We went to tell Frank Hilbaum about this and he practically threw us out of the office and . . ."

"I told you I didn't trust him."

"When Peter and George came out, two men attacked them. One took the articles."

"Damn..."

"George says he can compile them again."

"Where is Peter now?"

"Peter got arrested and is spending the night in jail. I'm in the trailer... alone. And there's more. I thought Gutierrez called you."

"No, no one contacted me."

"Gutierrez said Frank Hilbaum called today to complain about me working with Peter and George and is accusing Peter of being an eco-terrorist and being connected to the accident!"

"How did he come up with that malarkey?"

"And not only that, but Hugo, the sheriff and Frank were on the local TV today saying that they had evidence to show that the train wreck was a failed attempt by the eco-terrorists to destroy the chemical plant. Somehow the train ended up in town instead of at their site. He announced they had a suspect that had sent incriminating Internet messages, but they didn't mention Peter's name."

"You know Lassie, that's the key."

"What?"

"Remember we started going down this path before. Who diverted the train into town and why?"

"I thought the local FBI was following that trail."

"Exactly. I'll take the first plane out and be there in the morning. In the meantime, keep the doors locked and your gun close by."

"I don't need you. I can take care of myself."

"You need a partner now more than ever. These guys are very dangerous and we can't trust the local FBI."

"I didn't want to disturb you... are you feeling OK?"

"Yeah, I'm feeling fine."

"Who is that?" Julie heard a woman talking.

A muffled response from Sean "It's work dear, go back to sleep."

"Oh, I'm so sorry, I didn't know you had your friend over..." Julie said apologetically. She was embarrassed now to hear the woman's voice. She wanted to tell Sean how she felt, her fears and how she missed him, but she didn't now. She felt she had just intruded into his private life, of which she was not a part.

"Don't worry, she understands," answered Sean.

"OK, but really, I can take care of this."

"Never mind, I'll be there tomorrow."

"OK," said Julie. She hung up the phone. Her stomach had settled. Suddenly she felt calmer. She washed her dish, and went to bed. This time she fell asleep right away.

Chapter Thirteen

Feeling Whole Again

The next morning, banging at the door woke Julie. She ran to the window and saw Sean's reddish hair and now clear and relaxed face. She opened the door, and then realized she was wearing her nightgown, so she rushed to put on a robe. When she remembered that she didn't bring one, she grabbed her jacket.

Julie couldn't help giving Sean a welcome hug. Sean lightly returned the gesture, but he was holding back. Julie sensed his coolness and it upset her.

"Sean, how are you? You look . . . well . . . better. Are you OK?"

"I'm fine Lassie. How are you? What, are you cold? Why are you wearing a jacket? It seems warm in here."

"I didn't bring a robe."

"Why don't you go change? We should go into town."

Julie went inside to change into her clothes, but kept speaking.

"Did Gutierrez say it was OK for you to come here? Because, honestly, I can take care of myself, you don't have to come here to rescue me."

"I just had a terrible plane ride, with lots of turbulence. They didn't serve a meal and then I had to drive into this stinking town. A thank-you and a cup of coffee will help, Lassie."

Julie walked over to the tiny kitchen. "I can make a cup of instant."

"I guess that will have to do. Do you have some toast? My stomach is a shambles."

"Here's an old bagel and some cream cheese. You could have stopped to eat. I mean the situation wasn't that critical."

"I'll be the judge of that," said Sean, dunking his bagel in the black coffee as he wrinkled his nose. Julie's coffee was always too strong.

"You know, you continue to patronize me as if I just can't handle myself. I think it's time you started treating me like an agent!"

"Well, maybe you should act like one," said Sean, throwing the stale bagel into the sink.

"What the hell do you mean?"

"I mean that I had told you about Frank and that I couldn't trust him, and without checking with me, YOUR PARTNER, first, you went straight to the lion's den. Why? Did you forget what I told you?"

"I... well.. yes. And, I didn't want to disturb you at home."

"Didn't I send the piece of metal to the lab myself? Didn't I tell you I didn't trust him?"

"Yes, you did, but you never explained. I mean, they were rude to me, but I didn't think they were crooked."

"Well, they are!"

"Why are you yelling?"

"And what the hell were that Peter and George doing with you? Are they FBI? Why do you involve civilians?"

"Why don't you shut up and listen? They were going to present the evidence to the FBI. This wasn't a hostile situation!"

"Ahhh!" said Sean now throwing the rest of the coffee into the sink. "I think I'll go into town and get a proper breakfast!"

"You're in a foul mood! I already apologized for interrupting you last night. You don't have to come taking it out on me."

Sean opened the door and started out. Julie followed and yelled out the door. "Why the hell did you come back here? Go back to New York! I'm handling this myself."

Sean got into the car and took off.

Julie's eyes filled with tears, her hands shaking. "Bastard, you male chauvinist pig, you think you know it all," she said out loud. Her stomach knotted again.

When Sean drove into town he noticed it was buzzing with activity. The environmentalist groups had descended into Wilburn like a flock of Canada geese. They were everywhere. A group of local Greenpeace activists had organized a demonstration in front of the government building. "Stop the toxic trains! Stop producing toxic chemicals!" While this was probably not the right place to demonstrate, because, after all, what could local government do, it was the right place to get media attention. A television truck was parked right across the street and they were eating this up. A great show for the nationwide audience.

A group from the Circle of Knights, dressed in white sheets, but no hoods, approached the activists and shouted obscenities. "Go the fuck back where you came from. Jobs, not greens," they said.

The deputies were around ready to clobber any environmentalist who got out of control. They didn't bother to post any men near the white-robed group. The news truck parked across the street filming the spectacle unknowingly saved the necks of the activists, who would have been battered if they weren't there.

On Main Street, other groups were handing out leaflets about the toxic aftermath of the train wreck. People were congregating around a speaker who gave out information about the chemicals and told people where they could get free testing.

Sean drove past Main Street. There were crews still cleaning up broken glass and debris. Even after three weeks, the place was not totally cleaned out.

A local news crew was filming and interviewing residents near the wreckage site: "I'm a farmer, and our crops are ruined. This hit us before harvest and singed the corn to the ground. The fields that survived stink from that sulfur stuff! No one wants to buy crops from this town, after they heard what happened."

"So what are you going to do?" asked the reporter.

"Things are hard enough without this disaster. I'll have to sell and move on. The land will be contaminated for years, so I'll probably lose the farm. We need relief here – hear that, politicians! This is a disaster area."

Other environmentalists were walking near the plant, investigating the wreckage, taking pictures and making notes. A number of college students were studying the site. The HazMat crews were still working cleaning up soil. It was painstaking work, scraping up a thick layer of contaminated soil and dumping it into trucks.

A newswoman approached one of the people doing the cleanup and, pointing a microphone, asked: "Where are you taking this soil?"

"Well, right now it's being land-filled at the end of town, in an emergency landfill with a plastic liner. Later, it might have to be incinerated, but that will take time."

"Who's going to pay for this?"

"The town is footing the bill. The feds haven't come up with any money yet."

When the news reporter was done talking to the HazMat worker, she was approached by an elderly lady in a blue sweater

and knit pants. She had white hair and very wrinkled skin. "May I speak to you, dear?" she asked.

"Sure, but we're pulling out in five minutes."

"Don't leave yet. Come to the hospital and talk to 'Mushroom Man' as we call him. We have a story for you."

"What is it? We can't go see him now."

"His name is Rakky Basidia, our group's lead mycologist. He was poisoned by a toxic mushroom."

"Well, aren't mushrooms poisonous? We don't have time for that."

"I mean a perfectly edible mushroom that was contaminated by the chemicals. He is very sick."

"Start again. What's the story? Joe, turn on the camera." Joe started the live camera. "OK, now slowly and carefully, can you tell the audience the story?"

The old woman faced the reporter and made sure not to look at the camera. She knew how to handle herself and spoke clearly and slowly.

Sean was eating eggs and sausage at the local pub, downing a glass of milk and frowning. He was still angry with Julie, but what made him more upset was that he really didn't know why he was angry. Whenever Sean was angry, he ate and ate. Especially now that he no longer could calm his nerves with a drink.

He quickly finished his eggs, went to the bartender, and paid. He was ready to leave when Julie walked in the door.

"Hi... you forgot your travel bag at my place."

"Oh... thanks. Well, I was going to go to investigate the plant and nearby manufacturers."

"Well, I.."

"Hey, that's old Mrs. Southerland – my tenth-grade teacher!" yelled a man at the bar pointing at the television.

Their eyes turned toward the TV screen. An eloquent old woman was speaking.

"Our mushroom-picking group usually goes out on trips in the nearby woods, about ten miles from here. We went out yesterday and we thought it was safe. I mean, the wreckage was pretty far away. We didn't think anything of it. Rocky, our tour guide, is an expert mycologist. He knows all the species. He was showing us a patch of *boletus edulis* (the 'king bolete'). These are known as Porcini mushrooms, and they are a delicacy. He took a few home. We didn't take any because, well, we just go for the nature, and I can't take any chances with my digestion.

"The next day he called from the hospital. He was sick as a dog after he ate the mushroom. Turns out the lab showed the mushroom was contaminated with man-made chemicals. It had absorbed them and concentrated them in its flesh."

"So you're saying that the chemicals came from the wreck?" asked the reporter.

"Well, we don't know. We think that the woods are contaminated and the mushrooms and other foods dangerous," responded the woman.

"Thank you Ms. . . ."

"Abigail Sutherland."

"Where is your 'mushroom man' hospitalized?"

"He's at the local hospital in town. I'll meet you there."

"Ok, we'll be there a little later. Goodbye," said the reporter.

The old woman walked away in the background as the reporter turned to the camera and continued speaking. "Apparently, the spilled chemicals from the derailed train have affected much more than just the town. The nearby woods are

now contaminated with deadly chemicals. We'll interview 'mushroom man' later in this report. Stay tuned."

Julie and Sean turned their eyes away from the television and faced each other. They were quiet for a while and then Julie spoke.

"I think I should talk to that 'mushroom man'. What do you think?"

"You're asking me what to do, Lassie? Thought ye didn't need me."

"I'm sorry about that. I want to apologize."

"Well, you know, I haven't been myself since Buenos Aires. I blew my stack. I should be the one apologizing. Are we partners again?" asked Sean extending his hand.

"You bet," she said now pulling his hand and hugging Sean, her eyes filling with tears.

This time Sean held on for a while and Julie felt whole again. When she let go she had a smile on her face and Sean patted her back. "OK now?"

"Yes, I'm sorry for the outburst. I'm a bit emotional lately."

"Well, this is an emotional case...Look, I'm going to check the manufacturers. You check 'mushroom guy' at the hospital and see what you can find out."

Julie and Sean walked out of the pub with a renewed bond. They got into their separate rentals and drove off in opposite directions.

Before entering the hospital, Julie called and asked for Rakky's room. "Hi, Mr. Basidia, my name is agent Juliana Del Rio. I am an EPA consultant to the FBI. I saw the report on television about your mushroom poisoning incident and I was

wondering if I could come up to your room and ask you some questions?"

"Well, I'm still pretty shaky, but they pumped my stomach and the doctor says I'll be OK. I suppose it will be alright."

"I'm right outside. I'll be up in about five minutes, okay?"

"That will be fine."

Julie took the elevator to the second floor and walked past the open patient rooms. She was always apprehensive in hospitals, and now more so after her stay in Alaska. When she walked into room 211 she was surprised to see an athletic young man, with piercing blue eyes and an early case of male-pattern baldness sitting up in bed.

"Hello. Mr. Basidia?"

"Agent *Scully*. Nice to see you." He said smiling with his sure midwestern accent. "Is there something wrong? You seem to be staring at me."

"It's Julie Del Rio, thank you! You're not what I expected," excuse me for staring.

"I don't know what you mean."

"I thought you might be older. What I mean is, seeing Abigail, I thought I was dealing with a senior citizen's group."

"Well, this is an activity enjoyed by people of all ages. It's very common in Europe. We have a lot of Russian immigrants who join us. Mushroom-picking is something they do regularly at home. Anyway, how old do you think I am?"

"About thirty?"

"Heck, I'm nearly 50."

"Really? You don't look it."

"Well, I'm a vegetarian and I don't smoke, don't drink, and don't do drugs. I walk every day. The human body is supposed to look like this at this age, if you don't abuse it."

There was something about the loud tone and direct way Rakky spoke to her, always looking straight into her eyes that was unusual. Julie smiled at him and without realizing it, her eyes were drawn to the unusually clear blue-green eyes; she was staring at him again. Embarrassed, she quickly focused her eyes on the sample bag containing mushrooms, on Rakky's night table.

"Glad to meet you Rakky. So tell me, I understand you are a mycologist. Did you eat the wrong kind of mushroom?"

"No, I know my mushrooms. This one was a *boletus edulis,* a delicacy. We pick them all the time, right after the rains. It rained a few days ago, so naturally our group took a walk in the woods and we picked mushrooms. I found a wonderful new patch of these mushrooms, one I never had been to before. It's a great find because you come back again and again to the area and harvest them."

"So, how far was this patch from the train derailment?"

"About 8 to 10 miles. It was deep into the woods. I didn't think the chemicals could travel that far...or could they?"

"I don't think that's likely. Is there a lab report on the mushroom?"

"Here it is," Rakky handed Julie a lab report that was on his night table. "I got it today. But, my field is mycology, what do you make of this?"

"Hmm, nitrates, halogenated hydrocarbons, traces of arsenic, mercury in toxic concentrations. None of these chemicals could have come from the train wreck."

"So where did they come from?"

"They come from contamination in the soil. I know that in Asia, mushrooms are used extensively to clean up contaminated fields. The mushrooms have the capacity to absorb heavy metals and toxic chemicals from the soil and concentrate them in their tissues." When Julie stopped talking she found herself staring at his clear eyes again.

"Yes, mushrooms are the forest's clean-up crew," agreed Rakky still looking at Julie with a smile.

"And, it seems to me that these chemicals are not natural to the forest."

"I don't know where man-made chemicals could have come from. We were in the middle of the state park. This land has always been wild. Nothing was ever built there. It's pristine."

"Why do you go to these pristine areas?"

"Everyone who picks mushrooms knows they will absorb everything, and picking them near roads or industrial areas is not advisable."

"But has anyone who picked mushrooms close to a road been poisoned, for example?"

"Not that I know of. The pollutants are very dilute. I mean, if rainwater is washing off a road, it's not going to be absorbed by the mushroom. Mushrooms are the fruit of a fungus that grows underground. The fungus has a network of mycelia, which absorbs the nutrients from the surrounding soil. The only purpose of the mushroom is to disperse the spores. This is why runoff during heavy rains is not really a problem. The polluted water probably rolls off the wet ground and doesn't reach the underground fungus, or is filtered by the time it reaches it."

"So, this leads me to conclude that the only way the chemicals could have been absorbed by the mushrooms is if they had been buried under them," said Julie.

"I've been to that forest for years, Ms. Del Rio. There's never been a toxic dump there."

"Someone may have buried something in the forest that he doesn't want anyone else to find. We need to go back to the area and dig to find the evidence."

"That sounds pretty reasonable to me. I hope you're not planning to bring some heavy equipment into the area. You'll destroy my patch, and the forest"

"How else can we dig? We need to find out what's under that patch," said Julie surprised at Rakky's possessiveness of 'his patch' in the forest.

"I can enlist our group to assist you. We will dig in a responsible manner."

"Look, Rakky, if we find contamination, we need to strip all the soil and have it incinerated."

"Well, let's see what's there first before we do any major damage. That eco-system is very sensitive."

"OK, if you insist Rakky, but I want to get started tomorrow morning. Will you be all right by then?"

"I'm checking out today. I'll be fine. Now, if you don't mind, I'll make some calls. We can meet at the entrance to the state park tomorrow at six a.m. sharp."

"At your service Mr. Basidia," said Julie smiling.

"I'm sorry, I didn't mean... you know, we feel we are the keepers of the forest. We have a responsibility to preserve it. Can you understand that?"

"Sure, I've spent my life protecting the environment. I know how you feel, Rakky."

"I'll be there tomorrow," he said smiling at her, his eyes still staring right into hers.

Julie found herself somewhat mesmerized by his stare and lingering more than she intended.

"Well, I think I better go," she said.

"I'll see you tomorrow."

Peter's arraignment was scheduled for 2 p.m. and Julie was driving quickly to make it in time.

At the courthouse, Peter was standing next to his lawyer. "Peter Wells, you are charged with assaulting an innocent bystander and an officer of the law at this time. There are also charges of conspiring to destroy property as part of an eco-terrorist group. How do your plead to these charges?"

"Innocent on all charges, your honor."

"The defendant will remain in custody. The trail is set for the first Tuesday of next month."

"But your honor, Mr. Wells has a clean record. I ask that bail be set so that he has time to prepare his case."

"Mr. Wells has been accused of conspiring to commit a heinous terrorist act that has taken the lives of countless citizens of Wilburn. He is not a Wilburn resident, and in fact, he seems to have no permanent residence. We are still not sure of this his true identity. He will remain in custody. Court adjourned."

Peter was returned to jail and his lawyer shook his head as he walked out. Julie came running up to the lawyer, "Excuse me, I'm sorry I'm late."

"Yes?"

"I'm Juliana Del Rio, FBI. I was working with Peter Wells on this case and could be a witness for him."

"Well, Ms. Del Rio, he'll need all the help he can get. But it's the FBI accusing Mr. Wells. How could you testify for him?"

"I don't agree with the local office. I have worked with Peter on other occasions and I know he has the best intentions."

"Thank you, Ms. Del Rio, I'll be in touch. In the meantime, please do not visit Peter. There seem to be eyes and ears in that jailhouse and we do not want to alert the prosecution of our strategy."

"OK, but please tell him I'll watch the trailer tonight. He left it in my trust."

"I'm afraid that the FBI raided the trailer this morning and has taken all of his equipment into custody. Particularly the computers, for forensic examination."

"Oh no!"

"You mean you didn't know?" asked the lawyer, surprised. "I guess you guys don't work together."

"No, the local office and our group work independently."

Chapter Fourteen

Pitfalls

Justice was driving north on Main Street in his beat-up Chevy. Just outside of town he turned at the bar where he had saved George and Sean two weeks earlier. He parked the car behind the bar, and entered through the back door. Stopping behind a wooden coat rack, he paused to observe the clientele. At the end of the bar closest to Justice, Sean was sitting on a stool eating a sandwich. Justice carefully looked around the room, in case any of the thugs who had attacked them were sitting at one of the dimly-lit tables.

Satisfied for the moment, Justice walked up to Sean. At the sound of footsteps Sean turned, still holding his glass as if to sip his drink. When Sean noticed it was Justice walking toward him, he raised his glass and drank a long gulp and then turned back to stare at the mirror behind the bar. Justice stopped at the empty stool next to Sean and sat down. Justice stared into the mirror, as the bartender approached and asked, "What do ya' want, boy?"

Justice replied, "A draft beer," and the bartender grabbed a glass, from the stack next to the sink, and pulled the stout handle. The glass filled up, but with too much head. The bartender placed the glass in front of Justice, "That'll be four bucks!"

Justice reached for his wallet, but Sean grabbed Justice's wrist and said to the bartender, "Put it on my tab. And I think you made a mistake. A draft is only $2.50."

The bartender shook his head, mumbled back, "Sure," and walked to the other end of the bar.

Sean grabbed his sandwich, but before biting, he said to Justice, "You're taking a big risk coming in here again."

Justice sipped his beer. "Not as big a risk as you are eating this food."

Sean chuckled and finished chewing. "But how did you know I was here? The FBI doesn't even know I'm back in town."

Justice smiled, "We track everything going on at the trailer. Those cameras feed into our central server and allow us to stay in contact with each other."

Sean smiled back at Justice, "That's interesting, but how did you find me? This morning I was following Mr. Forsythe, but I left him when he went to OC Chemicals Plant, probably to see Mr. Arias. I haven't been back to the trailer since this morning."

Justice replied, "I was told you stopped drinking, but I figured it's hard to break the habit of going to the bar."

"I guess you're right. Anyway, there aren't many places to get a simple lunch around here and I wanted to get the local gossip. Maybe I would find out where these terrorists hang out," said Sean as he took the last bite of his sandwich.

"Maybe I can help you out with that. A mutual friend says we should check out a farmhouse several miles northwest of town. I have no specifics, but they supposedly meet there."

Sean shouted, "Bartender!" and handed him a twenty-dollar bill, waited for his change, and then walked toward the back door with Justice following. Justice added, "I suggest you don't go back to the trailer this evening. The feds have raided the place and it's no longer safe."

"Maybe you can keep an eye on Julie 'til I get back," said Sean.

Justice didn't reply, for he knew how difficult it was for Sean to ask for help.

As Sean and Justice walked into the parking lot, two men with weathered wooden baseball bats approached. One man, who was closest to Sean, wore a cowboy jacket. The other man, who was shorter, came from behind.

Justice said, "There are the guys who attacked you and George."

The cowboy said, "That's right, and now we're going play a little Louisville Slugger on you two."

Justice asked Sean, "Sean, you want to shoot these guys?"

Before Sean replied, the cowboy took a swing at him. Sean ducked and the bat smashed against the side of a pickup truck.

Sean said, "I prefer not to. That'll only get us arrested and they'd put us in jail."

The short guy angrily shouted at the cowboy, "Hey Tom! What are you doing? That's my truck." For a moment the two men stared at the dent, but then gripped their bats with both hands and charged. The cowboy swung at Sean and the short guy at Justice. Again Sean and Justice were able to jump out of the way.

Justice said to Sean, "There's no room to maneuver." He reached down and pulled out a stick tied around his left leg.

Sean raised his eyebrow and asked, "What's that?"

Justice replied, "It's a new titanium bo-stick," and he wound the rope around his wrist and grabbed the end of the stick.

The cowboy turned and swung from the upper right toward Justice. Justice raised his stick, making contact about two feet above his head. The bat thudded against the stick directly against the lower part of the bat label, but the stick did not move. Instead, the top part of the bat broke off, leaving only the short handle in the cowboy's hands. The cowboy's arms were shaking and he looked at the splintered end of the bat.

Justice smiled and said, "I think I have the bigger stick!"

The cowboy staggered back two steps, but at that moment the short guy approached Sean and swung at his legs. Sean jumped away in time to clear the bat, but he lost his balance and fell. The short guy raised his bat, preparing to give Sean a deadly blow from above.

From six feet away, Justice released his grip on his bo-stick, swung it around his head and out as far as he could so that the tip of the stick cut across the short man's left arm just above the elbow, ripping the jacket and opening the skin. Blood squirted out, dripping onto the ground next to Sean's feet. The assailant dropped his bat and screamed as he grabbed his left arm.

Sean rolled to his right and picked up the fallen bat as he stood up. He charged the cowboy, pushing the large round end into the cowboy's chest. The cowboy let out a full lung of air, dropped the bat handle and bent over, before falling to his knees.

Sean dropped his bat and grabbed Justice. "Let's get out of here before the authorities show up."

"OK, I'm going back to town." Justice got into his Chevy, drove left out of the lot toward town.

Sean got into his car and turned north on Route 19.

About five miles out, Sean pulled into a convenience store. He walked up to the soda counter and dispensed a cup of ice. At the counter he gave the cashier a dollar.

The cashier said, "There's no soda in the cup."

Sean replied, "That's OK, I just want the ice. Where's the restroom?"

The cashier gave Sean a quarter as change. "It's at the end of the freezer," and he pointed to the other side of the store.

Sean carried his cup of ice into the restroom. He pulled down about ten feet of paper towel and stuffed the ice into the center and folded the paper over the ice. He placed the iced towel onto

his left shoulder. Exposing the skin to the makeshift ice pack, it was easy to see the bruising he suffered when he fell.

Sean kept the ice pack on for ten minutes and then discarded it. He opened the restroom door and started to walk back to the cashier, when he spotted the pickup truck with the cowboy and his buddy pulling up. Sean ducked back into the restroom and waited, often peeking into the store.

The cowboy came into the store alone. He purchased a roll of bandages and a six-pack of beer.

Sean waited until the pickup pulled out of the lot. Then he quickly left the store and followed the pickup.

The pickup headed north on Route 19 for two and a half miles and suddenly turned right onto "East Fork River Road." Sean stayed a quarter a mile behind the pickup, but had to check every turnoff in case the pickup left the winding main road.

After he'd followed the pickup for a mile, Sean's cellular phone rang and he answered: "Agent Ryan."

"Sean. It's me. Where are you?"

"Julie, I'm following two suspects north of town on East Fork River Road. Why? What's up?"

"I just got back to the trailer and they took the computers! In fact, they left the place open and disabled the cameras and alarm system."

"Julie, who took them?"

"I assume it was Frank Hilbaum. Peter's lawyer told me that the local FBI searched the trailer earlier today."

"Did they take anything else?"

"I don't think so. They left Peter's publications and other materials untouched. I guess they really just wanted to stop any more snooping into the case. Frank isn't really interested in

investigating Peter, because then he'd only prove he didn't do this."

"Well, Lassie, was any of your stuff taken?"

"I was lucky. I had removed all my clothing and taken my computer with me this morning. Mrs. Gutierrez's instructions to stay away from Peter turned out to be good advice."

"Yeah, she always had excellent judgment. The good news is Frank didn't find any evidence that you were staying with Peter. That bastard would have used such evidence against you, and probably would have implicated you in a romantic affair with Peter. That would have been really bad for you."

"That's ridiculous. I'd have a better chance of implicating Frank and Peter. Peter is not romantically interested in me," Julie countered.

Sean paused before responding, "Well... I'm ... glad."

"Frank is an asshole. And we're going to prove he's a traitor. I'm investigating a lead tomorrow. 'Mushroom Man' discovered a patch of mushrooms growing in the National Forest over what I think might be a clue to where the explosives came from."

"I suggest you follow that lead and let me know what you find out. And, Lassie, I want you out of there. The trailer is no longer a safe place."

"OK. I'm going to get out of here as soon as I contact the home office. I'll check back with you later. Good-bye."

"Good-bye Lassie."

Julie walked to the back of the trailer and sat in the chair that used to face Peter's computer. She punched the FBI home office number.

"This is Agent Del Rio. I want to talk with Agent Drago."

"I'll put you through to his office. Please hold."

After a few seconds of silence Julie heard, "This is Agent Lazar, Agent Del Rio. Agent Drago left for Wilburn earlier today. He was going to start his investigation into the death of Agent Zack Greenburg. Can I help you?"

"I wanted to find out if you heard anything about the investigation on how the train was diverted. Frank Hilbaum said he was going to ask you to investigate this after he gave you his input."

"I'm sorry, but we haven't had any request from Agent Hilbaum's team."

"Thank you, Agent Lazar." Julie ended the call and punched in another phone number.

"This is Agent Del Rio. I want to talk to Mrs. Gutierrez."

"One moment, she's on the phone, but I'll tell her you're calling."

"Thank you," Julie closed her eyes and tried to relax.

After a minute of silence Julie heard, "Hello Ms. Del Rio, this is Assistant Director Gutierrez."

"Yes Ma'am, I wanted to tell you personally that Frank Hilbaum did not cooperate with the home office. He did not provide the information nor did he request an investigation into persons responsible for diverting the train through town. If you recall, it was Agent Hilbaum who said he would lead the investigation into this connection. It's been over a week and the home office has not been contacted. Remember what Sean said when we last met: this connection is an important lead to the terrorists responsible for the train derailment. There's got to be a reason that Agent Hilbaum doesn't want this investigation to proceed and I'm betting it's because he's protecting these bastards."

Gutierrez responded, "I agree. Between the sexual harassment charge and this dereliction of duty, I believe I have cause to bring in a team to investigate Agent Hilbaum. I'll have

a team there within twenty-four hours. As for Sean, I'll contact him and ask him to join the investigating team."

"Well, Mrs. Gutierrez, I don't know if I should say this, but Sean is already here in town. He is investigating Mr. Forsythe and company."

"I should have expected that. Sean is not one to easily give up his pursuit of a criminal, especially someone responsible for shooting him. But I'm disappointed he did it without contacting me. He could be disciplined for his disregard of orders."

"I know you can do that, Mrs. Gutierrez, but I think he came here because he felt I was in need of assistance. You can't blame him for that."

"Why, Juliana? Did you ask him to come?"

"Not directly. I did discuss the case with him yesterday, and then he showed up this morning."

"I won't take any action now, but after this case I'll look into this. Good-bye, Ms. Del Rio."

"Good-bye, and thank you, Mrs. Gutierrez."

Julie stood up and walked toward the front of the trailer. As she past the open bathroom door, she heard a footstep. Julie turned, but before she saw who was behind her she was hit on the head and slumped to the floor. The intruder paused over her fallen body. Satisfied she was unconscious, picked her up and placed her on the couch. He closed the door as he left the trailer.

Meanwhile, Sean followed the pickup truck for seven miles and saw it turn left onto a dirt road. He stopped at the side of the road and waited until the pickup was out of sight. A sign posted on a tree read 'Keep Out. Property of White Oak Farm.'

Sean drove past the next bend in the road and parked the car behind a row of willow trees. Leaving the car, he walked toward the dirt road, passing through a grove of trees, and followed a stone wall for a quarter of a mile before he saw two buildings.

One was a small house, built out of brick and stone and only large enough for one room. The other was a large, red-washed barn with two big corn silos.

Seeing no animals in the meadow, Sean suspected that whatever they might be hiding had to be in the barn. He needed to get a closer look, but the field leading up to the barn provided very little cover. He decided to wait until dark. He sat down behind the short stone wall, looked at his watch and noted that it would be two hours until sunset. Sean took out his cellular phone and called Julie; he wanted to tell her where he was so that she wouldn't worry, but there was no answer. Resting his head against the wall, he planned to try to reach her again in a few minutes, but instead he fell asleep.

Inside the farmhouse, several men had gathered, including the cowboy and his short partner. FitzPatrick arrived shortly after dark along with Ashland. They were sitting at a rectangular table looking over drawings and drinking.

"Jim, is Jeff coming tonight?" asked FitzPatrick.

"I don't think so, Bill. He said he had to make sure that Arias had taken care of his end of the deal. He'll join us tomorrow to go over the plan," replied Ashland.

Bill took a long gulp of his beer. "We don't have much time left you know; we're going to be doing this in two days."

"I know. Don't worry, Jeff will be ready."

"I'm not worried about being ready. I just like to know what everyone is doing. That way there won't be any surprises."

"Bill, there won't be any surprises. Everyone involved has too much at stake to be a Judas."

"Well, I hope you're right, Jim, because I'm not going to let them put me in jail!" Bill replied.

Sean awoke about two hours after sunset, with a stiff shoulder. He welcomed the short nap, but was upset at having lost the time. The moonlight made it easy for him to find his way to the farmhouse, using a small wooded area adjacent to the field. He stopped when he saw the silhouettes of two men with guns guarding the entrance. Sean circled around to the rear of the farmhouse, where he saw two cars and three pickup trucks parked by the back door. Someone was also guarding the door. Sean crossed back through the open field and was walking through the wooded area, when he stumbled as the footing beneath him gave way and he fell face-down into a large hole. His head hit the side of the hole as he fell. By the time he reached the bottom, he was out cold.

Julie gently touched the back of her head with her right hand. "Ouch," she winced, as she carefully stood up, took hold of the side of the trailer and walked over to the refrigerator. She took a tray of ice cubes out of the freezer, spilled the contents into a wash towel and placed it on the back of her head. She sat down and put her head down onto her right folded arm that was resting on the now-empty counter.

About fifteen minutes later, she walked over to the bathroom and cautiously looked in, not actually believing that someone was still inside. She could not believe she had let herself be tricked. She looked for any clues the attacker might have left, but found nothing.

Assured the place was safe, she wrapped a towel around her head and steadied herself on the counter before walking back to the couch. She closed her eyes and held back tears. Julie took her phone out of her pocketbook, stared at the numbers for a while as she struggled with her feelings of guilt and inadequacy, and then dialed Sean's number.

Sean's phone rang six times and then the answering service picked up. Julie listened to the recording, but didn't leave a message.

Julie took a deep breath "Oh God," she whispered. Again she was alone and vulnerable, the case now resting heavily on her shoulders until Gutierrez sent help. Sharon was in danger of being discovered by Frank Hilbaum. Peter was facing serious criminal charges by the FBI and Sean couldn't be reached. In the morning she was going to meet this 'mushroom man,' but she felt that this lead was going to be another dead end.

Julie left the trailer, making sure she locked the door. She got into her car and began to drive to the motel in the next town. The further she got from the trailer and the town, the better she felt. Soon her fears were under control.

"What's this?" Sean asked as he lifted his head out of the damp dirt and looked up at the top of the hole. He tried to stand but when he shifted his weight to his feet, a sharp pain raced up his left ankle. He stumbled back, hitting the wall. "Ouch, goddamit!" Sean cursed. He grabbed the side of his left foot with both hands and slowly twisted his ankle and bit his lip from the pain. "Great, I'm in a bear trap with a sprained ankle!" he said as he looked hopelessly at the top of the hole.

Sean's cellular phone faintly rang and he checked his shirt pocket, but it wasn't there. He searched the dark bottom of the hole, feeling each inch of the ground. The phone rang six more times, but he didn't find it. Frustrated, he picked up a baseball-size rock and tossed it into the corner. He tried to climb up one of the walls, to see if the phone was there, but his now-swollen ankle and the wet wall were too much, and he slid down.

Hearing footsteps as he rested against the wall, Sean crouched down and grabbed the rock he had just tossed into the corner.

A man said, "Steve, the ringing came from over there. I think I see something among those rocks. Let's take a look." The footsteps came closer. "Hey, look at the trap. We caught something," said Steve, who bent over the hole and peered down. Sean flung the rock at the man. It brushed him in the shoulder and caused him to fall back a step. Sean took out his gun, but the other man had circled around the hole, pointed his rifle at Sean's back and said, "Drop your weapon!"

"OK. I surrender."

Steve extended his arm and pulled Sean up while the other man kept his weapon aimed at him. Sean was surprised to see that the man pulling him up was Steve Howard, the man he had captured and left at the Forkbend Jail. Once Sean was on his feet, Steve dug his rifle into Sean's back as Sean hobbled to the farmhouse.

Matt opened the door and Steve pushed Sean inside. Jim Ashland was sitting at a small table. "Jim. We found Mr. Ryan in the bear trap. I know what I'd like to do to him as payback for our last encounter, but it's up to you," said Steve giving Jim Sean's gun and badge. Matt placed Sean's cellular phone on the table, "I found this on the ground next to the hole."

Jim replied, "Tie him up and gag him for now. I have to let Jeff know about this."

Jim took his phone and punched in Jeff's number. "Jeff. We caught one of the FBI agents sniffing around at the farmhouse. His name is Sean Ryan. Isn't that the same agent who followed you to Buenos Aires? What do you want to do?"

Jim listened for a reply from Forsythe.

"OK, we'll take care of that," said Jim. Breaking the connection, he told Steve: "You and Bob drive out to the road and find his car. Take it to Blind Bluff and make it look like an accident. Here take his badge and gun, too." Jim handed the items to Steve.

"Why not take him, too?" asked Steve.

"We're to use him as a decoy for now, and if necessary he can be our hostage. We only need another day and then we can kill him, but for now we can send the sheriff and the feds on a wild goose chase. It'll take them a while to realize he's not dead and that'll give us the time we need." Jim paused: "You have your orders; now go!"

"OK," said Steve as he and Bob left the farmhouse.

After checking into her motel room, in the nearby town, Julie immediately connected her portable computer and logged on to the Internet. She went directly to that special chat room, and typed, "Mama is hungry. Any news on Pop? Dinner is getting cold." She read the other messages on the chat and after two minutes a new message popped up. "Mama, Pop went to the woods to hunt possum, have not seen him since 2 p.m."

Julie remembered she had spoken to Sean about 2:30 and typed, "If anyone knows where there is good possum hunting let Mama know."

Julie waited three minutes before getting a reply. "Sorry, haven't seen any possum around here, but will ask around tomorrow and let you know. If you want, I can have Pop's cousin join in your hunt."

Julie didn't want to risk implicating Justice, so she typed, "Thanks, but that won't be necessary." She hoped that maybe Sharon could find out where the farmhouse was, but she did not want to wait until tomorrow.

Therefore Julie called the sheriff's office. "Is Sheriff Williams there?"

The deputy replied, "Sorry Ma'am, he went home. Is there something I can help you with?"

"I'm FBI Agent Juliana Del Rio and I'm trying to locate my partner, Sean Ryan. I last had contact with him this afternoon and he didn't call in and doesn't answer his phone. I was wondering if you have any reports this evening?"

"Nothing unusual. All I have on the sheet for today was a fight outside a bar at 2 p.m., a car accident at 8 p.m. outside of town and two DUI's " the deputy replied.

Julie said, "Can't be the DUI's and that fight was too early. Tell me about the car accident? Who was in the car?"

"We don't know yet. A deputy is heading there now. We responded to a truck that radioed he saw a car go over the ridge ten miles north on Interstate 81. We get a couple of hotheads who go over Blind Bluff every year. Usually there's not much left for us to do."

"I'm going out there. Tell your deputy that I'll join him in fifteen minutes."

"OK Ma'am, but you're not going too see much tonight."

But Julie had already hung up and grabbed her purse. She ran out of the room, slammed the door and headed to her car. She found the local map that she kept in the glove compartment and planned her route. She had become proficient in finding her way around; after all, she had spent almost two weeks in the area. To get to the spot that the deputy indicated, she drove north on West Virginia State Route 35 for eight miles and turned west on Route 19. The last two miles were uphill, heading to the higher slopes of the Appalachian Mountains. She slowed down at the entrance ramp of the Interstate, where she spotted the deputy's car and the deputy standing at the edge of the road. She parked behind his car. The deputy heard Julie's car as it crossed onto the sandy shoulder.

The deputy walked over to Julie, turning his flashlight on her.

"Miss Del Rio? The office said you were coming. I'm Officer Norton," said the deputy.

"Yes," Julie replied as she walked in front of the deputy. Facing the edge of the ridge she asked. "Have you seen what type of car is down there?"

"Not yet, but that's a long drop and it's too dark out tonight to get a clear look."

Julie took the flashlight from the deputy and leaned over the edge. The light bounced off the side of the mountain for about fifty feet, but beyond there were too many trees. "How can we get a look at the bottom of this ravine?"

"Daylight."

"You can't wait till daylight! My partner may be down there and he may need medical attention."

The deputy took the flashlight. "If your partner is down there, he doesn't need medical attention. No one ever survived a crash over Blind Bluff. It can wait till tomorrow."

The deputy walked back to his car and Julie followed. She stepped on something and bent over to pick it up. The deputy shone the light on what looked like a wallet. "It's Sean's badge!" said Julie, now fighting back tears. "Humm," said the deputy, as he walked back to his car.

"What are you doing?"

"I'm going back to the office and then home for some rest. I suggest you do the same thing."

"We need to get a rescue team tonight!"

"Not in the middle of the night. And besides, I doubt very much that wallet conveniently fell out of the car right here.

There's something wrong. I'll bring in the rock climber tomorrow morning. He'll be able to see what's down there.

"Deputy Norton, here is my cell phone number. Please call me as soon as you find out who's down there."

"OK. We'll be back here first thing in the morning and I'll let you know," he said, climbing into his squad car and driving away.

Julie stood at the side of the road for another ten minutes. She couldn't understand how the sheriff's department could just wait and do nothing and it hurt her knowing she had no other choice. It was a short drive back to the motel, but it was going to be a long night with little rest. This feeling of despair was not going to go away.

Chapter Fifteen

For The Love Of The Earth

"The purity men love is like the mists
which envelop the earth, and not like the azure
ether beyond."
Henry David Thoreau

The alarm clock startled Julie, interrupting a nightmare. She was wet with perspiration and glad to be awake. It was still dark outside. She jumped out of bed, plugged in the hotel's coffeemaker, and went into the shower. As she stepped out wrapped in a towel, she took a drink of the fresh coffee, switched on the hair dryer and dried her hair. When her cell phone rang, she dropped the drier and rushed to pick up.

"Ms. Del Rio, this is Deputy Norton. We checked the wreckage. We didn't find anyone down there. Whoever caused this accident wants you to think your partner is dead. Your team should take over the investigation from here. It may be weeks before we can get the car raised, especially with all of our resources devoted to the train wreck."

"Thank you officer. We'll take care of things from here on." Julie breathed somewhat easier knowing Sean might be alive. She glanced at her watch and realized that she had to hurry if she was going to keep her appointment with Rakky. She didn't wait for her hair to be completely dry. The humidity had turned her normally straight style into a mound of knotted curls. There was little time to fuss with it, so she gathered the curls on top of her head and held them in place with a large clip, letting some

hang loose around her face. She got dressed in jeans and a sweatshirt and ran out the door.

It took twenty minutes to reach the entrance to the National Forest Preserve. Through the trees she saw the golden rays of the sun diffused by the fine morning mist that hovered close to the ground. The air was thick and wet, and a chill swept through her sweatshirt and into her joints. In the distance she saw Rakky Basidia standing in front of a large black van. As she approached, Rakky cheerfully said to her, "Good morning!"

"Good morning Rakky, I ..."

"I like your hair that way! Natural," he said loudly, his clear blue eyes looking piercingly into hers. Julie blushed, afraid that the group behind the van had overheard the comment. The group consisted of two men and three women who looked like they belonged to the octogenarians' club. The men were wearing pants and sweatshirts, but the women wore colorful stretch pants and knitted sweaters. Among them was Mrs. Southerland, the retired teacher who had spoken on television about Rakky's poisoning.

"Julie, meet Joe McClawsky, Jim Brady and Abigale Southerland."

"Nice to meet you Mrs. Del Rio," said Mrs. Southerland extending her hand.

"It's Ms. Del Rio."

"Oh, you're not married," said the old woman looking at Rakky. Juliana blushed again.

"Julie, meet Winnie Gallo and Elizabeth Jones," said Rakky, pointing to the other two women. Elizabeth sat on an electric wheelchair.

"Hello, dear," they said in unison.

"Well... Rakky, can I see you alone for a moment? Excuse me gentlemen, ladies..." Julie walked far enough to be sure the

group did not hear what she had to say. Rakky followed, and stood close to her and smiled. He reminded Julie of a cat, with his clear blue eyes staring directly into hers, quietly and steadily. It embarrassed her.

"Rakky, these friends of yours are in their eighties. They look like they can barely walk, never mind dig out the site for evidence. What are you doing?"

"Julie, don't worry, they're stronger than you think; they go on hikes all the time," said Rakky still staring at her intensely. "Well, I hope you know what you are doing..."

But Rakky stopped her, pulling her toward him in one quick move and kissing her passionately on the lips. Julie didn't push him away but just let herself enjoy the moment. She took a deep breath when he let her go.

"I know what I'm doing Julie," he replied.

"Rakky, I think you may have misunderstood me. This is an official investigation, I am here on official business."

"Come on Julie, we're burning daylight. We don't want the other visitors to see us digging," said Rakky, as he handed Julie a shovel and some plastic bags – something she had not even thought of bringing. With an air of satisfaction, Rakky turned and signaled the group to follow.

Julie placed her hand on her forehead and pondered for a moment before moving on. *"En que me he metido ahora"* she mumbled.

Julie followed Rakky as he walked quickly, head high, back straight, toward the forest. She looked back at the seniors walking slowly behind them. She stopped for the group to catch up. Jim Brady dragged a small shopping cart loaded with the group's shovels. Mrs. Southerland walked behind, followed by Elizabeth, who was riding beside Joe McClawsky.

"Go ahead with Rakky, dear," said Mrs. Southerland, "We'll catch up. My arthritis flares up in the morning so it takes me a bit longer."

"OK, but are you going to be all right?"

"Don't worry." said Mrs. Southerland smiling. "You go ahead."

"Come on Julie, they'll catch up," Rakky yelled.

About five minutes later, Rakky and Julie arrived at a patch of beautifully shaped mushrooms covering a large area near an old tree. While Julie stood to admire their beauty for a moment, Rakky was already digging a hole in the corner.

"I've never seen anything like this," she said.

"I'm glad you appreciate them. They are nearly as beautiful as you," said Rakky admiring the patch of mushrooms and stopping to stare at Julie.

"Rakky, before we go any further I just wanted to say that what happened back there is..."

But Rakky interrupted her before she could say more. "Julie, I think that we should dig as quickly as possible. We don't know who may be watching. This area where I'm digging is where I picked the mushroom that put me in the hospital. We can try other areas, or maybe you want to take soil samples in a pattern around the patch."

"Rakky, stop. I want to make it abundantly clear that I don't appreciate what you did back there."

"You mean that I kissed you?"

"Yes! I mean, I didn't think you were the kind to... well, you didn't seem..."

"Seem what! I don't take advantage of women regularly out here in the forest, if that's what you're thinking. I just thought

you felt the same way about me. Back there in the hospital, I thought you liked me...." Rakky put down the shovel. "Oh, I get it, that's how you get men to cooperate with you; you bat your eyelashes and lead them on!"

"I'm sorry, but you got the wrong signal Mr. Basidia! Boy, did you get the wrong signal!"

Rakky resumed digging, ignoring Julie.

Julie stared at Rakky, admiring his physique, and almost regretted what she'd just said, but quickly turned away and continued digging.

After a few minutes, the octogenarians arrived. "Oh, aren't they beautiful!" Elizabeth rode her chair right up to the edge and got up with Joe's help. "Yes, they are as beautiful as they were the other day. It's been raining."

Rakky stopped digging, stepped in front of the seniors and said: "Grab your shovels and plastic bags from the cart. Each of you take a sample of soil from the edge of the patch, but be careful not to disturb the mushrooms. Note where the samples came from and put them in your bags. I'll continue to dig here, where we got the contaminated mushrooms. Julie, you may want to dig another hole a few feet away."

As they went to work, the forest got brighter and the mist dried up. Mrs. Southerland waved Julie over to the edge of the mushroom patch. As Julie walked over to her, almost stepping on one of the delicate mushrooms, she said "Oh, no dear, careful not to step on them."

Mrs. Southerland led Julie away from the group and faced her.

"What is it? Is something wrong?" said Julie.

"He likes you, you know."

"Yes, he let me know already."

"He's a very nice young man. He was one of my best students. Just wanted to let you know he's a real good man. He just won't stop talking about you."

"Yes, I know that, but I'm working for the FBI. I'll be leaving soon and I don't think there's a chance for us right now."

"Well, you never know what life will bring, Julie," said Mrs. Southerland smiling as she walked back toward the group.

"Julie, come over here please," yelled Rakky.

Julie ran back to the patch of mushrooms where Rakky had dug a hole about three feet deep. Her eyes widened when she saw what he uncovered.

"Oh my God!" said Julie. She slowly pulled a mat of cut-off wires; a corked glass container with some liquid still in it and a label that said 'Acid'; some plastic material, and lab glassware. There was a terrible smell around the hole now. "You're going to have to stop digging; these could be explosives Rakky."

"We have to take some material back with us as evidence don't we? I'll carefully dig around this with my hands."

"No, I don't want you to take a chance; you'll need special gloves for that."

But Rakky wasn't listening. "I'll use a plastic bag."

"Rakky, please don't."

As Rakky dug deeper with his hands in the plastic bag, the plastic started melting.

"You're right. We need protective gear for this."

Rakky got up and cleaned his hands with some loose dirt he picked up far away from the patch.

"Let me see your hands," said Julie, grabbing his hand and wiping the dirt off of it. "It's red! Are you OK?"

As Julie was examining Rakky's hands, a shot rang out. Julie ducked as Rakky grabbed her. "Oh God, Rakky, just take the group out of here! I'm going to see if I can chase that gunman or he might kill all of us."

"No, Julie, let me..."

Julie reached for the gun under her sweatshirt and held it out "Rakky, please, get out of here and take these people with you!"

Rakky signaled the seniors to leave.

"Rakky, go back, you need to protect the group."

"Don't worry, old Joe McClawsky carries a World War II rifle and he doesn't miss. They'll be OK." Rakky reached into his sweatshirt and pulled a gun. "I don't think you should be alone here."

"Is that legal? I didn't think you packed one!" said Julie.

"We always come protected. Some hikers have been attacked in the park."

"Look, I can't place you in danger," said Julie, before running off in the direction of the gunfire.

"I see him," said Rakky from behind one of the trees. He pointed the gun and shot toward the man. Julie ran toward the guy, but he ran faster and hid behind a tree. "Julie, stop right there! There could be more than one! Come back!" Rakky ran toward Julie and crouched behind a tree, very close to her. "Doesn't that agency believe in sending a partner with you? Do you have to do this alone?" he whispered.

"Sean, my partner, is missing. I went looking for him last night. The agency is sending a team to help out this afternoon."

Another shot came from straight ahead; the bullet hit a tree next to Julie.

Julie spotted two heads suddenly pop from behind thick bushes. She fired twice. Rakky shot from behind the tree, hitting one of the men, who screamed as he fell. But the other man disappeared from sight. As Julie ran toward the downed man, the second man reappeared and pointed a shotgun at her. Before he had time to shoot her, Rakky stood up and fired, but he missed. The gunman quickly turned and shot Rakky, hitting him in the shoulder. Julie fired three times at the gunman, hitting him once in the arm. The gunman fell.

Julie ran toward Rakky, but didn't see the gunman as he got up and aimed at her. Hearing a loud shot, Julie turned quickly and saw the gunman fall forward with blood gushing out of his leg as he fell. Behind the gunman was Joe McClawsky, holding his rifle.

Julie ran toward Rakky. She pressed against the wound on his shoulder to stop the blood. "Oh God, no!"

Joe walked toward them and put his jacket behind Rakky's head.

Rakky looked at Julie, his clear blue eyes now dull. Julie held his hand.

"I'm sorry." Rakky howled in pain as Julie pressed harder against his open wound to slow the loss of blood. Then he was quiet; he had gone into shock.

"Do you have a cell phone?" asked Joe.

"I can't call the local FBI; they might be in on this."

"That's all right, I'll call the fire department; my grandson works there."

Julie handed Joe the phone. As Joe dialed, he walked toward the downed man. "He's still breathing; I made sure not to kill him because we'll need his statement," he said.

"Hello, this is Joe McClawsky; is Billy there? Billy, you need to come to the National Park right away and bring a couple of

stretchers and the ambulance. Please, I can't explain, but don't alert the sheriff, you hear me!" Joe placed the cell phone in his pocket before heading back toward the mushroom patch. No one was there, but he noticed that someone had covered the hole that Rakky had dug.

When he reached the injured man, Julie was still pressing against the wound and checking Rakky's breathing. "They should be here soon. How's he doing?"

"He's in shock, but he's still breathing. I think I have his bleeding under control. Where are the others?"

"They took off. The samples will be safe with them."

"Rakky's breathing is erratic. Oh God he stopped breathing!" Julie was in a panic and her hands trembled.

"Honey, you need to calm down. Give him mouth to mouth or he'll die. He still has a chance."

Julie began administering mouth-to-mouth, and pushing down on the chest, but Rakky was not responding.

"He's choking on his own blood. Turn him over and open his mouth," ordered Joe.

Julie and Joe worked on turning him, and as they opened his mouth a trail of blood came pouring out. Julie turned him back on his back and continued pressing his chest and blowing air into his mouth. Suddenly she saw Rakky's eyes widen and she felt his pulse stop.

"Oh God, no!" cried Julie.

"Keep it up! Don't worry about that. The medics will be here any minute. I hear the siren."

Julie continued CPR, desperately trying to revive Rakky.

Almost immediately two firemen and a medic ran toward them carrying stretchers. "Grandpa, are you all right? What happened?" asked the young fireman.

"I'm OK, Billy, but Rakky needs help now."

"What happened to him?"

"That guy over there shot Rakky and I shot the gunman," said the old man.

"I'll take over Miss. I'm Billy, Joe's grandson," said a young man dressed in jeans and wearing a fireman's hat.

Two other young firemen set up the stretcher, and one dressed as a medic injected something into Rakky's arm as Billy continued pounding on his chest and blowing air into his mouth. One of the men went to attend to the gunman, who was still face down. "He's breathing, but in shock," said the young man.

"Put him on a stretcher and make sure he doesn't die! We'll need to find out who put him up to this," ordered Joe.

Suddenly, Rakky's chest began moving on its own. "He's breathing!" said Billy. Julie began to cry out loud, as she approached Rakky, and held his hand. "You took a bullet to save me...I'll never forget this," said Julie.

Rakky seemed to acknowledge her words, even though he was too weak to speak.

As the men were putting the gunman on the stretcher, Julie yelled: "We shot another guy! He should be behind those bushes."

One fireman searched the bushes. "There's some blood here, but the guy's gone."

The firemen carried the gunman and Rakky on stretchers back to the waiting ambulance.

Julie walked up to Joe and whispered, "Was the sheriff alerted?"

"No, don't worry. We all know the sheriff is crooked. The medics are friends of Billy's. We're going to keep this quiet until we can figure out what's going on," said Joe.

"You seem to know what you're doing Joe. Have you been an investigator at some point?"

"I served in the war, and for the police department years ago. You don't get to be my age and learn nothing."

"How old are you?"

"Well, I'm older than 80 years young my dear, but as you can see I can still shoot straight!"

The octogenarians had driven off in Rakky's black van. Joe got into the ambulance with his grandson Billy and his friends. Julie followed in the car.

At the hospital, the two men were rushed into the emergency room. Julie tried to go through the doors, but she was stopped. "Sorry, Miss, at this point, relatives only," said a nurse.

An older woman, with blond-gray hair and the same piercing blue eyes as Rakky, followed his stretcher into the emergency room. She turned her head and gave Julie a cold stare. The doors closed behind them.

Julie was left alone. Reaching for her phone, she realized that, in the confusion, Joe had kept it. She went to the nearest public phone and called her cell number.

"Joe, I think you kept my cell phone. Where are you?"

"Meet me at the local high school. I'll be at the entrance. Mrs. Southerland had the chemistry teacher analyze some of the material. You'll be interested to know what we found."

"Oh, no! We needed the FBI to test that."

"Don't worry. They didn't ruin the samples, just did some spot testing. Meet me there."

It took Julie only a few minutes to drive to the school. As she stopped next to Joe, he stuck his head in the window and said: "Park the car over there and follow us in."

The school was officially closed, so the group went in through the side door, which was guarded by a heavyset man in a uniform. As Joe and Mrs. Southerland passed him, he nodded. He didn't bother to look at Julie, who was carrying her small laptop computer. She took a deep breath. The old high school was cool and smelled fresh, in contrast with the hot, humid air in Wilburn. The high ceilings, shiny floors and long, empty hallways with brightly colored walls brought memories of her high school in Vieques and of her grandmother. Being with Joe and Mrs. Southerland made Julie feel safe.

When they reached the lab, one of the men Julie had met at the park, Jim Brady, was standing next to a laboratory setup, heating a blue liquid in a glass flask.

"Hello Mrs. Del Rio, welcome," said Mr. Brady, still looking at the various test tubes he had lined up on the laboratory bench.

"Hello, Mr. Brady," said Julie pretending to be interested in his findings. She was more concerned with the integrity of the samples; she fully expected to send these to the FBI lab as soon as she got them back.

"I know you want to get these samples to the lab. We, on the other hand, want to find out what is contaminating our mushrooms and if we can get rid of it, so we got busy on the analysis," explained Brady, as he continued to stir the blue liquid. Mixing beads inside the beaker clicked as he spoke.

"What did you find?"

"Well, we have the raw materials for simple nitroglycerine here and traces of plastic explosives. Looking at my analysis, I could say that whoever buried this material was building an explosive and a detonator. This board, for example, is a wireless receiver. It is a cheap thing, used to set up remote cameras and security systems. It can be bought from any catalog or electronics store. It might be used to detonate something on signal. There are some other components here that may have been part of a detonator," said Brady with an air of authority.

Julie did not respond, but looked skeptically at the board.

"Before he retired, Jim worked for the CIA laboratory in Washington," said Joe. "Well, you know, testing methods have changed a lot in the last few years," said Julie, now using her bifocals to look carefully at the serial number on the wireless receptor board.

"They spend a lot of money on high-tech devices because they don't have expert personnel to do the analysis I can do here," said Jim, now somewhat annoyed at Julie's skepticism of his methods.

Julie was not listening. Suddenly, she put down the board, opened up her computer and got into the Internet.

"What are you doing?" asked Joe interested in the device.

"Accessing the FBI lab site."

"You can do that from here?"

"I have wireless Internet, I can access the lab from anywhere," she said as she keyed the serial number and make of the board into a database. The system took a minute to respond before the name and phone number of a man in Wilburn, Virginia, appeared on the screen.

"That's it, the board was bought locally by this guy."

"You can trace that from your computer?" asked Joe.

"They could do that when I worked at the CIA, Joe. Except now the computers are smaller and wireless. The purchase of all devices that could possibly be used for explosives is recorded. Data is volunteered by the companies that conduct transactions," explained Jim.

"Joe, could I have my cell phone back please?" asked Julie.

As Joe handed her the phone he asked: "How is Rakky doing?"

"I wasn't allowed in. His mother, I think, went into the emergency room with him. I'll see what I can find out," said Julie as she dialed the hospital.

"Hello, can you connect me to the emergency room desk please?"

Julie took a deep breath as she nervously clicked on her computer keyboard. "Yes, this is Agent Juliana Del Rio, from the FBI. Two men were admitted to the hospital just about an hour ago, one was Mr. Rakky Basidia, and the other man had a gunshot wound to the leg. Do you know who the other man was?.... OK.

"And can you connect me to the nurse please? I want to check on Mr. Basidia's condition."

"Who is he?" said Joe worried.

"Yes, thank you, I appreciate this." Julie pressed the disconnect button and placed her phone in her purse.

"Rakky has been stabilized and the bullet removed. He's going to make it. The other guy's name is Jim Stark. He may not make it."

"Jim Stark is the name you just displayed on the computer," said Joe.

"Exactly, but what good is he to us if he's dead!" Julie took a deep breath, closed her eyes and put her head down on the table.

"Are you OK?" asked Joe.

"No, and neither is this case, nor my partner. He's missing."

"Why don't you call him?"

"I did but couldn't reach him. I can try again," said Julie dialing Sean's number.

At the farm, Sean was tied up and sitting on the floor in a corner of the room. Sean's cell phone and other personal effects were spread out on the table. When the cell phone rang, one of the men walked to the table and picked it up. "Hello, Sean Ryan here," he said and then smiled at his partner.

Julie realized immediately that the person wasn't Sean but she played along. "Mr. Ryan, why have you not reported back to headquarters? Where are you?"

"I was stuck in traffic ma'am, and frankly, I got drunk last night," said one of the young captors, laughing at his friend.

As Julie continued to play along, she clicked a couple of keys on her phone. She later clicked some keys on the wireless computer and brought up the GPS system.

"Well, Mr. Ryan, you are going to be reprimanded when you get back. We'll dock your pay. Don't bother to call us again. You're suspended from the force unless you can come up with a better excuse than that!"

"I think I'd like to lick you all over ma'am..." said the captor, laughing with his buddy.

"I'm sure you would! What else....You're making me so hot," said Julie, who needed to keep the man on the phone. "I want to chew on your..." The man continued his lewd suggestions as Julie grimaced, wishing the records she had called up would appear. Then Julie heard a door open and another voice in the background, an older voice.

Jeff Forsythe had entered the farm-house. "What the hell are you doing, Matt. Hang up that phone!" roared the Jeff.

"I'm just having a little fun..."

"Disconnect now or I'll shoot your dick off!"

The young man looked down the barrel of a shotgun and quickly ended the call.

"Bingo!" yelled Julie as she saw the record that traced the geographic location of Sean's phone.

A couple of clicks and the place appeared on a map.

"Amazing!" said Joe.

"It takes a couple of minutes for the system to trace the position, so I had to keep him on the phone."

"Good work, Agent Del Rio," said Joe.

"Thank you for your help. Could you put these samples in a safe place until I get back, and record your findings? Send the report to this fax number at the FBI headquarters. I've got to get some help and rescue my partner. It seems he's been captured. I'm praying they haven't killed him."

"Don't you worry, you go ahead. The samples are safe here," assured Jim.

Julie picked up her computer, and as she walked out the door she called Gutierrez. "Mrs. Gutierrez, Agent Del Rio. I went to the National Park this morning and found what I think is evidence of a detonation and explosive device buried under a contaminated patch of mushrooms.

"Locals assisted with the investigation. There was a shootout, and the mushroom expert who led the expedition into the forest, Rakky Basidia, was seriously wounded. We also shot the two gunmen, but one escaped and the other was sent to the hospital.

"I just connected John Stark, the man in the hospital, with the purchase of one of the electronic boards we found buried under the mushroom patch. Unfortunately, he's critically wounded and his accomplice is missing."

"Good work Agent Del Rio. We need to get a confession from Stark to corroborate a statement we recently got from one of the technicians at the train-switching station; he was apparently blackmailed or bribed to reroute the train. The new team has

been investigating the switching station operators and found computer records that clearly indicated the switch was done on purpose and was unscheduled. I've been trying to get a hold of Sean, but he's not answering."

"I found Sean, or at least his phone. I was able to pinpoint his cell phone to a location five miles from Wilburn. I don't know if his phone was lost and picked up by someone, or whether he was captured, but last time he checked with me, he was on his way to a farm outside of town. I'm just on my way out to see what I can find out. In case something happens to me, I've e-mailed you the coordinates and the map. Please be sure that the team arriving knows the location and comes to our rescue if I don't call again."

"The new team will be there in a couple of hours. Meantime, please lead the investigation and try to find Stark's partner."

"Ma'am, may I remind you that I am not a formally trained FBI agent and I just don't feel comfortable with this assignment at this point. I need reliable backup now! I'm all alone here!"

"Very well Ms. Del Rio. Please contact Agent Drago and ask him to back you up for now."

"But Ma'am, a couple of hours may be too late for Sean!..." said Julie, but Gutierrez had ended the call in her typically abrupt manner. Julie trembled. She took another deep breath and called Drago.

"Agent Drago, this is Agent Del Rio. I want to meet you at the Wilburn Hospital to discuss this case. Now!"

Chapter Sixteen

A New Purpose

Despite taking several deep breaths to regain her composure, Julie's heart pounded and her hands shook as she drove to the hospital. She remembered meeting Drago back at FBI headquarters, but she had no idea of what to expect and she felt helpless and alone without Sean around.

In the hot midday sun of a southern town, car air conditioners were having trouble keeping up; Julie's car was hot and steamy. She opened the window but there was little relief. She wasn't wearing dark glasses and the long stretch of scorching road ahead reflected a blinding light.

Her breath was rapid and shallow; her mind foggy. She found it difficult to keep the car in the lane. The road seemed to get narrower and on either side there appeared to be deep gorges. Suddenly a splitting headache make her head feel like it was in a vise. She lost control of the car.

A weightless and nauseous feeling in her stomach told her the car was now airborne. She was sure that she was falling over a cliff. She stomped on the brakes as she let out a deafening scream; her head hit the steering wheel!

"Come on, get up!" Matt yelled at Sean, soon after hanging up on Julie. He and his friend seemed oblivious to what had just happened. All he could do was smile with satisfaction at the hot exchange on the phone.

Sean said nothing and got up without a struggle. The tight ropes were cutting into his wrists, and his arms were so tightly tied behind his back that his shoulder joints were swollen and painful. But he was calmer now after overhearing Matt's phone conversation with Julie. *"Smart lass,"* he thought. She kept the

idiot on the phone at least five minutes, enough time to pinpoint the farm's location. He knew help was on its way, but not for some time. He guessed that Gutierrez wasn't going to get a team over to Wilburn for at least two or three hours. He only feared that Julie would take off on her own again to save him.

"Move now..." yelled Matt, pointing a gun at Sean.

"Lad, could you untie my legs? I can't walk with these tight ropes around my ankles," said Sean.

In answer to his request, Steve hit him hard on the side of the head with the handle of the gun. Blood poured down Sean's head and he fell to the ground.

Only then did Matt untie his feet, revealing red bloody gouges on Sean's ankles.

"Don't get any wise ideas. Don't even think about it. Walk out that door and toward the barn. I'll be right behind you," said Steve.

Sean got up slowly and limped out into the scorching midday sun. His eyes struggled to adjust as he walked toward the large red barn. He wondered why they were moving him. Without turning his head, he managed to look out of the corner of his eye and saw a silver sedan. He had seen that car before back in Wilburn, at the plant. The man standing next to the car was looking his way. It was Jeff Forsythe.

"Move!" said Steve, shoving the tip of his gun painfully into Sean's side. As soon as they entered the barn, Steve pushed Sean into one of the animal pens. He cut the ropes from Sean's hands.

Matt moved in front of Sean and said, "Put your hands in front of you. I'll handcuff you."

Sean was relieved to be able to move his arms around to the front and willingly let Matt handcuff him. With the handcuffs locked shut, Matt put a chain around the cuffs and a large pole and padlocked it. He didn't seem concerned at Sean's docility.

"You ain't going anywhere, so I'm not bothering with your feet," said Matt looking at Sean's bleeding ankles.

Sean couldn't figure out why Matt was actually giving him a break. He realized the red marks on his wrists and ankles and bleeding head presented a pathetic picture, but could Matt be feeling sorry for him?

When the car came to a full stop, Julie's head rested against the steering wheel. After a few moments, she looked up. She was by the side of a deserted road, lined by pine trees as far as she could see. The gorges she thought she saw earlier didn't exist. Her mind had played tricks on her. She took a deep breath and she let out a primal scream. Her eyes filled with tears and she started weeping uncontrollably. *"Dios, ayudame!"* she said as she cried.

"You've got to pull yourself together, Julie! Help is on its way. You've got to pull yourself together!" she screamed. For a moment, the vivid memories of the day's events replayed. First, she felt Rakky's wet and tender kiss, the sensations in her body as she surrendered briefly. Then, she felt the tightening of her gut with fear when gunman pursued her in the forest, and the echoing sounds of the bullets buzzing by her and ricocheting off the trees. She relived the agony of seeing Rakky nearing death before her eyes, the feel of his mouth on hers as she blew her life-giving breaths into his lungs. The robust, once vital body she couldn't take her eyes off was now limp, small and frail in her arms; it felt more like that of a baby. She could almost feel the wetness on her hands as she tried to stop the gush of blood from Rakky's trembling body as it twitched with pain. She dropped her head back on the steering wheel and cried for a long time – all of the tension, fear, and other pent-up emotions pouring out of her.

When the tears subsided, Julie lifted her head and saw a small fawn with a spotted coat and big shiny black eyes staring at her— almost looking into her soul. As she watched it, her eyes

cleared. Forgetting her own problems for the moment, she wondered if the animal was OK all by himself. For a second she thought there was a connection. Perhaps he knew what she was thinking? The fawn's mother soon appeared from behind the trees and looked briefly at Julie before the two deer jumped gracefully into the darkness of the woods and disappeared from sight.

Julie opened the passenger window; the cross-breeze brought some relief. She took a deep breath and smelled the pine scents, the chamomile and the grass. She looked up and saw an eagle soaring high across the now-clear blue sky. She was surprised to spot one still alive after all that happened. She thought for sure that the chemicals had killed wildlife for miles around. Nature's relentless ability to survive even the worst catastrophes surprised even her. Julie wiped her face, combed her hair and started the car. She suddenly knew what her purpose was on this case and in life.

She was on her way to the hospital. She was going to save her partner and solve this case.

Julie arrived at the hospital to find Drago sitting in the lobby. She could barely remember his face from their last meeting, but his attire spelled FBI. "Agent Drago, I'm Agent Juliana Del Rio," she said extending her hand.

"Nice to meet you again," said Drago shaking Julie's hand as he would shake that of a man. "I just heard from Gutierrez and she filled me in on the details. It seems that you've located Sean, and I understand you've connected John Stark to the materials you found in the woods. Good work, Ms. Del Rio!"

"I... you got all that from Gutierrez?" asked Julie, irked at his condescending, patronizing attitude.

"Yes. We can't interrogate Stark until he improves, but I think that it's possible that we can catch his accomplice."

"How do you propose to do that? We wounded him in the shootout and he escaped," said Julie, now studying Drago's dead-pan face. Trying not to reveal her thoughts with her expression, she put on a hypocritical smile. *"Men seen so damn sure of themselves! Why can't I be like that?"* she thought.

"Don't worry, he'll be along soon, to kill the very person who can turn him in and possibly take us to the leaders of this operation. We'll have to set a trap for him."

Julie nodded, and tried not to show her disgust at Drago's arrogant, assured tone. His self-assurance made her feel like a fool. She had just lost her composure out on the road and this guy was right on track. Now, she felt even more inadequate than she had in Alaska, when she first experienced the fear and stress that came with the job. Gutierrez had just assigned this guy to back her up, but all of the sudden he was taking over the operation. *"He's nothing like Sean. I don't like this guy at all,"* she thought. "So what's the trap?" she asked Drago.

"First, we'll call the sheriff and let everyone in town know that Stark is here, and then Hilbaum and myself will sit and wait."

"Oh, that's just fine! Didn't Gutierrez tell you the worst?"

"What?"

"Frank Hilbaum is suspected of working with the terrorists, Arias and Forsythe."

"I don't think you have any proof of that, do you?"

"Oh, I have proof! Frank had one of his accomplices beat up Sean and George, the local reporter. He then made sure he trapped Peter and had him jailed."

"How do you know the men who did this were working with Frank?"

"I saw him signaling them from across the room before they trapped Peter. They were the same men who beat up Sean and George."

"That's pretty lean evidence against a veteran FBI agent, don't you think? But I'll check with Gutierrez and involve the sheriff only at this point."

"Good, you do that! If you don't mind, I plan to save my partner from being killed. I believe he's been captured."

"Don't you think you better wait for more backup?"

"You're all the backup they gave me, I can't trust Frank, and the 'cavalry' won't be arriving for a couple of hours. By then Sean could be dead."

"I'm sorry I can't come with you. I have to get set up this trap and hang around for when Stark is able to give his confession. I advise you against going into a situation without backup. You're not a trained agent and these are dangerous criminals."

"Look, while I'm gone, I would appreciate it if you'd call the sheriff and get Peter released from jail. He's being held on suspicion of causing the train derailment. It's clear now that these gunmen are the murderers."

"I'll do so - as soon as I set the trap," said Drago. "But I'll have to call Gutierrez and let her know that you're attempting to go after Sean, alone. Sorry. Can't this wait until I'm done here?"

"Thank you for your vote of confidence! I'll might as well call Gutierrez myself right now." Julie turned around and walked out the door, leaving Drago standing in the hospital lobby.

Julie was furious at Drago's arrogance. *"He dismissed everything I said and has the nerve to threaten to report me!"* she thought. Riding an adrenaline rush, Julie was about to repeat the mistake she'd made in Alaska. She knew that rushing into a situation with no backup was dangerous and could get her fired.

But this time things were different. She was no longer thinking logically when it came to Sean. She needed him so badly that she didn't think of the risk to herself or to her career. She had to go and find him, be with him, save him. She never asked herself why she was so obsessed with him now, to the point of forgetting her duty. Her mind wouldn't let her go there at this point.

She didn't call Gutierrez; she would just order her to wait for the backup that was still two hours away. *"If I could only find Sean, I could create a diversion and keep him alive, at least until backup gets here."* But as she was about to get into the car, a hand on her shoulder gently pulled her back.

"Julie, don't go out there alone!"

Julie looked behind her. "George, what are you doing here?"

"Well, I was sitting in the hospital lobby, hiding behind a newspaper when I happened to hear the conversation you had with that agent."

"Yes, well, I was pretty angry. I'm not myself lately."

"Let me come with you, at least."

"I appreciate what you're doing, but don't get involved. You're in enough trouble already George," said Julie as she got into the car and started the engine.

"Wait. I talked to Basidia. He's OK."

Julie stopped the engine. "Oh, thank God. I didn't go to see him; I don't think his mother wanted me around."

"His mother had quite a story to tell me about OC Chemicals. We should talk to her later. She's disabled from exposure to Cynoff and Diazinon in 1994. She used to be a nurse for OC Chemicals. She hates Arias and Forsythe and she can be a great deal of help to us. She doesn't trust the FBI because she thinks they're crooked – I mean, the ones she has met."

"I don't blame her – it's getting to where I can't trust anyone myself."

"Look, Julie, it's not my business, but I don't want anything to happen to you. Don't you think going out there alone is dangerous? I mean, what weapons do you have? What's your plan? When it comes to Sean, you're no longer thinking rationally."

"Look George, I know what I'm doing."

"I know how you feel about Sean. You're not helping him by barging in without a plan!"

"What do you mean, you know how I feel?"

"You're in love with the guy. It's obvious to anyone who sees you together. This is an emotional decision you are making here, *Agent Del Rio.*"

"I don't want to hear any more of this nonsense. Sean is a good friend, and I admit I care about him, as a friend. Any time a woman is trying to do her job, her duty, she's accused of being emotional or irrational or being in love with someone! If I were a man, this would be a *brave* thing to do!"

"OK, so you don't want to admit it. I'm going with you whether you like it or not!"

"OK George, then get in!"

"And by the way, Sean will be OK. He's a veteran. Why would those guys kill Sean? Then they'll have no bargaining chip."

"George, I'm a big girl. I wear a badge. I have a gun. I don't need you to hold my hand, but you're welcome to come along – for now."

Julie drove, following the location indicated by the GPS system.

"So what do you have on these guys from the plant?"

"George, you know...I can't..."

"Come on, I'm helping you out, and besides, if something happens, someone other than you and Sean should know the story. Do you really think those other FBI agents are going to tell the truth?"

"Look, Forsythe and Arias have a nice business going, creating so-called 'chemical accidents' for various reasons. Forsythe's technology allows them to infiltrate and control a plant wirelessly, from anywhere in the world. They create these spills for insurance fraud, terrorism or to gain contracts cleaning up. They were doing this in Argentina. We caught Forsythe there demonstrating the technology to organized crime and trying to make a deal, but we couldn't implicate him. He claimed he was just demonstrating technology to clients, for *legitimate* purposes."

"What about the train wreck?"

"We suspect this guy Stark, who took a shot at me today. But that's not proven. Drago is setting a trap to get the accomplice to show up at the hospital. He's going to try to get a confession out of Stark when he's in condition to talk."

"And Hilbaum?"

"We know he's up to something. Assistant Director Gutierrez, my boss, asked him to investigate the reason why the train was diverted through town, instead passing through the plant as usual. Hilbaum never bothered to follow up. When Gutierrez sent an agent to the railway control center, they were able to trace the switch through the computer right away. The guy responsible worked for the railroad, and he was also working for someone who we believe is working with Stark. But we can't prove anything yet."

"Why would they divert the train and cause this horrific accident? What could they possibly gain?"

"That's what Drago is supposed to be finding out."

Julie saw the sign to White Oak Farms and pulled in. The long road, lined with pines, stretched for more than two miles. Julie pulled the car to the side of the road and drove into the woods, until the car was well hidden. *"We can hide here until dark. The GPS system indicated that the call was from this property. Maybe the new FBI team will arrive by then,"* she thought.

[Lunchtime a Wilburn bar]

"Hey Joe, put on the local news, it's time for highlights from last night's ballgame. Maybe they'll show the home run I hit," shouted the young man sitting at the bar.

Joe the bartender tuned to the local TV station and turned the volume up. He said, "There you are, Bob. But I still can't believe you hit a home run."

Bob looked and listened to the station, which showed the local newsman: "Last night the Wilburn Devils beat the Appalachian Beavers five to four. The winning run came on a home run by centerfielder Bob Farmer in the tenth inning. We go now to the highlights."

A picture of the ball field appeared, and Bob shouted, "Yeah, here it is!"

But the view of the ball field changed abruptly to one of the newsman, who was saying, "We have a special report!"

Bob shouted, "No, not now!"

The newsman told the story, "The FBI has just announced that they have caught one of the persons responsible for the train derailment. The person's name is John Stark, a member of the local Circle of Knights group. Authorities say the suspect was shot, but was in the hospital recovering from his wounds. They expect to question the suspect shortly and say they found the explosives that were used by the terrorists. Further information, they say, will be available later today."

The picture of the newsman faded and the ballfield reappeared, "....so it was an exiting finish. Tomorrow the Devils will host the Gilmore Bears," the sports report ended.

[That afternoon, at the OC Chemicals Plant]

"Yes Jim, the communications are set up and I'll be there soon." Bill FitzPatrick said loudly. "Hey Jim, don't worry, the FBI won't know what hit them. They'll be too busy responding to our diversions to be looking for us." Bill hung up the phone and shut off his laptop computer.

Sharon had seen him use the laptop several times today and now walked up to him, "Are you interfacing your laptop to the plant's computer system?"

Bill eyed Sharon intensely, wondering what she'd heard, but chose to dismiss his worst thoughts. "No. This is a Forsythe Company computer they gave me to keep track of employee man-hours and project schedules." He put the laptop in a soft leather carrying case and placed it under the desk. "It has nothing important," he said as he left the office.

Sharon followed Bill to the door and watched him as he walked down the hall and into the restroom. She quickly returned to his desk, took the laptop out of the leather case and turned it upside-down. She unscrewed the cover to the quarter-size clock battery, removed it, and placed it into her jeans pocket. From her other pocket she took out another nearly identical battery disk, placed it into the slot, closed the cover and put the laptop back in its case and under the desk. She quietly walked back to her desk and sat down, just as Bill returned.

"I'm going to be gone all afternoon, Sharon. I have a meeting with Mr. Ashland," said Bill as he walked over to Sharon. He put his right hand gently on her shoulder. "There isn't much going

on today, so if you want you can take off early, I won't say anything."

Sharon paused before replying, "Thanks, I appreciate that Bill."

Bill walked to his desk, picked up the leather case and left the office.

Sharon remained at her desk, staring at her computer screen. She clicked the Netscape icon, typed in the Web site so that she could communicate to Julie and Peter, and read the chat room talk.

Sharon typed, "Mama are you there? Is baby brother with you?" She waited five minutes but there was no reply. She typed another message. "Baby brother, this is baby sister, are you OK?"

She waited five more minutes, but again there was no response.

Sharon typed, "Mama tell Grandma, that the boys are going to do something bad tonight. I don't know where but I'll be watching." She closed out of the Web site and went to the parking lot to feed Grady, who had been left with the guard to keep him cool. The Guard was happy to oblige for the company.

"George, you stay here; I have to make a call," said Julie

Julie got out of the car and stepped far enough away so that George couldn't hear. She dialed Sharon's cell number. "Sharon, it's mama. How are you doing?"

"It's OK, I'm in the car feeding Grady. Things are OK. I overheard FitzPatrick on the phone with Ashland. They were preparing for a big operation, but I didn't get the details."

"Look Sharon, Gutierrez assigned Agent Drago to the case temporarily until backup arrives. He promised he was going to call the sheriff and get Peter out of jail once he was able to talk

with the suspect we shot this morning. Could you just check with the sheriff to make sure Drago did what he promised? I'm a little busy right now."

"Drago knows nothing about me, right?"

"That's top secret. No one knows about you except Peter and Sean. Sean's been captured at White Oak farmhouse about 5 miles from town. I'm there now, but I haven't told Gutierrez yet."

"I heard the name White Oak Farms today, when FitzPatrick was on the phone. Look, Julie, take care of yourself. I've got to get back to the plant. I'll let Gutierrez know what's going on and I'll be sure they speed up the arrival of the cavalry. Sorry I don't have more details about what's going down tonight, but I have plenty of evidence now to prove these guys were involved in many remotely activated chemical accidents."

George looked serious as Julie got back into the car. "So, you still don't trust me. You have to make your phone calls all the way out there."

"George, I can't get you involved, you know that. I do trust you, or you wouldn't be here. At this point, George, you seem to be the only guy I can trust!"

"Gee thanks. Will you marry me?" asked George sarcastically.

"Maybe I should, and quit this damn job!"

"If you ever decide to drop that red-haired narc, any time," said George.

Julie smiled and shook her head. "You know, I think I'd better call Gutierrez!"

George smiled when Julie dialed the number from inside the car.

"Assistant Director Gutierrez, Agent Del Rio here. I'm at the farmhouse where Sean is being held."

"Agent Del Rio, you're on your own now. The FBI team was called off by one of my superiors. My hands are tied. It seems that Agent Hilbaum may have called a buddy of his. He's retaliating against me because I called for his investigation. I think the pollution-for-profit organization has friends high up in the FBI, people who fought this department all the way. Now I know why.

"Julie, do what you can. Sean may or may not be safe. I'll make sure a team goes out there as soon as I can, but it may not be FBI. I have to call some of my own friends in Washington. They aren't going to stop Anna Gutierrez. I swore that when I saw my little girl die in my arms of leukemia. They aren't going to stop me, Julie!"

"Anna, you have our full support. I'll do my best here until you send backup." Julie pressed the disconnect button and closed her eyes.

"What?" asked George.

"The cavalry is not coming, at least not within the next few hours. We're alone here and Sean's in danger. Gutierrez has been stopped, at least for now, by someone higher up in the FBI."

"So, what do we do?"

"Let's wait until nightfall and then try to sneak in."

"Well, I promised I would help, and here I am."

As evening approached, Julie watched the road. The car was well hidden from view. She gave George a nudge once in a while to stop his snoring. She saw a car go by with two men wearing light robes and hoods that partially covered their heads. A few minutes later, another car passed with four men wearing robes and hoods.

"George, wake up!" she whispered nudging him.

"What, what?"

"I just saw two cars headed to the farmhouse. The passengers were wearing hooded robes."

"Oh... that..."

"You know what that's about?"

"Yea, it's a regular meeting of the Circle of Knights."

"I've heard of them. It's a white supremacist group. At first Peter and I suspected such a group may have had something to do with the train wreck."

"Why did you think that?"

"Well, the toxic materials killed so many blacks. I thought it was part of their agenda, you know, because Forsythe and Arias are members?"

"Why would these guys want to destroy their very own property? They mostly rent those homes to black tenants. Lots of them own businesses and they depend on labor from residents in downtown Wilburn. These people have been living here for years. Their agenda is mostly political and business. You know, keeping the contracts in their club, that kind of thing. Keeping the blacks out of their business turf, but using them whenever there's an opportunity for minority-owned business contracts. COK actually has some black members."

"That's sick. Anyway, I bet this is where Forsythe sets up his pollution-for-profit dealings! Why the robes?"

"Well, only those wearing robes can attend the meetings. The robes are given only to members of the organization."

"You seem to know a lot about them."

"They make sure they invite me to their meetings for the P.R."

"Do you wear a robe, too?"

"Yeah, I mean, you know, when they invite me. I have a special membership as a reporter. Usually they read some

speech, they make announcements, and then the members split up into their own private meetings. I'm hardly ever invited to those."

"Could you go to this meeting today?"

"Yes, but my robe is at home, and you won't be allowed into this meeting."

"I attended a political rally this white supremacist group was holding. They didn't stop me then."

"That was a public meeting; this is members only."

"Well, we'll need two robes," said Julie determinedly, as she took the gun from her holster and loaded it.

"What are you going to do?"

"Get the robes."

"Julie, these guys are armed."

Julie walked to the side of the road, holding her gun in one hand and her badge in the other. When one of the cars passed, she shot at the tire and it immediately deflated, forcing the driver to stop. As the passengers got out, Julie walked toward them, pointing her gun and flashing her badge. "FBI. Don't move. You're surrounded."

"This is a legal meeting. It's been announced. You have no reason to arrest us."

"Shut up and do what I say and you won't get hurt!" snapped Julie, shooting at the ground next to the men. Visibly shaken, the two bald, middle-aged men put their hands up.

"George, get over here and bring some of that rope in my trunk." George appeared behind Julie, holding the rope.

"Now you guys, strip! Completely!"

"What is this?"

"I said STRIP damn it!" and this time she shot closer to their feet.

The men disrobed, letting their clothes fall to the ground.

"All of it off, the shorts too and don't say a word or the next one is in your crotch."

The two men took off their underwear and stood completely naked in front of their headlights. "George, tie their hands and legs together." George did as he was asked. "Now, hop over there," said Julie seemingly enjoying the feeling of power she had over these two pathetic guys. "George, tie them to the tree."

Julie waited until the men were securely tied to the tree before she continued. "Now, George, grab this guy's shorts and tear them up into four pieces, and then stuff the material in the guys' mouths. I don't want anyone to know they are here." Turning to the men she added, "Sorry guys, hope your shorts were clean."

When George finished he picked up the two robes, grabbed the clothes and put them in their trunk. Julie got into the men's car and drove it into the woods, making sure it was well hidden. She put on one of the robes and George put on the other.

"Julie, I think you better hide in the trunk and sneak in after we pass their checkpoint. By the way, you enjoyed that too much back there," said George as he got into the driver's seat.

"Yes, I definitely did!" she answered, without apologies. Julie got into the opened trunk and held the cover closed, but made sure it didn't lock.

Once at the farm, they parked near the other cars. A man wearing a robe, but no hood, approached. Julie crouched down in the trunk and George got out of the car quickly. "And who are you?"

"Press, I was invited," said George flashing his press card.

"Press, I didn't know we invited anyone today."

"I'm a member, I've come to other meetings."

"OK, go ahead," said the man turning his attention to other cars that were arriving.

As the man walked away, George knocked on the trunk to let Julie know she could get out of the car now. She covered her face with the hood before she and George headed for the building.

"I'll check out that barn over there and see if I can find Sean," she whispered. There was no moon so she crossed the open field unnoticed. George walked to the meeting with the rest of the hooded members.

Julie had brought her flashlight and used it to get around inside the barn. Fearful of meeting someone, she walked silently and carefully. She was checking the animal stalls when she noticed a metal chain around a post. Looking inside, she found Sean asleep on the floor. Julie rushed over and knelt beside him. "Sean, Sean," she whispered, nudging him and shining the flashlight in his face. Sean's eyes finally opened. "It's Julie, wake up."

"Julie, how did you get here?"

"George helped. He's a member of that group, you know."

"I was hoping you wouldn't risk this alone."

"I had to. Gutierrez ran into some trouble in Washington. Hilbaum has friends in high places. Come on, I have to get you lose."

"See if you can find an ax or some pliers."

Julie found some tools at the end of the barn. "Here, wire cutters." She walked over to Sean and used them to cut the link between his cuffs. "Let's go. I have a car in the parking lot. We'll hide in the trunk and leave with George."

Sean nodded. Once outside, they looked around, and since no one seemed to be around, they headed for the car with Julie

leading. But as they were about to get into the car, Sean felt the cold hard end of a rifle on his back. "Stop or I'll shoot."

At the meeting, the congregation of the COKs hushed when the grand chairman called order. Their hoods where down; their faces visible. George was sitting a few rows from the front taking notes. He looked for Forsythe or Arias, whom he knew attended the meetings. The fact that they were nowhere in the room worried him.

After a few welcoming remarks, the chairman spoke:

"Many of our members have been affected by the recent train accident. We'll be devoting this meeting to discussing the issues that affect the COK community. Discussion is open to the floor."

Several of the men raised their hands and the chair recognized one. A middle-aged man with a mustache and glasses went up to the front and stood glancing at the congregation before reading a prepared speech.

"Recently, the Circle of Knights has been accused by the media of direct responsibility for the train accident. We are all suspects." A loud response from the audience caused the speaker to pause.

"News that two members of COK have been arrested in connection with causing this terrible accident has just been picked up by the media. It's no secret that the FBI has been investigating the incident for weeks. We know that if any COK members were involved, they acted alone. This organization does not support acts of terrorism. It's our membership that has lost friends, employees and relatives in this accident. Let's go around the room. Each member please share with us how this accident has affected you." The man with the mustache glanced at George first, to see if he was taking notes, then his eyes moved to someone in the back who raised his hand.

"I lost my friend Joe, my business and three employees. My family and I went into town to help get people out. Since the

media accused our group of causing this accident, people are calling me a racist, even a murderer. It's not true."

Another man stood up. "The explosions shattered my windows and killed two employees; one got trampled. I was around the corner. I transported as many people as I could out and helped in the shelter. Now the families of the dead employees are threatening to sue me because of my involvement in what they are calling a racist organization. COK has done a lot for my business, but being associated with this group makes me an accomplice to a terrible evil. My own children are calling me a flaming racist! I take these robes off today and quit. If members were involved, they'd better not meet up with me."

Another man spoke. "I agree. I just heard the news announcement by the FBI about a half hour ago. They mentioned who was involved. There was a shooting in the National Forest. An FBI agent was attacked and a good friend of the family, Mr. Basidia, was nearly killed by two COK members! It turns out they may have been the ones who caused the accident."

"Who told you these men are members of this group, Thurton?"

"Someone I respect, someone who was there! This is the 21st century and I've outgrown this kind of rhetoric. You promised respect for our race, as if we were under attack. Meanwhile, you use our political power for your own selfish, dirty dealings. You know who came to my wife's aid when the fumes overcame her? A black firefighter. He saved her life and didn't care that she was the wife of a COK member. I apologized to that man and I am out of here too!"

"This is a small community, blacks and whites depend on each other. My crops were destroyed by this racist atrocity and my field will be contaminated for years. Who was watching out for the environment here? Not you white power assholes! You didn't come to my aid when the field was burning. It was the farm help that put the fires out, black farm help."

"Gentlemen, order! I assure you that if those men you know about caused this accident, they had their own personal reasons and did not act for this organization. Our philosophy has always been to respect one another, and be proud of our race. We are trying to make sure we are not discriminated against for being white. We don't do that by destroying our black brothers! We should be proud of our race, our accomplishments and our contributions to the betterment of this community."

Another man, not waiting to be recognized, yelled, "I ain't proud now! I'm sick, literally. I haven't slept or felt good since all hell broke loose with that chemical spill. You let these criminals into this group and now we're all blamed."

George was frantically taking notes, realizing that he was probably witnessing a turning point in this old organization. It could be worthy of a national story. *"This is my ticket out of stinking Wilburn,"* he thought.

Some of the members walked out, dropping their robes on the floor. The Grand Master tried stopping them. "If you walk out of here today, there could be consequences to your business. You know the rules; those that don't join us live as outsiders."

One of the men pulled out a gun and pointed it at the Grand Master, who was now blocking the door. Two other men drew handguns. "You can't do any more damage than this. You have destroyed what we had left. Now get the hell out my way!"

The door slammed behind the three men who stormed out. More than half of the members threw down their robes and walked out.

Chapter Seventeen

Poetic Justice

While Grady was eating, Sharon took her cellular phone and dialed Peter's number. Getting no answer, she stopped the call, dialed another number, and waited for a reply.

"This is Deputy Norton; can I help you?"

Sharon responded, "Yes, I'm looking for someone, his name is Peter Wells. Is he being held in jail?"

"Yes Ma'am."

"Are you sure?"

"Why, yes Ma'am. He's been here for a couple of days. He doesn't look like he's going anywhere."

"Deputy, I'd like to speak to the sheriff. Is he there?"

"Yes Ma'am, but he's very busy right now."

"Deputy, it's very important that I talk to him. You just tell him that."

"OK, Ma'am, but who should I tell him is calling?"

"I'd prefer not to say to you."

Curtly the deputy placed Sharon on hold and punched in the sheriff's extension.

"Sheriff, I have a woman on the phone who says it's important that she speak to you. She won't give me her name."

The sheriff waved at the three deputies in his office and pointed to the door. As the last man left the office, the sheriff replied, "OK, put the woman on."

He answered on the first beep. "This is Sheriff Williams, what can I do for you?"

"Sheriff, you don't know me, but I'm an FBI agent working undercover in town." Sharon spoke softly and with the most cordial of southern accents.

The sheriff rolled his eyes and responded, "What! Is everyone in town now an FBI agent?"

"No, Sheriff. But this one has it from inside sources that the person responsible for the train crash is in the town hospital. I was also told this information was supposed to be passed on to you so that you could release Peter. However, I now know that you weren't told, and I suspect something went wrong at the hospital. I can't go investigate without blowing my cover, so I need someone who can."

"So you want me to check it out!" the sheriff said.

"I appreciate you volunteering, Sheriff; you know how to make another southerner feel welcome." Sharon sounded very seductive; the sheriff couldn't say no.

"The hospital did inform the office of a patient admitted today with a gunshot wound and it's normal practice to investigate. I can send a deputy over to take a statement and check it out."

Sharon raised her voice, "No Sheriff, don't send a deputy. There are too many people involved and it's difficult to know whom you can trust. Please do it yourself. There is Agent Drago, who was to interrogated the suspect and set a trap to catch his accomplice." Then softly she added, "I don't want this getting out to others."

"OK, I'll check it out personally," the sheriff acquiesced.

"Thank you, Sheriff."

The sheriff hung up the phone, grabbed his jacket and left his office. He stopped to tell the deputy on duty, "In case anyone is asking for me, tell them I'll be out for a while."

The deputy, who had been writing a report, looked up at the sheriff and started to open his mouth to ask where the he was going, but decided instead to answer, "OK." The deputy recalled that the sheriff often liked to be alone and was annoyed when he had to provide his deputies with his itinerary.

The sheriff drove down Main Street to the hospital, which was once a small local clinic. But as the number of chemical facilities around town increased, the hospital required additional space. It was the local Business Association that donated the land for the required expansion. To most in town it seemed to be a win-win situation for the town and the chemical plants. The town got the needed medical facilities and the chemical plants got a lot of good will and a large tax write-off.

However, a few years later, an article by George Reed in the local paper had raised doubts about the purpose for the donation of land. He tried to prove that the land had been a dump site for chemical wastes from the plants, and that if the companies had retained the property they would have been faced with a potentially long and expensive site cleanup. But George couldn't provide documented proof and the story quickly died.

It was late afternoon when the sheriff arrived at the hospital and parked in the emergency parking lot. He had been at the hospital many times, but usually in the evening or at night. This time he noted that there were many more people entering and leaving. He remembered three weeks earlier, when the train had derailed, the activity was almost frantic, because the hospital had to be evacuated and patients transported to nearby towns.

The sheriff walked through the emergency entrance without being stopped or noticed. The usual security guard wasn't present, and the nurses were too busy to look up. Today there was order. Nurses were doing their job and patients were quietly waiting, but there was also a sense of overwork. Since the train

derailment, the hospital had seen a thirty percent increase in emergency room traffic, but it didn't have the budget or staff to effectively handle this increase.

The sheriff walked to the main lobby and up to the information area. Ignoring the two other persons talking to the receptionist, he said, "I'm looking for a patient that was brought in earlier today. He was admitted by the FBI."

The receptionist's mouth was wide open as he turned to see the sheriff's stone face. The receptionist quickly turned to the others and said, "Excuse me for a second." Turning back to the sheriff, he said, "Do you know the patient's name?"

"No. He may be listed as John Doe."

After looking at a list of names on the computer, the receptionist said, "We have a patient brought in at 10 a.m. When they brought him in he was listed as John Doe, but his name is John Stark. He's on the third floor, in critical condition, recovering from surgery."

The sheriff quietly turned and walked toward the elevators.

"You're welcome," called out the receptionist in a tight voice. The sheriff responded by shaking his head, but didn't look back.

It was a long wait for the elevator, and when the sheriff got on, it was packed. The sheriff, a couple and an elderly man with a white beard got off on the third floor. He walked down the long corridor to his right until he reached a series of double doors. As the sheriff slowly walked through the first set of doors to the recovery room, a nurse met him. "Can I help you, sheriff?"

The sheriff raised his eyebrows as he saw the nurse, "Why Mary, imagine running into you."

"Well I do work at the hospital. Are you looking for someone?"

Before he could answer, loud beeps from the adjacent room made Mary turn and enter the room. The sheriff followed and

waited till Mary reached over the bed and adjusted the control of oxygen to the patient.

"I'm looking for John Stark. He was brought in this morning. He may have had a gunshot wound."

"We finished operating on him four hours ago, and then he was in the recovery room for a while. Two FBI agents came in and took him out."

"Mary, do you know where they took him?"

"Sorry sheriff, I didn't ask. But I don't think they took him out of the hospital. He wasn't in any condition to travel."

"Thank you Mary," the sheriff said with a smile as he turned and left the recovery room. He stood outside the double doors and looked down the corridor. He walked a short distance, stopped, looked into a room at his right and noticed a pair of empty beds. An attendant was busy mopping the floor. "Can I help you?"

The sheriff turned without answering and continued down the hall, passing an occupied room on his left before coming to a closed door. He started to walk further but when he heard footsteps from inside the room he stopped. He opened the door, stood in the entrance and stared at the person inside.

"Close that door, sheriff!" shouted Agent Hilbaum. He was standing between the two beds waving a gun with one hand and had the other arm around a tall, thin man who was handcuffed and had a gag stuffed in his mouth.

The sheriff let the door close. "Frank. What the heck are you doing with that man?" Behind the far bed another agent was holding a needle and appeared to have just given the person in that bed a shot of something. Looking directly at the other agent, the sheriff asked, "And who are you and what are you doing?"

"Cut the crap, sheriff. These are the two men responsible for the train derailment." Frank said. "The man behind the bed is Agent Drago. He helped capture these two."

The sheriff moved farther into the room, "What are you going to do with them? Do you want me to take them to jail?"

Frank replied, "No, not now. That one needs hospital care," nodding toward the man on the far side of the room.

"What about the other?" asked the sheriff.

Taking a step toward Frank, the sheriff asked again, "Can I take this other suspect?"

Frank waved his gun, "No, sheriff. Look, these guys are not worth it. We're going to take care of this."

The sheriff backed off a step, "OK, then I guess I'll be going," and he turned toward the door.

"What brought you to the hospital, sheriff?" asked Frank.

The sheriff didn't turn around but responded, "I was told there was a gunshot victim here and I came to get a statement."

"Who informed you, the hospital?"

"Sure. It's standard procedure."

"But isn't it unusual for you personally to take a statement, sheriff? And your timing is just too coincidental with our capture of this second suspect only minutes ago." Frank tightened his grip on the suspect.

The sheriff shrugged his shoulder and said, "Well, I guess you realize that someone else is aware of your intentions." Suddenly, the sheriff spun around, holding his gun chest-high and against his body.

Frank didn't see the gun until the sheriff fired. The recoil jerked the sheriff's body back a foot, but the bullet hit its target, ripping into Frank's right shoulder. Frank lost his grip on the suspect he was holding and fell on top of him. The sheriff had a chance for a second shot, but this time he missed Frank. The bullet hit the oxygen tank on the other side of the bed, causing the pressurized gas to begin leaking out of the tank.

Drago crouched down behind the bed and pulled out his gun. Meanwhile Frank took a half-sighted aim and fired at the sheriff while shouting, "You bastard! Drago, you have to stop the sheriff."

The sheriff narrowly escaped the bullet as he dove behind the empty bed nearest the door. The bullet logged in the door. Drago fired at the sheriff as he ran out the door. The bullet grazed the sheriff in the left leg.

The sheriff raised himself up and peered over the bed at Frank, who had grabbed his wounded shoulder with his gun hand.

"You're hurt bad Frank. Give it up!" the sheriff snapped.

Frank slowly responded, "I can't."

The sheriff leaned his head around the end of the bed, rose up with his gun and fired another shot. This one hit Frank in the left side of his chest, causing him to drop his gun. The sheriff cautiously circled around the bed and grabbed the fallen gun. He saw the suspect lying on the floor between the beds, still handcuffed and with his feet tied. Frank was now slouched over the other suspect in the bed.

The sheriff took Frank's head in one of his hands. "This was foolish, Frank."

Frank was bleeding from two chest wounds. Barely conscious he asked, "Why?"

The sheriff held Frank, "It's just wrong Frank. The FBI knows you're involved. They have someone on the inside. They probably don't know that Agent Drago is involved too." Frank drifted into unconsciousness and the sheriff remained there looking at him until two security guards pushed open the door and shouted, "Drop your weapons!"

"It's all clear. I'm the sheriff."

The guards, still cautious, came in with guns aimed directly ahead. When they saw the sheriff, they lowered their guns and said, loudly enough for those in the corridor to hear, "It's OK, but we need some nurses and a doctor in here."

The doctor checked Frank. "He's dead." Moving to the patient in the bed, the doctor said, "He's dead, too. He appears to have been drugged." The doctor examined the suspect on the floor. "This one's OK. Just a few bruises. Help me get him up."

The guards bent down, untied the suspect and lifted him up.

"I want him in custody and taken to jail," the sheriff told the guards, as one of them escorted the man from the room.

The doctor turned to the sheriff and asked, "What about you?"

"You tell me. You're the doc."

The doctor looked at the sheriff's leg. "You'll be OK sheriff, but we need to clean this wound." Turning to the other guard, the doctor added, "Put him on the bed."

As the nurse cleaned and dressed the wound, the sheriff took out his phone and called his office.

"Sheriff's office," answered a deputy.

"This is Sheriff Williams. I've been shot and am at the hospital. There's a suspect loose here. Send two cars, I don't want him escaping."

When he hung up, the sheriff turned to the guard. "Have someone at each entrance and alert them to check everyone leaving. We're looking for a white male. He's an FBI agent, about six-feet one-inch tall with black, short hair. He's wearing a suit and is armed and dangerous, but I want him taken alive. My deputies will be here shortly to take charge."

When the guard didn't move, and the sheriff shouted, "Go. Do your job!" Turning to the doctor the sheriff asked, "How soon can I walk?"

"You could walk now, but I advise you to rest that leg today."

The Sheriff waited for the nurse to finish wrapping the bandage, then he slid off the bed and stood up. "I don't have the luxury doc. There's too much happening and I need to find answers sooner rather than later. These FBI agents have been screwing around with this case long enough. It's about time I did my job."

"It's your leg that will hurt."

The sheriff limped out of the room. From inside the maintenance closet, Drago watched through the slightly opened door as the sheriff entered the elevator. Once the sheriff was gone, Drago took out his cellular phone and punched a number. He spoke softly. "Hugo, this is Drago. The sheriff killed Frank and has the hospital closed off. I heard him tell Frank an FBI Agent working undercover tipped him off about us, so be careful. I don't think the FBI knows about our plans, but you better make sure they don't find out. You know what you have to do. Good-bye brother." Drago ended the call, took off his suit and buried it in the bottom of the clothing bin.

He put on one of the fresh doctor's uniforms that were stacked on the shelf, checked the hallway, and seeing no one, walked quietly to the stairs. He walked down three flights and made his way toward the busy emergency entrance. About thirty feet from the exit he saw a deputy and a guard standing watch. He ducked behind one of the many curtains that separated the Emergency Room from the rest of the ward. He peered at the exit from behind the curtain and was surprised when he heard, "Doc, can you help me?"

Drago turned, and saw a teenager sitting on an examination table and said, "What's wrong?"

The boy shook his right foot; "I hurt it during baseball practice. I can't walk on it."

Drago took the foot and applied gentle pressure along the length, "Tell me when it hurts."

The boy remained still, but when Drago pushed the back of the heel the boy painfully yelled, "Yea, that's the spot."

"Looks like you sprained it. You'll have to stay off of it for a week. I'll have to bandage it tightly. You lie back and rest; I'll be back shortly."

The boy put his head down and sighed.

Drago stopped at the chair and picked up the boy's jacket and cap and carried them out of the area without the boy noticing. He walked down the corridor and entered the public restroom.

Back in the barn, Forsythe was tying Julie to a chair after he tied Sean to a post.

"I need to know how you knew I was here, Ms. Del Rio, and who else knows about us." He twisted her wrist behind her back.

"We've been trailing you and the FBI knows all about your toxic dirty dealings. You're the worst kind of criminal, for crimes against the environment are crimes against humanity. You'll be tried by an international court and could be executed. Killing us won't save you; it will make things worse. How can you live with yourself after causing that train wreck? The blood of this whole town is in your hands."

Sean very gently tapped Julie's foot with his, to signal her to be quiet.

"Those idiots acted alone and almost screwed up our plans. They blackmailed us and came through with their own dirty threat," said Forsythe, who was stroking Julie's face and eyeing her body as he finished tying the knots.

"So you knew and said nothing and warned no one to protect your ass," spat Julie. Sean again tapped her foot.

"I'm getting a bit tired of your mouth, nigger," said Forsythe grabbing Julie's hair tightly in his hands.

"Leave her alone!" said Sean trying to loosen the knots tying his hands.

Julie was like a madwoman, out of control. She continued yelling at Forsythe. "You are responsible for murdering hundreds of people in this town and destroying the environment, leaving toxic materials that will sicken generations to come. How can you even look at yourself in a mirror?"

At this Forsythe grabbed Julie's face and squeezed hard enough to cause her to scream from the pain.

"I don't want to mark that pretty brown face. I know how to shut you up, though. Don't worry, after I'm done with him I'll have you to myself, brown sugar."

Forsythe kicked Sean in the stomach and punched him in the face. "No, stop!" yelled Julie, to no avail. "Please, do anything you want to me, I promise I won't fight you, just don't hurt him any more!"

But Sean was on the ground, bleeding and out cold. Forsythe turned his attentions to Julie, unbuttoning her blouse and caressing her as he spoke.

"You'll do this for your partner. You're such an environmentalist. Let me tell you, the environment isn't in danger, we humans are. We're making ourselves sick. I don't cause the pollution, the legitimate businesses do. I just profit while I can, because tomorrow, we die...so why not have some fun now?"

"What are you planning to do tonight?"

"Tonight, tonight, we'll see the sky be bright. There will be fireworks for all of us. The plant is going to blow and while the townspeople try to put out the fire, some of them will choke to death slowly. We'll be off with the plates and enough money to buy our own island in the Pacific."

"What plates..."

As Forsythe ripped Julie's blouse he said, "The printing plates for hundred dollar bills. Maybe I can take you with me, baby." And he buried his face in her chest as Julie bit her lip and

tears ran down her cheeks. "Remember, if you fight me, he dies. I always wanted to have me an FBI agent."

Forsythe's partner Arias entered the barn, as Forsythe was about to ejaculate his evil seed into Julie. "God damn it! What are you doing?"

"Having a little fun."

"Get off of her. We have to get moving. The train will be passing through in about two hours. It's not safe here. The Circle of Knights members are quitting in droves since the fucking announcement that one of their members was responsible for the train accident, and we have no backup. Kill them and get out of here."

"We can't kill them. They'll be useful hostages. And besides, I want this bitch for myself," said Forsythe.

"We'll take them with us to the warehouse. The feds know about this place. They're going to be here any minute. Move it!" shouted Arias.

"We'll meet again, sugar," said Forsythe as he buttoned his pants. He untied Julie's hands, covered her half-naked body with Sean's jacket and buttoned it. "I don't think we'll need to tie your hands any more." She said nothing, while eyeing Sean, who wasn't moving.

"Get up!" said Arias, kicking Sean in the ribs. But Sean was unconscious and lay limp on the floor. "I need some help here," Arias said to one of the men outside.

Julie was blindfolded and Sean carried and thrown into the back seat of the car. Forsythe drove them to a nearby warehouse. Two men brought Sean's limp body into a room and dropped him on the floor. Forsythe led Julie to the room. At the doorway he placed his hands on Julie's hips and brought her closer to him. "Why don't you join us?"

Julie stared at him and said nothing.

"Come on," said one of the men and Forsythe threw Julie into the room with Sean and locked the door.

There was a connection for a hose in the corner. Julie was able to get some water onto a piece of what was left of her skirt.

She sat on the floor and carefully untied Sean's hands, noticing the marks around his wrists. As she pressed the cold compress on his face, she cradled him, as she would a baby and lightly kissed his face. She looked at her legs, noticing the dark bruises on her thighs that Forsythe had left as he raped her. She suddenly realized that the environment around Wilburn was about to be raped as well. She saw the face of Jeramiah's little girl, the flames, the people gasping for breath and she wept as she stroked Sean's face, feeling helpless to stop the terrorists and the imminent catastrophe.

Bill FitzPatrick parked his car at the back of the warehouse and entered through a small door that was part of the much larger two-door garage. Inside were five four-wheel drive vehicles and two large vans. Two of the four-wheel drive units had machine guns mounted on the back, while the other three were loaded with munitions and automatic weapons. Ten men were busy loading the vehicles and didn't pay attention to Bill as he walked past them and into the room with Jim Ashland, Matt and Steve.

"Hi Jim. Are you ready?" asked Bill.

"Of course I'm ready! But I've been worried about you."

"Don't worry, Jim. I told you I'd be prepared," said Bill loudly as he put the leather case on the table and took out the laptop. "I have everything I need in here. The laptop is hooked up with a wireless modem and the location of the explosives is indicated on the software. I can blow up any part of that chemical plant or the train tracks whenever I want and wherever I am, and in any order I want, with a single touch of this button."

Bill touched the button, and Jim lunged toward him. "What are you doing?" he shouted.

"You're too worried Jim, the computer isn't on. Here have a beer." Bill grabbed two beers from a six-pack on the table, and handed one to Jim.

"Why shouldn't I be worried? We're holding two FBI agents; we're going to hold up a federal train and blow up a chemical plant," replied Jim as he took a long swallow. "We'll be lucky to stay alive, not to mention get away with the plates and the money."

"You have to relax. There's no turning back now. Anyway, we have all the surprises we need in this computer. Don't worry. Besides, the only people who know the whole plan are you, Jeff and myself. Even Hugo doesn't know the details. Have another beer." For thirty minutes Jim and Bill drank and looked over the map that was laid out on the table.

Jeff entered the room. "The men are ready. It's time to start. Set your watches to exactly 8 p.m. Bill, get that laptop operating."

Bill placed the laptop on the table and turned it on. He clicked an icon and a map of the OC Chemicals plant appeared on the screen. "Jeff, I'm ready."

"OK Bill, blow up the large storage tank," ordered Jeff.

"You want to have the honors?" asked Bill as he offered Jim the computer.

Jim looked at Bill and closed his eyes before replying, "No, that's your job."

Bill pressed the button and looked at the screen.

Jim said, "What do you expect to see on the screen? You'll not going to see it blow up."

"No, but I did get a confirmation that the signal was sent and received," answered Bill.

"Come on. It's time to go," signaled Forsythe to Bill and Jim.

"Matt, Steve; you two stay here and watch our guests. We can be reached with this phone," said Jeff handing Steve a cellular phone. "Press star one to reach me. If you're discovered, blow up the place with the two FBI agents. You can do that by pressing star nine."

Steve nodded and placed the phone on the table.

The rest of the men, including Jeff, Jim and Bill, got into the vehicles. The two large garage doors opened and the convoy drove out.

Julie listened to the conversation that Bill and Jim were having in the other room, but returned to Sean's side when she saw him move his arm and open his eyes. "How are you feeling?" she asked.

"Like hell," said Sean placing his hand on his head. "My head is pounding and I think that asshole broke a rib." He started to sit up gingerly. "What's the matter?" asked Sean, on seeing Julie weep.

"Nothing. I just didn't know if you were ever going to wake up."

"It takes a lot of pounding to bring Sean Ryan down Lassie," and he wiped her tears as he stroked her face. "I know what you went through for my sake, Julie. I'm sorry, I tried to get up but I passed out."

"If it wasn't for me maybe he wouldn't have beaten you. I should have kept my mouth shut when you warned me."

"He was going to beat me anyway." Sean looked around the room and asked, "Did I miss anything important?"

"The terrorists left about fifteen minutes ago."

"Tell me everything that happened," said Sean, as he looked for an exit.

"It was dark when we left the farmhouse. They blindfolded me and threw you in the back seat. The trip from the farmhouse

had to be less than twenty minutes and we were moving very fast, so I think we were on the highway. As soon as we got here, they locked us in this room and another man arrived and sat in the next room with Ashland. He was very loud and they talked of blowing up the chemical plant as a diversion so they could rob the armored train carrying master plates and hundred dollar bills. I couldn't hear the details but it seemed that this other man had a computer that was linked to explosives." Julie watched for Sean's reaction.

"Sounds like the same thing they did in Buenos Aires, but on a larger scale. Julie, do you know how many terrorists there are?"

"I heard several vehicles drive off, maybe five or six, when they left the warehouse. I think a couple of men remained because once in a while I hear voices from the next room."

"Is there any way out of here?" asked Sean.

"Only through that door, and it leads to the other room. Do you care to try?"

"That's OK, we'll wait for an opportunity." Sean stood up and checked the door. "Unfortunately there's no window," he said as he sat down next to Julie. "Things don't look too good. The terrorists are ready to strike *again*. The town is in jeopardy *again* and here we are helpless to do anything about it *again*. I guess you think our efforts are quite pitiful. I know it seems that the more we try to help the town, the more trouble there is." Sean rubbed his face and continued, "and the more pollution and environmental damage is done to these innocent people."

Julie placed her right hand on Sean's shoulder. "Sure, these people are victims of terrible environmental acts, but the one thing I have learned from this case is that people don't have to be innocent bystanders and many are doing something about it. Once it's clear who the enemy is, the people join in the fight. They've gone into the forest to find evidence; they've protested

and lobbied the politicians and press," Julie sighed and continued, "but, yes, I do feel quite helpless at times like this."

Sean stood up and whispered, "Did you hear that?"

"Hear what?"

Sean said, "It sounded..." but stopped to listen.

"This is the FBI. Give yourselves up and come out now," shouted the voice through the bullhorn.

In the next room, Steve turned to Matt: "It's time to get out and blow this place."

Sean pulled on the doorknob and yelled. "You're trapped. The place is surrounded. Open the door!"

"You and your FBI buddies can have this place. After we blow it up there won't be much left. People will think it's just another Waco, but this time it'll will be the FBI guys who die," said Steve, grinning. "Matt, let's go through the underground tunnel. It'll let us out at the river's edge. Take the phone and we'll blow this place up once we're out."

"What about the two in that room?" asked Matt.

"They won't feel a thing. Now let's go!"

Matt ran to the adjacent room and opened the door. Steve turned around and shouted, "What? You fool!" and grabbed the phone from the table.

As soon as the door opened, Sean ran out and rushed toward Steve, who dropped the phone, and started to raise his rifle. Before he could pull the trigger, Matt hit Steve in the back of his head with the butt of his shotgun and Steve dropped his gun and followed it to the ground. As Sean grabbed the rifle, Matt turned to him and said, "I'm on your side."

The announcement took Julie and Sean entirely by surprise. "I didn't know we had someone on the inside," said Julie

"I'm not an FBI Agent. I live in Wilburn but I'm a member of CAP. Peter thought it would be useful to have a local go undercover, so he contacted me before he arrived in Wilburn," explained Matt.

"OK, I get the picture. Now help me tie his hands," ordered Sean while pointing to Steve lying unconscious on the floor.

Sean used his handcuffs, which were on the table, to cuff Steve. Matt and Sean lifted Steve from the floor and shook him until he was conscious again. The four of them walked out of the warehouse and into the parking lot. Two FBI agents holding rifles with night scopes immediately approached them. Eight other agents, who had surrounded the warehouse, converged on the group within minutes.

An agent with a mobile phone approached Sean. "Mr. Ryan, are you OK?"

"It's good to see you again, Agent Martinez. We're tired but fine."

Martinez approached Julie. "I have the Assistant director on the phone. She wants to talk to you, Ms. Del Rio," said Martinez, handing the phone to Julie.

"Agent Del Rio here."

"Ms. Del Rio. I'm glad our team finally got to you."

"But Mrs. Gutierrez, how did you find us? Was it George?"

"No. It was Sharon. She gave us this location using a tracking device she planted in one of the computers that the terrorists are using."

"Mrs. Gutierrez, the terrorists are planning to blow up the plant by remote control as a way to divert attention from the train robbery."

"What train?"

"The train that's carrying the treasury bills and plates. It's passing through town tonight. Ma'am, the terrorists don't care that they'll cause widespread environmental damage. I'm afraid we're facing a Bhopal- type accident right here in Wilburn, the likes of which this country has never seen before."

"Julie, it's already begun. An explosion of a storage tank has caused a huge fire at the plant and there's likely to be more explosions, from what you're saying. Unfortunately, when the news stations broadcast earlier today that they had caught the persons responsible for the train accident, the FBI security team left the plant."

"Why did they leave?"

"Agent Warrant Fieldman and his team were sent to investigate the threatening letters received by Arias a few weeks ago. Their investigation was inconclusive. Based on Sharon's reports, I have confirmed my suspicions that Arias and his associates likely planted those letters. That's why I didn't want the local FBI and authorities to know about Sharon. With some help from some good friends in the agency, I was able to reassign Agent Fieldman's team to this rescue team. That's how I was able to get backup for you in spite of my foes high in the agency."

"Thank you for finally sending in the cavalry, Mrs. Gutierrez, but we need to hurry now."

Julie handed the phone to Martinez, and stood next to Sean while Martinez listened to Mrs. Gutierrez.

"Yes Ma'am, Agent Ryan told me that the terrorists had plans to rob a train," said Martinez. "OK Ma'am, my team will contact the treasury department and find out which train is carrying the money and plates. Our priority will be to stop the terrorists from robbing the train." Martinez ended the phone conversation.

"You should take Matt with you; maybe he can help identify the terrorists. We'll lock Steve up at the sheriff's office," Sean

told Martinez. Turning to Matt, he asked, "Can I borrow your car?"

Matt handed his keys to Sean and pointed to a vehicle parked on the side of the warehouse. Matt left with the FBI team, leaving Sean and Julie with their prisoner.

Sean led Steve into the back of the pickup and locked one side of the handcuffs to a large tool chest that was permanently mounted to the vehicle. "We ought to hurry, Lassie," said Sean as he waved Julie to the truck and painfully got down from the box.

"Wait a second. I need his shirt and maybe even his pants."

Sean unlocked Steve and pointed a gun at him. "OK, you heard her! Strip!"

"A bit big, but I'll need some coverage at the plant!" Julie took the clothes and went into the pickup to change. Sean again locked Steve, now wearing only a pair of boxer shorts, to the pickup and got into the passenger side.

"You drive, Lassie," said Sean, handing Julie the keys. Julie was surprised by Sean's request, but placed the key into the ignition, took a deep breath, and drove out of the warehouse as fast as she could.

"What are we going to do about this chemical disaster? How are we going to stop these terrorists?" asked Julie.

"I don't know, Lassie; just drive to town."

"Sean, What's up? I got the feeling you wanted to say something back there."

"Something doesn't feel right and I didn't want to say anything in front of Agent Martinez. I just don't think Martinez is going to stop the terrorists from blowing up the plant."

"What do you mean?"

"You heard Martinez. He said he was going to locate the train. He's assuming the train is where it's supposed to be. What if it isn't? Just like the train that derailed in town."

"If that's true, then he may be too late! But what can we do? We're heading back to town."

"We have to stop the one who controls the bombs. Julie, do you have a phone?"

"I picked up your phone at the warehouse. Take it; it's in my pocketbook. Who are you going to call?"

"I'm calling Sharon," said Sean as he punched in Sharon's cellular number.

"But you'll blow her cover!"

"For all we know they've already found her out," answered Sean, waiting for Sharon to pick up.

"This is Sean Ryan. Sharon, is that you?"

"Yes, Sean. Are you OK?"

"Yes, Julie and I are fine. You seem to be in a noisy place Sharon, can you talk?"

"Yes, but we're trying to put out a large fire at the storage tanks."

"I know about the explosion. Do you know who's controlling these bombs?"

"I think the bombs are detonated from Mr. FitzPatrick's computer. The same computer that has the tracking device."

"Good! Can you give the location to Justice? He might be able to disable the computer. Can you do that?"

"Yes, I'll head back to my office and run the tracking program."

"Julie and I will be there soon. How are things at the plant?"

"Very confusing; the fire department and most of the sheriff's department is here, and I don't think we can handle any more chemical explosions," replied Sharon, as she abruptly ended the conversation and hurried back to the control room.

Sean sniffed the now pungent air and said to Julie, "I smell burning gasoline. We need to go directly to the plant."

"What about our prisoner?"

"He'll be fine; we'll lock him to the vehicle," said Sean with a smile. "I have an idea. It's going to be a madhouse at the plant. Park the car in the contractor's lot, next to Sharon's truck."

Julie turned into the contractor's entrance and drove to the end of the lot. A soft breeze was blowing smoke across the parking lot, making it difficult to see the cars. From the far end of the lot, Sean and Julie heard a dog bark. It was Grady, tied to a shady tree next to Sharon's truck. Julie parked the pickup and asked, "What do we do now?"

"Untie Grady; we're taking him into the plant. I worked with Grady several times in our war on drugs, but before that he sniffed out bombs," said Sean.

Julie untied Grady and handed the leash to Sean.

"You can't leave me here. Take me to the sheriff's office," shouted Steve.

"I don't trust anyone, so tonight you're staying here," answered Sean.

Sean and Julie ran, as Grady led the way into the guardhouse.

"What's that dog doing in here?" shouted the surprised guard.

"He's coming into the plant!" Sean shouted back.

"No he's not! No dogs allowed, by order of the plant manager," the guard replied.

"Then get me the plant manager," ordered Sean. "I'm with the FBI and we need the dog. He's a specially trained canine agent."

The guard dialed the phone and looked at Grady. "He's a nice-looking dog, but orders are orders. Maybe if the plant manager says it's OK...," said the guard while waiting for someone to answer the phone.

"They said the plant manager was not answering his page. You know they're busy fighting a fire and he could be tied up right now."

"So a terrorist can get into this plant, but a dog can't!" bellowed Sean ready to pull a gun on the guard.

But Julie put up her hand out to stop Sean. She leaned over the counter and said, "Since the plant manager is not available, why don't you make the decision? This dog can find bombs, maybe even a bomb here in the control room. If he finds a bomb you'll be a hero and if he doesn't no one will ever know he was here. So you have nothing to lose and a lot to gain."

"Putting it that way, I guess it'll be OK to let him in," replied the guard as he rubbed his chin.

Julie quickly kissed the guard's forehead and then hurried into the plant, with Sean and Grady right behind.

"Nice job," said Sean.

"Now Grady is all yours. So where to?"

"We have to find Sharon."

Julie stopped a worker and asked, "Where's the control room?"

"It's the short building next to those two columns," said the worker as he pointed down the road.

"Thanks," shouted Sean as he and Julie ran toward the indicated building.

The flames from the storage tank were visible in the distance and thick black smoke obscured any stars and moonlight. The pungent smell of the burning gasoline got stronger as they approached the control room; it was difficult to breathe or see. Julie covered her face and tried to hold back the coughs, her eyes tearing from the acrid smell. Suddenly, a second explosion shook the ground. From the storage area, a large mushroom-shaped orange cloud reached far into the black sky and lit up the plant with a blinding light.

"Oh God, no! Those bastards are blowing up the storage tanks one by one!" shouted Julie.

"Come on Lassie, we better get inside now!"

Justice had been driving south on Route 33 when his cellular phone rang. "Justice here."

"Hello, Justice, it's Sharon. Where are you?"

"I'm headed to the chemical plant, I saw an explosion and wanted to help."

"I just talked to Sean. He says the terrorists are going to rob a train and he wants you to stop them from using the computer to set off any more explosives in the plant. The FBI is going after the terrorists but Sean thinks they'll be too late to prevent them from setting off the bombs. And one more thing: he said to tell you that Matt was with the FBI team, and that you would know what that means."

"Yes I do, Sharon. So where do I find this computer?"

Sharon typed a set of commands on the computer screen.

"The computer is five miles south of the Interstate on Route 22. If it moves I'll let you know. You better hurry; things are pretty bad here at the chemical plant. We had a second explosion only minutes ago."

Justice made a U-turn, turned right at the next intersection, and pushed the gas pedal to the floor. He drove several miles

before he neared the location Sharon had provided. He hid the car on the side of a mountain lined with thick trees. He took a high-powered rifle, some ammunition and several hand grenades from the trunk, wrapped a munitions belt around his chest, and put on night visors.

He climbed to the top of the mountain, stopping at a small clearing. At the bottom on the other side of the mountain he saw train tracks and a narrow dirt road running parallel to the tracks. He switched on the heat sensor on his visor and looked along the mountain ridge. The visor detected two bodies perched on the top of the ridge about six hundred yards to the north. From the size of the heat signature he could tell they were either human or a pair of black bears. Justice switched the visor to light sensitivity and saw that it was indeed two men, and both of them were looking down at the tracks.

Justice walked parallel to the mountain ridge until he was behind and beneath the two men and close enough to hear their conversation. Before he could get closer, there was a loud explosion, followed by second and third lesser explosions. Justice could see that the two men were looking at the explosions. He quickly identified one as Jim Ashland. The other was Bill FitzPatrick, who was typing on a computer that he was holding.

Justice removed two large darts from his belt, inserted them into his rifle and aimed through his visor. He shot the first dart at Bill, hitting him in the butt and forcing a scream from his lips.

"What's wrong?" asked Jim, as he looked at Bill.

Bill grabbed the dart and fell forward, losing consciousness. Jim caught him as he fell and placed him on the ground. Just as Jim turned toward the woods, Justice fired again, sending the second dart into Jim's left shoulder. Jim grabbed his chest and fell to the ground. He tried to move, but was asleep from the tranquilizer within seconds.

Justice ran up to the two unconscious men. There was the screeching of a train whistle and Justice looked over the

mountain ledge. In the valley below, a train, consisting of a front and rear engine, two passenger cars and five boxcars, was stopping.

The bright headlights on the front engine illuminated two hundred feet of track, but further on the rays of light were diffused. Justice switched his visor to heat sensor, saw the signature of two smoke bombs and knew now why the rest of the tracks were obscured. He also saw that the cloud was expanding. The train reversed direction, backed away from the smoke, and stopped five hundred feet from the bombs.

Switching his visor back to night vision, Justice saw a man jump off the rear of the train and run down the track. It was a conductor. He began to inspect an area of the track that had been torn apart by the first explosion.

Justice took out his cellular phone, called the sheriff's office and told the deputy, "An AMTRAK train has been stopped and is about to be robbed. It's near Route 22, twelve miles north of Wilburn."

"What's your name?" asked the deputy.

"My name is Justice Linden. Can you send some deputies?"

"Most of our officers are at the hospital and the chemical plant, where there have been several explosions and a huge fire. Everyone here is busy, but since it's an AMTRAK train I can notify the FBI."

"The FBI already knows, but thanks," said Justice as he ended the call and put the phone back into his belt. He found the computer resting under Bill; it was still on and there was a visual display of the train route. It showed that four bombs were located along the tracks: the first was behind the train, two were directly in front, and a fourth, not yet detonated, was located one mile toward town, at the point where the tracks crossed over the Little Run River.

Justice clicked the tab titled 'chem plant' that was at the bottom of the screen and a new visual appeared. It displayed the chemical plant and the location of eight bombs; two, located on storage tanks, indicated that they had been detonated. Six other bombs, indicated as 'live', were at various locations in the plant: next to the reactor vessel, in the main power building, on the feed pumps, at the sulfur facility, the main entrance, and the last one at the contractor's entrance.

Justice took out his cellular phone, punched in a number, and waited. The phone rang three times but there was no answer. Annoyed he said, "Sharon, answer the phone!" After the fifth ring, Justice placed the phone back into his belt. Justice studied the screen, memorizing the location of each live bomb and then turned off the computer and threw it over the side of the mountain. He then tied up Bill and Jim before the effect of the drugs wore off.

At the train below, another engineer, along with an armed officer, walked up the tracks toward the smoke. As they reached the cloud of smoke, two four-wheel drive vehicles sped through the smoke and up the dirt road. The engineer and the officer turned and ran, but were shot before they reached the train.

Helpless to stop the assault from his perch on the mountainside, Justice watched through binoculars as the terrorists held up the train. At the front and rear of the train, illuminated by the engine's headlights, he saw three federal officers with rifles firing at the approaching four-wheel-drive. The conductor was busy inspecting the rear tracks, but just as another four-wheel-drive vehicle and two vans sped up the dirt road from the rear of the train, he ran back and jumped onboard the rear engine. As the armored vehicles converged on the train from the front and rear, their passengers tossed smoke bombs into the front and rear locomotives. Smoke filled the compartments, forcing the armed officers to drop their weapons

and stagger out, coughing and covering their eyes. The terrorists surrounded them and pushed them to the ground.

One terrorist remained to guard the captives while two others boarded the train and two more boarded the four-wheel drive vehicles. Two others opened the doors to the boxcars, while one of the men in a four-wheel drive fired three quick shots into the air. Two vans came speeding up the dirt road and stopped next to the two boxcars. Men jumped out of the vans and began helping unload bags from the train and place them into the back of the vans. A perfect robbery it seemed, for as the rest of the town was busy fighting the series of plant explosions, the terrorists would be able to get away.

At the chemical plant, Sean and Julie entered the control room, passing operators who were frantically trying to shut down equipment. They didn't see Grady, or Sean and Julie, as they ran toward Sharon's office. Sharon wasn't there, but her pocketbook and cellular phone were on the desk next to her computer, which was still on.

"We need to find Sharon," said Sean.

"Yes, but where?"

Sean heard a noise and rushed over and grabbed a man who was behind the nearby control panel. He led him over to the desk.

"Who are you?" asked Sean.

"I'm Clyde, a plant operator. I heard you were looking for Sharon."

"Yes! Do you know where she is?" asked Julie.

"Yes Ma'am. I saw her leaving the building with Mr. Arias, the plant manager, a couple of minutes ago."

"Do you know where they went?" asked Julie.

"No, but they put on coveralls and hardhats and took masks."

"Thanks," said Sean, and he picked up Sharon's bag and held it to Grady's nose. "OK Grady, let's find Sharon."

Julie grabbed Sean's arm and pulled him into the hallway and over to the dressing area. She handed Sean a pair of coveralls a hardhat and an air mask. "Here, put this on. Do you know how to use the mask?" asked Julie.

"I've seen you use it at the train derailment site," replied Sean.

"Listen carefully!" said Julie and she put the mask over her head. "Make sure the fit is snug and you can breathe normally. The filter should last for one hour. Remember to keep the mask on!"

"OK, I've got it."

"I'll stay here and communicate with Justice and the FBI. Good luck!"

Sean left the control room and waited while Grady sniffed the outside air. Sean thought of his days in the Narcotics Division when they used these dogs for finding dope. A good sniffing dog was able to trace the scent through the air, leading them to the source. Soon Grady started to lead Sean toward a row of large furnaces and then past two tall columns. Grady stopped at the staircase next to the large reactor vessel.

Sean bent down and patted Grady, then slipped his mask to the side so he could speak, "OK Grady, good dog. Now where?"

Sean put the mask back on and tightened it. Grady sniffed around Sean and then started up the staircase, passing the first and second levels. When he got to the third level, Grady walked around the large reactor and stopped at an open platform. Sean tightened his hold on the leash as he saw Sharon being held against the outer railing next to an open catwalk. Arias had a gun to her head. Neither Arias nor Sharon saw Sean as he placed Grady's leash around the top of a small temperature gauge on the side of the reactor.

Sean quietly approached Arias from behind, while holding his gun in one hand. When he got within twelve feet, he was in Sharon's direct line of sight, but she didn't move. When Sean got within eight feet, Arias swung around, placing Sharon between him and Sean, and pointed the gun at Sharon' head.

"Ah, Mr. Ryan, those bright orange coveralls of yours make a great reflection in the mask. I think I have the advantage here. Why don't you put down your gun?"

"Why should I? You'll only kill us both."

"You're correct, Mr. Ryan, but if you do it my way, I won't have to splatter this pretty head all over the area," shouted Arias over the noise of the reactor, as he waved his gun at Sharon's head.

Grady barked, and Sean turned to him and shouted through his mask, "Stop Grady."

The dog bounded toward Arias, pulling the leash loose. Running at full speed, Grady leaped over Sharon and knocked the man backward. Arias stumbled over a ten-inch pipe that ran along the bottom of the walkway and fell over the railing. Sean ran to the edge of the railing and saw Arias plunge forty feet before landing on top of a large centrifugal pump.

When Sharon reached down and patted Grady's head, she noticed that his breathing was labored.

"It's over. Are you OK?" asked Sean.

"I'm OK, but Grady isn't good. He's been breathing this polluted air. He needs clean, fresh air."

"Let's get back to the control room."

Back at the train, the terrorists were busy transferring the bags of money from the first boxcar to the vans. The boxcars were standard 50-foot steel cars with double steel doors and the Union Pacific Railroad emblem on the side. When the first

boxcar was emptied, Jeff ordered the captives to get into the boxcar. One of the men locked the sliding side double doors while the other terrorists started unloading the other boxcars.

The sound of sirens pierced the air, and the terrorist in the four-wheel drive fired three shots into the air to signal that the authorities were approaching. The terrorists slammed the van doors shut and sped off, leaving one four-wheel drive behind and two terrorists onboard the train.

The terrorist at the rear of the train called on his radio, "Jeff, aren't we getting off now?"

"Tom, I'd rather take my chances on the train. I have the plates. I'll start the engine and get out of here before those feds can get on board."

"OK, Jeff. I'm with you."

Jeff throttled the long stick on the diesel engine and the train started to move forward, reaching the area of the two smoke bombs in just seconds.

Justice continued to watch from the mountainside as the robbery unfolded. He was surprised when the train continued along the track, but then remembered the diagram that showed a fourth bomb located a mile up the tracks.

The FBI, with sirens blaring, reached the remaining vehicle and found the bodies of the engineer and treasury officer, which were the only traces of the recent robbery. The last FBI car stopped next to the vehicle, while the other agents continued on the dirt road in pursuit of the fleeing terrorists.

Justice dropped his visor and ran south along the ridge. The tracks wound around the mountain and the train was going to have to slow down as it turned. Justice reached the bottom of the ledge just as the train was making the turn. He put his rifle on the ground, stood at the ledge and jumped the twelve feet between the ledge and the top of the last boxcar as it passed. He landed on his feet and rolled over as the car made its turn.

Holding onto the roof walk to avoid falling over the side, he heard banging coming from inside. Justice crawled along the top of the car until he reached the top of one of the double doors. He hung over the side of the car and kicked the handle, trying to open one of the doors.

Tom, who was standing between the rear engine and the last boxcar, had seen Justice jump onto the roof of the boxcar. Tom climbed onto the top of one end of the boxcar and aimed his rifle at Justice. Justice jumped when a bullet hit the roof of the car no more than one foot from his head. He looked down the roof and saw Tom aiming his rifle. It was difficult for Tom to steady himself, as the train swayed from side to side as it made the turn around the mountain. Tom fired a second bullet that hit the top of the car and bounced past Justice's head. Justice hung over the edge of the car and hand-walked his way toward the front of the car where he was able to grab the side ladder. As he held on to the ladder with one hand, he drew his handgun and looked over the top of the car.

Tom slowly walked toward the front of the car, his rifle ready. Justice poked his head and gun just above the car and fired. The shot missed Tom by a couple of feet, but he fell on the top of the car and lost his grip on the rifle. It bounced several feet in front of Tom, and Justice climbed up the ladder and reached the top of the car while Tom crawled over to the rifle. As Justice aimed, Tom grabbed the rifle and swung the butt end at him. The rifle hit Justice in the right leg, dropping him to his knees and causing him to drop his gun. Both weapons bounced off the top of the car and over the side to the ground below.

Tom stood up and approached Justice. Although Justice was on his knees and exhausted, he managed to take out his night stick. He swung the club at Tom, hitting him in the left forearm, causing Tom to stagger to the side. Regaining his balance, Tom lunged at Justice before Justice had a chance to swing the club again. Tom clutched Justice and the two of them rolled as they struggled. Tom managed to wrap his hands around Justice's neck. But as Tom stood up, Justice kneed him hard in his groin

and flipped Tom over, causing him to scream from the excruciating pain in his back. Tom was lying flat on the roof of the boxcar, trying to catch his breath.

Justice walked over to the middle of the car and slid over the side until he was able to reach the steel door handle. He unlocked the handle and one of the captives inside slid the door open. Inside were the eight captives. Justice yelled, "You can get out now. You'll have to make your way to the passenger cars. You're on your own. I have to stop this train." Justice again carefully crawled along the side of the car and to the side ladder. He climbed up the ladder and was about to grab the brake wheel when Tom grabbed his arm and started to push him off the ladder. Justice could not move his right arm and his left hand was holding the ladder. He twisted his legs so that they were tight against the ladder rail. With his left hand, he was able to grab Tom's long hair. With a sudden jerk of Tom's head Justice threw Tom over the front of the box car. Tom landed on his back again, but against the track that was beneath the couplers. Justice's last recollection of Tom was the fear he saw in his eyes right before the car wheels ran over him.

Justice walked on the roof of the other boxcars. Reaching the passenger cars, he climbed down and swung open the door that led to the front engine compartment. It was empty. He rushed to the train controls, but they were locked. He tried to remove the rod that was jamming the dead-man's switch, but it had been locked in place. Grabbing the heaviest wrench from a nearby toolbox he banged on the bar several times.

"OK, that will be enough!" ordered Jeff, from behind the engine compartment.

Justice reached for his gun, but then remembered he lost it in the last struggle with Tom. He turned and faced Jeff, who was pointing a handgun.

Jeff said, "It's a good thing you didn't have a gun there; otherwise you would be dead right now, boy! I assume you killed Tom." Jeff paused, but Justice did not reply.

"Nothing to say, boy? You just stay comfortable while I give the orders." Jeff punched a number on his cellular phone, but got no answer. "You're pretty good, boy. You must have gotten to Bill and Jim, too. I guess I'm just not going to be able to blow the bridge. That's OK; I'll still be off the train with my plates." Jeff kicked a bag marked 'US Treasury' that was leaning against the compartment. "You won't be able to stop the train and it will blow up just the same at the end of the line." Jeff threw a key over the side of the train as he spoke, "But just in case..."

At that moment, Justice flung the wrench at Jeff, hitting his gun and causing it to fire as it fell to the floor. The bullet hit Justice in his left forearm. Justice fell back from the force of the gunshot, while Jeff grabbed the bag, turned around and ran to the back of the engine and onto the outside steps. Two officers who were freed from the boxcar came rushing through the passenger car door. The first man lunged just as Jeff, with bag in hand, jumped from the train as it started over the bridge. The officer got a hand on the bag and pulled it out of Jeff's hand, but he couldn't hold it and it dropped over the side. The officer didn't see where Jeff landed, but he did hear two faint splashes.

The second officer approached Justice and said, "Let me see that wound."

"It's not that bad," Justice replied, but the officer ripped open the torn shirt and tied his handkerchief around the wound to stop the bleeding.

"That will have to do until you can get medical treatment."

Justice asked the officer, "Where's this train headed?"

"It's was routed directly to Fort Knox. There's no scheduled stop along the way."

"We can't stop the train. The controls have been frozen and the dead-man's switch is locked."

"You have a cellular phone. We could have the authorities clear all traffic and divert us to run until the diesel is exhausted."

"That's sounds too easy. Forsythe expected this train to blow up," said Justice, taking out his phone and calling Sharon.

But Julie answered. "Hello, this is Agent Del Rio."

"Julie, this is Justice, I was calling Sharon."

"Oh Justice, Sharon isn't here. She left her phone; Sean is out looking for her. What's happening out there?"

"We managed to break up the train robbery. The last I knew, the FBI agents were chasing the terrorists. I got onboard the train and stopped one of the terrorists, but Forsythe may have gotten away. Right now, the train is headed south and we can't stop it. I need to get in touch with central control right away."

Julie sat down at the computer. "I'm checking the phone number for central control. I'll make this a conference call, so hold on for a while."

"Better make it quick. I suspect we have less then ten minutes before we reach Wilburn."

"Hello, this is Agent Del Rio of the FBI. I need to talk to Supervisor Defazio." Julie waited for ten seconds. "Mr. Defazio, this is Miss Del Rio, I have someone onboard a train that needs to confirm the train's routing. It's an emergency, so I would appreciate your help."

"Agent Del Rio, I'll do what I can. Your party can begin," Defazio said.

Justice spoke, "We're on a train, heading toward Wilburn. The officers say it is routed directly to Fort Knox. Can you confirm from your tracking that this is correct?"

"I'll check our board; it will take a few seconds."

Justice looked at the two officers, "How are the rest of the passengers?"

"They're fine; they're in the rear engine," one answered.

Defazio came back on the phone, "We show your train heading south, but it apparently turned off from the correct route about ten miles back. There was a switch that was thrown in the wrong direction. Currently the train is headed directly toward Wilburn. Our board shows it is on a line that will go through the OC Chemicals plant."

"Can you route it back onto the main track?" asked Justice.

"I can make the necessary changes but not until the train has passed through Wilburn." Defazio replied.

"If it gets through!" Justice sounded disgusted. "Thank's for your efforts. I'll keep you informed."

"Good luck," replied Defazio and he ended his connection.

"Julie, you need to find out where the train tracks in the plant lead to. Call me back as soon as you find out. I have to try to stop this train," said Justice.

"Any ideas?" asked the first officer as he looked at Justice.

Justice paused before replying, "I believe the terrorists planned to have the train crash and burn, to kill the eyewitnesses and destroy any evidence. First thing we need to do is prevent those onboard from getting killed."

"But we can't stop the train, and they can't jump," the second officer added.

"Yes, but we might be able to stop the cars," added Justice.

"At these speeds it's nearly impossible to uncouple the cars," said the second officer.

"Maybe we can increase our chances," said the first officer.

"What do you have in mind?" asked Justice.

The first officer moved to the controls and turned the intercom system on. "Good, the intercom is still functioning." He held down the button and spoke, "This is Jack. Can you hear me?"

"Yes, Jack, this is Bob. What's up?"

"We have to slow down the train. Is there any diesel in your engine fuel tank?"

The engineer looked at the gauge. "Jack, the engineer says it's near the bottom of the tank. It's hard to tell how much, but there should be fifty gallons or more."

"That's OK, we only need enough to counteract our forward momentum for a minute or two. Start the engine and put it at full throttle."

Jack told the second officer. "Joe, get over to the passenger car and get ready to release the coupling." Jack turned to Justice and added, "You, too."

Justice replied, "No, you go. I have to see if I can stop this engine. If it explodes anywhere in the plant, we'll have even more environmental damage."

Jack shook his head and answered, "OK. Good luck." He ran to the back of the compartment and onto the passenger car. As the rear engine reached its top output, the train started to slow down. Jack and Joe, removed the two backup chains that held the car to the engine and then released the pin holding the couplers. The front engine and the passenger cars separated quickly, each part of the train now under the power of its own engine. The officers waved to Justice until he was out of eyesight.

Justice's cellular phone rang. "Justice here."

"This is Julie. The train tracks in the plant go past the warehouse and then through the storage facilities and then out of the plant."

"That sounds like good news," said Justice.

"Not really," replied Julie. "There's a big fire in the storage facilities. The tracks have been burning for hours. We don't even know if there are any tracks. You could be heading for a fiery graveyard."

"Are there any side rails in the plant?"

"There's a spur that ends at the water treatment pond and an abandoned large storage tank."

"What about the storage tank? Will we hit it and, if so, is anything in it?"

"According to the plant plot plan, the tracks go directly around the tank, but these tracks are old and if the train is going too fast it could jump the track and plow through the tank before it reaches the pond."

"Is there anything in the tank?"

"No, the tank has been drained and cleaned out. It's currently being dismantled because of defective welds."

"Then that's it. Set the switch to divert the train to the pond. With just the engine, my speed has increased and I should be there in three or four minutes."

"What about you, Justice? How are you going to get off?"

"Will the train still go past the warehouse?"

"Yes."

"Then hook a worker's harness to the end of one of the plant's small cranes and line it up over the tracks at the warehouse. I'll grab onto the harness as the train goes through. You'll hear the engine whistle when I reach the plant."

As Julie ended the call, Sean and Sharon entered the office.

"Sean, it's Justice. The train will enter the plant and pass by the warehouse before it heads to the storage tanks. We have to

throw the switch located after the warehouse but before the tanks, so the train will plunge into the water treatment pond and not the burning tank facilities. We have just three minutes.

"Sharon, we need a crane with a harness attached to the end over at the warehouse. Justice is going to grab it as the train goes by."

"OK I'll take care of that; you two throw the switch." Sharon patted Grady and tied him to the desk. "You be a good dog and stay here."

Sharon went into the operators' room and approached Clyde. "I need a crane right now. Do you know where to get one?"

"Follow me." As they left the control room, Sharon grabbed an extra pair of coveralls. She said to Clyde, "These will have to do; I don't have time to get the workers harness from storage."

Clyde pointed to a pair of cranes that were across the road at a small construction area.

Sharon ran over to the first crane and tied the orange coveralls to the end of the hoist. She climbed onboard and started the engine. She put the engine in gear and pointed it up the main road and toward the warehouse.

Wearing orange coveralls and air masks, Sean and Julie ran to the switch, which was located three hundred yards before the storage tanks. Although the switch was away from the fire, the area was busy with fire-fighting equipment and other company vehicles coming and going. When they reached the switch, Sean tried to throw the switch; it wouldn't budge. Julie joined Sean in pulling the lever; still no luck.

The train whistle breached the noise of the chemical plant as Sharon drove the crane to the end of the warehouse. She raised the end of the hoist to eighteen feet above the tracks and positioned the chain with the coveralls to twelve feet. She was glad that as a teenager she had practiced handling heavy machinery on her father's farm and knew how to handle the

tricky controls. She locked the hoist in place as the engine came into view at the other end of the warehouse tracks. She saw Justice as he climbed to the front of the engine. The orange coveralls would be easy to spot, but Sharon didn't know if they would hold his weight or whether Justice could grab the coveralls.

As the train got closer, Sharon grabbed the hoist lever with both hands to hold it in place. Justice stood directly into the wind and jumped into the air. He grabbed the coveralls first with his left hand, but his arm was weak from the gunshot wound and his grip was poor. He slid down six inches before his right hand grabbed the leg of the coveralls. He swung his legs up as the engine sped out from under him. Justice was clear of the train and was spinning around on the chain. Sharon lowered the hoist until Justice was about four feet above the ground. He let go and landed on his feet. Sharon climbed down from the crane and hugged Justice, and they began to walk back to the control room.

The engine passed the warehouse area and headed toward Julie and Sean, who were still trying to throw the switch at the abandoned storage tank. Sean had grabbed a long metal pipe lying alongside the switch and jabbed the rod between the track and the switch rail. He levered one side on the permanent metal rail and the other against the movable metal rail. He pushed hard, trying to separate the two rails enough to loosen years of rust due to nonuse. The train was only thirty seconds up the track. Sean took the metal pipe, went back to Julie and the lever and placed the pipe over the lever, thus providing more leverage. Together Julie and Sean pulled on the lever and the switch finally moved to the right just as the engine swept past them. The wind blew both of them off their feet. Sean landed on against the cement containment wall of the nearby storage tank, hitting his left arm hard and causing him to scream from the pain. Julie hit Sean as she landed and was hurt more by the screams of her partner than the fall. They remained on the ground as they watched the train speed by.

The speed of the engine was too much to completely make the final turn, and the engine jumped the track, just missing the side of the large empty storage tank, and continuing for one hundred yards before plowing into the center of the water treatment pond. There was no fireball or explosion. Instead there was a whoosh, as the water engulfed the engine, leaving just the top visible above the pond.

"It's over," said Sean, as he and Julie slowly walked back to the control room.

"I think I need an ambulance, Lassie," said Sean when he reached the control room. As he sat down, he passed out from pure exhaustion.

Chapter Eighteen

Environment Lost

The windows in the hospital were wet with summer raindrops. Sean was sitting in his room watching a television reporter standing in front of a charred chemical plant that was now empty. The air was visibly brownish and smoggy.

"This was truly a Worst Case Scenario. The residents of Wilburn, who recently endured a terrible train wreck, which killed hundreds of residents in town and spilled toxic materials for over two miles, suffered a second disaster last night. A series of explosions released hundreds of thousands of pounds of toxic chemicals stored at the OC Chemicals plant into the nearby river, air and soil. The FBI is investigating a major terrorist plot and there have been arrests. Details are not yet being released to the public.

"Fortunately, there were few injuries this time, because the plant is a few miles from town. However, all residents with asthma and other ailments were told to leave town and move to a hotel several miles away, where the government is setting up a shelter. Even the dead had to be handled with special care because the toxic bodies could not be buried in cemeteries but must be interred in special sites equipped to handle the hazardous chemicals trapped in their corpses.

"But the massive spills will plague this town for years. The force of the explosions has spread the material far and wide, and it will be deposited over fields, rivers, soil, and homes. Many farmers might lose their livelihood because the contaminated soil can't be used to produce food or raise livestock.

"Harry Jones is the director of the HazMat team that responded to the *train wreck emergency three weeks ago. He is now back at Wilburn responding to an even larger toxic spill. Mr.

Jones, can you tell us about the accident, and the long-term effects to this community?"

Harry wiped his forehead and removed the mask hanging from this face and spoke directly into the camera. "This is the largest spill of the kind ever experienced in the United States. Half of the one point two million gallons of chemicals stored in this plant have been released into the environment. The force of the explosions has spread them over a large area. Cleanup will take a long time and cost taxpayers billions. But, even with the best techniques, we'll never be able to clean it all up. Towns as far as 20 miles downwind are smelling the chemicals, and residents have been told to stay inside and take children and the elderly who suffer from asthma or other ailments to visit relatives or to shelters in other towns."

"What is going to happen when it rains?" asked the reporter.

"We're fighting the clock here. It's beginning to rain now, as you can see. Rainwater will wash more of the chemicals into the streams and eventually the river. What we are trying to do is divert rainwater to ditches so we can pump as much of it as possible into containers for cleanup and neutralization. Already there have been huge fish kills from chemicals that settled in the water after the explosions.

"With the previous accident, we were able to stop the leakage from the train wreck and save the river, but this incident is just too large a spill and we couldn't stop the rivers from being contaminated. Unfortunately this river discharges into the ocean, where pollution will affect fishing for years to come. What happened here is equivalent to what happened in Kosovo, when refineries were bombed and materials spilled into the Danube. It is truly an environmental crime of the worst kind."

The reporter looked at Harry as if he had just had touched the most politically incorrect topic on his list.

"You say this was a crime? Do you mean this wasn't an accident Mr. Jones?"

"Accidents like this don't just happen. This was a criminal act. The perpetrators have been identified and arrested, but unfortunately the authorities couldn't stop them before much of the damage was done. The plant didn't have enough security to stop the men who were working on the inside, creating the explosions."

"What was the motive? Was it a politically or racially motivated?"

"I'm not allowed to talk about the nature of the crime or the motives. The FBI will release details at a later time. But while I'm not allowed to discuss motives, I can say that we need laws to protect citizens from this kind of incident. Chemical plants are time bombs open to any freak who wants to blow them up. Most are safe, but security is lax in too many areas. Past regulations have been inadequate, asking companies to police themselves. Regulations such as the Process Safety Management and Risk Management Plans require only paperwork. Safety is up to each plant. We see here how inadequate these regulations are in preventing criminal actions by terrorists."

"Thank you Mr. Jones. And that concludes this report on the Wilburn accident, or maybe as we just heard the Wilburn 'terrorist incident'. Back in the studio, we are interviewing George Reed, a local reporter who has written extensively on these incidents. Mr. Reed will soon be releasing his book, 'Worst Case Scenario,' the story of the conspiracy that led to the worst chemical disasters in US history."

Julie walked down the long hospital hallway carrying a bouquet of red roses. The place was buzzing with activity as nurses rushed to treat the overload of patients suffering from chemical inhalation. As she passed by the rooms, she could see young and old struggling to breathe under oxygen tents. Fortunately, the wind had blown most of the toxic fumes away

from town, but not before many residents inhaled enough corrosive smoke to burn the lining in their lungs.

Now the air in this area was more breathable. Julie stood quietly outside the door of Sean's hospital room, watching as he dressed. His back was to the door, so he didn't notice her standing there. She admired his broad shoulders and long, straight back. He had lost weight in the ordeal and the change was very becoming. She took a deep breath and let it out slowly before she walked in.

"How are you doing, Lad?" she asked Sean, who was now packing his few belongings into a plastic bag.

Sean turned, smiled, looked into Julie's eyes for a moment, and finally said: "Flowers, for me?"

"I think it's better to get them while you're still alive, don't you?"

"What's the news out there?"

"The rains washed all of the chemicals into the streams. The HazMat team is pouring lime along the rivers in an attempt to neutralize the acid waters before they reach the bay. We were fortunate there were no human casualties this time. But in spite of our efforts, half the chemicals stored in the plant were released into the environment. There was one casualty - Sharon's dog Grady."

"He seemed OK last night!" said Sean turning to Julie.

"I know. He died this morning. The vet said his lungs had filled with fluid as a result of the chemical burns caused by breathing the fumes. We may see some human casualties in the next few weeks if some of these victims don't recover from similar burns to their lungs."

"I'm sorry."

"If we hadn't worn our masks, we would be suffering a similar fate. Too bad we didn't have one for Grady... By the way, Gutierrez called, and she has another case for us."

Sean turned his back to Julie and looked out the window for a moment before responding. "I'm not going back to the FBI. I'll e-mail my resignation in tomorrow. This case was a dismal failure. The criminals were always two steps ahead of us and in the end, look what happened. My poor old body can't take much more!"

"But you bounced back as you always do," argued Julie. "You're a strong man, Sean Ryan. You're no quitter. We caught the polluters, so at least they won't be able to cause any more damage."

"Stop it! My God, look at you, your face scratched, your bruises, and you endured the worst back there for me. Go back to your desk job at the EPA, you'll live longer."

"Well, who knows if there will be a job over there for me now. This new administration is cutting back on environmental enforcement, you know. The papers devoted more text to that than to this horrible accident. It's as if they don't want the public to know what's going on. There is still a budget for this at the FBI and I'm thinking of joining Gutierrez's division permanently."

"Well, isn't that great of our government! You put your heart and soul into the job and now they don't think the environment is worth saving. The bastards! You should be working at a big law firm, instead of wasting your life on this government job. Julie, take off those blinders!

"The world is going to hell and we're going right along with it. This case was a failure. We can't stop these polluters and now no one in power wants to do anything about them. They couldn't stop our own home-grown terrorists with the Oklahoma City bombing; we couldn't stop this. When we needed help, the agency just got caught up in its own corruption. It turns out our own

agents were working with Hilbaum to help these bastards Forsythe and Arias. They don't give a damn about the environment or anything else. They were after a cushy retirement. I hope they croak from cancer before they reach 65!"

Julie moved toward Sean and stood quietly beside him as he looked out the window.

Sean continued, "Look at that brown grass and those dead trees. I can't even see a bird out there. I don't mind if we kill each other in our own sick wars, in Belfast or Beirut. But we're killing innocent animals, the plants, all of God's creation. I'm sick of it. We are a bad bunch, we humans. Maybe we deserve what we're getting."

Julie turned to face Sean, put her arms around his waist and hugged him as she had back in the trailer: "Sean, I believe you have finally turned."

"What do you mean?"

"You're now an official card-carrying environmentalist. And you said this job was for wimps and didn't care when you joined the group."

"Hey, we saved Alaska didn't we?"

"That we did."

Julie pressed her lips to Sean's chest. Sean tilted Julie's head up and softly pressed his lips to hers.

Julie looked at Sean and brushed his reddish hair from his face. "I thought I was going to lose you back there."

"You'll not lose me, Lassie," he said before kissing her again.

A nurse walked in and coughed. "Mr. Ryan, I believe you're checking out today. Here's your wheelchair."

"Oh, I don't need that missy."

"Sorry. Hospital rules."

Julie escorted Sean to the wheelchair. "Come on Sean, sit and enjoy the ride." Then she turned the conversation back to Sean's apparent belief the world was going to hell and nobody cared. "There is hope for the earth yet; you can't quit."

Sean sat in the wheelchair and the nurse began pushing.

"I'll take over from here 'missy'," said Julie, smiling at Sean as she started wheeling him to the main lobby.

"Sean, think before you turn in your resignation. I mean, where would you find such an exciting, low-paying job as this? Look at the medical benefits we have. You've been in the hospital three or four times already this year and it's 100 percent covered!"

"I think you're crazy, but if you're going to stay, so will I. So what does Gutierrez have in store for us now?"

"Well, first of all, the good news. She got promoted."

"What?"

"She finally got those traitor bastards at the FBI kicked out. Thanks to the sheriff, who caught Drago as he tried to leave the hospital. As fate would have it, the Sheriff spotted him because he was wearing the sheriff's son's high school football jacket over a doctor's gown. Hilbaum's bunch of friends, including Drago, will be facing a Senate hearing soon. In addition to conspiracy, they were supplying FBI guns to the terrorists. The only retirement they'll be getting is a prison sentence. Hopefully, for the rest of their lives.

"That's good news?"

"And, this accident finally woke up some people in Washington. The president is personally supporting legislation to improve security at all plants. He's even thinking about naming a special task force to protect against such terrorist attempts."

"Well, that may end our careers, if environmental criminals can't operate."

"Don't worry, Gutierrez already has a new case for us. You are not going to believe this one!"

As Julie and Sean passed one of the rooms, Julie stopped. "Look, it's Jeremiah's little girl. Hi, Jeremiah? May I come in? Juliana Del Rio, and my partner Sean."

"I remember you," said Jeremiah, extending his hand. "You came to investigate the first accident. We briefly met at the hospital."

"How is your little girl doing?"

"She has to come back to the hospital and be placed in oxygen every day. They say she is healing. Fortunately, this time, the fumes didn't hit us, but I've lost my job at the plant. My brother lost his farm. Thousands of gallons of benzene and other stuff rained down in his field when the plant exploded. It soaked right through. The only way to get it out is to strip the soil. But it probably filtered down to the well, so his farm is now a toxic wasteland. We're moving to New York to live with relatives until I can find a job."

"I'd like to keep in touch and see how your little girl is doing."

"We'll see each other. I'm suing the government for our suffering. It turns out they had clues all along, but no one was watching out. How can they let these corrupt people run our government? I mean, who is watching out for us? Two COK members blew up that train that hurt my little girl. We've been complaining about that organization for years, but what has the government done? They held their racist meetings. Now they claim they had nothing to do with it. They nurtured those criminals and fueled their hate. Now it's too late."

"Well, any way I can help."

"You'd be testifying against your own people."

"Not my people, just the rotten apples. We need to clean house, but believe me, most of the organization is made up of good people."

As Julie and Sean walked out of the hospital, Sharon, George, Peter and Justice met them. Sharon handed Sean a large bouquet of flowers.

"What? More flowers?"

"We just wanted to wish you well, and to thank you."

"For what? Just doing my job and so were all of you. Sharon, you did a great job. I'm sorry about Grady. And Peter, Justice, well, you basically gave us the 'intelligence' we lacked in our own organization. Any time you need our help just let us know. And George, I see you finally published one of your stories on the newswire and some national papers and magazines picked it up. Julie mentioned you looking at a book deal? Congratulations! Guess you'll be moving out of Wilburn, finally?"

"Definitely, to Washington. I'll be following the FBI corruption case and the new legislation that will be needed to stop this type of environmental crime. I finally made it out of this hellhole."

"Maybe you'll be thinking this place is a bed of roses once you live in Washington," said Julie, chuckling.

Julie and Sean got into their sedan and drove. The air was breathable, but the sky looked brown. They passed trucks and cranes and heavy equipment working round the clock to clean up the massive spill.

Julie turned to Sean and said, "This may be the end of the case for us, but it's just the beginning of years of cleanup for this town." Sean nodded, and as they drove out of town they quietly contemplated their future.

Postscript

Morning of September 11

The flight to New York was rough, and turbulent. Sean couldn't calm his nerves with whiskey, so he held on to his seat, his palms sweating. Sean was relieved to have landed safely, and rested at the terminal. Julie grabbed him by the arm and said, "Hurry, it's eight-thirty; we have a 9 a. m. meeting at the EPA's office New York with Gutierrez and we're going to be late,"

Sean and Julie hailed a yellow cab from La Guardia airport. As the cab dropped them off at the office a crowd was gathered, watching as the second plane hit the top of the World Trade Center. Sean drew closer to Julie and they watched for forty minutes, mesmerized at this horrific act of terror. A thundering sound rocked the pavement as a tower collapsed into itself. Sean pulled Julie into the nearest open door. They were inside a delicatessen. Julie held on to Sean tightly this time, as they both watched the black cloud pass through. Darkness and an irritating dust enveloped New York.

We will never forget

End of Case 2